MW00583411

Jackals
BRONZE AGE FANTASY ROLEPLAYING

THE FALL OF THE CHILDREN OF BRONZE
A GRAND CAMPAIGN

John-Matthew DeFoggi

OSPREY GAMES

OSPREY GAMES
Bloomsbury Publishing Plc
Kemp House, Chawley Park, Cumnor Hill, Oxford OX2 9PH, UK
29 Earlsfort Terrace, Dublin 2, Ireland
1385 Broadway, 5th Floor, New York, NY 10018, USA
E-mail: info@ospreygames.co.uk
www.ospreygames.co.uk

OSPREY GAMES is a trademark of Osprey Publishing Ltd

First published in Great Britain in 2021

A catalogue record for this book is available from the British Library.

ISBN: HB 9781472837684; eBook 9781472837691; ePDF 9781472837707; XML 9781472837714

21 22 23 24 25   10 9 8 7 6 5 4 3 2 1

Originated by PDQ Digital Media Solutions, Bungay, UK'
Printed and bound in India by Replika Press Private Ltd.

Osprey Games supports the Woodland Trust, the UK's leading woodland conservation charity.

To find out more about our authors and books visit www.ospreypublishing.com. Here you will find extracts, author interviews, details of forthcoming events and the option to sign up for our newsletter.

None of this book is open gaming content.

Acknowledgements
To my wife, Trisha, without whom I could never have attempted this. I adore you.
To my son, Zane; you are a constant wellspring of inspiration and wonder.
Thanks to all my playtesters: Darlene Avery, Trisha DeFoggi, Madeline du Breuil, Becky Cleveland, Jonathan Cleveland, Paul Cross, Rachel Cross, Ben Feehan, Jess Feehan, John Ford, JD Ford, Evan Franke, The Gentleman's Society (Jon Crenshaw, Terry Cruse, David Howse, Michael Howse, JP Meisenburg, and playtest coordinator and Loremaster Greg Nagler), Lily Giddings, Azver Hussain, Derek Krebiel, Rebecca Lauffenburger, Kevin MacGregor, Christopher Pileggi, Jervaise Pileggi, Mark Pileggi, Corey Reddin, Nathan Reed, Richard Rohlin, Sophie Rohlin, Joshua Kelly, and Thomas Thompson.

CONTENTS

CHAPTER I

INTRODUCTION

Gone is the gate and gone are the walls
Their foundations lie below
The dry and arid desert sand –
Once an empire, long ago.
Cast down by foes both base and weak,
Children made of bronze.
Time will bring their trials to naught
And all will be made pawns
Of the Iron Crown which will arise
To once again be placed
Upon a brow so dread and fair –
Our fate shall be erased.
Rebuild the gate, rebuild the walls
Oh, chosen of the east.
Arise and claim the onyx throne.
The Mou'alin wish to feast.

~Prophecy of Mou'alin, Kinesh of Mikro, Year of Fallen Seeds~

Welcome to *Jackals: The Fall of the Children of Bronze* (abbreviated hereafter to *Fall*), the first campaign for *Jackals*. Within these pages are 14 adventures spanning nine years of the Zaharets, broken up by year and region. The goal of this book is to give Loremasters a grand arc of a campaign, while leaving plenty of space to add in their own adventures along the way. It tells the story of the fall of one of the War Road's city-states, as they are subsumed into a new kingdom of the Luathi.

CAMPAIGN ASSUMPTIONS

Fall contains several assumptions, of which Loremasters should be aware from the beginning.

ASSUMPTION 1: THE CAMPAIGN TELLS THE ROLL OF YEARS, NOT A STORY

This campaign is not an adventure path, where each adventure tells one part of a story. Rather, *Fall* tells multiple stories along the War Road in the years leading up to a great war. Although some of the adventures connect, the majority do not. They build on each other, but in subtle ways, advancing towards the conclusion. We recommend that you, the Loremaster, read the entirety of this book before running *Fall*. Of course, if this does not appeal to you, you can always pick and choose the adventures you wish to add to your own long-term *Jackals* campaign.

ASSUMPTION 2: THE JACKALS WHO BEGIN THIS JOURNEY WILL NOT END IT

These adventures span nine years, which means – whether due to death or Kleos – Jackals might retire over the course of *Fall*, possibly even before its end. Throughout the campaign you will see *Retiring Benefits* in many years – these are additional incentives for players to allow one Jackal to move up in the world, while another steps onto the War Road. These benefits are not cumulative; they apply to those who retire in that year – in addition to the usual retiring benefits (see *Jackals* page 193).

ASSUMPTION 3: ALTHOUGH FALL IS THEIR STORY, IT IS NOT THE ONLY STORY

There is much going on behind the scenes in *Fall*. Many potent beings of Law and Chaos have turned their eyes to the Zaharets. The players might begin to catch glimpses of other grand plots, while you as the Loremaster will receive more insight into them. This is intentional – to convey the scope of the world as well as provide seeds for the stories and adventures that come after *Fall*.

ASSUMPTION 4: YOUR FALL WILL BE UNIQUE

The longer a group plays through *Fall*, the more you should expect your story to deviate from the presented campaign. After all, your Jackals leave their mark on the world. Non-player characters (NPCs) might live or die, or the Jackals might radically affect their lives in other ways. To account for this, the adventures in the first five years follow a different structure from those in the last four. The farther along in *Fall* you progress, the looser the adventure structure grows. This provides you as Loremaster the most structure in the early years and the most flexibility in the later years. In the end, think of *Fall* as but one view of the future of the Zaharets. Yours may be quite different.

YEARLY FORMAT

Each year provides an outline for Loremasters to follow, which sets the scene for the year and introduces the major players and developments, as well as a series of adventure hooks to help flesh out the other adventures of that year. The general format of the year is as follows:

- **Introduction:** the overview of the year, which gives a high-level view of the adventures and reveals which, if any, other adventures in *Fall* are tied to it.
- **Theme:** the themes of this year's adventures.
- **Important NPCs:** the important NPCs for this year.
- **Events:** other goings-on in the Zaharets the Jackals might hear about but that do not tie into *Fall's* narrative.
- **Adventure:** the adventure(s) for the year.
- **Hooks:** ideas for other adventures in which a Jackal can participate this year.

HOOKS

Fall is a grand campaign with many moving parts, big plots (both on and off the screen), and several NPCs. You will find story hooks below to tie Jackals closer to the story of *Fall*. Each of these story hooks provides a Jackal a unique tie to the campaign, which can pay off in a variety of ways as they move through the story. Throughout *Fall*, you will find ways to bring these hooks to the fore, giving that Jackal a spotlight scene or adventure. Have each Jackal roll on the following table when they make their character. As Jackals retire, if their hook is unfulfilled, they may choose to pass it to a newer Jackal to discover the end of their tale.

JACKAL HOOKS		
d100	Name	Effect
1–8	Family Heirloom	The Jackal possesses a strange necklace, passed down from mother to child. It is a silver chain with a black wooden pendant in the shape of an acalana tree in bloom. The necklace provides a +5% to Willpower checks.
9–16	Born Under a Strange Sign	The Jackal's birth occurred under a unique sign. Twin comets blazed in the night sky, while the Skyriver waxed deep indigo. The Jackal may choose to gain one Fate Point (bringing their total to 4) at the cost of gaining 4 Corruption.
17–24	Hunted by Shadows	The Jackal is cursed, having drawn the attention of a Rathic that is bound to slay the Jackal. Once a year, the Rathic makes an attempt on the Jackal's life. The reason for the curse, and what the Rathic might gain from slaying the Jackal, is unknown.
25–32	Ancient Grudge	The Jackal's family bears a grudge against another family. They can be from any culture, but fate conspires to bring the families together. The results of these confrontations serve only to purchase an extension of the blood debt.
33–40	Treasure Map	The Jackal purchased a trinket from a trader many years ago. Although it was worthless, the old piece of leather in which the trinket came wrapped held a strange map. The Jackal has yet to decipher it, but it seems to hold the path to an underground ruin.
41–48	Spirit Companion	A spirit, like a Ba, an ancestor, or an Umbalnani, attached itself to the Jackal. Most of the time it is invisible, watching over the Jackal. But at times it can manifest, alerting the Jackal of danger or great reward.
49–56	Guiding Dream	The Touch of Law is upon the Jackal's soul, and each night when they head into the Silent Lands, Law guides their path. They received a guiding vision, one which will bring solace and focus to their path.
57–64	Nightmares of the East	Each night Kauma is full, the Jackal receives the dream of an obsidian throne. Each time, the throne is more defined, resolving slowly over the months and years into a terrible symbol of a coming king.
65–72	Terrors from the Night	Even if the Jackal is not Gerwa, an Ukuku from the Silent Lands visits them in their dreams. This Ukuku always attempts to transmit a message from the beyond, but the experience is harrowing for the Jackal.
73–80	Doom	The Jackal is fated to die a horrible and ignoble death. No retirement or respite awaits them at the end of the War Road. Roll on the table below to discover the doom: 1 – Long ago, the seeds of the Jackal's fall were sown deep within their flesh. And from their flesh, darkness will consume them. 2 – As Tracal was severed and creation was ordered from its body, so too shall the Jackal be severed to bring about something new. 3 – The rime will grow, frost will form, and dust will cloak their head. From their heart, twisted vines will twine, to choke those they use for beds. 4 – The sins of the child will be avenged upon the heads of the elders, and coals like rain will be heaped into the laps of those who do not deserve it.

| 81–89 | Mantle of the Ancestors | When the Jackal was born, it was prophesied they would follow in their ancestor's footsteps, bring glory back to their people, and destroy the beasts of the East and end their tyranny. They march with that burden hanging around their neck. Each day it grows heavier, and each day they find it harder to breathe. |
| 90–00 | Blood of the Old Kingdoms | The Jackal has darker hair and is taller than most. People frequently wonder aloud at their lineage, commenting about giant blood. Often, when they see the memorials and sites of the Children of Silver, they feel a strange longing. |

EXAMPLE HOOK: GUIDING DREAM

The sun rises in the east, spreading its light across the golden sands of the Luasa to your left and the green Aeco Plains to your right. You stand upon the summit of Mihshalnim, the holy mountain. As the light of day spreads out, and Alwain's blessing flows over you, you feel a soft voice speak to you. "All that you see, I created. Everything that exists has its root in me. I raise up those I will; and I set them against those who stand against my Law. You I have chosen; you will stand in the light against those in darkness." To the [insert direction of adventure], you can feel the darkness growing – its shadow begins to creep along the ground. You know what you must do. Leaping off the summit, you are born aloft on a fierce wind, and begin flying towards the growing threat, the warmth of the sun on your face.

EXAMPLE HOOK: NIGHTMARES OF THE EAST

Disoriented, you stand before a wind-blasted plinth. The light of the setting sun glows like the red of a furnace behind you. The howling wind does nothing to mask the steady dripping noise of blood slipping free of your mangled hand to the black sand below.

The storm's gale slowly erodes a block of blackest obsidian from the rock face. The wind pulls at the earth, forcing it away to free what lies beneath. It reveals more and more of the stone, showing the block to be raised on three of its sides. At length, as the wind reveals the back of the object, you finally recognise what it is: a black throne. A twisted crown of black iron lies on the seat of the throne, marked with unfamiliar runic inscriptions. In your mind, you hear a voice, cold with the chill of the grave, "You will take it, or you will kneel."

THE TALE OF TWO TREES

Fall is the tale of two trees standing ever in the minds of the Luathi people. In the west stands the Shalla Tree. Shumma states:

> *The children of Anoh reached the shores of the sea, and great weariness overtook them. Their burdens drove them to the sand, and their laments rose to the heavens. They cried out against Alwain for driving them to their deaths. And Alwain's heart was grieved when he heard their cries and saw their desolation "Look. Humanity followed our decrees and laboured long in their journey. It is our will to shelter them here, to build from them a great people, and to draw forth the spear from their midst for us to cast. Therefore, let us provide respite for them and grant them rest."*
>
> *And the Shalla Tree sprang up among the children of Anoh. Its long, waving limbs shaded them in the cool of its shadow, and its fruit was sweet and refreshing. And the hearts of the children were restored, and once again they praised Alwain.*

~ Shalapher – **Beginnings** *~*

The Shalla Tree symbolizes Alwain's bounty for humanity and Law in the world. It bridges the space between earth and heaven. Luathi work this symbol into their robes and homes. When the Takan ruled the land, the trees withered and died, and the Takan ripped them from the soil. However, after the Uprising, the Shalla grew and bloomed once again in the land. The Shalla grows a yellow fruit that tastes like a tart berry and blooms nearly year-round. The Luathi craft a refreshing wine from the fruit. Most Hasheer staves and Alwainic altars are crafted from Shalla wood. The Luathi say that one who sleeps beneath a Shalla Tree will be sheltered in the hands of Alwain from foreign dreams and the claws of wolves.

In the Luathi mind, the Shalla Tree contrasts the image of the Ironbound Tree of the East. From the *Futheniad*:

> *Fuenten pulled his spear from Ibbi-Suen's neck,*
> *and death's dark shadow came and veiled the Priest-King's empty eyes.*
> *Fuenten strode with Alsipur, beside him Huenten,*
> *Into the throne of Mouadah, the dark and the reviled.*
> *Behind the onyx throne, there rose a dark and mighty tree,*
> *Stripped of leaf and rendered bare, yet twisted and alive.*
> *Its limbs were bound with blackest iron, which dug into its flesh –*
> *Alsipur cried out, "My lord, it bleeds!", for surely it did weep.*
> *Sap flowed free and wine-dark to stain its wood and bands*
> *Like the fangs of the sheep-killing wolf.*
> *But none dared approach the hungry roots, of the ironed tree*
> *For malice homed beneath its limbs, and hatred in its bark.*

Branded into the skin of the Takan, worked into their banners, and painted on wagons at massacre sites, this tree stands in opposition to the Shalla Tree. The Ironbound Tree represents the chaos and darkness of the east, its corruption of flesh and nature, and its desire to bind all living things beneath its rule.

Two trees, two poles of the Zaharets – Law and Chaos. Each tree represents the mediation of heaven and earth, but with two different outcomes. In *Fall*, each tree is represented by an NPC working in the background. Toara, Hasheer of the Scriptorium, represents the Shalla Tree in this campaign. She works to aid the forces of Law in the Zaharets, and to provide a place where the Luathi can rest and thrive, safe from the harshness of the world. Avsalim, a fallen Kahar, represents the Ironbound Tree. He seeks to raise the ancient gates of Mouadah and subjugate the Zaharets beneath his will.

These trees are ever-present in the background of daily life in the Zaharets; likewise, Toara and Avsalim are ever-working behind the scenes. These two, although they do not yet know it, work against each other. Jackals might meet Toara, but they will not see Avsalim directly. Yet his hand affects much of what they do and see. Toara and Avsalim's story comes to the fore in later Zaharets stories; but, for now, events, adventures, and hooks that are part of their tale are marked by their tree. As you proceed through *Fall*, you can see their influence on the Zaharets.

CHAPTER 2
YEAR OF
FALLEN SEEDS

Here marks the site of the victory of Melekbolan III, king of Kelesh across the mountains, against the Takan hordes in the 16th year of his reign. Upon the hill of Muanjin, Melekbolan sets this Ebenezer in remembrance and warning. Never again shall the Eastern Wave crash upon … [inscription breaks off here].

~ **Partial inscription on a stele in the Luasa Desert** ~

INTRODUCTION

The Year of Fallen Seeds is Year One in *The Fall of the Children of Bronze* campaign. Here, you will find the first pebbles that herald the avalanche of the Unification War, the rise of the Daughter Beneath the Earth, and other events. Here, new Jackals take their first steps out on the War Road to discover that the Zaharets is much deeper than they knew, and even their lives are seeds a hand greater than theirs planted for a purpose. Is it not said, *"Never does Alwain's grain fall by accident, nor is his harvest unplanned."* ~ Shalapher ~

THEME

The theme of the Year of Fallen Seeds is the hidden depths of the earth. In both **Mine of Atem** and **The Stone Garden**, Jackals must uncover the earth's secret knowledge of threats from the ancient past of Kalypsis, which might rise once again to threaten the Zaharets.

The central conflict of the Year of Fallen Seeds is communal needs. For the north, this means securing a new source of tin, one of the key components of bronze. It highlights the danger inherent in exploring a world such as Kalypsis, where the current communities are not the first residents of the area. Jackals provide an essential service for the communities of the War Road, but they often cause problems, as well.

For the south, the need is more personal. Sar Japeth has fallen ill. Nabal provided an old Alwainic rite to save the Sar's life, but the items necessary for it are rare, and no one has seen them since the foundation of Sentem. Here, the story of the south begins with the Jackals searching for the asa rose.

IMPORTANT NPCS

Abishai, Hasheer of Rataro: Abishai is a young Hasheer who was banished to Rataro. Once an arrogant scholar, a run-in with Takan several seasons back shook her, and her superiors exiled her to Rataro as punishment. Her discovery of possible tin in the north revitalised her. This renewed confidence led her to hire the Jackals.

Arishat, Hasheer of Sentem: After training at the Scriptorium, Arishat served three generations of the Yesim family. She is working with Nabal to uncover any information on the ritual of exorcism. She knows the location of the Stone Garden and the asa rose.

Ba-en Nafar: (See page 183 of *Jackals*.) Ba-en is Sameel's eyes and ears in Sentem. If the Jackals participated in *The Lost Children* adventure, Ba-en is already aware of them and will approach them to actively search for the ritual material.

Hen-he-net: A Gerwa trader who travels along the War Road, peddling wares, trading rumours, and spying for Ger and for a Mouathenic named Avsalim. The Gerwa trader fell under the Mouathenic's power years ago and, since that time, has worked as his agent in the world. Hen-he-net receives orders from Avsalim through dreams; these orders are always cryptic, yet she follows them without hesitation. Persuading someone like Atem (see the adventure below) to dig in a specific area is one example of Avsalim's far-reaching plans. So far, her orders from Avsalim have not contradicted those from Ger, but she knows it is just a matter of time before she must choose an allegiance. (See *Jackals* page 183 for more information on Hen-he-net and her patronage.)

EVENTS IN THE NORTH

- A Rathic possesses Kinesh of Mikro and delivers the prophecy given at the beginning of this book.
- Orsem Ven begins to send gems to Ameena Noani. The miners discovered azurite and malachite, as well as beryl and chalcedony, leading many to believe they will find tin in the mines.
- Mellou and Aldimir enter the Ligna Hualla and begin to breach the Mouadran chamber site there for information on the Vault of Ur-Takan.

EVENTS IN THE SOUTH

- Wolves (bandits) begin to raid the trade road between Ameena Noani and Sentem.
- Gerwa merchants bearing a writ of contract from the Kiani of Narhi, the westernmost city in Ger, begin to come north. He is offering silver shekels in exchange for two years of service fighting against the Ungathi tribes that harass his city and temple.

RETIREMENT BENEFITS

None for this year.

NORTHERN TALE: MINE OF ATEM

An adventure for Unblooded Jackals, set during the month of Isten, in the rainy season.

OVERVIEW

Three seasons ago, Atem, a Gerwa miner acting on insight from Hen-he-net, discovered a small cave in the foothills north of Orsem Ven. Exploring the cave, he found a wealth of azurite and beryl. So, he began to mine it further and take his findings back to the Orsem. Hen-he-net provided him additional help, as well as guards to protect his claim. Last season, Atem made an even more startling discovery as he followed a small vein of gold – worked stone! Thinking he had discovered an ancient tomb of some sort, Atem began to excavate the wall. Soon, he discovered a door and, breaking the seal, he entered deeper into the mine. Weeks passed, and Atem unearthed a shrine. While exploring the shrine, Atem discovered a series of sealed amphorae, and in breaking one, released a part of the essence of Mealil, a Labasu (a Rathic of disease). The Hulathi of the kingdom of Lukka bound Mealil beneath the earth centuries ago. Atem – now gripped with the spirit's fever – fled the mine and headed to the closest mining camp, seeking healing. Within a week, his guards, miners, and the entire camp were dead, and the sickness slowly spread among the miners and settlers of Orsem Ven. Atem, possessed by Mealil, fled south, spreading the Rathic's disease as he went.

This adventure begins with the group in Rataro, where the Hasheers delve the ruins beneath the city in search of knowledge. While searching for ancient rites and lore, one Hasheer, Abishai, discovered a room full of Hulathi tablets that seemed to be old trade reports. Although seemingly worthless, Abishai diligently reassembled the tablets and discovered reports of tin being shipped to Ameena Noani from Kibeth-Albin, an old Hulathi city in what is now the Vori Wastes. Kibeth-Albin, lost to the waters of history, once sat in the Vori Vana. After months of research in Rataro and the Scriptorium, Abishai narrowed down the location of the old city to the area north-west of Orsem Ven. She hopes its mines are still there and hires a group of Jackals to investigate it for her. Unaware of the plague and the spirit of Mealil, Abishai sets the Jackals on a path north.

TOUCH OF THE MINES

Mealil causes the disease that has come to be known as the Touch of the Mines, and the newly released spirit's power spreads with each infected and slain person. The disease manifests with chills and fever after physical contact with the infected. Within a week, Mealil's mark appears in the bone of the infected person's forehead, growing darker each week the disease progresses, becoming visible as a black blotch after the second week.

Below are the stats for the disease. (Refer to *Jackals* page 159 for rules about diseases.)

DISEASE: TOUCH OF THE MINES

Vector: touch

Cycle: 1 week

Damage: Vitality and Wisdom (divide the damage between the two)

Intensity: 4

Increase the intensity of the disease by one level per 4 Corruption the target possesses. This only applies to the check difficulty, not the damage.

After the disease reduces a target's Wisdom below 9, the target begins to hear whispers drawing them north to the mines. Each day at sundown, the target must make a Willpower check to resist heading into the mine. Jackals make this test against the disease's difficulty. The quarantine is the only thing preventing those infected within in the Orsem from travelling to the mines. Mealil's voice whispers to the souls of the infected, drawing them north for some unknown reason.

ACT 1: RATARO

The adventure begins in Rataro, where the Jackals hear about a Hasheer seeking a pack for a journey to the north.

Reasons for meeting with Abishai could include:
- A desire for a Hasheer patron
- A desire for closer ties with Ameena Noani
- They possess the *Treasure Map* hook, and want information
- The simple promise of reward – silver, information, etc.

Once in Rataro (see page 138 of *Jackals* for more information), the Jackals are directed to one of the many excavation sites around the town. Red-robed figures fill the chambers beneath the town, as well as labourers clad in loincloths, who are clearing rubble, stacking tablets, and assembling fragments. The frantic noise of work and the sounds of collaboration between Hasheers is staggering. Abishai is in a small chamber off one of the main chambers, studying a series of fragments spread across a wooden table. Abishai is a severe-looking young woman, and she is covered in the same red clay dust that coats everything on the site.

Read or paraphrase the following:

The Hasheer does not turn as you enter the small room, engrossed as she is in her studies of the tablet fragments she has painstakingly assembled. Once she notices you, you see the ragged scar that crosses her face.

"From your smell, you must be Jackals. No, I mean no offence. You are the only ones who smell of the outside. I am glad you came; I have need of Jackals to explore something I discovered. It may perhaps aid us all in our fight against the Takan.

As I am sure you know, we get most of the copper for our weapons and armour from the A'hule Asa. However, to make bronze, our redsmiths combine it with a grey dust found in the Vori Wastes. The dust is dangerous to find, transport, and combine with copper. It gets into the lungs, and it means most redsmiths live short lives and die horrible deaths. Tin, what we need is tin. It, too, makes bronze, but it is rare here in the north. Traders say Sentem has ready access to tin, but that is neither here nor there. For now, those mines lie beyond our reach. We must secure our own supply.

The tablets and artefacts here are from an ancient kingdom which once held these lands. These are merchant's reports and records of its trade and taxes. What I have found here could indicate a source of tin in the north. I, and the Sar of Ameena Noani, want to have these records investigated."

Abishai can provide the Jackals the following information:

- The Hasheers of Ameena Noani will pay good silver for information on the availability of tin in the Vori Vana – 200 ss each for investigating the Vori Vana, plus 200 ss more if they bring back evidence of tin.
- The Hasheers can provide food provisions (provisions for two weeks) but nothing in the way of an advancement on the funds. The Hasheers cannot fund an expedition without certainty. This is a reconnaissance mission.
- The journey from Rataro will take just over a week.
- She recommends skirting the Vori Wastes, for the dust contains dangers beyond mere toxins.
- She can provide a contact at Orsem Ven: Hen-he-net, a Gerwa who has worked with the Hasheers before.
- Some of these artefacts are from the inhabitants of Kibeth-Albin and Lukka, whereas others are from Luathi of that time, such as talismans in the shape of bulls. They were found in one of the lower chambers, and she is deciphering the text.
- Kibeth-Albin is probably long gone, fallen with the kingdom of Lukka millennia ago. However, Hulathi ruins often have ways of resisting the ravages of time. She suspects there are some remains beneath the earth.
- There is nothing in the tablets about what happened to Kibeth-Albin, but Abishai knows Kibeth-Albin disappeared from history long before Lukka did.

If the Jackals seek to find out more about Abishai, other Hasheers can share the following information:

- Abishai was sent to Rataro as punishment for some of her theories.
- Her scars are from a Takan attack. She led a group of Jackals into the wastes to prove a theory, and only Abishai and one of the Jackals returned.
- Her theory is on the nature of the wastes and the destruction of Lukka.
- She is obsessed with the legend of Lukka – a kingdom which predates Barak Barad – and a spirit named Nimnamula.

Once the Jackals are ready, the journey to Orsem Ven takes between 10 and 15 days, depending on their route. If the group heads straight across the wastes, the journey takes 10 days and requires five Survival checks against the wastes' difficulty (rules for travel found on page 73 of *Jackals*). This option might cause Corruption. If the group skirts the wastes, they must make seven checks, five against the Plains' difficulty and two against the Mountains' difficulty. After allowing the characters to explore Rataro and resolving the travel checks, proceed to Act 2.

ACT 2: ORSEM VEN AND ENVIRONS

The Vori Vana rise in the west of the Zaharets and are not nearly as tall as the A'hule Asa. They have flat, stunted peaks which barely break the timber line. Broken rows of foothills and ravines flank these squat, brown mountains. These hollows hide monstrous creatures – Takan and wolves – as well as various mining shafts. Some mines were exhausted long ago, whereas others are home to miners associated with Orsem Ven or Kroryla. The opportunities for adventure in the Vori Hills are numerous; see the *Hooks* section at the end of this year for ideas.

Eventually, the Jackals come upon the remains of a miner's house. The group spots a funeral pyre smouldering in the distance long before they see the ruins. Other miners started the fire when they came upon the site of a Takan attack in the home. They mounted the Takan heads on spears outside the home and burned the bodies of the three miners within. Inside, the aftermath of a slaughter greets the Jackals. If they search through the remains of the pyre, they find six skulls – three human, and three Takan – all with the same dark mark on their foreheads.

Eventually, the Jackals reach Orsem Ven. There, they see several dozen bodies around its perimeter, some burned to nearly black ash and some with javelins still sticking out of them. The gates to the orsem are closed. The guards above the gate stand with their javelins at the ready.

Read or paraphrase the following:

The squat fort sits on the edge of the foothills. Although the stones are painted to resemble the green stone of the other orsems, it fools no one. Those who have seen true orsems know Ven for an imposter, for the fading light of day does not set the tower ablaze with pale light. The great wooden gates, banded with thick bronze, are shut, even though there is a small group of miners and traders gathered outside Orsem Ven. Strange lumps pock the hard-packed ground at the base of the fort's walls, and guards stand vigilant at its ramparts. The group of miners at the gates yell at the guards, but none of them seem to care.

Approaching the crowd, the Jackals see that most of the miners and traders are listening to one person, a short Gerwa woman flanked by two Melkoni warriors. The woman is Hen-he-net. She is trying to calm the crowd, speaking oil over their turbulent souls. [Should anyone attempt an Influence check to determine Hen-he-net's goals, a success gives them the impression Hen-he-net is out of her depth trying to calm an angry mob. A critical success reveals her words might soothe for now, but they do not address the issue. If the crowd's anger is not quelled, it could return seven-fold stronger.]

Aiding Hen-he-net requires a difficult Influence check. A fumble could lead to a short outburst of violence!

Luathi and Melkoni make up the crowd. They look haggard, dirty, and hungry. Most bear scars and wounds consistent with mining and panning – bruises, ragged cuts from sharp rocks, and burn marks.

Any member of the crowd can impart the following information:

- The orsem sealed its gates three weeks ago.
- The guards killed Old Laemon for trying to scale the walls.
- The guards say there is a plague inside the city, but the last body they threw over the wall was four days ago. The Sar is trying to keep the plague out.
- Orsem Ven is the only place to resupply food and wares within a week's journey.
- Starvation is their main fear – there is no plague out in the crowd.
- Hen-he-net is helping as best she can, but the merchant arrived a week ago, and her food is almost gone as well.
- Some of the outlying mines have gone silent, mainly to the north of the orsem.

Hen-he-net is a short Gerwa woman with dark kohl under her eyes and a magnificent braid she keeps oiled. When she ponders matters, she is prone to stroking her braid. Her two Melkoni guards, Persephora and Herkadon, are kitted out in leather and bronze. They never let Hen-he-net out of their sight. Usually, one is at the carts while the other stands watch over their mistress.

Hen-he-net can impart the following information:

- She has been coming to Orsem Ven for eight seasons now.
- Her trade route goes from Kroryla to Sentem. She likes to spend the wet season in the north and the dry in the south.
- She mainly trades in grains, ores, and precious metals, but she has a brisk trade in ferrying messages and goods along the War Road.
- She has heard of Abishai's wild thoughts on Kibeth-Albin, but she has found no evidence of a city in the area.
- However, she has heard of a miner named Atem, who discovered a strange statue of a weeping woman in his dig site.
- Atem was the first to show signs of the plague.
- She can give directions to Atem's mine: it lies two days north-west of the orsem.
- She is shocked by the fact that the orsem is closed; she cannot believe the fort would deny people food. No one in Ger would be treated so.

Hen-he-net has several goods to trade, should the Jackals be interested:

- A jade figurine of an Ukuku bird. 15 ss
- Two bronze khopeshes of Gerwa manufacture (one provides +1 damage but gives a –5% penalty to Melee Combat due to its unbalanced nature). 100 ss and 120 ss for the unbalanced one.
- 20 javelins. 50 ss each.
- A bronze necklace set with lapis lazuli. 250 ss.

If they speak with the orsem guards (which requires a difficult Influence check), the Jackals can discover:

- The orsem has been closed for three weeks.
- The guards sealed the fort on Nawsi Hamar's orders.
- The goal is to keep out the sick, and to deal with the plague inside.
- Hamar is Hasheer-trained, and believes the sickness is a spirit of plague. The Hasheer's rites are proving effective at keeping the plague at bay.
- The gates will not open until they go ten days without incident.
- The first to get sick were from the mines to the north, specifically a Gerwa miner named Atem.
- They can give directions to Atem's mine (see above).

If they investigate the lumps around the walls, the Jackals discover that they are bodies, wrapped in linen and packed with salt. The guards have been throwing the sick, some still alive, over the edge of the wall for weeks. In total, there are some 35 bodies around the walls of the orsem. The linen around the forehead of each body is stained black, as though they all died from the same sort of wound. Should the Jackals attempt to unwrap a body, the guards from the walls shout at them. If they persist, the guards fire one warning shot, then make attempts to bring the Jackals down (Ranged Combat; 65%; 1d8 damage). Some trinkets were buried with the dead. Jackals wishing to steal from the dead (and gain Corruption, per page 151 of *Jackals*) must make a Stealth check. Should they succeed, have them roll on the following table:

MINE OF ATEM: WHAT IS ON THE DEAD BODY	
2d4	Discovery
2	The plague! Roll versus the Touch of the Mines – see page 20.
3	An onyx statue worth 18 ss
4	A small opal-hilted dagger worth 15 ss
5	A ring worth 6 ss
6	A necklace worth 12 ss
7	A small Rephaim statue worth 15 ss
8	A small malachite statue of a kneeling woman with her head bowed and her hair covering her face worth 30 ss.

ACT 3: MINE OF ATEM

The Jackals should have no issue finding Atem's mine after their encounters at Orsem Ven. The mine is about two days to the north-west of Orsem Ven, in the Vana foothills. Travelling there requires one Survival check against the Mountains' difficulty (see page 73 of *Jackals* for travel rules). Should the check trigger an encounter, the Jackals meet a wandering Takan pack consisting of 1 Oritakan, 1d6 Mavakan, and 2d6 Norakan. These Takan all bear the same weeping wounds on their foreheads as those found on the dead outside Orsem Ven.

Atem had no homestead; rather, he slept just inside the entrance to his mine – a cave set in the side of a cliff 130 cubits (1 cubit = 1.5 feet) above the plains. Atem set up climbing ropes from the cave mouth down to a nature path, about 30 cubits from the entrance.

Kauma is high in the evening sky at this moment, casting much of the cliff face in blood red hues. The ascent is a simple one, requiring only time (no need for a skill check). A successful Perception check reveals fresh claw marks in the cliff. A successful Survival check identifies them as Takan.

1. Entrance

What a Jackal's senses reveal:

Sights – completely dark. Walls made of sedimentary rock, bearing the smooth markings of water erosion near the front of the cave and recent chisel marks near the back. The ceiling near the front is stained black by smoke.

Smells – smoky, sweaty, sickly smells. The bedroll is the source of the sweat and sickly smell. The hole in the back of the room possesses a dry smell.

Sounds – dripping water, the wind howling, the flap at the front of the cave snapping in the wind. A successful Perception check at the hole reveals the sounds of shuffling in the dark.

Atem made his home in the entrance of his mine, which is curtained with a thick hide blanket spiked to the mine itself. The remnants of a small firepit occupy the centre of the room near the entrance. Eight small clay figurines are arranged in a semi-circle around the head of the bedroll (these are representations of the Eight of Ger). Mining tools, all bronze, lie along the wall, as well as baskets which once held foodstuffs. These were recently torn apart. Pus-soaked bandages lie next to the bedroll.

The side of the room farthest from the entrance contains a hole down into the hill, as well as buckets. Atem sorted the gemstones he discovered into these wooden buckets, set around the entrance to the next level. The buckets contain the following gemstones:

- Spinel – 15 ss worth
- Fire agate – 60 ss worth
- Beryl – 35 ss worth

Note that the worth given is for the raw stones. Should these gems be cut and polished with a successful Craft check (a failed check ruins the gem), they double in value; a critical success triples it.

The Jackals can access the next level of the mine via the hole and the ladder within.

2. Upper Mines

What a Jackal's senses reveal:

Sights – completely dark. Some walls are made of sedimentary rock and bear the marks of chisels and pickaxes. Others are the dark grey stone of the mountain. Atem used timber to shore up the tunnels between the naturally occurring caves. In torch light, parts of the walls glitter with metallic and mineral deposits [silver and gemstones]. There are strange rocks that look like eggs; they are hollow and look like their insides were scraped out.

Smells – dry and foul smells. The tight confines trap older scents.

Sounds – dripping water and scrapes in the darkness. The sounds of rock fragments being kicked about by careless feet.

These were the first areas Atem opened at the start of his dig. The relative ease of digging through the sedimentary rock helped him expand the mines. Little did he know, he was exploring an old mine, which flooded and was sealed a millennia ago. Atem dug out the new rock from one of the old mine tunnels.

There are four main areas in the upper mines, joined by tight tunnels that make it difficult for Jackals to bring heavy weapons to bear (+1 Clash Point cost to all attacks with heavy weapons while in the tunnels). Takan also infest these tunnels, drawn here by the spirit of Mealil.

Three of the areas are identical – large caves where the sedimentary rock has not been completely excavated. Atem grew frustrated as he struck the older shafts, subconsciously knowing he was digging through someone else's site. There are remnants of broken tools, old meals, and other detritus of the age. A successful Perception check allows a Jackal to roll a d6 to discover what might lay under the debris. A critical success gives them a +2 to the roll.

	WHAT IS IN THE MINE?
d6	Found
1	Nothing of interest
2	Bone fragments
3	Bronze pick-axe head – cracked
4	Blade to a bronze dagger, the hilt wrapping haven fallen away to dust. It bears the mark of the shield with the sunburst. 5 ss.
5	A silver coin bearing the image of a regal woman on one side and the shielded sunburst on the other. 5 ss, or 15 ss if sold to a Hasheer in Rataro.
6	A small silver bracelet set with polished amber stones. 50 ss.
7	A small piece of lapis lazuli in the shape of the eye of Djhutemos – Atem's. 45 ss.
8	A small statue of a weeping woman. For a Hasheer or Kahar, this statue provides +4 Devotion Points per day, which renew at sunrise.

The final room in this level holds two additional points of interest. First, this is where Norakan burrowed into the mine, drawn by Mealil's released power. There is a hole in the cave wall, piles of dirt pushed out around the opening, and Norakan (two per Jackal) crouched at the edge of the descent. If the Jackals are noisy while exploring the other areas of this level, the Norakan hear them with a successful Common skill check. In this case, the Norakan ambush the Jackals. If the Norakan flee, they run into the tunnel that leads back to their warrens, not further into the cave.

The other point of interest is the entrance to the lower mines. Atem discovered this by accident, when he uncovered the sealed door during his excavation of the mines. A large stone slab lies next to the hole that leads into the lower mines, etched with marks made when Atem ripped it out of the wall. It is covered in strange iconography. There are bulls at the four corners of the slab: the top two are magnificent specimens and face outwards, whereas the bottom two, standing in a river, are emaciated and face inwards. In the centre of the slab is a bare-chested, powerfully built man holding lightning in each hand. He sits on a mountain top, poised to strike the emaciated bulls.

A successful Ancient Lore check reveals this is an image of Ashkagael, one of the local Luathi gods before the revelation of Alwain through Shumma. Beyond the slab, a set of rough-cut stairs descends further into the mountain.

Studying the slab grants a Jackal +2% to Ancient Lore.

3. Lower Mines

What a Jackal's senses reveal:

Sights – completely dark. The walls transition to older, worked stone. See individual location write-ups for descriptions of the walls.

Smells – there are few scents here; the air is dry and old. Every so often, however, the Jackals pick up a hint of something bestial.

Sounds – a successful Perception check at the entrance reveals shuffling sounds in the dark and the sounds of metal striking stone.

Features of this area include:

Geodes – geodes are rocks with crystal formations inside. Several large geodes contributed to the finds Atem sorted into buckets; these are the empty egg-like rocks the Jackals found above. To discover that the egg-like rocks are geodes, Jackals must specifically look at them. Opening them requires a successful Craft check to preserve the gems inside. There are several large geodes scattered throughout this level: each area has 1d4 – 1 geodes. A geode is worth 1d10 ss as a raw gem. Use the rules found in Area 1 for cutting/refining them.

Signs of Atem's digging are not visible here. The stone door above sealed off this area for centuries, leaving the lower area undisturbed.

THE STORY BEHIND THE LOWER MINES

Ancient Luathi also excavated in this area and uncovered the old Hulathi sanctum, where the Children of Silver buried Mealil the Labasu. When Mealil manifested and consumed the lives of all who lived in Kibeth-Albin, the Hulathi captured and bound Mealil beneath a mine per the rites of the Alwainic faith. They sealed the shrine, which was buried under a landslide during the Wars of Heated Death. One of the Luathi tribes of the Ausueda found this shrine a thousand years ago while digging in the area. However, the Ausueda feared the sites of the Children of Silver and sealed it. This seal was broken by Atem.

The large area of this level was the old Luathi dig site. Here, the old Luathi kings found tin, but they fled the mine as soon as the old Hulathi ruins were discovered. Wooden carts lie abandoned, along with primitive mining tools cast from bronze (200 ss worth of bronze, but they are bulky and weigh down a Jackal with 5 Encumbrance). With a successful Lore or Craft check, a Jackal knows the old bronze can be melted down and recast. Should the Jackals spend an hour digging around the area, a successful Perception check turns up several rock formations with black mineral deposits in them. Tin! However, the quantity of tin here is quite low, confirming the mine was exhausted long ago. With a successful Lore check, a Jackal can work out that there is about 25 shekels' worth of tin left in these rocks, which can produce about 250 shekels of bronze! That is enough to craft five fine spear heads or four leaf-bladed swords. Although this might not seem like a lot to the Jackals, it should stress the importance of finding a larger tin supply for Ameena Noani.

On the far side of the cave stands a door in the rock. In front of it, about 50 paces out from the door, is a low stone circle set in the ground. The rock around the door is sedimentary and carries past the door, giving the appearance that whatever structure was once attached to the door was swallowed up by the earth. The door is made of hestul, which catches and amplifies the light from the Jackal's torches.

There is also a group of Takan, which entered through the Norakan tunnel in the level above and is attempting to open the door to the shrine. The Takan have yet to notice the break in the roof above the door which Atem used to enter and exit the shrine. An Oritakan oversees the group, while a Mavakan and a handful of Norakan (one per Jackal) attempt to pry open the doors. The Mavakan wears a pair of silver armbands in the shape of wolves' heads, each worth 95 ss, and carries a bronze spearhead of fine Luathi craftsmanship, which it picked up from this area. The spear head is etched with prayers to one of the Balim, but the name is worn away with time. If a Jackal attaches the spearhead to a long spear, its keen edge adds +2 damage. The Mavakan also wears a boar's-tooth helm, inlaid with silver and fire opals, worth 75 ss.

Once the Jackals deal with the Takan, they can investigate the door. The door's relief is of a kneeling woman facing those who approach the door. Her head is bowed, and her hair hangs down in front of her head. A pair of fountains spring up on either side of her knees. Behind her, the sunburst of Alwain is prominently displayed, as if bathing her in its light. At the base of the woman's knees is an inscription. In Hulathi (which requires a difficult Lore or normal Ancient Lore check to discern), the inscription reads:

> Like a river, I flow from my head –
>> following the paths
> Of crags and cliff. I fall like rain
>> To strike the earth below.
> Though my water is bittersweet,
>> often you will find
> That though it flows both free and fast,
>> Laughter follows behind.

The door is sealed, and resistant to the weapons of the Takan and Jackals alike.

There are several ways to enter the shrine:

- Notice the opening in the roof behind the door, which Atem used. This requires a successful Perception check.
- A Kahar or Hasheer can attempt a rite to open the door. This requires a successful Lore check and the expenditure of 3 Devotion Points.
- Decipher the riddle of the door and call out the words 'Tears' in Hulathi: *Ula*.

In any of these cases, the Jackals gain access to the shrine.

4. Hidden Shrine

This is the room where Atem freed the spirit of Mealil. Massive hestul pillars support a tall roof. The pillars are carved into the shape of masts, and the floor bears fine-grain marks reminiscent of wood, although it is stone. A small, boat-like altar, marked with the full sunburst of Alwain and flanked by two statues of malachite in the shape of the weeping woman with a bowed head, dominates the centre of the room. One of the statues has been shattered by Atem and lies broken at the foot of the altar. A large chunk of malachite is missing from the broken statue: specifically, its hands. A sense of melancholy and sorrow seems to flow from the other statue. On the altar is a series of what seem to be broken amphorae, marked with a shield and a sunburst within. This is the symbol of ancient Lukka.

The amphorae are broken and empty, but there lingers within a rancid oil – the medium in which Mealil was bound. Any Jackal touching the oil must roll immediately against the Touch of the Mines at +2 Potency.

The friezes on the walls show scenes of the Binding of Mealil by the shining knights of Lukka. These warriors bound the spirit in chains, rendered it down in seven burning cauldrons, and poured its remains into seven amphorae. A successful Perception or Lore check gives the Jackal the impression this shrine lies east of the city of the warriors (which is Kibeth-Albin). Also, there are only six amphorae here, all broken. The seventh appears to be missing (see *Mirim Mahazra* on page 123 to discover what happened to the seventh amphora).

A successful easy Culture (Own) check is enough to know that diseases in this world come from one of two sources: a spirit of disease or a messenger from the gods. This is clearly the work of the first.

A successful Lore check gives the Jackal an impression of the importance of the missing amphora. If it holds Mealil's power, then possessing it would be Mealil's sole goal. If Mealil could destroy the seventh amphora, the Labasu's power would fully manifest. But if its power remains bound within the oil, the Jackals can track Mealil's essence and contain it with the correct rites. Rites which, unbeknown to the Jackals, Abishai is close to uncovering (see *Mirim Mahazra* on page 123 for the next part of this story).

A successful Perception check reveals something hidden within the broken statue. When Atem, possessed by Mealil, feverously lashed out to destroy the image of the Labasu's tormentor before fleeing in madness, he inadvertently revealed a means of binding the spirit's essence. Within the statue of the woman lies a pair of sealed alabaster jars. A honeyed substance imbued with herbs fills each jar. This substance, found after Kibeth-Albin fell to the plague, can drive Mealil's essence from its victim's body. If the Jackals break the other statue, they find another two jars, for a total of four. Each jar contains four doses of the medicinal unguent, which must be applied to the mark of Mealil on the victim's head.

Each statue is made from close to 20 talents' worth (60,000 shekels) of malachite. Should the Jackals wish to carry off both statues to sell them, this is akin to grave robbing. However, taking a sizable chunk of the broken one (at 1 Encumbrance; worth about 200 ss) seems acceptable to Alwain.

Aftermath

Having discovered the mine, possibly some tin, the remains of Mealil, and the unguent, the Jackals probably want to inform Abishai of their findings. Should they deliver the unguent to Orsem Ven, Nawsi Hamar gives them 150 ss each in reward, as well as a place at his table whenever they journey this way. He also resupplies them and re-opens the orsem.

The return journey follows the same rules stated in Act 2. When the Jackals return to Rataro, Abishai pays them for their journey and for any tin they brought back (100 ss each). While disappointed that the tin mine is exhausted, Abishai is fascinated by any mention of the woman, as well as by the existence of Mealil. She believes she has seen that name before and begins delving the catalogues for more information.

When the adventure is over, the following is true:

- The Jackals should know Atem released something into the Zaharets and it fled.
- Some of them might be marked by Mealil – either spiritually or physically (diseased).
- Tracking the spirit is difficult.
- It seems the spirit was originally bound by the Children of Silver.
- Relapse in the Year of Chill Winds picks up this story thread naturally. However, should your Jackals pursue Mealil now, use that adventure when the Jackals seek to find more information about the spirit and the Hulathi.

Advancements

- 1 for discovering the existence of Mealil
- 1 for discovering the tin is exhausted
- 1 for ending the threat of plague for Orsem Ven
- Ending the threat also increases each Jackal's Kleos by 1

SOUTHERN TALE: THE STONE GARDEN

An adventure for Unblooded Jackals, set during the month of Isten, in the rainy season.

OVERVIEW

Sar Japeth aben Yesim is a tormented man. For the past six months, a spiritual malady has claimed his mind and body. Dark spirits haunt him day and night, reducing the once great man to a wild beast penned in his room. His hair grew long, his nails are like claws, and he howls at apparitions only he can see. The affliction is so great, Sameel locked his father away and took up the mantle of the Sar of Sentem in all but name. Kahars, healers, and Hasheers are unable to cure his father. Yet, a month ago, Kahar Nabal discovered a possible rite to save the Sar. It is an ancient exorcism rite, one which Nabal found in his temple. However, it requires rare and unusual ingredients: an asa rose, the freely given heart of an Aeco ayal, and a piece of hesoa – a stone from the old Hannic moon road. When Sameel discussed this with his advisers, Hasheer Arishat revealed she may know where Jackals could find an asa rose.

Arishat knows of a strange location, high in the mountains of the A'hule Asa, which she refers to as the Stone Garden. It is a massive dome of thick granite which rises from the top of a mountain plateau. Although no one is sure of its origin, Arishat knows that during her youth, the Stone Garden was a place in which the asa rose grew. However, there were never many roses to begin with, and she has not visited the location in three decades.

With the raid on Bartak Kentak on the horizon, Sameel's steward, Ba-en Nafar, makes the decision to hand off this mission to Jackals, to ensure the raid is not compromised.

This adventure begins while the group is in Sentem, after the events of *The Lost Children* adventure in *Jackals*. Nawsi Sameel of Sentem is looking for Jackals to aid him in a sensitive mission as he continues to prepare for the upcoming cleansing of Bartak Kentak. Sameel is worried for his father, whose physical and mental health continue to degenerate. Hired by Ba-en Nafar, the Jackals must journey into the A'hule Asa, seek out the legendary Stone Garden, and find the rare asa rose. Armed with knowledge – and perhaps a rough map – the Jackals must brave the A'hule Asa during the rainy season to recover this secret of the earth to save Sameel's father.

[See *Jackals* page 126 for a description of Sentem, page 183 for background on Ba-en Nafar, page 185 for background on Sameel, and page 139 for secrets of Sentem.]

ACT 1: SENTEM

This adventure assumes the Jackals participated in *The Lost Children* scenario. If this is not the case, the Loremaster can use a similar setup to the one found at the beginning of that adventure for drawing the Jackals into this one.

Ba-en Nafar calls for the Jackals a week or two after they have rested from their previous exploits. He sits just inside the gate, where he can watch the road into Sentem, the Aeco Plains, and the inner courtyard where the elders gather.

Read or paraphrase the following:

Ba-en Nafar stands there, within the shadow of Sentem's gatehouse, watching you approach. The man's eyes never seem to linger long in any one spot, yet always seem to snap to you when you enter his vision. The inner square is filled with the sound of the town's elders meting out wisdom, advice, and justice in low murmurs, punctuated by the occasional shout.

Nodding at you, Ba-en withdraws a fish spine from between his teeth and waves you closer. As always, the Gerwa man gets straight to the point:

"Iiwey*, Jackals. I have need of your services again, and there is silver to be made for my tasks. What I have is a need for secrecy. Sameel is preparing the people for a strike at the festering nest of Bartak Kentak, and nothing can disrupt their confidence. Am I clear? Good. You may have heard about Sar Japeth, as the people of Sentem tend to trade in words more than goods. It is true, the Sar is sick, but Kahar Nabal thinks he may have a rite to drive off the spirits. Sameel cannot go himself, with the upcoming raid. He needs Jackals to go get this ingredient for him. And only Arishat, our Hasheer, knows where it is."

He pulls a small wooden token from his belt and hands it to one of the Jackals. It is a smooth wooden disc, marked with the Yesim family symbol on one side and an Ukuku bird on the other.

"This is my token; it will get you in to see Arishat. Speak with her and no one else. Jackals who scare off wolves get fed; those who yelp too loudly get driven off, or worse. Do I make myself clear? Good."

*"Welcome" in Gerwan.

Ba-en Nafar can share the following information:

- Nabal has gathered almost all the rite's components, but the last couple are so rare they are nearly impossible to obtain.
- The raid preparation is going well. Sameel is taking the information discovered in *The Lost Children* under advisement.
- Although the raid is important, so is getting the Sar back on his feet.
- Trouble is brewing on the War Road – Ba-en can feel it in his bones.
- Wolves (bandits) are harassing caravans to the north. Two such raids happened in the previous season. Ba-en is worried they are pushing south, towards Sentem.
- Ba-en Nafar can pay the Jackals 150 ss apiece to search for the Garden, and a further 150 ss each if they find an asa rose and bring it back.
- This task must be undertaken with discretion. Although the town knows the Sar is sick, there would be panic if the people found out he was sick enough to need a rite.

Arishat's rooms are within the Yesim fortress. The fortress stands tall in the middle of the town – the oldest building there. Some of the Sentemites whisper that the giants of the mountain carved the fortress out of the living stone of the earth for the first of the Yesim line. Ba-en Nafar's token gets the Jackals into the fortress, and the guards can provide directions to Arishat's living quarters. They are on the top floor of the far southern side of the fortress, since Arishat loves to go up onto the roof to chart the stars. The wooden door to her room is marked with a rough carving of a short staff. She answers any knock with rough grumbles, and the sound of shuffling soon after. Arishat is a rough-cut woman in her later years. She keeps her grey hair braided down her back, and she wears a Hasheer's red cord over her left shoulder. She offers wine to the Jackals after she opens her doors for them to enter.

Read or paraphrase the following:

"Come in, come in. Plains children never move fast enough for me." Arishat moves to the side of the door, welcoming you all inside. The Hasheer's rooms in the fortress are nearly as large as some of the houses of the crafts folk in the town below. Three large rooms, joined in the middle, are visible as you enter. The first seems to be a sitting room and library – the walls feature alcoves filled with scrolls. Looking beyond, you can see and smell a workshop. The earthy odour seems to come from there, and you glimpse a stout, wooden ladder which leads to the roof. A woven curtain blocks the door to the third room. It bears the staff and flame of the Scriptorium.

Arishat moves slowly, but with purpose, gathering cups and wine for the Jackals.

"So, what brings Roadwalkers to my door?"

Arishat listens to the Jackals, nodding all the while as she pours the wine. When they mention why they are here, read or paraphrase the following:

"Ah yes, Nabal's ritual. I am not even sure it can work, but Sameel is grasping at hope like straws. Very well. I will tell you what I know. What Nabal requires is an asa rose. It goes by many other names – Jahazanrab to the Trauj, Mountain Bloom or Ahanilanta to the Hulathi of old. They all refer to the same thing. A stone flower which blooms on the side of the highest peaks of the A'hule Asa. The old scrolls say they were more bountiful in the old days, during the time of the Grand Kingdoms. Perhaps the Hulathi were better tenders of the world than we. Bah, much has passed, and much has been lost. Where was I? Oh yes, the asa rose. These stone flowers bloomed where the light of Alwain was strongest, the earth responding to the light like seeds in a ploughed field. Those who came before felt that these roses, should they be harvested correctly, bore the power

and strength of the mountain with them. And should one know how, they may impart that vitality to another."

She pauses for a moment, as though gathering her strength.

"I know of one spot in the mountains where the asa rose may still grow, although it has been many years since I was last able to make the journey. Then, there were less than a dozen blooms growing in the Stone Garden. But, if there is one to be found in the A'hule Asa, the Stone Garden is where you will find it."

Arishat can impart the following information:

- The old Hasheer has worked for the Yesim family for three decades.
- She does not know what plagues Japeth, but fears it is a Rathic of some sort.
- She visited the Stone Garden when she was a young woman.
- The strange place is a half-dome of stone that rises out of the earth. She believes it is Nahunum work, but she has no idea what its purpose is.
- Transporting the asa rose is delicate work, but she knows the rites to prepare a stone bowl to help them do so. The Jackals can harvest the rose with a knife of stone, which she can loan them.
- If the Jackals are willing to bring two roses back, should two exist, she will pay them handsomely: 150 ss apiece.
- She is willing to part with 1d4 + 1 doses of acalana resin before their journey into the mountains, but drops the reward she offers by 30 ss per person for each one the group takes.
- She warns the Jackals that the Stone Garden is holy ground, and they should treat it with the proper reverence.

Once the group is ready to head into the mountains, proceed to Act 2.

ACT 2: THE ASCENT

The A'hule Asa, or the Great Mountains, tower above the Aeco Plains and divide the lands of the Luathi and the desert of the Trauj. Home to Nephalim, Wolves (bandits), and other creatures, a trip into the mountains means leaving behind what safety one can find among the settlements of Sentem and Densom. The A'hule Asa's foothills quickly rise into sharp ravines and defiles, with few paths into the higher regions. It is rough going for the Jackals.

Once the Jackals are ready, the journey to the Stone Garden takes between four and seven days. This journey requires one Survival check against the Mountains' difficulty, found on page 74 of *Jackals*.

As Ba-en Nafar suspected, there are Wolves in the mountains. A band of Wolves, known as the Qayim, harass caravans and peddlers along the War Road. Because the towns and villages are independent or only loosely affiliated, the Qayim find the area easy to plunder. Their leader, Hanni a Luathi of the Geshrun Tribe, grows complacent, and starts to ponder the riches of the south. The rumours of Sar Japeth's illness reach his ears, and he sends his second, a Trauj warrior named Tamu, to scout the region. Tamu sets up a small camp in a cave in the mountains; from there, the Wolves can scout down into the plains. Her band, while part of the Qayim, take the mark of two black nails as a sign within the Qayim that they are loyal to Tamu. She grows restless and raids two traders in the plains, slaughtering all witnesses and leaving evidence behind to mask their presence. Sentem believes Takan are behind these raids, but Ba-en Nafar suspects differently.

Halfway into the journey, or as a random encounter, read or paraphrase the following:

The journey is rough going, almost as if the A'hule Asa's indifference to your presence has turned hostile. Sheer cliffs and rough defiles replace the lush grass and gentle hills of the Aeco Plains. You follow the path of a small mountain stream, which eventually joins up with others below to flow into the Asa Etho. The shear sides of its paths fall away suddenly, and you find yourself in a broad mountain clearing where the stream meanders, resting after its journey from the peaks before it continues its rush to the plains.

Something feels off, however. The mountain sounds are strangely silent here, and you can see wooden crates stacked against the side of a low cliff. Someone is here.

If the Jackals were moving silently as they travelled up the mountain, they sneak up on the Wolves, as the stream masks their noise. However, if the group made no such declaration, roll once – using their Common group skill of 45% – to see whether the Qayim lookout notices them. On a success, the Qayim lay an ambush for the Jackals.

In the event of an Ambush:

Follow the rules for ambushes found on page 62 of *Jackals*. The Qayim, in this case, roll for Stealth with a skill of 65%. After the initial volley of arrows and javelins, Tamu offers the Jackals the chance to leave with their lives. This only costs the Jackals all their gear. (Tamu is honourable, for a Wolf, and should the Jackals comply, they are allowed to leave with enough food to get them back to Sentem. This gives Tamu time to relocate the Qayim. However, should a Jackal choose violence, the Qayim will fight [one Qayim, plus one per Jackal. Use the stats for Wolves from page 209 of *Jackals*].

In the event the Jackals approach the cave without the Wolves spotting them:

The Qayim are all resting in the cave from the heat of the day – save for their lookout, Asan, who has grown lazy, as he has never seen anyone but his fellow Wolves in the area. Should the Jackals approach with successful Stealth checks, they come across a sleeping Asan. Should anyone fail their Stealth check, Asan makes a Perception check with the negative trait *Sleeping* (add an extra 1s die to the roll and take the worst result). On a success, Asan wakes and calls out a warning to Tamu and the rest of the Wolves [one Qayim, plus one per Jackal. Use the stats for Wolves from page 209 of *Jackals*].

The Qayim will not fight to the death in either case. When their morale breaks, they surrender to the Jackals, hoping for mercy. This episode sets Hanni against the Jackals – no matter how they respond – and sets the Qayim leaders' eyes upon Sentem.

Tamu speaks for the Qayim. Their recent plunder resides in the cave, but Tamu is far more concerned with getting word to Hanni. She sends one of her Wolves through a secret path out of the cave to warn the commander.

Within the cave, the Jackals find the spoils of the Qayim, as well as the plunder from two recent raids on caravans.

Personal plunder:

- Set of silver figurines depicting Ahote and Djhutemos, 100 ss each
- Four rings, 20 ss each
- Dried fruits and meats – enough food for a Jackal for four days. 5 ss.

Merchant plunder:

- A golden necklace set with rubies, 300 ss
- Three talents of cedar wood, 500 ss
- A silver crown set with lapis lazuli and onyx stones, 450 ss
- 50 talents of Gerwa bronze, 600 ss

Should the Jackals keep any of the merchants' goods, they gain Corruption per the banditry corruptive action (see page 151 of *Jackals*). They do not gain Corruption for taking the Qayim's personal plunder, but they do gain a total of 15 Corruption for taking all the merchants' goods. The Jackals can avoid taking this Corruption if they bring the goods back to Sentem and turn them over to Ba-en Nafar.

Once the Jackals deal with the Qayim, (remember, leading the Wolves back to Sentem takes an extra two days' travel time and provokes another travel check on the way to the Stone Garden), they can continue their journey to the Stone Garden. If the Jackals have hirelings, they can send them back to guard the Wolves, instead.

ACT 3: THE STONE GARDEN

The Jackals eventually spot the Stone Garden in the distance on the fourth day of travel out of Sentem. It is a grey dome that rises against the towering walls of the A'hule Asa and continues to reveal itself as the Jackals climb higher into the mountains. The stone arc is nearly 200 cubits high at its apex and stretches out nearly 400 cubits from side to side. Its surface is smooth, unmarred by any scars or damage; but, as the Jackals approach, they see what appear to be a half-dozen growths on the northern side of the sphere, about 60 cubits up along the curve.

These growths are asa roses, which are made of a mineral that grows into the shape of a rose over centuries. They are a concentrated form of the power of the Law of Alwain, which only grow in sacred places in the A'hule Asa. However, the Takan of the mountain tribes routinely come through here and scrape off the flowers, or at least those they can reach. Therefore, Nahausteta – a Nahunum – has settled near the Stone Garden. The Garden's need drew her, after she renounced a life of violence. She sits here, year upon year, tending the Garden and guarding the Asa roses from all intruders… including the Jackals.

Read or paraphrase the following:

The grey dome rises to the heavens as you approach it. Its base merges with the stone of the A'hule Asa, and its apex brushes the sky. There, on its western arc, you can see what you came for – a slight hazing on the surface of the smooth stone: the asa roses of the Stone Garden. As you near the great dome, an explosion of sound and stone fragments to your left catches your attention. A Nahunum, one of the giant-kin, slowly walks towards you out of the shadow of Mihshalnim's peak, already hefting another stone.

"Settle! Come no closer to the garden of earth. Who are you and for what reason do you come?"

Nahunum are dangerous foes, especially for Jackals new to the War Road. Should the group try to fight Nahausteta, it will most likely end in many of their deaths. However, Nahausteta is a guardian, not an adversary per se, and she is willing to talk. Nahausteta is intrigued by the Jackals' approach, as they are the first humans to appear in the short while she has been guarding the Stone Garden.

Nahausteta was not the guardian of the Stone Garden when Arishat visited this place decades ago. There was no guardian then; only in recent years did the Garden summon Nahausteta to protect it from the depredation of the Takan.

Nahausteta's disposition towards the Jackals starts off as neutral. She will only allow the Jackals to harvest the asa rose from the Stone Garden once she is friendly towards them.

Jackals can accomplish this in the following ways:

- Influence checks. Nahausteta delights in conversation.
- Simple Perform checks. Nahausteta, like all Nahunum, enjoys a well-told story. Attempts to sway her with a story about the Jackals' valour or their people goes a long way towards showing Nahausteta who they are.
- Explain their need – this also requires an Influence check, but it is a difficult check. After all, she is a guardian.
- Talk about slaying Takan – this is a free success (limited to once per negotiation).
- Speak well of the Hulathi, Children of Silver, or the sea – this is a free success (limited to once per negotiation)
- An Athletics check to engage Nahausteta in a contest of strength or rock throwing.

Loremasters can apply a trait to these checks for good roleplaying on the player's part. However, Jackals can also lose favour with Nahausteta by doing any of the following:

- Intimidation checks – these are an automatic failure.
- Threats with weapons – Nahausteta attempts to convince the Jackals to put them away. The Jackals in question must make a Willpower check. Should the Jackals succeed, they have the option of putting their weapons away quickly. If they do not, count this as a 'failure' for the scene.

The Jackals need to accumulate **six successes** (critical successes count as two successes) before they incur **three failures** to persuade Nahausteta to let them claim the asa rose. It is up to each Loremaster to decide whether to keep the skill challenge requirements a secret from the players or to share them.

Nahausteta might ask the following questions during the discussion:

- Who are you?
- Does silver still shine among the plains below? (She is asking whether the Hulathi have returned. Play this fact close to the chest.)
- Why are you here?
- Who is this? (In relation to Sar Japeth, Sameel, Ba-en Nafar, etc.)
- Why must you take the rose? They are so few.
- Tell me, what stories do you share among those of your kin?

Nahausteta can relay the following information, granting one answer per successful roll:

- She is a Nahunum.
- There are others of her kind in the holy mountains, but she was cleaved from them.
- The Garden called to her, and she came to find stillness.
- Her past is an avalanche of bodies and a river of blood, but here she finds stillness.
- The Garden is a sacred place upon a sacred place. In the shadow of Mihshalnim (the holy mountain), the stone's bounty is close to the surface.
- She guards the Garden and the roses.

Should the Jackals accumulate **six successes before they gain three failures**; read or paraphrase the following:

Nahausteta nods, thoughtfully considering your words. When she speaks, a smile breaks across her face for the first time during these negotiations. "Very well, it seems your need for the rose is great. As a guardian, it is my role to shield against those who wantonly destroy the earth or seek to steal the rose for their own selfish ends. However, my role does not concern those who approach me in true need. Take the rose(s) you need."

In this situation, the Jackals merely need to gently scrape the rose(s) away with the stone knife and set it in the bowl. They might need Nahausteta's help – the roses are high up, and the smooth stone grants no purchase for climbing or setting a rope, which makes this a difficult check. If a Jackal engaged in a contest of strength/rock throwing with Nahausteta and won, the Nahunum gifts them her stone sword (see below).

Should the Jackals accumulate **three failures before they gain six successes**; read or paraphrase the following:

Nahausteta shakes her head. With a heavy sigh, she speaks, "I am sorry. I cannot lay aside my guardianship and allow you to take the rose. Its beauty is a rarity on the earth in such times. I will allow you to stay and pray, but when the sun mounts its chariot in the morning, you must be off." She stands and walks back towards the shadow of the mountain from where she originally emerged.

The Jackals have several options here, but negotiations are of no more use:

- They can leave empty-handed. Nahausteta shares her food with them – simple fare of apples, figs, honey, and flat bread – but states she has made her decision. The will of a Nahunum is like carved stone, and they are quite intractable once they reach a decision.
- They can attempt to take the rose via stealth. Kauma is high in the evening sky now, and casts everything in the south in its red glow. However, there are hours between sunset and moonrise that would give the Jackals an opportunity to steal the rose. Nahausteta cannot see any better in the dark than a human; still the Jackals must deal with the difficulty of the height at which the roses grow. Additionally, stealing the rose gives the Jackals 2 Corruption each, with the actual thief gaining an additional 2 Corruption, for a total of 4.
- They can attempt to take the rose via force. This is a difficult fight, and the Loremaster should pull no punches. The great-sized bow Nahausteta fights with requires a Strength of 21 to pull and allows the wielder to add their damage bonus to ranged attacks. She also has a stone sword, crafted from the heartstone of the A'hule Asa. It, too, requires a Strength of 21 to wield, and is worked with Nahunum runes of cunning, granting the wielder +10% to Melee skills. Once per day, the wielder can call upon the strength of the earth for aid, restoring 1d8 Wounds and 2d6 Valour. It costs 2 Clash Points to invoke this ability in combat. If the Jackals slay Nahausteta, they each gain 3 Corruption for the murder of a Lawful being.

AFTERMATH

Once the Jackals are ready, the journey back to Sentem takes about the same time as the journey to the Garden did, and it requires one Survival check against the Mountains' difficulty (see page 74 of *Jackals*). Should the Survival check generate an encounter on the way back to Sentem, the Jackals run into scouts of Bartak Kentak: 1d4 Oritakan and 3d6 Norakan. Point out the snake badges and brands these Takan possess.

Upon returning to Sentem, Ba-en Nafar greets the Jackals at the gate. Should they have the rose, he hurriedly ushers them to Arishat. The Hasheer prepares and stores the rose per the rituals found on Kahar Nabal's tablet, and then pays the Jackals (if they returned with an extra rose). Should any Jackals wish to make Ba-en Nafar a patron, they can enjoy a one-time bonus of +15% to the Influence check for the Acquire Patron action this season.

If the Jackals did not bring back a rose, Ba-en Nafar pays them for their time, but is not happy with them. He attempts to recover a rose himself, disappearing for the rest of the season. He has a 70% chance of returning; should this roll fail, Ba-en Nafar dies at unknown hands in the mountains and plays no additional part in this campaign. In any case, Ba-en Nafar is unavailable as a patron for this season.

Hearing that the Wolves are so close to Sentem (or having some delivered to him for questioning) disturbs Ba-en Nafar. He begins to recruit more guards from Densom, and more Jackals, as he fears what this might mean for Sentem and Nawsi Sameel.

ADVANCEMENTS

- 1 for dealing with the Qayim Wolf Den
- 1 for discovering the Stone Garden
- 1 for returning with an asa rose (one or two), which also increases each Jackal's Kleos by 1.

HOOKS

A Border Dispute: Sedeq and Bodi argued before the village elders for weeks about boundary markers. The matter was considered settled, but then Sedeq turned up dead and Bodi fled to the temple of Alwain, claiming refuge. Bodi swears he is innocent of Sedeq's murder, and that it was the Dead of the Aeco Plain that killed him. He is willing to part with shekels to prove his innocence. Unfortunately, no one has seen the Dead near their land in the past year.

Raid!: Sameel is preparing for Sentem's annual raid against the Takan of Bartak Kentak. The events of *The Lost Children* have him worried; still, the beasts must be culled. He often hires Jackals to flesh out the raiding party.

Wolves in the Hills: in the north, a new group of bandits is starting to harass the caravans between Kroryla and Orsem Ven. Heraklydes Bloodsandal, a Melkoni veteran, leads them. He and his followers fled from western Melkon to Kroryla, but Glykera swiftly kicked them out of the city for starting riots.

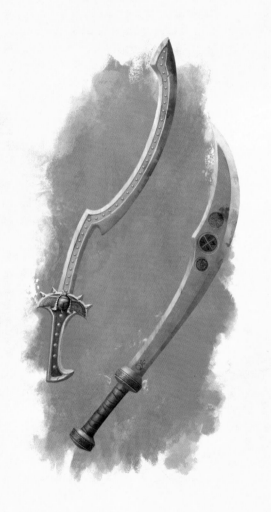

CHAPTER 3
YEAR OF SHROUDED HEARTS

The light of Alwain, reflected in the stars and the moons, forced the Rathic to seek out places of greater darkness. It was at this time the Skessh gathered in the first city, which was named after Almaj. Almaj and his brood ruled over the city, and they were first among all the Skessh. It was Almaj who discovered the 17 verses of power. Almaj begat Bedojin, first of the Skessh to bring the beasts of the land into the first city. Also, he begat Qithar, first of the Skessh to play the harp. Also, he begat Baru, first of the Skessh to draw bronze into useful shapes. And for a time and times, the line of Almaj ruled over the Skessh, and there was peace in Almaj.

The Umari Ungato ~ **The Fifth Tale** ~ **Emari Unjo**

INTRODUCTION

The Year of Shrouded Hearts is Year 2 in *The Fall of the Children of Bronze* campaign. Here, Jackals delve deeper into the wider world of the Zaharets. They encounter a secret Skesshic cult in the north; while in the south, Densom and the secrets of the dark Aeco Woods await.

THEME

The theme of the Year of Shrouded Hearts is loss. In **Shadow Over Mikro**, the people of Mikro are under the sway of a dark entity that overrides their free will; in **The Sacred Hart**, the Jackals search for the last of the ayals – sacred deer the Takan are hunting into extinction. During both scenarios, Jackals must deal with communities in the throes of mourning. Perhaps these Jackals discover that the true measure of a person, or culture, is how they deal with loss. Do communities rally through the pain and lift each other up, or do they turn against each other?

The central conflict of the Year of Shrouded Hearts is against the darkness which came before. For the north, this means dealing with an uncovered ancient evil which is corrupting the hearts and minds of the town of Mikro. This year also deals with the dangers of Corruption in the Zaharets; it is insidious, and should it take root, dealing with it can be arduous. Jackals, detached as they are from the communities they aid, are often the best-equipped to deal with such issues.

For the south, the depredations of the ancient Takan cause trouble for Sentem and those concerned for Sar Japeth. Having (hopefully) recovered an asa rose in **The Stone Garden**, the

Jackals must now travel to Densom and the Aeco Woods. Here, they seek the heart of an ayal, the sacred deer of the Aeco Woods. It is said that the heart, freely given, possesses a strange grace. But the Takan lust after the flesh of ayals even more than the flesh of their enemies. Are there any still alive? If so, is healing Sar Japeth truly the best outcome?

IMPORTANT NPCS

Arishat, Hasheer of Sentem: see page 18.

Ba-en Nafar: see page 183 in *Jackals*.

Kinesh: Kinesh is a priest of Alwain whose sanity was shredded by exposure to Naahpasswee's gaze. Kinesh's insanity makes him an easy target for spirits to possess. However, he might be the Jackals' best hope for discovering what lies behind the strange disappearances in Mikro.

Namgidda benna Amar: Namgidda is the Sari of Rataro, where she oversees the Hasheers at the behest of Toara of the Scriptorium. Namgidda works for Toara, not only searching the ancient tunnels beneath Rataro, but keeping an eye out for other dangers and opportunities in the region. She is keeping a wary eye on the situation in Mikro.

Avi, Sari of Densom: see page 187 of *Jackals*. Sari Avi is the Jackals' best hope for finding the ayal. Her family has kept the rites and secrets of Densom even from the Yesim family. However, in exchange for her aid, Avi seeks something even grander than the restoration of one man. She seeks the renewal of the Aeco Woods, something her town and the plains greatly need.

EVENTS IN THE NORTH

- A fresh wave of refugees from Western Melkon flood into Kroryla. Glykera orders the Krorylians to help the refugees establish a new town to the northwest, along the woods.
- Now that the Jackals dealt with the eastern Wolves, Sari Phamea announces her intent to bring wood from the Ligna Hualla to build ships for trading goods with Ger and Melkon.

EVENTS IN THE SOUTH

- Nabal continues restorations on the Temple of the Morning Lord. As such, he announces he will consecrate the altar during a great feast in the next season.
- Reshpar – the Feast of Harvest – will be celebrated on the 1st Yomoura of Sebe.

EVENTS ANYWHERE

- Wherever the Jackals are on the War Road – Deborah of the Torch and her pack take down a rogue Nahunum who was attacking caravans.

RETIREMENT BENEFITS

If a player retires their Jackal in this year, their new Jackal gains +4 advancements due to the pack's renown attracting better recruits.

NORTHERN TALE:
SHADOW OVER MIKRO

An adventure for Tolerated Jackals, set during the month of Sebe, in the dry season.

OVERVIEW

As mentioned on page 135 of *Jackals*, Mikro is under siege. It fell under the control of an ancient entity known as a Skessh. The Skessh were elder beings of great power, which once ruled the great empire of Keta. Those who ruled the Zaharets before the coming of the Takan – the Hulathi of the Grand Kingdoms – came into conflict with this Skessh, who is called Naahpasswee. At the time, Naahpasswee held sway over a vast slave kingdom, having bound the Luathi of the region to her will. Death could not end Naahpasswee, for her power was too great. So, the Hulathi, with shining spears and songs of power, drove Naahpasswee from the land. They chased the Skessh back to her temple, sealing her in the temple's *kella*, or centre. The Children of Silver then razed the temple to the ground, assuming this dealt with Naahpasswee for good. However, few know a Skessh cannot be slain in this fashion, and Naahpasswee entered the *ekruannak* – the deathless sleep – waiting for a time when the stars were right and she could return to claim her lands and slaves once again. She is currently bound behind Hulathi wards and struggles to emerge from the *ekruannak*.

Five months ago, Leodias, a young shepherd of the town, discovered Naahpasswee's resting place while searching for a lost sheep. After locating the sheep, Leodias found himself too far from home to return, so he spent the night under the stars – and over the kella where Naahpasswee slept. When the sleeping shepherd's mind began to wander the Dream Road, the Skessh was waiting. Naahpasswee scoured Leodias' spirit, rebuilding the youth's mind in her own image. When the sun mounted its chariot the next day, Leodias returned to Mikro as the high priest of the ancient Ketian being. Slowly, so as not to rouse suspicion, Leodias brought others from Mikro out into the wilderness. There, they uncovered the ruins where Naahpasswee dwelt. Some of those he brought are bound beneath the fetters of the Skessh's foul will. But Leodias cast any who possessed the purity of spirit or strength of resolve to resist the Skessh's influence into a pit, where their dreams feed Naahpasswee during her moments of near wakefulness. Takan soon answered the Skessh's silent call, and Mikro is now a town under siege from within and without. Waking and freeing his goddess is Leodias' primary goal. He removed a hestul sealing disc, allowing Naahpasswee's spirit and influence to grow beyond the kella. He is currently searching for a way to destroy the seal and free his mistress.

Eilene, daughter of a brickmaker in Mikro, noticed her neighbour acting strange. When the strange behaviour spread to her father, she fled to find aid. She encounters the Jackals and tells them her tale of missing people, strange lights, and bizarre changes in the town of Mikro. Can the Jackals stop the spread of the shadow over Mikro, keep the trade road open, and prevent an ancient evil from claiming the northern end of the War Road as its own?

This adventure begins with the Jackals moving towards Mikro, either going to or coming from Orsem Yahan or Rataro. Mikro is one of the major towns that lies along the eastern trade road (see pages 124 and 135 of *Jackals* for more information on Mikro).

TIMELINE OF THE ADVENTURE

Month of Sina, second month of the Year of Shrouded Hearts

2nd Dark day (day 17): Naahpasswee begins to stir in her sleep.
3rd Water day (day 28): Leodias' sheep goes missing and he discovers Naahpasswee in his dreams.

Month of Erbe, fourth month

2nd Chief day (day 11): Leodias brings his first convert to the site. Leodias steals the seal of Ennuki.
3rd Gai day (day 24): excavation of the kella begins.

Month of Hamis, fifth month

1st Earth day (day 10): Leodias restarts the building of Mikro's walls.
2nd Kauma day (day 13): Kinesh confronts Naahpasswee and loses.

Month of Sedis, sixth month

3rd Water day (day 28): Philon is taken.
3rd Path day (day 29): Eilene heads to find help.

Month of Sebe, seventh month

Start of Sebe: Jackals become involved.

Month of Samane, eighth month

1st Chief day (day 1): if the Jackals fail, Leodias finishes his conversion of Mikro.
2nd Bull day (day 16): the walls are completed, and Leodias installs Naahpasswee's statue in a new temple dedicated to her.
3rd Dark day (day 27): Naahpasswee awakens fully, and the Skessh becomes the ruler of Mikro. She then begins to expand her influence.

Zadon's Week, year end

Zadon's Week: Leodias breaks the seal of Ennuki, freeing Naahpasswee from her prison. Once again, a Skessh of Keta walks the world.

ACT 1: EAST OR WEST

Depending in which direction the Jackals are headed, this scene can take place in either Rataro or Orsem Yahan. If it is in Rataro, Namgidda benna Amar reaches out to the Jackals; if in Orsem Yahan, Nawsi Namar does. Emissaries of the NPC put out the word that their patrons have need of Jackals. The promise of silver shekels for simple reconnaissance should be enough to lure the Jackals into hearing more.

Read or paraphrase the following [adjust for location]:

The runner brings you all to [the Hasheers' palace/Nawsi's chambers] where [a tall woman in robes with a knotted red cord/the Nawsi of Orsem Yahan] waits, talking with a young woman. The runner bows and retreats from the room, closing the door as they leave. [Namgidda/Namar] nods at the young woman.

"Welcome Jackals, it seems we have need of you. Have you heard of Mikro? It is the town [east/ west] of here. We rely on Mikro to supply much of our wool and bricks, but I am not surprised if you have not heard of it. It is a small, seemingly peaceful town." Motioning to the young woman, [Namgidda/Namar] introduces her.

"This is Eilene, she is the daughter of Philon, one of Mikro's brickmakers. She tells a different story of Mikro. Go ahead, Eilene, tell these Jackals what you told me."

Eilene gives you a smile befitting her name. "Hello. I, I mean I came here looking for help. My father said that the people here have always treated him right. Which is why when… Something is wrong at home. Some people have gone missing, while others, others have changed. My father noticed it, and we were looking to leave, but then… he changed too. Oh, you must help us. Please!"

Namgidda is a middle-aged Hasheer of the Scriptorium, as well as the Sari of Rataro. She is never seen without her knotted scarlet cord, which identifies her as an elder in the Scriptorium or staff of office.

Namgidda can share the following information:

- Mikro is an important source of building materials for Rataro.
- There are many ruins throughout the area, some of which lie hidden beneath the lands for centuries until just the right confluence of events occurs.
- People going missing is not all that strange, but the pervasive change in personalities worries Namgidda. That smacks of corruption and spiritual influence.
- She wants the Jackals to investigate Mikro while she keeps Eilene under observation. If it is a possession or corruption, Namgidda wants to make sure Eilene is not here to help it spread.
- She offers the Jackals 150 ss and an acalana resin each to investigate Mikro. If they can bring back evidence that something was going on and they dealt with it, she will pay them an additional 350 ss each.

Namar is a young man, which is surprising considering his high rank. He is usually seen in his leathers, stamped with the three bulls of Ameena Noani.

Namar can share the following information:

- Mikro supplies much of the wool and bricks for the orsem.
- Namar knows Philon, or at least of him. The man has one foot. He always seemed to be a good man, even though he worshipped those foreign Melkoni gods.

- The strangeness in Mikro worries him. With the Ligna becoming hostile (see page 75), and the incident with Wolves last year, Namar has more than enough to deal with in the east. He needs to know that the route back to Ameena Noani is secure.
- Although he cannot spare his people, he can free up some silver to send the Jackals to deal with the situation. He can pay the Jackals 150 ss each.
- He wants them to escort Eilene back to Mikro and investigate.
- If there is something going on there, and if they can bring it to a swift end, he will pay them 350 ss each. The supply road must be safe if Orsem Yahan is to survive.

Eilene is a young woman, with sharp, striking features. Her hands are red and cracked from working with clay bricks. She tries to keep them hidden at all times. She seems skittish, possibly because of the events in Mikro and being in an unfamiliar place.

Eilene can share the following information:
- She and her father first noticed their neighbours starting to act strange about three months ago:
  › People abandoned their normal jobs to work on the walls.
  › Devout Alwainites no longer attended the shrine or the daily rites.
  › Old friends suddenly acted completely differently (becoming secretive, seductive, or dismissive).
- Kinesh, the local Kahar, was acting strange before that, but Philon and Eilene became suspicious when Hector, the fisherman, began to head out into the wilds each night and attempted to get them to join him.
- Leodias was always a shy shepherd, but recently he became bold and a powerful leader of the town.
- Rebecca and her husband began to distance themselves from the community when they discovered they were expecting.
- Philon and Eilene noticed the town seemed to be dividing along lines of those who followed Leodias and those who lived life as it had always been.
- They also noticed strange healings and recoveries in those who followed Leodias, reversals of old injuries and the like. But the healings always left the recipients… off somehow.
- Eilene was worried because her father had lost his foot in the wars in the west.
- At first, Philon was the one pushing to leave, but once Eilene saw people being healed, she began to voice her concerns.
- When she awoke 10 days ago and saw her father walking around with two feet – the new foot covered in faint green scales – she knew she had to flee!

Once the Jackals are ready, the journey to Mikro from Orsem Ven or Rataro takes two or four days, respectively. Both journeys take place along well-travelled paths, and use the Plains' difficulty, found on page 73 of *Jackals*.

After resolving these checks, proceed to Act 2.

ACT 2: MIKRO

Mikro is a small town that lies along the Asa Amwa, as it flows out of the Rekiti Vana on its journey to the sea. Across the broad and fast-flowing river, the dun-coloured hills of the Wuma Ejo fill the vale between the mountains, shielding Mikro from the worst of the desert winds. The hills also provide plenty of hiding places and secure lairs for the Takan. Mikro's red brick walls face south, towards the Red Ford, and guard against this threat from the hills. The red river clay makes up most of the town's buildings, which stand huddled between three hills. One hill is bare, with a shrine to Alwain becoming visible as you approach the town.

Townsfolk stand along the river's edge, pulling bounty from the waters. Along the banks, small rows of fish dry in the sun and a few townsfolk repair rafts, although the area seems to be less active than expected. Many parts of the bank are overgrown, and old huts can be seen among the weeds.

This act is fairly freeform – the Jackals must find out what is going on in Mikro. The places and people of interest listed below are the Jackals' best clues for discovering the presence of Naahpasswee. At the end of the act, the Jackals should know something strange is happening in the town and something supernatural is causing it. They should also (hopefully) know what to do about it – find an Anzaim or return the seal – and need someone to show them the ruins where Naahpasswee lives (most likely Leodias or Philon).

I. Walls of Mikro

The two gatehouses of Mikro, to the west and east, are still under construction. The walls are slowly being completed, but a low wall (3 cubits) does encircle the town. The walls rise to a full height of 10 cubits along the southern section.

2. Shrine of Alwain

The tallest, yet smallest in circumference, of the three inner hills holds an open-air shrine to Alwain, although a successful Culture (Luathi), Survival, or Perception check reveals no one has used the shrine or altar for months. There is a 50% chance the Jackals can find Kinesh here at any time. The mad Kahar is usually crying to Alwain or raging impotently against the stone of the altar.

3. Leodias' Home

Leodias claimed the Sar's home on top of Durab Hill (the southeastern hill) in Mikro. The Sar now lives in a newer building at the foot of the hill in the village. There is a 35% chance the Jackals can find Leodias here, but only during the day. He spends much of his time at the kella to the north, communing with his goddess. Within the home are carvings of a woman and snakes, although Leodias is a poor carver and all are very crude. Additionally, Leodias stores the following goods in his home (taken from the kella and the town):

- A hestul sealing disk that bears twin short spears and the sun of Alwain. An Ancient Lore check reveals this is the symbol of Lukka, one of the Grand Kingdoms. The seal is worth 2,500 ss to the Hasheers. Leodias must find a way to break this seal to free Naahpasswee from the kella.
- Bronze plates and utensils from the Shrine of Alwain, 300 ss.

- A squat, ugly statue of a creature with a snake's body and a toad's head – this is one of Naahpasswee's spirit servants, and the statue was found in the kella. It is worth 500 ss if melted down. While carried, it functions as a Nightmare Token (see page 87 of *Jackals*) that bears the name of the person carrying it.
- 450 ss of jewellery offered by the town.
- A black, stone dagger chipped from obsidian (inflicts 1d6 + 2 damage). It always scars those it cuts (if it inflicts Wounds, add +15% to the Scarring check; always perform a Scarring check, even if the recipient is still in the first row of Wounds. See page 71 of *Jackals*). The dagger provides 2 Devotion Points for each cut inflicted (up to the character's maximum Devotion Points). This counts as blood magic. Worth 700 ss.

4. Lake

Nestled between the three hills of Mikro is a small lake. It is filled with fish, which come up from underground streams. This lake ensures Mikro has a safe and usable water supply in the event of a siege. There is a 50% chance the Jackals can find Kinesh here, cavorting and dancing along the shore or swimming naked in the lake.

5. Philon's House

Eilene's directions to her father's house are easy to follow. The large work yard, where red clay bricks dry in stacks, also makes it clear this is Philon's house. The door to the house is carved with the twin spears of Lykos, but they were recently altered to have a more snake-like appearance. There is a 65% chance that Philon is here (otherwise, the Jackals can find him working in the kella). He is working on new bricks for the kella and has drawn up some sketches for a grand stairwell. Additionally, Philon keeps the treasures he pulled from the kella here:
- 60 mouahalan coins, 300 ss.
- A black mask in the shape of a serpent's head, 1,200 ss.
- A metal sceptre/club designed for someone much larger than even a Trauj (inflicts 2d10 + 2 damage with –10% to hit due to its size).
- Hack silver, 500 ss worth.

NPCs in Mikro:

Philon

Philon is a Melkoni veteran of the wars to the west. When he lost his foot, he brought his wife and their daughter east, staying for a time in Kroryla, but eventually making a home in Mikro. His wife, Penelope, died in a Takan raid four years ago. His home still looks as though someone recently packed for a journey, as it has only been a few days (at most ten) since Leodias took him before Naahpasswee. The Skessh regrew his lost foot. Philon's loyalty to Naahpasswee is deeper than others in the town due to this act; he is not under spiritual domination, but worships Naahpasswee of his own free will. Since then, he has spent much of his time in the kella, renovating its entryway to enable Leodias to bring more people down there.

He appears to be a relaxed, slow-speaking individual, save for when someone brings up his foot or his daughter. He refuses to talk about or show his foot, becoming agitated if the Jackals persist. As for Eilene, he is initially interested in her location, but soon reverts to indifference if she is not in the town.

Philon can share the following information:

- Mikro is a fine place to live.
- He moved here from the west about seven years ago.
- There is still fierce fighting to the west.
- He settled here with Penelope and Eilene.
- Eilene ran away about a week or so ago.
- No, he was never missing a foot, why do you ask?
- He is building a new stairwell for the house.
- Leodias is not someone he has spent a lot of time around.
- No one acts strange around here. That is superstition. Everyone here is the same as they always were.
- Rebecca has been giving people the evil eye, or so the townsfolk say.
- [If the Jackals push for more information]: He has seen Leodias sneaking around to the north and could show/tell the Jackals where.

Kinesh

Kinesh was the Kahar of Mikro. The night he confronted a horror of the ancient world broke Kinesh's mind. He now wanders the town, seeing the world through whatever spirit possesses him at the time. Sometimes, his old self shines through, and Alwain chooses to speak truth through this jar of clay. Other times, Naahpasswee walks among her people, unseen in her broken vessel. When the Jackals find Kinesh, the information they receive depends on with whom they are speaking. Whenever Naahpasswee or a messenger of Alwain possesses him, Kinesh tries to make for the kella. Canny Jackals can follow the mad Kahar.

Kinesh can share the following information (roll 1d6 to see who is in control of the Kahar):

1. Naahpasswee: Kinesh burns with fever whenever Naahpasswee possesses him. This is the corruption of the Skessh. Using Touch of Law or Paths of the Moon does not kill Kinesh, but does drive Naahpasswee from him for 1d6 hours.

- Come to me. Speak with me. I will give you your heart's desire.
- So long, so long without the moons.
- My priest will aid me, and soon light itself will fail.
- Where is he who awoke me?
- There are many things that hide in the paths of dreams, from times former and times yet to come.
- I see you, mortals. Your spirits burn like torches along the great path.
- My great vengeance – born of dreams and portents – I already planted in your world. Soon, it will be born in blood and water. (See the *Aftermath* section below.)
- My power will soon shatter the lock; then, once again, I will be free to tread my path.

2. Kinesh: Kinesh is a broken man, who – through his pride – has become a vessel of something greater than himself. He alternates between weeping and ranting. Kinesh has control for only a couple of questions before you must make a new roll on this table.

- It is hopeless, he has failed in his duties. The rites and the altar of Alwain are neglected. It (Naahpasswee) burns him.
- She is in his mind; she sees the town through him.
- Who is she? She is the one that waits in the darkness and in dreams.
- What does she want? She wants the town and the torches in the town – that light – for herself. She wants the silver seal to be shattered (the Hulathi seal).
- He is without hope. They should kill him. Kill him and end her threat.

3. A Trauj Ancestor: This can be the Ancestor Spirit from *Mantle of the Ancestors* or *Spirit Companion,* should any Jackal possess either of those hooks. In this case, allow the Jackal to question their ancestor or spirit. The Yahtah wander the great Dream Road after they die, so they can watch over the Trauj. The presence of a Great Serpent has drawn this Yahtah, so it seeks to aid those who stand against the serpent.

- An evil from the north once again threatens the great realms.
- The evil struggles to awaken, but is bound by chains of sleep, for now.
- Its poison stains this one's soul.
- The poison can be drawn, but the evil must be sent back to sleep.
- None could kill it in past ages, and this age is lesser; but the gift of death could be granted.
- Sleep or Gift, death must be given back to this serpent or it will raise its banner once again.
- The giants left a way to keep the evil bound. The wards they placed were moved – the seal must be found.
- More wander the Dream Road than have been seen in an age.

4. Mouadran Priest-King: This mad spirit is also struggling to wake and is incoherent. It should not give the Jackals any real information, just rant and rave.

- All Hail the Great Spirit of the World.
- The Gates which have fallen will rise again.
- The Night Without Dawn will fall over the arc of the world and the great enemy will be blinded.
- I once bred the beasts without souls, which broke the back of the world. These and greater beasts will I unleash for the utter ruin of the world!

5. A Spirit from the Dark: This can be the Ancestor Spirit from *Mantle of the Ancestors* or *Spirit Companion,* should any Jackal possess those hooks. In this case, allow the Jackal to question their ancestor or spirit. This is a good set-up for other adventures you might plan for the War Road.

- I will have my vengeance. –Random Spirit
- I see you. My touch will soon burn in your bones. –Mealil
- Why, why have my bones been left unburied? My soul wanders, I am lost. –Random Gerwa or Melkoni spirit.
- The light, it calls to me. –Random Luathi spirit
- Delve deeper, seek me out. I will reward you. –The Daughter Beneath the Earth (see page 122)

6. Messenger of Alwain: This messenger brings hope to Kinesh, Mikro, and all who would listen. Kinesh's whole demeanour changes when this spirit speaks through him. The feverish and frantic nature of the other missives, and the pain in which Kinesh lives, all disappear. For the moment, he is at peace. When this passes, he seeks to head to the kella.

- Be at peace. Alwain has not forsaken or forgotten you.
- The beast that seeks the light shall ever be denied it. For it seeks what it does not know, and so ever walks in darkness.
- The Silent Lands will only receive the beast if a spear made from the claw of an Anzaim pierces its breast.
- You may banish the beast back to the Dream Road, should you replace the seal of Ennuki on the door (the hestul sealing disc in Leodias' house).
- Only Alwain speaks into the Silent Lands; and here, Alwain speaks through this clay vessel. But heed Alwain's words, draw this thorn, lest its venom spread through the north.

Leodias

Leodias, son of Heraklydes, was a shepherd. This changed when one of his lambs went missing (see page 46). Since his meeting with Naahpasswee, Leodias has become the most important person in Mikro. After settling some old debts with bullies and the like (they were his first converts or victims), he set upon the idea of quickly finishing the walls. Leodias knows that as soon as word gets out about Mikro, Jackals will arrive. He is attempting to convert the entire town and move Naahpasswee to Mikro, but he has run into a complication: he is unable to break the seal on the kella. Should the Jackals meet him in town, the seal is most likely in his home on Durab Hill.

Leodias can share the following information:

- He is a herdsman.
- The Sar offered his home to Leodias after Leodias had a vision sent from heaven.
- He is a simple man, one who had greatness chosen for him.
- He just wants to live a simple life and bring peace and prosperity to Mikro.
- He has no plans to leave Mikro.
- Who sent him the vision? Why, one who treads the great Sky Road above!
- Alwain? Perhaps. Who can say what forms or names the god uses?
- The grantor of the vision heals those among the town through him.
- He goes into the wilds to commune with his god.
- He can give an abridged version of the Introduction – he followed a lost sheep and had a vision from a power in the world. He still goes there to receive more visions, but the power now works through him.
- He has not noticed anyone acting strangely, save for poor Kinesh.

Leodias can also share the following information, assuming the Jackals can make a successful difficult Influence or Deception check:

- The Jackals can persuade Leodias to heal a Jackal's scar. If so, the Jackal automatically fails the Willpower check to resist Naahpasswee's influence. The scar heals, missing limb regrows, etc. However, after 1d10 days, the Jackal manifests some sort of serpent twist to the healed area and gains 1d6 Corruption.
- The Jackals can persuade Leodias to show them where he receives these visions. Leodias leads the Jackals into an ambush – see Act 3.

LEODIAS

Type:	Humanoid	Location:	Mikro
		Wounds:	50
Defence:	70%	Protection:	4 (snake-like skin)
Combat:	65%	Move:	15
Knowledge:	60%	Initiative:	15
Urban:	50%	Clash Points:	4
Common:	50%	Treasure Score:	2
		Corruption:	15

Special Abilities

Inured to Darkness: Leodias suffers no penalties due to absence of light.

Gifts of the Serpent: Naahpasswee gifted Leodias with some of a Skessh's natural abilities in reward for his service. This ability counts as a trait for all Combat and Defence checks.

Combat Range

1–20%	*Ketian War Cry:* Leodias lets loose the war cry of ancient Keta. The war cry affects targets equal to the ones result on the attack roll (e.g., if Leodias rolls an 18, the war cry can affect up to eight targets). Those affected must make a hard Willpower check. On a failure, the target takes 1d12 (6) Valour damage; on a success, the target takes half that damage.
21–35%	*Serpent's Strike (2 attacks):* Leodias lashes out with his dagger, striking with the speed and danger of a serpent. 2d6 (7) damage each.
36–50%	*Hypnotic Gaze:* Leodias catches a character's eye, forcing a hard Willpower check. On a failure, Leodias takes control of the character's actions and Clash Points for one round.
51–65%	Venomous Bite: Leodias bites his target for 1d12 (6) damage. Additionally, he pumps a potent venom into the wound. The target must make a difficult Endurance check. On a failure, the Jackal takes an additional 2d6 damage, ignoring Protection.

Townsfolk

There are many townsfolk in Mikro; some have come under the influence of Naahpasswee, whereas others have not. Many of the townsfolk seem tired and distracted during the day, when Naahpasswee's influence is weakest. This part of the investigation should be mysterious and people may shift their alliances; essentially, they have joined a cult that dominates their personality. People can change overnight, which should be disconcerting to the Jackals.

Use the following table to determine the characteristics of any townsfolk the Jackals talk to:

TOWNSFOLK OF MIKRO	
d6	**Culture**
1–3	Luathi
4–5	Melkoni
6	Gerwa or Trauj
d6	**Profession**
1	Brick worker
2	Clay gatherer
3–4	Fisher
5	Miner
6	Shepherd
d6	**Influence**
1–3	Naahpasswee
4	Normal, but Naahpasswee will take them that night
5–6	Normal… for now

Those loyal to Mikro can share the following information:

- Some townsfolk are acting strangely. (They can point the Jackals to those Naahpasswee has converted.)
- People started acting strangely a couple of weeks back. They forget important things, leave their spouses and children, and even abandon their work.
- They walk around during the day in a fugue.
- At night, they build the wall.
- Leodias is the new de facto Sar of the town.
- He was a shepherd until recently; no one ever paid him much mind.
- Some are thinking of leaving (both sides) and heading for Rataro or the orsem.
- The strange ones are seen going north into the wastes, about once every ten days or so.
- They always try to get others to go with them.
- Rebecca and Nahan's baby is born healthy; they will name her in a day or two. [The Pantheon, Alwain] blessed them with this child.

Those loyal to Naahpasswee can share the following information:

- Everything is normal in Mikro, why do you ask?
- [Upon the Jackals noticing some freshly healed wound, which seems to be flaking into scales]: This? I was born with this. Kinesh said Alwain blessed me because of it.
- Many have stories of how Leodias came and healed them when they were wounded, sick, or dying.
- He is 'Her' priest.
- [In response to 'Her?'] Yes, she is an emissary of light, come to illuminate the Zaharets.
- If you are interested in Her, you should speak to Leodias.
- If the Jackals make any disparaging remarks about Leodias or 'Her', the townsperson flies into a rage.

Those converted to Naahpasswee since the last time the Jackals spoke with them can share the following information:

- I was mistaken, nothing seems to be wrong.
- I sat down with them, and you know, what they say makes sense.
- If you are interested in Her, you should speak to Leodias.
- It was all a big misunderstanding, you should go.
- These townsfolk react to disparaging remarks with rage.

Should the Jackals be too heavy-handed in their inquiries, Leodias attempts to have them killed. During the night, or while they are travelling, he sets [2 × the number of Jackals] possessed townsfolk on them (use the Guard stats from page 206 in *Jackals*).

Once the Jackals decide they are finished exploring Mikro and are ready to travel to the ruins, proceed to Act 3.

ACT 3: PORTAL TO THE UNDERWORLD

At this point, the Jackals should know something is going on in the town, and that they must put whatever is behind it to rest. Finding a spear with an Anzaim claw on it (or crafting one) is an adventure in and of itself (see the *Hooks* section at the end of this adventure). However, the timeline in the Overview shows what is likely to happen if they leave the adventure at this point.

The ruins to the north are in a small hill about one day's travel from Mikro. At this point, there is nothing to distinguish it from the surrounding hills, save for a half-dozen wind-worn huwasi (standing stones) around its apex. It appears as though someone recently displaced the stones. A successful Craft or Survival check reveals two of the stones fell due to natural causes, but someone uprooted the rest. A successful Survival or Perception check alerts the Jackals to the presence of many tracks; mostly human, but some Takan. The huwasi are worn, and their carvings are difficult to discern; however, the twin spears and the sunburst are still visible. An easy Lore check informs the Jackals all cultures use standing stones like these today. They are designed to call a god's attention to a place, and to stand as testaments or reminders of the past.

Near the top of the hill, within the circle circumscribed by the huwasi, lies the entrance to Naahpasswee's resting place. Leodias and Philon hide it, covering the entrance every dawn with wooden slats, hides, and dirt from their digging. A successful Perception check reveals this, as does any clever investigating the Jackals do, for although the entrance is hidden from view, there are clues to its presence (the way it sounds when one walks over it, for example). If the Jackals came here with Leodias, Philon, Kinesh, or a possessed townsperson, they could point out the entrance to the Jackals. Once the Jackals discover and remove the camouflage, the way is opened.

Resting Place of Naahpasswee

What a Jackal's senses reveal:

Sights – completely dark. Clay bricks make up new additions: stairs, pillars, and walls.

Smells – earthy scents. Drying clay, mould, and the sweet stink of unwashed bodies.

Sounds – faint moans echoing from The Pit, whispers on the edge of hearing, and strange echoes.

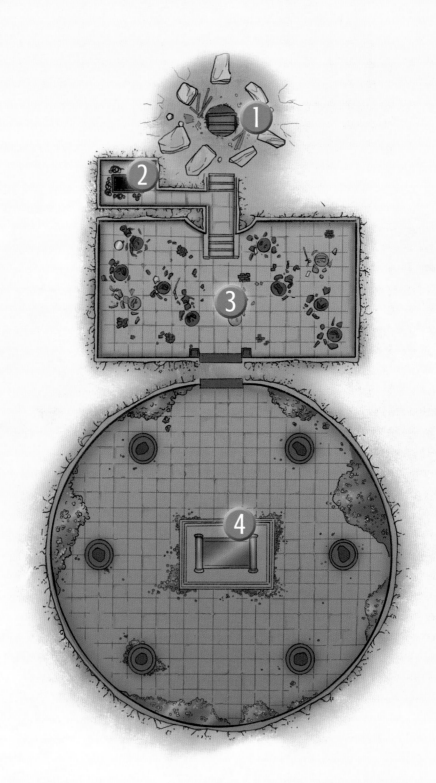

1. Entrance Well

Newly shaped clay bricks line a black pit in the ground, and a large, wide stairwell descends into darkness. If the Jackals revealed their intentions in town, or travelled here with Leodias, Philon, or a possessed townsperson, Takan lie in ambush for the Jackals when they descend the stairs [1 Oritakan, 2 Mavakan, and 2 Norakan for each Jackal in the party above four]. Use the ambush rules from page 62 of *Jackals*. These Takan came to worship Naahpasswee and bear the chaotic marks of their obeisance. Black and green scales peek out from under mangy patches of fur. Many have serpent's eyes or forked tongues as well. If no ambush is set, these Takan are resting in the entry well.

The Takan's treasure from raiding the region is here, waiting for the day the Great Chamber opens and they can lay it at the coils of Naahpasswee:

- A silver armband worked with the three bulls of Ameena Noani, 170 ss.
- 100 ss worth of copper ore taken from a trader.
- Set of three armlets with sapphire settings, 75 ss each.
- A stained, curved sword notched at many places along the blade – Nagek-rihn. This is a foul blade of Barak Barad. The Takan forged these blades by quenching them in the blood of slaves, Takan, and the venom of Giant Scorpions and Aburrisanu. These blades are potent Oritakan weapons from when they ruled over the Luathi.
  - › This blade is heavy and unbalanced; it causes a penalty of –20% to Melee Combat unless the wielder's Strength is 19 or above. It causes 1d10 + 3 damage.
  - › This blade is corrupt. Jackals wielding this blade gain 2 points of Corruption per season they carry it. Additionally, when Luathi see this blade, all Jackals must make all peaceful uses of the Influence skill at extreme difficulty. However, should the Jackal attempt to influence Takan, this blade grants them a +15% to all checks. Note: This can cause Corruption, see *Jackals* page 151.
  - › This blade is envenomed. Wounds caused by the blade are very painful. Each successful attack inflicts a –5% skill penalty (cumulative) to the target, as the venom burns painfully in their bodies. This penalty lasts for five days.

2. Holding Pit

This is where the Takan and Leodias keep those townsfolk of Mikro who resist Naahpasswee's will. The people are emaciated and weak from lack of food, Takan beatings, and the fact that Naahpasswee feeds off their dreams. There are currently a dozen villagers in the pit. Slop buckets containing the 'food' the Takan feed their prisoners line the rim of the pit, as do thick, knotted cables of rope. A small group of Norakan taunt the prisoners, throwing handfuls of the slop into the pit [three Norakan per Jackal].

The prisoners know little, but can relate the following information:

- They all dream about the same thing, a creature with the head and coils of a massive snake, and the scaled torso and arms of a woman. She comes to them in their dreams and feeds off them, eating their dream selves night after night.
- She calls herself Naahpasswee. She says she sleeps now, but soon will awaken.
- They are weak, too weak to travel back to Mikro on their own.
- They know the creature is close, it is behind the great doors.
- Leodias is the one who betrayed them all.
- He seeks a way to free 'his mistress'; he believes the door has been enchanted shut.
- Aneal, a Hasheer from Mikro, says: "He stole the seal. I heard him say it is the lock and the key". Aneal also relates the likelihood the seal on the door was keeping Naahpasswee asleep. If the Jackals can find it, perhaps they can restore the seal. Leodias took it from this place.
- They warn the Jackals to steel their wills, as she can influence those who enter her presence. Even now, her reach is greater than when they first arrived.

3. Lesser Chamber

This large area is where the Hulathi sealed Naahpasswee into her temple. Stacks of clay bricks lie scattered around the area, and the Jackals can see where Philon was repairing the façade. Statues lie broken around the chamber. Some are clearly inhuman: Skessh, Takan, and other strange hybrids. There seem to be more animal features than human among the wreckage. There are also statues of marble. They were once graceful figures of women and men in antique armour; some of the armour pieces are made of actual silver (500 ss worth). The marble statues face the great door as if preparing to fight whatever emerges from it. The Takan and Leodias recently defiled these Hulathi statues, ruining them. At the far side of the chamber is a clay façade, two towers in the earth that flank a large stone door. The door is engraved with the image of a chained Skessh, coiled over a pile of broken weapons and skulls. Bronze bars overlay the doors, meeting near the centre, where a bronze lock rests. A large, empty, disc-like shape indicates something is clearly missing from the lock. The bronze is etched with familiar symbols (Hulathii and Luathii share the same script), but in unfamiliar combinations. A successful Lore check reveals the symbols as Hulathii, and a critical success gives the reader the sense that the words are apotropaic in nature (that is, they have the power to avert evil influences). A successful Ancient Lore check reveals the name of the bound creature, *Naahpasswee*, and that the script is a prayer to keep the ancient terror bound in sleep.

Studying all this for an hour grants +5% to Ancient Lore. Should the Jackals attempt this before sealing the door, they must make Willpower checks for Subsumation – see below.

Naahpasswee's power floods the chamber, drawing it partially onto the Dream Road. The Jackals essentially tread along the road of dreams once they enter the chamber. Much of what happens here is based on dream logic. Shadows pool and grow, ever moving about in defiance of torch light. Distances seem to stretch and collapse without reason. Voices and whispers seem to come from great distances.

Subsumation

The will of a Skessh is a powerful thing, and though she sleeps, Naahpasswee's will is still dreadful. Those who enter the chamber – except any who are touching the hestul seal – must make a difficult Willpower check to resist her influence. Jackals must make these checks every 10 minutes, as Naahpasswee's influence rolls out in waves. Those who were warned about this effect (from the prisoners in the pit) can steel their will and make the roll at +10%.

Critical Success: the character's will is too strong for Naahpasswee to break… for now. The Jackal is immune to further Subsumation checks for 24 hours.

Success: the character barely retains their hold on their will. Naahpasswee's attack against their spirit causes 1d4 Mettle damage.

Failure: Naahpasswee momentarily dominates the Jackal. They are under the Loremaster's control for one round, during which Naahpasswee speaks through them. The Jackal gains 2 points of Corruption from this foul presence inhabiting their mind.

The possessed Jackal can impart the following information:

- Naahpasswee is still sleeping, she reaches out from the depths of the Dream Road.
- She once ruled in splendour, with peace throughout her kingdom. All were subject to her will. It will be as such again.
- She invites all the Jackals to renounce their gods and worship her.
- Bound as she is, she cannot die. She merely sleeps, waiting for the time when the stars are right for her return.

See the details about Kinesh above for additional information a possessed Jackal can impart to their allies.

Fumble: Naahpasswee completely dominates the Jackal. They gain 1d4 + 1 Corruption. Naahpasswee is likely to keep this Jackal as a sleeper agent (see the *Aftermath* section below).

If the Jackals have not yet confronted Leodias, he emerges from the shadows to bar their attempts to reseal the doors. There are two Tsutakan and one Ba with him (plus one Mavakan for every Jackal in the party over four). This is a tough fight. Ignore the morale rules for this fight, as Leodias and the Takan will fight to the death to defend their goddess.

4. The Great Chamber

Jackals can only enter this area if they sunder the seal of Ennuki. Without a spear crafted from the claw of an Anzaim, they are doomed!

The chamber beyond is egg-shaped, curving out in all directions. Six pillars – carved in the likeness of Skessh battling writhing, inhuman shapes – stand throughout the room. In the centre, upon a dais of gold, lies Naahpasswee, the great Skessh. She is already awake, her hands curling on the haft of a spear with a long, curved blade. Golden scales lay piled like coins throughout the chamber, offerings from her servants long ago.

NAAHPASSWEE			
Type:	Skessh	**Location:**	Kella; Outskirts of Mikro
		Wounds:	160
Defence:	80%	Protection:	4 (snake-like skin)
Combat:	120%	Move:	30
Knowledge:	80%	Initiative:	18
Urban:	50%	Clash Points:	8
Common:	80%	Treasure Score:	see below
		Corruption:	20

Special Abilities

Inured to Darkness: Naahpasswee suffers no penalties due to absence of light.

Chosen of Jahamah: this ability counts as a trait for all Combat and Defence checks.

Dark Rites: Naahpasswee has access to all the rites of the Mouathenics listed in Jackals. Whenever she may invoke a rite (see combat range), the Loremaster can choose to invoke a different rite from those listed below. She can also call out the names on the spear instead of invoking a rite.

Wild Skill: Naahpasswee possesses a combat skill of 120%, which means she has the Quick Reflexes advanced talent and reduces the cost of Sweeping Arc attacks by 1 Clash Point.

Subsumation: Jackals in the Great Chamber are subject to Subsumation rules (see above) unless they bear a piece of the hestul seal.

Corruption: Skessh – beings between worlds – do not suffer Corruption in the same way as mortal beings. Rites such as Touch of Law or Path of the Moons deal only half damage or one-quarter damage on a save.

Immortal: Skessh cannot be permanently slain, except by the weapon of their doom. In Naahpasswee's case, this is a spear made from the claw of an Anzaim. Should she be reduced to 0 Wounds, she enters the ekruannak for a year and a day. Even if her body is destroyed, it reconstitutes itself, re-emerging at the end of this time.

Combat Range

1–20%	*Ketian War Cry:* Naahpasswee lets loose the war cry of ancient Keta. The war cry affects targets equal to the ones result on the attack roll (e.g., if Naahpasswee rolls an 18, the war cry can affect up to eight targets). Those affected must make a hard Willpower check. On a failure, the target takes 2d8 (9) Valour damage; on a success, they take half that damage.
21–40%	*Ketian Spear (2 attacks):* Naahpasswee whirls her spear, striking with the speed of a serpent. 1d12 + 1d8 + 2 (13) damage.
41–50%	*Spit Venom:* 2d8 (9) damage. The target must make a difficult Endurance check; on a failure, the Jackal takes 2d6 damage, which ignores Protection.
51–60%	*Venomous Bite:* Naahpasswee bites her target for 2d12 (13) damage. Additionally, she pumps a potent venom into the wound. The target must make a hard Endurance check or suffer 3d6 damage, which ignores Protection.
61–70%	*The Scouring of Jahamah (Ketian rite):* Naahpasswee's eyes flare with dread light, and fires scorch her target's bones. The target must make a difficult Endurance or Willpower check (whichever is lower). On a failure, they suffer 3d6 Wounds and 2 Corruption for each 5 or 6 rolled on the damage dice; on a success, they take half that damage.
71–80%	*Mouathenic Rite:* Naahpasswee can cast either the Scouring of Jahamah or any Mouathenic rite from Jackals (see pages 101–103)
81–90%	*Crushing Coils:* Naahpasswee entangles her target with her snake-like body. 3d10 (16) damage. Additionally, the target moves with Naahpasswee and must make a hard Endurance test at the start of each round (before deciding Initiative order). The target takes 3d12 (19) damage each round from being crushed; a successful save means the target takes half damage. On their turn, a crushed target can make a hard Athletics check to break free. On a failure, one of their arms slips and is caught fast between the coils. A second failure (or a fumble on the first attempt) means they are completely caught within the coils and unable to take actions. An ally can make a hard Athletics check to free a caught character.

Treasure:

- Piles of golden scales, 8,000 ss worth. Encumbrance is 80.
- Naahpasswee's two-handed spear. The haft is a single piece of carved, polished bone. Twin snakes carved into the bone twist their way from the butt to where the head joins the blade, their scales providing a solid grip for the wielder. The spear's long, slightly curved blade protrudes from their mouths. The blade is a dull, white metal, which neither catches nor reflects the light.
  - › 1d12 + 2 damage.
  - › The blade can cut through stone as easily as flesh.
  - › Calling out the name *Jahamah* after a successful attack causes one of the snakes to leap forward and strike the target. The target must make an immediate difficult Endurance check. On a failure, they take 2d8 damage; on a success, they take half that damage. A Jackal can call upon Jahamah three times per week.
  - › Calling out the name *Hamahaj* protects the wielder from the powers of the Rathic. The wielder gains +3 Protection and +20% to all Defensive skills versus Rathic attacks and powers. The wielder can call upon Hamahaj three times per week.
- Staff-sling made of golden scales. +1 damage and + 1 Clash Point.
- Heavy iron stabbing sword. +2 damage but causes a –5% penalty to Melee Combat (penalty increases to –10 if the wielder's Might is 11 or less).
- A golden censer in the shape of a Yammim's head. When filled with incense, the smoke billows out in ever-increasing waves. This is enough to fill a 30-cubit × 30-cubit space in three rounds. The smoke blinds those within it, and all Willpower checks are made at +1 level of difficulty.

Aftermath

There is no way to fight or defeat Naahpasswee without the spear. Although this might feel initially unsatisfying to a group, it is the way of the world. Kalypsis holds wonders and terrors to which the current age gives no answers. The best the Jackals can do is return the seal, deal with Philon and Leodias, and free Mikro from Naahpasswee's shadow. Replacing the seal does this and frees the villagers (and any Jackals) from Naahpasswee's influence. Replacing the huwasi also helps seal Naahpasswee's power away. The villagers all act as though they are coming out of a time of poor sleep, seemingly troubled by horrible dreams that quickly fade from memory. There might be some complications.

Replacing the seal does not free Philon, for he was never truly bound. When Naahpasswee restored his foot, she won his undying loyalty. He waits for a season, acting like his old self, before sneaking out to the site and reopening it. Eilene returns to Mikro and becomes the first of Naahpasswee's new converts. The cycle might begin anew if the Jackals do not pay attention. Additionally, children born during this event are exceptionally sensitive to movements along the Dream Road; some might even become prophets for good or ill.

The Fate of Kinesh: replacing the seal does not prevent Naahpasswee from touching the Kahar's spirit, nor does it repair the mental and spiritual damage inflicted upon Kinesh. If he takes part in slaying Naahpasswee, this helps restore part of his mind; but, truly, only the blessing of Alwain can heal this Kahar. Kinesh needs the aid of Alwain, such as can be found in the Temple of Alwain in Ameena Noani. Should the Jackals leave Kinesh to his own fate, Kinesh finds his way into Avsalim's service within six seasons.

Dark Birth: one of Naahpasswee's secret gifts was to open the womb of Rebecca, a Luathi woman. She and her husband, Nahan, conceived a child almost immediately. This child is a vessel – an assalu – which carries a fragment of Naahpasswee's power and personality. Should the child grow to adulthood, it becomes a powerful Mouathenic of the Ketian Way, someone in whom Avsalim is interested.

Sleeper Agent: should one of the Jackals fumble their Willpower check against Subsumation, they are still under the will of Naahpasswee. Within a season, their new mistress contacts them through their dreams. Loremasters should use this as they like, as Naahpasswee controls the Jackal while they sleep.

For additional ideas about what can happen in the wake of the **Shadow Over Mikro**, see the *Hooks* on page 71.

Advancements

- 1 for dealing with the Takan/Leodias
- 1 for discovering the influence of Naahpasswee
- 1 for sealing the Great Chamber

SOUTHERN TALE: THE SACRED HART

An adventure for Tolerated Jackals, set during the month of Tise, in the dry season.

OVERVIEW

Once again, Ba-en Nafar calls upon the Jackals to aid the Nawsi's father. If Ba-en Nafar died during the events of **The Stone Garden**, Nabal replaces him with Naitgadda, a former Jackal loyal to Nabal. This time, the ritual requires another ingredient from legend – the freely given heart of an ayal. Arishat knows nothing of these beasts, save that they died out long ago, but Ba-en Nafar hopes that Sari Avi of Densom might possess knowledge lost to the rest of the plains. In truth, she does; however, Sari Avi hopes for a different miracle from the last ayal's heart. She would see the ayals restored to the woods and the Aeco Plains.

Legend says that ayals, green-furred deer, once ran throughout the Aeco Wood. The ayals were liminal beings, creatures that roamed between this world and others. The stories say that when a person possessing a great need found an ayal, the beast might freely give up its heart to aid that need. The ayal would then be reborn from the heart of one of the greatest trees in the woods a year and a day later. However, when the Takan came to the Aeco Plains, they hunted and slaughtered the ayals, craving their flesh even above that of the Luathi. No one has seen an ayal since Densom first sprang up along the edge of the woods.

The Sars and Saris of Densom harbour secrets from the rest of the plains, secrets concerning the fate of the ayals. Sari Avi, as possessor of those secrets and prophecies, can set the Jackals upon the hunt for the last ayal. However, dark forces align against them, seeking to prevent the discovery of this sacred beast, and perhaps corrupt it for dark ends. In the end, saving the ayal, convincing it to give up its heart, and deciding what to do with that heart is in the hands of a group of Jackals.

See *Jackals* pages 129 and 133 for information on Densom, page 187 for a background on Sari Avi, and pages 129 and 131 for information on the Aeco Wood.

ACT 1: SENTEM

The Jackals begin in Sentem, at the start of the season, with the Sar still struggling. Whether or not this year's raid has occurred yet is up to the Loremaster. However, following their success in dealing with the first ingredient, Ba-en Nafar (or Naitgadda) summons the Jackals to procure the second. (If they failed, the Loremaster can either find a reason for Sameel to involve them again – perhaps Ba-en perished procuring the first item after they failed – or can have Sari Avi approach them to procure the heart for her purposes – see below.)

Ba-en Nafar can impart the following information:

- Nawsi Sameel is grateful for the work they did in securing the asa rose.
- The next ingredient they need is as obscure as the first – the heart of an Aeco ayal, freely given.
- He does not know what that means, save for ayals were a type of deer that once roamed the Aeco Woods.
- He wants the Jackals to go to Densom and speak with Sari Avi about the ayals.
- Although Densom is under the protection of Sentem, it is still autonomous. The Jackals must handle this matter with subtlety.
- Sameel does not want his allies to know that Japeth is doing poorly, although they obviously know something is wrong. Hence, he is sending the Jackals.
- As with the previous job, Ba-en Nafar will pay the Jackals 100 ss apiece to search, and 100 more if they find a heart and bring it back.
- Arishat might know more if they wish to inquire with her.
- Should the Jackals manage to complete this task, Sameel plans to meet them in person.

If the Jackals wish to speak to Arishat, the Hasheer can impart the following information:

- Sari Avi is the leader of Densom. Her husband, Hanno, is one of the town's healers.
- Despite living so close to Bartak Kentak, the town thrives. It does so because of the Yesim line's covenant with the town and the peace it enforces.
- The ayals were more spirits of the earth than true animals. They were the forest's life and essence given flesh.
- According the lore she has studied, Arishat knows the ayal could be reborn – provided the one to slay it invoked the proper rites.
- She possesses the stone knife and knowledge of the ritual required.
- She is willing to share the proper rites with a Hasheer or Kahar (or with an invoker of another culture, should the Jackal succeed at an Influence check). Learning the rite grants the Jackal +2% to Ancient Lore.
    - › The rite requires a stone knife, an invocation, burning the remains of the ayal and – most importantly – that the ayal freely gives up its heart.
    - › The invocation is in Hannic, but Arishat translates it into Luathii: *'Great Forest hear my plea, let your flesh manifest come speak with me.'* If the ayal chooses to hear you, it will come lay its head in your lap. You must verbalise your need to the ayal – it will either open its heart to you or leap away.
    - › If done correctly, the ayal will be reborn in one year and one day.

- The Takan hunted down the ayals, feasting on their flesh and preventing their rebirth.
- She has heard rumours for years that one last ayal survived. Foresters of Densom claim to have seen it. But the last of those tales came almost 10 years ago, back when Hirrom was still with them, before he disappeared. (Hirrom was Japeth's oldest son.)

Once the Jackals are ready, the journey from Sentem to Densom takes three days and uses the Plains' difficulty.

ACT 2: DENSOM

The town of Densom sits across the Wuma Amwa from the mist-covered ruins of Bartak Kentak, and within the shadow of the Aeco Woods. Two gates stand at the south and east ends of the town. The eastern gate faces the woods. The gate and the start of the palisade stand 11 cubits above the ground. The palisade is incomplete, covering only about a third of the town. The southern gate is stone and stands half again as tall as the wooden one. It faces the Wuma Amwa and the ruins. The walls extending out from it protect the southern quarter of the town, but they are in desperate need of repair.

Finding Sari Avi is a simple thing, as the elderly Sari comes to meet the Jackals once word reaches her. If this is the Jackals' first visit to the town, she politely but forcefully demands to know their business in Densom; if not, she welcomes them more warmly (depending on how their last visit went).

NPCs of Densom

Sari Avi

The Sari of Densom is a handsome woman, well beyond her youthful years. Nearing 40, the Sari spends most of her time lovingly tending to the town's needs as a shepherd tends to a beloved flock. She becomes wary when Jackals begin to speak of the heart of an ayal, removes them from the market of Densom, and takes them back to her house to speak.

Avi and her husband Hanno live in a simple, four-room house. At the front of the house is a covered yard with several benches, and bunches of herbs hanging to dry. Inside, Sari Avi demands to know why they are looking for an ayal. Should the Jackals attempt to lie to her, they must succeed at a difficult Deception check. If they fail, she tells them she knows they are liars and dismisses them. Only a successful Deception check, the truth, or excellent roleplaying can convince her to tell the truth: that an ayal yet lives.

Sari Avi can impart the following information without revealing the truth:
- Wonderful and terrible things fill the Aeco Woods.
- The ayals were spirits of the earth – existing in, but not of, the mortal world.
- She can impart most of what Arishat knows of the ayals (see above), save for the ritual.
- The last ayal died when her grandmother was a child, hunted to extinction by the Takan (false).

Should the Jackals gain her trust, she can further impart the following information:

- She fears something is wrong with Japeth (should the Jackals mention his malady).
- There is a prophecy, handed down from Sar to Sari in Densom.
- Tirisht, the fifth Sari back from Avi, had a dream. In it, she saw black vines threading through the forest, choking the life from the trees. Suddenly, a green fire spread through the wood, harming only the vines. The fire's edge was shaped like a multitude of ayals.
- Tirisht, and the Saris and Sars who came after, believed this was a vision from Alwain. They believed the ayals would return to the forest one day to wage a war against the darkness that lies beneath it.
- Avi has seen the last ayal three times over the course of her life. All the sightings were a day's walk, or deeper, into the forest. She suggests the Jackals follow the Wuma Amwa deeper into the forest, as it provides an easy path into the heart of the woods.
- She has no special knowledge about how to attract or find the ayal. Each time she saw it, she was wrestling with a difficult decision or time in her life.
- She asks a boon of the Jackals – one which cannot be bound by oath. She asks them to restore the ayals to the forest.
- She knows there must be a way, although she cannot see a path that does not involve risk.

Hanno

Hanno, Densom's herbalist, is the same age as his wife, Sari Avi. A man who is just starting to be bowed by his years, Hanno greets those around him with a smile and a kind word. There is a 75% chance Hanno is home, working on some concoction. Otherwise, he is out and about in Densom and on the farms, healing those who need his help. Should a Jackal make a successful Perception check, they notice Hanno's jars are all marked with colours and small, simple slash marks. The healer is illiterate and created his own symbolism to keep track of his ingredients and recipes.

Hanno can impart the following information:

- He has not heard about the ayals for many years.
- His interest in the woods is more earthy.
- He will always pay Jackals for fresh acalana. He pays 25 ss for five vials of resin, or trades a prepared dose of acalana resin for the same amount.
- His wife is wiser than he, and a wonderful Sari to the village.
- Every year, the raids seem more effective. Still, the Takan are cunning beasts. Hanno worries they now hide better than the Sar of Sentem realises.
- He can sell the Jackals up to four doses of acalana resin for 45 ss each.

Gan

Gan is a spy in Densom. A Jackal's careless actions put mouahalan coins into Gan's hands, and these coins corrupted the young man's spirit. He has begun to spread his corruption, and the Daughter Beneath the Earth now speaks to him through his dreams. Gan seeks information to aid his dark mistress in her return to the world, and so opened a hostel in his home for Jackals. Jackals who wish to spend the night in Densom find the villagers directing them to the House of Gan.

Gan's home is a standard, four-room Luathi house. Although it is smaller than Sari Avi's, it possesses a second floor. He asks the Jackals about their business in Densom and subtly probes them, trying to divine their purpose in the town and the woods.

Gan can impart the following information:

- He can put up the Jackals for whatever they are willing to spare; he does this to honour the Jackals who saved his life five seasons ago, when Takan attacked his caravan.
- He is a trader, moving through the woods from Densom to Sentem and bringing goods back again.
- Once, when he was younger, he travelled farther south, as far as Ger. Once, he even passed through Jehumma's Gap to trade with the Trauj.
- He asks the Jackals of news of Sentem, the plains, and the wider world.
- Should any Jackal possess the *Family Heirloom* or *Treasure Map* hook, Gan is especially interested in them. He mentions he has seen that symbol on ruins in the wood (*Family Heirloom*), or he recognises one of the features on the map from deep in the woods. He recognises them as important to his mistress and sends her dream messages about the Jackal and what he discovered.

Once the Jackals are ready, the journey into the Aeco Woods takes three days and uses the Woods' difficulty.

ACT 3: THE HART OF THE WOODS

The Aeco Woods are a densely packed forest. Travel is slow going, as hills and knolls rise and drop, thick vegetation carpets the ground, and tree roots attempt to trip and block the Jackals' passage. See page 129 of *Jackals* for more information on the Aeco Woods.

Once in the woods, tracking the ayal is no simple task. There are several paths open to the Jackals. They can use Survival and Perception checks to search for the ayal. They can attempt Willpower or Lore checks to cast their need out into the forest to attempt to summon the ayal. Each check represents four hours of work, as tracking a lone deer in the forest proves to be quite difficult.

The Jackals need to accumulate **six successes** (with critical successes counting as two successes) before they incur **three failures** to summon the ayal from the forest.

For every two failures, the Jackals encounter something in the forest. Roll a d6 on the Aeco Woods Encounter Table to see what they stumble across. Roll for treasure normally for these encounters.

AECO WOODS ENCOUNTER TABLE	
d6	Encounter
1	Takan Patrol: two Tsutakan
2	Desecrated Ground: two Rapiuma per Jackal
3	Wolf Pack: two wolves (animals) per Jackal
4	Nahunum Scout: one Nahunum per two Jackals
5	Wild Aburrisanu: one Aburrisanu per Jackal
6	Wolves: one Wolf (bandit) per Jackal.

Should the Jackals succeed at the check, they find the ayal's tracks. Should the Jackals fail the check, they stumble upon the tracks of a group of Takan who are also tracking the ayal!

The tracks lead the Jackals deeper into the Aeco Woods. The ground grows ever rockier and broken. Finally, the ground gives way to a little ravine, where a small spring pools and flows out to eventually join the Amwa. Should the ayal be alone, it stands near the pool at the far end, drinking peacefully. Otherwise, the Takan have pushed the ayal back to where it stands in the pool, frantically looking for an escape. The Takan advance on the ayal, whips in hand. They all bear the brands and marking of a black tree. There is one Norakan per Jackal and one Mavakan per Jackal.

When the Jackals approach the ayal, the beast is strangely quiescent. It waits and watches them. At this point, they must begin the ritual. The ayal can only approach one person, so the Jackal who initially invokes the opening line of the ritual is the speaker. Invoking this ritual is tiring. The Jackal who does so must either spend 12 Devotion Points or suffer –2 Mettle for the rest of the season. No roll is necessary if the Jackals follow the ritual outlined by Arishat. Should they not know the ritual, or forget it, have them make Lore checks to intuit the correct path. The real question here, once the Jackals find the ayal, is what will the Jackals do? They know they need the heart for Sar Japeth, but they might also know this ayal could eventually bring back all the ayals. They have the ayal here and now, the chance they might find it again if it runs away is slim, and the timing is tight for the ritual to heal the Sar.

Once the Jackal states their need, the ayal turns to bare its side to the Jackal. As they watch, the skin and muscle unravel into fibrous, plant-like tendrils, and the ayal reveals its heart. If removed with a stone knife, the heart comes free and the ayal collapses.

Should the Jackals attempt to take the heart without the ritual, they are successful. They are Jackals after all, and the ayal's power is in its life-sustaining nature. The last ayal dies, and the forest becomes a much darker place (see the *Aftermath* section below).

Once the Jackals have the heart, they must burn the ayal's remains and return the heart to Sentem (for Sar Japeth) or to Densom (for Sari Avi).

AFTERMATH

The aftermath of this adventure depends on the Jackals' actions. Should they take the heart correctly, the last ayal is reborn in a year and a day. Should they take it by force, the last of the ayals is gone from the world forever, and the Daughter Beneath the Earth frees herself four seasons earlier than she would have (see page 99).

Should the Jackals bring the heart to Sar Japeth, their contact awards them properly, and Nawsi Sameel sends a message for the Jackals to dine with him soon. Additionally, the cost to take the Acquire Patron seasonal action for the next 1d4 seasons is reduced by 50% for Ba-en Nafar, Nabal, or Nawsi Sameel.

Should the Jackals instead use the last heart as Sari Avi wishes, sending the ayal to bring back more of its kind, two ayals are reborn next year; each year after, they return in twice as many numbers (up to 144). This action has far-reaching consequences for the southern campaign. First, it means Sar Japeth might succumb to the malady that afflicts him. Depending on the Loremaster's wishes, there might not enough time to wait for another heart, although the Jackals do not discover that until next year. However, the forest becomes a more peaceful place, and the Daughter Beneath the Earth finds herself restrained by the ayals' presence, emerging weaker than she expected. Sari Avi, upon hearing the news of the ayals' rebirth, offers a sacrifice to Alwain and prepares a feast for the Jackals. She also compensates them for their troubles – 175 ss each. Additionally, the cost to take the Acquire Patron seasonal action for the next 1d4 seasons is reduce by 50% for Sari Avi; however, the Jackals cannot take the Acquire Patron seasonal action with Ba-en Nafar, Nabal, or Nawsi Sameel for the same amount of time, since they hear of the Jackals' actions.

ADVANCEMENTS

- 1 for dealing with the Takan
- 1 for finding the ayal
- 1 for bringing the heart to Sentem for Japeth's treatment
- 1 for restoring the ayals to the Aeco Woods, which also increases each Jackal's Kleos by 1.

HOOKS

Discouraging Scouts: Both sides of the War Road begin to scout the other end, to see what is happening. Jackals might be tasked with hunting down these scouts and discouraging them from completing their missions.

Finding an Anzaim: Finding one of the Anzaim should be a quest. It should take three Find Rumour actions over the course of three seasons for a Jackal to discover they might find one in the Luasa Desert. The first rumour should point them to Orsem Yahan, where a Trauj named Baya resides. The Jackal discovers that Baya claims to have seen an Anzaim. Travelling to Orsem Yahan for a seasonal action enables the Jackal to question Baya. Baya tells them she saw one on her coming-of-age quest for the Arrow Tribe. She cannot say where it was, as only the Yahtahmi of her clan, the Ashan Mudi, can say where the clan's sacred ground lies. Finally, the Jackal must journey into the desert and convince the Ashan Mudi to take them to the sacred site. This could entail a Find Rumour check, or a quest to become part of the tribe and take the tribal elder as a patron.

Breaking the Seal of Ennuki: Sundering the seal takes effort and requires a Research downtime action. Striking it with an enchanted blade, specifically one crafted from the claw of an Anzaim (see the *Aftermath* section in **Shadow Over Mikro**), would do it. A successful Ancient Lore check reveals if they submerge the disc in the sea of Futhia at sunset; then burn it over an altar fire made from Shalla wood, tamarisk, and cassia; the disc will become brittle, making it easy to snap.

Once More into the Mines: Abishai, the Hasheer of Rataro, hires the Jackals to take her to Atem's mine to research the Labasu-Rathic released there.

CHAPTER 4
YEAR OF RECOVERED FAITH

Gai shelter me!
Kauma shield me!
Lord of the heavens,
Send your servants to hedge me in –
For my enemy hunts and seeks to snare me.
Darkness is his lair; the night is his home.
He scoffs as he raises his hand
Against your chosen servant.
Rise, oh Lord, mount your chariot,
Rush out of the eastern gates with the dawn,
Bring salvation to me with your mighty hand,
Shelter your humble servant.

~Fragment of a psalm of Nabal

INTRODUCTION

The Year of Recovered Faith is Year 3 of *The Fall of the Children of Bronze* campaign. Here, Jackals discover some of the land's ancient history, encounter figures whose shadows loom over the Zaharets, and dig into the inhuman history of the land as they deal with Umbalna – king of the Ligna Hualla – and seek an ancient moon road of the Hann.

THEME

The theme of the Year of Recovered Faith is mystery. In both **Forgotten Covenant** and **The Moons' Road**, Jackals encounter inhuman wonders. The spirit, Umbalna, stands apart from the rest of the Zaharets and time itself; while the Hann – although long departed from the Zaharets – left behind artefacts that defy the Hasheers' understanding. In both scenarios, the Loremaster should focus on the mystery and the alien natures of both the Hann and Umbalna. This means Jackals might find themselves with a lingering sense of incompletion, as if they are only getting part of the story; this is purposeful, as the mystery draws them in and inspires wonder to fuel their desire for knowledge.

The central conflict of the Year of Recovered Faith is ignorance versus knowledge. For humanity, history is something they have often sacrificed for survival. In these adventures, Jackals must learn from and come to terms with some piece of lost history for the good of the War Road. For the north, this means understanding a past covenant to save lives in the present. For the south, the Jackals must race to find the final component of the ritual needed to save the Sar's life: a piece of a Hannic moon road. However, finding such a road proves quite difficult, as the Hann built them according to their own rites and insights.

IMPORTANT NPCS

Ba-en Nafar: see page 18.

Nawsi Namar: see page 185 of *Jackals*. Namar is the Nawsi of Orsem Yahan and a man loyal to the Sars of Ameena Noani. However, he is a simple soldier. Fighting spirits of the forest is beyond his comprehension. He needs those familiar with such matters to step in and aid the fort and its burgeoning town.

Hen-he-net: see page 18. Hen-he-net is set up in Mayrah Vedil at this time of year, hawking her wares at the southern end of the road.

EVENTS IN THE NORTH

- A group of Hasheers in Ameena Noani begin to practise the Twisted Path. They start kidnapping the poor off the streets in small numbers to provide the blood needed for their rituals.
- Nikominda, a corrupted Melkoni, arrives in Kroryla seeking a true Warrior of Lykos.
- A small bout of sickness spreads in Kroryla, but the Rylareia contain it.

EVENTS IN THE SOUTH

- Ger begins to send merchants bearing messages of contract north to Sentem, offering 250 ss to those who travel to Ger as mercenaries. Apparently, they need more bodies for their war with the Ungathi tribes to the west.
- Strange Rathic from the Luasa Sands attempt to corrupt Anahalulf, the well of the world. Trauj clans unite to stop the Rathic and their Takan allies.
- A pack of Jackals boasts they are going to claim Orsem Kitan as a den for themselves.

EVENTS ANYWHERE

- There is a solar eclipse on the 1st of Isten, the first day of the year. Although the Hasheers predicted this, it is still an ill omen to start the year.

RETIREMENT BENEFITS

If a player retires their Jackal this year, their new Jackal gains a single piece of gear with two traits. The increase in trade means there is better-quality gear for purchase in the Zaharets.

NORTHERN TALE: FORGOTTEN COVENANT

An adventure for Recognised Jackals, set during the month of Eser, in the rainy season.

OVERVIEW

Before humans or Hann lived in the lands of the Zaharets, Umbalna, the Forest King, dwelt among the cedars of the Ligna Hualla. For ages unmeasured, it preserves the forest through its power and might. None living know the measure of its days or strength. For as long as the Ligna Hualla has been, Umbalna was. Umbalna and its offspring, the Umbalnani (see page 217 of *Jackals*), dwell in the forest, safeguarding it from intrusions of Chaos from the Vori Wastes and the Luasa Sands.

When the Luathi reclaimed the northern end of the Zaharets, they settled Orsem Yahan – which sits on the edge of the Ligna Hualla. For a time, humanity was unwelcomed in the Ligna, with the Umbalnani chasing off any who crossed its threshold. However, that changed 100 years ago, when Hasheers discovered references to an old covenant between the kingdom of Lukka and Umbalna. Tirisht, one of the Hasheers, braved the forest and summoned Umbalna, claiming the old covenant stood. The forest spirit, for its own inscrutable reasons, agreed, and opened the forest to the Luathi. There were missteps at first, but soon the Luathi of Orsem Yahan developed an understanding of what the spirit would and would not allow within the confines of its demesne, and Orsem Yahan began to enjoy the bounty of the forest.

However, the Luathi now stand in breach of that covenant. Unbeknown to them, Mouathenics entered the forest in the Year of Fallen Seeds, disturbing two sites under Umbalna's protection. The first was on the border of the forest (see **The Wolves' Lair** in *Jackals*). With the information gathered at that site, the two Mouathenics – Aldimir and Mellou – discovered the second site, deep within the forest. The two are searching for something called the Vault of Ur-Takan, and they believe these sites are part of the puzzle left to them by the Priest-Kings of old. Two months ago, they entered the Ligna Hualla, slew a score of Umbalnani, and violated the wards placed on the site. Although they escaped with their lives and some knowledge, they awakened the wrath of the forest. Mellou lost a leg to the grasping roots of a cedar, and an Umbalnani took one of Aldimir's eyes. Umbalna, enraged by the violent intrusions and the wilful violation of the sites, sees the covenant of old as broken. Umbalna attacks any Luathi who spends the night in the Ligna with increasing ferocity, stalking the woods with its retinue of spirit monkeys.

Three days before the Jackals arrived, while attempting to harvest cedar from the woods, Diokles and his son, Shapan, stumbled upon the site the Mouathenics discovered. While exploring a shallow cave for more water, Diokles triggered ancient magics in the cave, trapping his spirit. Shapan fled with Diokles, leading his father back to the orsem.

The Jackals, called to Orsem Yahan because of the deaths, must either repair the old covenant or make a new one – otherwise, Umbalna will seal the bounty of the forest from the Luathi again.

ACT 1: A CALL EAST

Word reaches the Jackals that Nawsi Namar is offering silver in Orsem Yahan. If the Jackals participated in **The Wolves' Lair** or Namar hired them in the past, Namar might send a runner to them, specifically. The message is simple: men and women are dying north of the orsem; Jackals are needed.

Once the Jackals are ready, have them plan the route for their journey to Orsem Yahan. See pages 124 and 137 of *Jackals* for more information on Orsem Yahan.

When the Jackals arrive, one of the orsem's elders immediately ushers them into the Nawsi's presence. Namar, still holding council in the old Alwainic shrine, can share the following information:

- The Ligna Hualla is a major resource for the orsem and for Ameena Noani.
- The wood, herbs, and other natural materials in the forest help support the orsem.
- For the last century, the Hasheers ensured an accord between the spirits of the forest and the Luathi, enabling them to harvest.
- Three seasons ago, a subtle shift occurred. The spirits grew more restless and aggressive. Each season, the hostility has grown.
- Three months ago, the first of the gatherers failed to return. Soon, others disappeared. Then, the Luathi began to find body parts of those from the orsem along cutter paths.
- Namar forbade people to travel into the forest, but many still sneak out to try to gather what they need.
- A father and son returned from the forest three days ago. The father's mind is broken, but the son might have some information for the Jackals.
- Namar needs to find out what caused the covenant to be broken (he can share the story in the overview).
- His guards are well-suited to protecting the orsem from Wolves and Takan, but spirits are not something they know how to handle.
- This is vital to the survivability of the orsem; he is willing to pay 300 ss apiece if the Jackals can rectify the situation.

Visiting the House of Healing

A pair of Luathi – Barqan, a Kahar, and Huldel, a Hasheer – now manage Orsem Yahan's house of healing. This is where the Jackals might have visited Baya in **The Wolves' Lair**. The two woodcutters returned from the Ligna three days ago, Shapan leading his father back from the north.

Barqan and Huldel

Barqan and Huldel have heard of the Jackals and are grateful for their intervention. Either can share the following information:

- These are the first survivors to return in over a month. The rest simply vanish.
- Something is wrong with Diokles – some malady of the spirit.
- He says nothing, eats only when fed by Shapan, and stares north.
- Not just north, but to a specific point in the north. When moved, his eyes shift to this point.
- Shapan is all right, physically. The young boy is only eight years of age, and he led his father on the journey out of the woods back here. He is harrowed by the experience.
- Barqan thinks it is a spirit that plagues Diokles. He believes it is Umbalna's work (false).
- Huldel is wary to say, but she believes it could be some dark rite (partially true).
- They can allow the Jackals to speak with Shapan for no more than half a bell. The boy must rest.
- They will not allow the Jackals to take Shapan back into the Ligna. Convincing them to let him go requires a hard Influence check.

Diokles and Shapan – Woodcutters

Diokles is clearly Melkoni. He sits cross-legged on a cot, staring north – his eyes unwavering in their focus. His left hand grips an amulet around his neck, which he rubs compulsively with his thumb. His son, who seems to have a touch of Luathi blood in him, holds his father's unresponsive hand, whispering that it will be ok. If the Jackals come to talk to him, his eyes widen with excitement. Shapan asks and can share the following information:

- Are you truly Jackals?
- The young boy questions them incessantly about their lives. He is fascinated, and unless discouraged, will probably take to the War Road when he is older.
- He was helping his father prepare a felled cedar, two days into the forest.
- His father assured him the spirits would not bother them, as they had their amulets.
- The forest got very quiet, and his father saw something by the upturned earth near the cedar.
- Shapan did not see it, but there was a flash of light, and then his father was like this.
- The Umbalnani went silent and fled after the flash of light.
- He spent a night waiting to see whether his father would recover, but then set out, leading Diokles back to Orsem Yahan.
- Shapan is worried; his father does not eat unless forced, and he grows weaker by the day.
- Diokles is looking back towards the Ligna.

- Shapan can show the Jackals where the site is – this requires an Influence check to convince him to go.
- If the Jackals do not convince him, Shapan can share that his father leaves marks on the trees so he and Shapan can return to their previous harvesting areas. This mark, a small half circle, is usually placed at the south side of the tree, up where the first branch extends.

Diokles' amulet: Diokles holds a small, bronze amulet of twin lightning bolts intertwined like snakes. A successful Culture check (Own or Other, as appropriate) reveals it is one of the symbols of Araton, the head of the Melkon Pantheon and father of Ryla. His cult has not travelled this far east; to see an amulet like this is strange, even to Melkoni. The amulet has apotropaic powers, and it is the only thing keeping Diokles' soul bound to his body. It gives the wearer +15% Willpower and 3 Protection from non-Melkoni rites.

Once the Jackals are ready, the journey from Orsem Yahan to the site where the attack occurred takes three days. The journey takes them across the Rekiti Vana and should use the Mountains' difficulty.

ACT 2: THE SECOND VAULT

The Ligna Hualla is a world of its own. A viridian haze fills the forest during the day, as the leaves break up the light that trickles down onto the forest floor. It is difficult for Jackals to maintain a sense of time or space within the forest's borders. The edge of the forest quickly disappears, leaving only trees as far as the eye can see. The light brightens and dims with little regularity, never completely fading, even at night. It is the realm of the Forest King, Umbalna, and mortals should tread its paths with care.

What a Jackal's senses reveal:

Sights – cedars, a green tint to other Jackals, remnants of strange monkey-men statues, darting figures in the branches of the trees that move too quickly to focus on them, and Diokles' half-circle marks.

Smells – cedar, loam.

Sounds – faint silences broken by the distant cry of monkeys, along with the rustle of the branches when the wind kicks up, or as if something invisible moves among them.

Following the woodcutter's marks into the forest requires a hard Perception check. A failure means the Jackals wander for a day, each suffering the loss of 1 Mettle, before picking up the trail again. A fumble means the Jackals have an encounter with a group of Umbalnani [two per Jackal] before moving on.

When the Jackals finally track Diokles' marks back to his camp, they see the scene Shapan described. A large, felled cedar dominates the small clearing, partially de-limbed. A small forest stream winds its way through the clearing, and a dark cave mouth sits low on a rise that forms the eastern edge of the area. A successful Perception check reveals the furrows and scars of other such fellings from prior seasons. Several tree stumps, and masses of upturned roots, lay scattered about the clearing. One stump, of an old and gnarled tree, frames a shallow pit underneath it. It seems it was recently dug out and is just large enough for a Trauj to squeeze through. A critical success also reveals what look like the rotting remains of a human leg from the knee down, trapped within a maze of roots at the base of one of the trees. A faint amaranthine (purple) light flickers under the root network, as well.

Searching the clearing reveals several logging tools left behind when Shapan led his father back to Orsem Yahan. Three bronze axes of different sizes, 100 feet of rope, and a bronze saw lie near the cedar. Broken shovels and a pickaxe lay near the strange stump. Inside the cave, the Jackals find the remnants of a small camp: two blankets, a bronze pot, a clay pot filled with dried dates and figs, and a Melkoni short spear. Should the Jackals search the back of the shallow cave, they can see it extends back about 15 feet and ends. The clearing remains quiet, although the feeling that something is watching the Jackals increases.

Beneath the stump lies a tunnel, leading down about 12 feet into a small, hemispherical stone chamber. The floor cants heavily to the northeast, making it difficult to traverse. Rubble, roots, and vines choke a small portal to what seems to be a stairwell, blocking the only visible exit. The dome of the chamber depicts a night sky unfamiliar to the Jackals. Mountain peaks reach up like grasping fingers around the rim to the vault of heaven. Black stars shimmer against the light of torches in unfamiliar constellations. The carvings show the moons of the Zaharets, but mottled with brown veins, pallid spots, and ominous dark stains. A successful Lore check allows a Jackal to recognise the Dura Jahamah – a mountain range far to the northeast of the Zaharets – on the wall, suggesting this whole scene lies somewhere far beyond this place. A successful Ancient Lore check reveals a fragment of a legend from before the rise of Barak Barad, a prophecy about the Black Dawn:

> When I have placed my enemy
>> beneath my frozen throne,
> And all his servants bow to me,
>> I – the Lord – alone.
> Then, shall I spread my bleakest cloak
>> Across all heaven's halls.
> The daughters, and the stars above,
>> shall my name exalt.

The patterns in the dome depict new constellations in shapes just on the edge of understanding. Studying the patterns for 10 minutes grants a Jackal +4% to Ancient Lore and forces them to make a difficult Willpower check. If they fail, they take 1d3 Corruption. A fumble on this roll gives the Jackal 4 Corruption.

A large, stone pillar rests in the centre of the chamber. The pillar is in the shape of a worm rising out of the floor. A dozen flat, spade-like teeth line the edge of the top of the pillar, forming little alcoves along its rim. One of the alcoves holds a small, clay statue. A successful Perception check reveals the squatting, grotesque figure is an image of Diokles, his mouth open in a rictus of terror. In the centre of the pillar sits an amaranthine gem, the smaller twin of the one found in **The Wolves' Lair** (see page 252 in *Jackals*). This one, however, has a large crack running through its left side.

Breaking the Statue

If the Jackals attempt to break the statue of Diokles, it lets out a tortured scream of pain. Should the Jackals continue, the statue is easily destroyed, as it is made of a soft clay. However, doing so destroys Diokles' mind, making the state he is currently in permanent. This also applies to any Jackals bound by the Hazukamna (see below).

The Gem

The gem is a prison for a Hazukamna, a powerful Rathic, bound here long ago in servitude to Mouadah. It aided them in their charting of the Sky Road and the stars long ago. In return for its aid, the Priest-Kings sacrificed servants and prisoners to it, binding their spirits within the gem so the Hazukamna could torture and feed on them. Once every 10 minutes, the gem's power flares, potentially catching the eye of one random person in the room. Have each character make a Dodge check to avoid looking at the light. The character who fails (or rolls the lowest if all characters make their roll) sees the light of the Hazukamna. Immediately, a small clay figurine with indistinct features appears. The character must then make a hard Willpower check each round or begin to lose their mind. With each failure, the statue's features refine more and more into the character's own. Three failures (with fumbles counting as two failures) result in the Hazukamna trapping the character's mind inside a small screaming statue, rendering them as simple as Diokles. A successful check means the Jackal is immune to the Hazukamna's ability for one day.

Jackals can break the gem, either with the Touch of Law rite or with brute force. The gem counts as stone (see page 69 of *Jackals*); but, due to the crack, only two successes are required to shatter it. However, shattering it releases the Hazukamna bound inside, which immediately attacks the Jackals.

Hazukamna, Stealer of Breath

During the height of Keta and Mouadah, those who travelled the Twisted Path found many teachers in the Silent Lands. Many of these spirits ended up in the service of their students, bound by the very rites they gifted. This Hazukamna is one such entity, bound in a gem for a thousand years by the Priest-Kings, and then for a thousand more by the power of Umbalna.

HAZUKAMNA			
Type:	Spirit	Location:	Everywhere
		Wounds:	65
Defence:	65%	Protection:	4 (insubstantial)
Combat:	75%	Move:	18
Knowledge:	80%	Initiative:	12
Urban:	70%	Clash Points:	5
Common:	70%	Treasure Score:	0
		Corruption:	10

Special Abilities

Inured to Darkness: the Hazukamna suffers no penalties due to absence of light.

Feed from Pain: the Hazukamna is fierce in both its anger and its hunger. It feeds on the torment of mortals, as Zadon gifted to it at the dawn of time. The Hazukamna inflicts +2 damage and recovers 1d6 Wounds at the start of its turn for each enemy within 25 yards that has taken Wounds.

Rathic: the Hazukamna is an insubstantial being – as such, it enjoys a high level of Protection from normal weapons. Its attacks generally ignore the physical Protection of their enemies. Additionally, Jackals cannot simply slay a Rathic. When its Wounds reach 0, it flees, driven away by the battle. Slaying a Rathic permanently requires a ritual and is feat of legend.

Combat Range

1–15%	*Enervating Flight:* the Hazukamna passes through the target, stealing a bit of their breath as it does so. 1d4 (2) Wounds, which ignore Valour.
16–35%	*The Hungry Cry (1d3 targets):* the Hazukamna screams, causing terror in those around it. The targets must make a hard Willpower check. They suffer 3d6 (11) Valour on a failure, or half that on a success.
36–65%	*Binder of Breath:* the Hazukamna can attempt to steal the breath of a Jackal. Have the Jackal make a Dodge check to catch their breath. If the Jackal fails, the Hazukamna begins to steal their breath. Immediately, the character suffers 1 Wound, ignoring Protection and Valour. The Jackal must make a difficult Willpower check at the end of each of their turns. Three failures (with fumbles counting as two failures) mean the Hazukamna steals the Jackal's breath and captures them in a small screaming statue, rendering the Jackal a mindless creature. A successful check means the Jackal is immune to the Hazukamna's ability for one day.
65–75%	*The Hungry Breath:* the Hazukamna releases the fullness of its hunger into the world, drawing the life from all those around it. All creatures within 25 yards must make a hard Willpower check. Those who fail start to suffocate, as the Hazukamna draws their breath from their bodies. 2d8 (9) damage (ignoring Protection) and 1d6 (4) Wounds (which ignore Valour). A successful check still inflicts 2d4 (5) damage (ignoring Protection) and 1 Wound (which ignores Valour).

When the Jackals defeat the Hazukamna, the clay statues it possesses turn to sludge. Those it trapped are freed, their minds remembering their time interned in clay as endless torture. The Jackals can also remove the statues from the chamber. The Hazukamna's hold on the souls dwindles with distance, failing when the statues leave the forest. When the Jackals drive the Hazukamna back into the Silent Lands, proceed to Act 3.

ACT 3: THE SPIRITS OF THE FOREST

When the Hazukamna falls, the forest goes from eerily silent to boisterously noisy. The cries of the Umbalnani ring out melodically among the trees, as if they are singing to a tune just on the edge of perception. They perch in the trees that surround the clearing, hopping from branch to branch, watching the Jackals intently. The birds in the trees break their silence as well, their chirps and calls blending with this music. Soon, the Jackals hear a rumbling harmony to the song from the north, and see a large light moving through the trees. If the Jackals flee, allow them to do so with no penalty. The Umbalnani let them go. Proceed to the *Aftermath* section below.

Should the Jackals stay, the forest floor begins to roil around them, the earth flowing and rippling like water. Each cedar is a fixed point in that sea, as the dirt seems to lap against their trunks. All Jackals must make an Athletics check to remain standing. As the light approaches nearer, it bathes everything, including the Jackals, in a soft golden light.

Read or paraphrase the following:

As you watch, what can only be Umbalna enters the clearing. The ancient being stands taller than three Trauj, yet it does not need to bow its head to move through the forest and its branches. It is vaguely man-shaped, with the feet of a vulture and hands like the paws of a lion. You stare up into its simian face and notice its features are like knotted rope, as if one could augur the future of the world from its expression. Twin horns, like those of a bull, jut from its head, and a golden light fills its mouth and eyes. When it speaks, its voice rolls over you with a force like an avalanche, yet it does not drive you away.

"Who are you, Children of Bronze? And why do you violate the boundary of my forest halls? Our covenant is broken!" It gestures to the place where the strange chamber lies.

Umbalna is not a monster, despite its curious and hybrid form. It is the guardian of the Ligna Hualla, placed here as penance for some great crime beyond the scope of mortal understanding. It is willing to discuss matters with the Jackals, yet is wary of them, as Mellou and Aldimir violated the covenant by breaking into the Mouadran chamber and stealing a potent artefact from where Umbalna sealed it.

Umbalna can share the following information:

- It is Umbalna, guardian of the forest by order of the Law of Heaven.
- It wards the borders of the Ligna, wherever they may be. It notes the forest is sometimes larger and sometimes smaller, as dictated by various needs and covenants.
- Its children are attacking the Children of Bronze because they broke the ancient covenant.
  - › When? Two great turnings ago (approximately a year).
  - › How? By breaking Umbalna's seal and violating the protection terms of the covenant. By stealing something inside and invoking dark spirits within the bounds of the forest.
- The chamber is part of a watchtower of darkness, built many great turnings ago. The lords and ladies of the west warred with the darkness out of the east. They are the ones who asked Umbalna, by the faithfulness of the covenant, to extend the forest and bury the site.
- It fears the time of covenants is at an end, for the Children of Bronze make weak promises, and the forest has need of protection. It plans to seal the forest from all outsiders.

Umbalna wishes to have the aid of the Luathi in protecting the Ligna, for it senses a great change upon the wind; but it is a proud being and will not bring this up unless the Jackals speak of it first. Should the Jackals wish to talk with Umbalna and negotiate a new covenant with it, they must begin to make Influence rolls. Other Jackals can make Lore rolls to uncover a bit of lore or other historical fact to bring to bear in this negotiation and aid their companion.

The Jackals need to accumulate **eight successes** (with critical successes counting as two successes) before they incur **four failures** to establish a new covenant.

With a covenant, each party makes a pledge to the other. For every two successes, the Jackals can claim a promise from Umbalna; for each failure, they must give up a concession to Umbalna. Below are sample promises and concessions to use as guidelines for the negotiation. The first promise and concession are good starting points to return to the status quo. Loremasters should feel free to add their own, as fits their campaign.

FORGOTTEN COVENANT	
Promises	Concessions
Humans can once again enter the forest	Orsem Yahan will help defend the Ligna from threats when Umbalna requests aid
Umbalna will increase the bounty of the forest – food, herbs, and trees	Humans will limit what they take from the Ligna to half of what the previous covenant allowed (approximately 80 trees a year)
Umbalna will provide shelter and succour against the Takan to any who come into the forest and call out its name	The Jackals will return within nine seasons with the two humans who unsealed the chamber
Orsem Yahan can use the covenant branch (see below) to call on Umbalna for aid once a year	Any human who spends the night in the Ligna can be slain
Umbalna will bury one thing within the forest for the Luathi	The Jackals must help reseal the chamber – which marks them by the dark forces that entered the chamber

Umbalna gives the Jackals a token to carry back to Orsem Yahan as a symbol of the new covenant. It is a flowering branch, plucked from a cedar by Umbalna's own hand. So long as the branch blooms, the Luathi can trust in the covenant. The covenant is sealed by the shedding of blood. At least one Jackal must make this oath on behalf of Orsem Yahan. Each Jackal in the group who joins in the ritual oath receives the following benefit:

Like the Cedar of Ligna Hualla: The covenant of Umbalna marks the Jackal. Over the next year, the Jackal takes on a visible mark symbolising this. Umbalna always places its mark where it is difficult to hide, such as on the forehead, cheeks, back of the neck, or hands. This mark takes the shape of a dark green discolouration in a vague shape which resembles either a monkey's head or the branches of a cedar. Those who bear the mark can call upon this covenant as a new Cultural Virtue, once per season.

There are no stats given for Umbalna. It has existed since before the sun and moons rose over Kalypsis and remembers the day Zadon drank the forbidden waters from the seven and one fountains on Tracal. If it can be injured or slain, it is not today, nor is it by the hands of beings such as the Jackals. If they choose to fight, give them one chance to back down. If they continue, Umbalna kills one Jackal each turn; it lets them go if they try to flee.

Aftermath

Upon returning to Orsem Yahan, Namar and Shapan greet the Jackals based on how they did. Should the Jackals return with a new covenant in place, Namar is pleased. Even with major (up to three) concessions, Namar is still understanding. In his mind, access to the forest is worth any price. He makes the trek to the Ligna and takes the covenantal oath, as well. The token of Umbalna remains with Namar for as long as he lives, and it becomes a symbol not only of the Nawsi position, but also of Orsem Yahan in the future. He gives the Jackals the silver he promised and offers them a place to stay for the rest of the season.

Should the Jackals defeat the Hazukamna without destroying the clay effigies, they return to find Diokles alive and well. Grateful for his renewed life, Diokles offers to make the group apotropaic amulets of their own. It takes him a season to do so, but he keeps them for the Jackals until they return. Shapan, enamoured by the Jackals who saved his father's life, turns to the life of the Jackal in about five years. Should any player wish to play as Shapan, they can start with 12 active advancements to represent the lad's preparations.

ADVANCEMENTS

- 1 for dealing with the Hazukamna
- 1 for discovering what happened to Diokles and the others in the Ligna Hualla
- 1 for saving Diokles
- 1 for negotiating a new covenant, which also increases each Jackal's Kleos by 1 (or by 2, if they give no concessions)

SOUTHERN TALE:
THE MOONS' ROAD

An adventure for Recognised Jackals, set during the month of Tise, in the rainy season.

OVERVIEW

Once again, Ba-en Nafar calls upon the Jackals to aid the Nawsi's father. It is time to recover the final – and perhaps the most elusive – ingredient for the ritual: a piece of hesoa stone. The Hann used hesoa to create their moon roads, ancient ways they used to travel the breadth of the Zaharets and Kalypsis. Arishat knows of the roads, how they are only visible to humans during certain times of the year and certain moon cycles, and how the Imil-Ajas – the dread shadow over the arch of the world – shattered most of them long ago in its wars against the Hann. She believes she knows where to find one, or at least part of one. She sends the Jackals back out into the mountains to Mayrah Vedil, a tin mine run by those loyal to the Yesim family, where they can find the last piece of the ritual to save Sar Japeth. Ameena Noani is also interested in the town, and the Jackals might have a chance to save a Sar loyal to Sentem while they are there.

ACT 1: MEETING WITH SAMEEL

The summons from Ba-en Nafar is different than before. This time, the Gerwa advisor invites the Jackals to share a meal with himself, Arishat, and Nawsi Sameel in the fort. It seems Sameel is eager to meet the Jackals who have returned hope to his heart. This meeting happens at the start of Tise, for the group must be at the mines no later than the 18th of Tise – when Oura is full and can reveal the moon road to the Jackals.

When the Jackals answer the summons, they are escorted through the fortress by two of The Thirty, a group of personal warriors loyal to Sameel that act as his guards and retinue.

Gashur and Yoseph, the brother and sister pair, are jovial with the Jackals, excited to see Sameel so hopeful. They take the Jackals to a large room with a broad balcony, which overlooks the plains to the west. Sameel sits waiting for them, as servants set out a rich meal. Bread, dates, figs, oil, wine, and several roasted and herb-crusted lambs are set out on the low table. Arishat and Ba-en Nafar are already in attendance. Sameel greets each Jackal by name and, if possible, asks them a question about a specific deed they have done in the service of his family. Once the introductions are done, the meal begins.

Sameel provides the following information in response to Jackals' questions:

- His father is not doing any better. The fevers and fits have grown worse.
- They believe his affliction to be a spirit tormenting him (true).
- Nabal believes Sar Japeth will not live to see Senon unless this ritual is performed.
- He is grateful for the Jackals' help. He would go himself, but Sentem needs him.
- Between the annual raids, keeping the plains peaceful, and other issues (he looks north), his role as Nawsi and Sar in his father's name keeps him occupied.
- Should the Jackals bring back the last ingredient, Sameel will reward them with 500 ss each, and another 500 each should his father survive.
- Sameel sent word to Sar Barqan in Mayrah Vedil to prepare for the Jackals' arrival.

Eventually, Sameel turns the discussion over to Arishat. The Hasheer can share the following information:

- The final ingredient of Nabal's ritual is a piece of hesoa.
- Nabal believes Japeth is being tormented by a Rathic. This ritual will exorcise it from him.
- They need a piece of stone as large as a fist.
- Hesoa was the stone of the Hann, much like hestul is to the Hulathi.
- Little is known about the Hann. They ruled these lands before the coming of humanity.
- They were intimately tied to the moons of Kalypsis. Some of the Hasheers' rituals come from studying their works.
- One such tie is the moon roads. These were paths paved with hesoa that only revealed themselves to non-Hannic eyes at certain times of the year, under the light of the full moon to which they were bound.
- Legends say the roads allowed the Hann to travel great distances in a single night, crossing the length of their once great empire.
- What happened to the Hann? We did. Or perhaps more accurately, time did. The Hann warred with many to push back the darkness. The Skessh, the Rathic, our forefathers. In time, some – like the Hulathi – converted to allies, but the damage was already done. Their people suffered too great a wounding in the wars of their time, and the greatness of the Hann slowly bled out. Alwain alone knows whether they still exist in this world.
- Arishat believes she knows of a moon road, or a fragment of one, far from Sentem to the north. There is a town, Mayrah Vedil, which lies north of the Ouwa Ejo. Sameel's grandfather settled and helped to garrison it, as it possesses a mine rich in tin on the far side of the Aeco Plains.

- Miners speak of glowing silver stones, whose glimmer fades long before they reach Sentem. She believes these are part of an old Hannic road bound to Oura. Oura is full from the 2nd Water Day through the 3rd Kauma Day of Tise. That gives the Jackals six days after they reach Mayrah Vedil to find the road, recover the stone, and return it here.
- She and Nabal will prepare the ritual; if the Jackals return in time, they will be ready.
- Many Hasheer tales speak of a guardian of the roads, even though none of the miners have spoken of one. She cautions the Jackals to be wary.

Once the Jackals are ready, the journey from Sentem to Mayrah Vedil takes 5 days. The journey takes them across the Aeco Plains, and uses the Plains' difficulty. After resolving these checks, proceed to Act 2.

CARRYING HESOA

Hesoa only remains potent when it is part of the works of the Hann or under the light of the moon to which it is bound. Once removed from the path, if the hesoa is not renewed under the light of the full moon of Oura each night, the magic fades in 1d6 + 3 days. This means the Jackals must obtain the stone and get it back to Sentem before Oura's full moon wanes. After that, unless it is treated by obscure Hasheer rites, the stone's magic disappears forever.

ACT 2: MAYRAH VEDIL

Mayrah Vedil is a small settlement, just over a week north of Sentem, at the edge of what Sentem nominally claims as its territory. Although it is independent from Sentem, two decades of trade and a few important battles won against the Takan have forged a tighter bond between the two towns. Mayrah Vedil is built against the base of a spur of the A'hule Asa, an old ruin the Luathi and Gerwa renovated into a fortified home. The plains below the town are fertile, but the town's real wealth is in its mines, for they hold tin. This key component in the making of bronze enables Sentem to wage its war against the Takan without worrying about the sickness caused by the grey dust from the Vori Wastes – used to make tin in Ameena Noani. This fact has not gone unnoticed by the northern city. Sari Phamea of Ameena Noani sent Huldel to investigate the town and its loyalty to Sentem. Phamea wants the tin from Mayrah Vedil and will stop at nothing to secure it for her people. Barqan, the Sar of Mayrah Vedil, has been dealing with Huldel for two weeks when the Jackals finally arrive in town. Barqan is loyal to Sentem, but in the face of the wealth of Ameena Noani, he finds that loyalty tested.

1. The Walls

Mayrah Vedil, like many villages and towns along the War Road, was built upon the ruins of a previous settlement – in this case, an old Gerwa settlement from the time of the 3rd War between Ger and Keta. The walls rise around a small, flat promontory, and are adorned with obelisks, statues of the Eight, and carvings depicting a Gerwa Kiani leading an army south. If the Jackals study the walls, they see the army travelled with a procession of bound and defeated enemies, many of which were some sort of serpent-folk. A successful Lore check reveals these creatures to be the Skessh, a powerful and dark race of serpents that ruled Ruined Keta to the far north. A successful Ancient Lore check reveals these carvings are most likely a triumphal record of the battle of Kammen, when Ger broke the Kings of Keta and claimed this area for a time. Studying the carvings and the statues for an hour grants a Jackal +3% to Ancient Lore. One great gate is set into the walls, which the inhabitants of Mayrah Vedil rebuilt with the help of Sentem. The newer walls are made from cut mountain stone that rests on top of the foundation of clay bricks and fitted stone blocks.

2. The Well

Mayrah Vedil is built around a large cistern deep below the main plaza, which provides water for the town.

3. The Town

Mayrah Vedil is not laid out like a typical Luathi town, as the Gerwa built it centuries ago. Broad streets crisscross the town, lined by trees taken from throughout the War Road and Ger. A dozen strange obelisks bearing memorials of a Kiani's great deeds are scattered across town; twice that number of bases mark where others once stood. The houses show signs of Luathi touches and reconstruction, but the civil planning still bears the mark of Gerwa forethought. It is clear the town was once larger than its current population of about 300 people.

4. The Sar's Residence

Across from the well is a fine residence in the Gerwa style. A successful Culture (Other) – or Culture (Own) for Gerwa Jackals – check reveals this was probably a personal temple for a Kiani or one of their family. It is now where Sar Barqan resides.

5. Temple to Alwain

This building is in the process of being constructed, but already shows promise of becoming one of the finest in the south. The people of Mayrah Vedil are pouring their wealth into its construction.

6. Mines

The mines – the reason Japeth's father supplied the initial settlement – are nestled against the A'hule Asa. The entrance is surrounded by a low wall about 4 cubits in height, and Barqan posts two guards there at all times. The mine is rich in chalcedony, beryl, sard, agate, and – most importantly – tin. This area has a wealth of tin, with about 40 shekels' worth of the metal coming out of the mine every season. This might not seem like much, but it is enough to craft 400 shekels' worth of bronze gear! Additionally, if need be, Barqan can increase this production by fourfold for a season, with a 45% chance of collapsing the mine and putting it out of commission for a season. This is where the Hannic road lies.

7. Huldel's House

Barqan gave this house to Huldel, allowing the emissary from Ameena Noani to stay here – under supervision – while he considered her deal. Should the Jackals become suspicious of her, they can attempt to break into her house. A successful Perception check reveals a disturbance under the large woven mat in Huldel's sleeping area. Beneath the mat is a small hole, recently filled in. Should the Jackals dig up the area, they discover two identical bronze lockboxes, each about two hand spans wide and one deep. Huldel locked each of them and warded them with a Hasheer glyph. The boxes require a successful Thievery check to unlock, and removing the wards requires a hard Lore check. Should the Jackals gain access to the boxes, they find the following:

Box 1: 80 shekels' worth of gold bulls – coins freshly minted in Ameena Noani. Each shekel of gold is worth 20 ss.

Box 2: Three vials of a strange, amber liquid. It smells faintly of charred wood. A successful Craft check reveals that it is Nehusta's Blood, a potent poison [vector: ingested; cycle: quick; intensity: 9; damage type: physical].

Between the mine's tin and gems, Mayrah Vedil is a prosperous town, trading with Sentem and Gerwa traders (see *Hen-he-net* in the NPC section below).

NPCs of Mayrah Vedil

Sar Barqan

Sar Barqan is an older man that has ruled over Mayrah Vedil for 20 years. He petitioned Japeth's father to help open the mine. Two decades of hard labour show on Barqan, who remains muscled despite his age. He rules over the town from the old Kiani home, and he spends most of his time overseeing trade deals and making sure enough grain and fruit flow into the town. He is attempting to acquire a redsmith of renown and is slowly converting the old Gerwa town to a Luathi one. He started building the temple to Alwain. Having never been or hired a Jackal, he is wary of new packs, unless they make it clear Sameel sent them.

Once the Jackals gain an audience with Barqan, he can impart the following information:

- He can give much of the information above; however, he is wary of doing so to outsiders. Questions concerning the wealth of the town, the mine's output, or his deal with Sentem require the Jackal to make an Influence check first. If it fails, Barqan politely tells them to let it be. If they ask a second time, he concludes their meeting.
- He has heard of Sar Japeth's illness. He prays and makes sacrifices to Alwain weekly to plead for the Sar's recovery.
- He is utterly loyal to the Yesim family. He states this, but a successful Influence check reveals it is not as true as it sounds.
- He has seen the stones his men bring out of the mine. Initially, the hesoa is pretty, but it is too hard to use for anything, as bronze cannot shape it. It eventually fades in lustre and hardness within a week (see *Carrying Hesoa* above).
- One can find hesoa in a variety of places in the mine, but he has never seen a road.
- If one of the Jackals mentions being a redsmith, Barqan wants to speak with them and question them about their ability. If they possess at least 75% in Craft, the cost to acquire Barqan as a patron is halved, as is the cost of building a home or foundry here.

- If asked about Huldel, Barqan relates his worries. The emissary from Ameena Noani came two weeks ago with many gifts and a desire to trade for most of the tin coming out of the mine. Though Barqan refused on the grounds of his covenant with Sentem, Huldel would not take no for an answer. She returns every few days with new and greater promises. At least once, the promises skirted the edge of threats. A difficult Influence check reveals that Barqan is close to giving in to the pressure. Should the Jackals discover this and wish to deal with it, they need to shore up Barqan's belief in Sentem and remind him of his covenant (see below).
- He gives the Jackals access to the mines – under guard – if they present their need as Japeth's. If the Jackals mention hesoa and Japeth's need, Barqan tells them about the sealed tunnel where much of the hesoa is found. It is one of the shallower tunnels, close to the surface. He warns the Jackals that those who go there are plagued with strange dreams. Some people have even died after being in there. Barqan sealed the tunnel about four seasons ago. Barqan assigns four guards to watch the Jackals and ensure they take nothing but the hesoa from the mines (see page 206 of *Jackals* for stats on the guards, if needed).

Barqan's Loyalty: Barqan is a good man who knows he only has his position because of the Yesim family. However, Huldel is good at her job and has the backing of Ameena Noani. Already, cracks are starting to show, and Huldel is quite certain she can break Sentem's hold on Barqan. If she cannot, she has orders to return with an Adept of Anu and replace Barqan with someone Ameena Noani can control. Should the Jackals become aware of this, they can attempt to influence Barqan to remember his covenant with Sentem. The Jackals need to accumulate **six successes** (with critical successes counting as two successes) before they incur **three failures** to remind Barqan of his vows and reinforce the man's loyalty. Barqan is a stubborn man in the seat of his power; therefore, any use of Intimidate, no matter what a Jackal rolls, counts as an automatic failure. This is the time for subtlety and grace, not brute force. Reminding him of Sentem's aid in opening the mines counts as an automatic success (usable once).

Should the Jackals succeed, Barqan is once again firmly in the Sentem camp and does not waver again. He sends Huldel away from Mayrah Vedil politely, yet firmly. If they fail, Barqan begins to turn his eye north. He increases production and starts selling the difference to Ameena Noani traders. This affects later adventures (see pages 153 and 173 for the fallout).

Hen-he-net

The Gerwa trader is setting up her wagon west of the well and pool in the centre of town. She brought many goods, fruits, and other surplus items to Mayrah Vedil, and people are already gathering to purchase them. If the Jackals met Hen-he-net before, she waves them over to chat as she sets up her area. She offers the Jackals 20 ss in trade to help her set up, and 15 ss a day to stand guard and aid her in her trade. She has a breadth of items for sale, including a couple of fine Gerwa pieces, but no magical items. The Loremaster can design specific pieces or roll them randomly using the tables on page 164 of *Jackals*.

Hen-he-net can impart the following information:
- She passes through here about twice a year – once each way along the road.
- Barqan makes it worth her while and has gifted her with a home here.
- She knows Barqan is desperate for a redsmith.

- She hears rumours that come up from the mines. There are areas Barqan has ordered sealed, due to the presence of rocks that glow with the light of the moon. The miners say those who spend too much time in the tunnel or carry the stones back with them are troubled with strange dreams. Some were unable to sleep ever again, and they wasted away.
- She can impart hearsay and rumours of the events and adventures from the northern end of the War Road over the past couple of years.
- She hopes the road stays open, but the two powers of Sentem and Ameena Noani are looking warily towards each other.
- If the Loremaster has an adventure they need a patron for or want to foreshadow, this is a perfect time to do so.
- If asked about Huldel, she goes quiet. An Influence check can drag the following information out of Hen-he-net:
  › Huldel is a former Jackal who has risen quite high in the esteem of Sari Phamea of Ameena Noani. If she is here, she is serving her Sari's interests.
  › What is one of the Sari's eyes and ears doing down here in Yesim land? Hen-he-net tries to sow seeds of suspicion at the feet of Huldel, where they belong, but also regarding Barqan (any man's loyalty can be bought) and Ameena Noani (why this town? It is known the city needs tin). In this aspect, she serves the will of Avsalim, sowing discontent among the Luathi.

Huldel

Huldel the emissary of Ameena Noani is a rare beauty, with long brown hair, high cheekbones, and wide hips. Her missing hand and scars add to her allure. She received permission from Barqan to set up in one of the homes near the gate. Huldel is dressed in the finest robes and jewellery of Ameena Noani and carries a short spear topped with a black spearhead. The spearhead always glistens as if freshly oiled, and a spicy smell fills the air when it is present. She openly talks with all the townsfolk, gathering information and spreading Phamea's coin throughout the town. Whenever she can, she speaks with Barqan about acquiring Mayrah Vedil's tin.

Huldel can impart the following information:
- Her hand was taken by a Mavakan. She slew it as it choked on her fist.
- She retired from the War Road, and now serves the great city of Ameena Noani.
- She is here in the south to scout and establish trade with the towns along the coast.
- She visited Jabalem three weeks back – see **The Bronze Bell** in *Jackals*.
- She is here to see the town of Mayrah Vedil for herself, as rumour of it has reached the north. It is as wonderful as she heard.
- She will not discuss her business with Barqan; if asked about it, she coldly tells the Jackals they should not interfere in matters of this scale. 'Go back to rooting around the bones of the dead.'
- Huldel always keeps a seal of Ameena Noani on her, hidden in a pouch on the inside of her robes. A hard Thievery check allows a Jackal to filch it without her noticing.

Once the Jackals are ready to enter the mines, proceed to Act 3.

ACT 3: A PATH THROUGH

The Jackals need Barqan's permission to enter the mines. Without it, they must deal with the guards.

1. Main Chamber

Barqan and his people initially carved out this space. It serves as a sorting and processing chamber, where materials from the lower mines are brought up and reviewed by the miners.

2. Tunnels Down

Six shafts descend deeper into the mountains. Four are proper tunnels, whereas the other two are water wells that were drained to allow access to deeper chambers by way of ladders. The sounds of mining and workers yelling at each other filter up from below.

3. Storage Chambers

The wealth of the mountain is stored here, as it is chipped free from the stone of the A'hule Asa. Guards are posted in this area to watch over Mayrah Vedil's wealth.

4. The Sealed Tunnel

A large stone slab, roughly hewn, blocks this side branch. The stone bears a wax plate with the seal of Sentem in the centre. Moving the stone requires a difficult Athletics check (remember the rules for aiding another, found on page 58 of *Jackals*). The tunnel leads back for a good while, then heads up, rather than down. Eventually, the Jackals can smell fresh air in the tunnel.

5. The Road

The tunnel leads to a narrow defile, which opens to the sky. It appears as though the roof of this cavern collapsed, or perhaps this place once existed beyond the mountain, but a landslide cut it off from the outside world. Forgotten tools litter the ground. The walls are the rough stone of the mountain, but grass covers the floor. The narrow beams of sunlight that reach this area do not account for the lushness of the grass, which is as fresh and green as it would be in the plains. There are no stones, save for the mountain rocks. A Perception check reveals the existence of miners' marks on the walls, holes in the ground where bronze tools tore chunks of dirt free, etc. But nothing of the Hann or their road.

Gathering the Hesoa

The hesoa stone of the moon roads is only visible under the full light of the moon. The Jackals will find nothing unless Oura is full in the sky. Should the Jackals wait for or arrive under these conditions, they witness a gleaming silver path of stone float into existence. It is as if the moon fills a dry stream with its own liquid light. It stretches into the rock face to the north, and flows backwards down the tunnel, fading from view once it is cut off from the moonlight. The road is wide enough for four to walk abreast, save for where its path is broken. There, the stones that pave its bed are missing. But, under Oura's silver light, the path of the moon is revealed to the Jackals.

Gathering a stone from the moon's path is difficult. There are several obstacles:

First, the Jackals need to break off a piece from the path. Hesoa counts as iron for the purpose of breaking (see page 69 of *Jackals*), and Jackals can only break off a piece where the path is already damaged. Any attempt to break the path in another spot shatters the tool used in the attempt.

Second, hesoa only remains imbued with Hannic magic for a limited amount of time.

Third, the path flows. If a Jackal stands on the path, there is a chance it may sweep them away. The Jackal must attempt a difficult Willpower check. If they succeed, they resist the force of the path, flickering briefly and moving only a few feet up or down the path. If they fail, they find the force of the current too great and are swept back to Area 1 or just outside the walls of Mayrah Vedil to the north. On a fumble, the path sweeps them away 1d6 × 10 miles to the north or south.

Finally, there is the matter of the Istanil, or path warden. The Hann bound spirits to their paths, because of the dangers to and on them. Their enemies attempted to use the paths, so the Istanil served to bar the way for those who were forbidden from using the paths. This Istanil emerges as soon as the first blow falls against the path. She appears as a tall woman whose robes flow into and out of the path. Parts of the being are missing – little tears, rips, and cracks in the essence of her robes and features. Her features, while feminine, are liquid – it is difficult to focus on any one aspect. When she speaks, her voice is light and silvery, yet it resonates with a deep and powerful magic.

The Istanil asks the party the following questions:
- Who are you?
- Where are the Children of the Moon? What has become of them?
- What are you doing here?
- Do you wish to travel? You do not bear the mark of Imil-Ajas.
- Where, where are the Children? Why do they not travel the rivers of moonlight as they once did?
- [Once the Jackals reveal they want a piece of the road]: Why would you take what is given to others?
- What gift would you give in return?

The Istanil can reveal the following information, but her memory is fragmented. Outside of the below items, things get hazy for her. Make it clear the Istanil laments the passage of time and the disappearance of the Hann:
- She is one of the Istanil, the guardians of the paths.
- This is one of the moons' roads – it can take them far.
- When the Hann fell to earth, they arrived amid the tears of the Daughters of the Moon. They gathered these tears, and some were used to make rivers throughout the world.
- This is one such river.
- She will not fight them, because Imil-Ajas has not touched them.
- Imil-Ajas is the shadow under the arch of the world.
- What happened to the Hann? The world has forgotten them. Their memory, like sand, is scattered. Their works are dormant beneath the bones of the world. Soon, all will forget their greatness, their sacrifice, and their beauty. All that is beautiful will pass from this world, until the marring in the north is healed.

Convincing the Istanil

The Istanil is bound to the path, so taking a stone from the path wounds it. However, as a creature of the Hann (and an aspect of Oura), she possesses more than just a sense of self-preservation. She knows the time of her masters passed, and could be convinced to give up a part of her essence to save another.

Jackals can make Lore checks to remember stories of self-sacrifice from the Hann or to remind the Istanil about the Hann's war against the Rathic. They can use Craft to create an item of beauty or a poem to give to the Istanil as a worthy trade. They can use Influence or Perform to enhance the tales of Japeth, Sameel, the deeds of ancestors, or even the Hann's own stories. A promise to spread the Hannic tales among the Jackal's people is also worth a free success (one time only).

The Jackals need to accumulate **four successes** (with critical successes counting as two successes) before they incur **two failures** to convince the Istanil to part with the hesoa willingly.

Should the Jackals succeed, the Istanil allows a part of her to be taken, giving up the stone from the path without further need for the Jackals to roll to break it. The fist-sized stone comes away from the path easily. Jackals who are watching notice that a similarly sized rent appears in the right sleeve of the Istanil's robe. Should the Jackals fail, they must take the stone by force. If they take the stone by force, the Istanil does not fight the Jackals. She does, however, curse the stone and tell the Jackals the day will come when they wish Japeth had died rather than be freed from his madness. See the *Aftermath* section below.

Once the Jackals have the stone, they must race back to Sentem in time to complete the ritual. The journey takes them across the Aeco Plains, and uses the Plains' difficulty.

AFTERMATH

Should the Jackals return with the hesoa stone in time, Nabal and Arishat successfully invoke the ritual of exorcism on Japeth! The Sar still needs seasons to recover, but he is no longer under the influence of the Rathic. Arishat also needs time to recover, but she is never truly the same after this struggle. The old Hasheer loses some vital energy she once possessed, and slowly moves towards retirement. After two seasons, a Jackal could take this advisory role.

Should the Jackals return with a cursed stone, all seems to be as above. However, the stone's curse eventually brings out Japeth's worst qualities, polishing them to a blinding sheen. By the Year of Chill Winds, he is well on his way to becoming a tyrant (see page 110 for this potentiality).

Should the Jackals fail to recover the stone in time, Japeth dies after raving during his final hours. The ravings of Japeth contain mysteries of dark and terrible portent, and Nabal faithfully records them. These mysteries, which deal with a powerful Rathic, or the ruler of the Rathic far to the north, grant anyone who reads them +5% to Ancient Lore and 1d4 + 4 Corruption. Should someone not take these from Nabal, he falls to Corruption by the Year of Chill Winds (see page 100 for this potentiality).

ADVANCEMENTS

- 1 for discovering Barqan's loyalty and preventing him from taking the deal with Ameena Noani
- 2 for recovering the hesoa stone, which also increases each Jackal's Kleos by 1
- 1 additional advancement for recovering the hesoa stone without using force

HOOKS

A Deep Darkness: The chamber beneath the Ligna Hualla connects to a larger and deeper complex – an ancient tomb or research site of the Mouadran Priest-Kings – which is home to a Rephaim.

The Hunter in the Dark: The Jackals are hunted by the Hazukamna they freed in **Forgotten Covenant** and must find a way to banish or destroy it forever.

A Test of Valour: As time goes on, Sameel needs to restore lost members of The Thirty. He tests one or two of the Jackals to see if they are worthy.

Forgotten Roads: If the Jackals use the moon road to head north, it deposits them somewhere strange. Ameena Noani or somewhere in the mountains north of Kroryla are possibilities, as are even more remote and strange locales.

Perhaps to Dream: The Jackals are plagued with dreams of a city far to the north – one which lies ruined before a great stone gate set into the side of a mountain. It could be Eki Ezeru, a Hannic mansion mentioned in the old sagas of the Grand Kingdoms. What treasures and terrors await mortals beneath the mountain?

Assassins in the Night: If Barqan rejects Ameena Noani, Sari Phamea marks him for death. The group might be able to stop the nobleman's death, if they catch wind of the plot.

CHAPTER 5
YEAR OF
CHILL WINDS

The Skessh made a womb of the whole of the world. After a time, when the fullness of their sins gave birth to obscenity piled upon obscenity, they delivered onto the face of Kalypsis the Takan, their favoured offspring. This was the chief and greatest of their sins, damning them forever in the eyes of the Light.

~ **Anahalis,** *Third Discourse of the Histories of the Descent* ~

INTRODUCTION

The Year of Chill Winds is Year 4 of *The Fall of the Children of Bronze* campaign. In **Relapse**, fallout from the **Mine of Atem** plagues the Jackals. The Jackals expand the edge of civilisation for Sentem, and in doing so, discover the threat of those who walk the Twisted Path. This is also considered the last of the 'good years' in the campaign. Beyond this, the paths of the War Road lead towards the growing conflict between Ameena Noani and Sentem.

THEME

The themes of the Year of Chill Winds are cold and darkness. For the cultures of the Zaharets, both are linked to the powers and entities of Chaos. In both **Relapse** and **Orsem Reclaimed**, the threats are creatures or people claimed by Corruption. Mealil returns from the Year of Fallen Seeds, snuffs out the light of a Hasheer, and spreads Chaos through the streets of Rataro. Meanwhile, in the south, a Mouathenic in service of the Daughter Beneath the Earth claims an old Hulathi ruin on the edge of Sentem. The darkness of the upcoming years is starting to press into communities the Jackals protect and support.

The central conflict of the Year of Chill Winds is light versus darkness. While Jackals are scavengers of the dead, they also serve as light bringers – carrying the knowledge and light of civilisation out to the edges of the world. Sometimes, Jackals bring back the darkness; sometimes, they drive it out. Either way, they bear a burden of responsibility for the communities to which they often do not belong. In these adventures, the Jackals begin to deal with their role in the fight between Law and Chaos, and perhaps begin to see the hands behind much of what they have encountered over the past few years.

IMPORTANT NPCS

Abishai: the Hasheer from **Mine of Atem**. Abishai worked for the past three years to uncover more about the Rathic Mealil, and her research bore fruit. She discovered how to deal with a Rathic like Mealil and now summons the Jackals to aid her.

Hen-he-net: see page 18.

Nabal: see *Jackals* page 184 – Nabal, Kahar of Alwain, is troubled by dark dreams about Orsem Kitan. He turns to the Jackals – who aided Sentem in the past – to cleanse a growing darkness on the Aeco Plains.

Namgidda benna Amar: see page 44.

Toara: see *Jackals* page 184 – Toara, of the Scriptorium, begins to take interest in Abishai and the Jackals. Events are unfolding in and around Ameena Noani, and she wishes to keep loyal and competent eyes on them.

EVENTS IN THE NORTH

- A great fire rages in Ameena Noani, in the Grand Track. Everything burns to the ground over three days in Sina, during the eclipse. Sari Phamea vows to rebuild, as a sign of her greatness.
- Unknown to all but the most trusted people, a group of Mouathenics broke into Gilead as the fire raged and stole many items from beneath the fortress. One dead ritualist bore the token of Sentem and the Yesim family. Among the items stolen was a piece of an iron gate that has laid in the vaults since before the Uprising.

EVENTS IN THE SOUTH

- After millennia, the Daughter Beneath the Earth frees herself from her prison beneath the Aeco Woods. She retreats into the A'hule Asa, to an old holdfast, and begins to regain much of her might.
- If Nabal recorded the dying ravings of Japeth, his Corruption reaches a point where he grows more paranoid, convinced a threat is coming to Sentem. He begins researching powers, rites, and entities that might be able to save Sentem. The Daughter Beneath the Earth visits him for the first time.
- People begin to look north with wary eyes. With hushed whispers, they speak of the reach of the Sar of Ameena Noani, and her desire for the plains.
- Wolves that attack caravans reportedly bear the mark of black nails.

EVENTS ANYWHERE

- The rainy season is unseasonably cold. The harvest from that planting is about half of what it should be. Prices for food for this season are doubled.
- The second solar eclipse in three years (16th and 17th of Sina) lasts for two days. There is also a total eclipse of Oura, the silver moon (21st of Erbe). Panic grips the people during both events.
- [On the same end of the War Road as the Jackals]: Deborah of the Torch is given accolades by the Sar of the city.

RETIREMENT BENEFITS

If a player retires their Jackal in this year, their new Jackal gains +2 advancements due to the pack's renown attracting more skilled Jackals. They also receive a minor magical item (see *Jackals* page 169).

NORTHERN TALE: RELAPSE

An adventure for Regarded Jackals, set during the month of Eser, in the rainy season.

OVERVIEW

The Zaharets are not lands at rest. Each action bears fruit, and sometimes that fruit can be bitter. In the years since the events of **Mine of Atem**, Hasheer Abishai of Rataro works to discover more about the spirit of disease that nearly wiped out Orsem Ven. She travels to the Scriptorium, scouring the tablets both there and in Rataro, and journeys to the mine herself, under Jackal escort. She learns many secrets about Mealil over these years, and about others that dwell in the Silent Lands. She believes she might have found a way to deal with the Rathic. She sends messengers to find the Jackals she worked with all those years ago to aid her.

However, Mealil is not dormant during this time. Possessing Atem, the Rathic journeys west near Kroryla and the burial site of the Luathi chieftain who stole the last of its amphorae, but Mealil is unable to break the warding rituals on the king's grave. Since then, Mealil searches for knowledge it can use to gain access to the grave; it discovers a seal of the bull – one of the talismans Abishai possesses – could be used to break the warding ritual. Mealil abandons Atem's body, which is corrupted beyond hope of disguise. The Rathic then possesses Ganak, a young Hasheer of the Amar tribe. Mealil suppresses its Corruption as it hunts for Abishai – both for her seal and the knowledge she has gained about it.

ACT 1: RETURN TO RATARO

The Jackals, wherever they are in the Zaharets, eventually meet up with others who have messages for them. The Jackals are Regarded at this point in their travels; many recognise them or have at least heard their tales, which makes tracking them down a bit easier.

Although it is clearly from Abishai, the note is purposefully cryptic. The message is simple: *I have found more concerning the sickness you fought in past years. Aid in curing it needed. You know where to find me.*

Once the Jackals are ready, they must journey to Rataro. This is a good point to have a Jackal's Animosity encounter (page 175 of *Jackals*). A group of Takan, including at least two Atakan, ambushes the Jackals as they travel towards Rataro.

Once in Rataro, finding Abishai is no longer as simple as returning to the dig site. When the Jackals arrive, they find the Hasheers guarded by men and women bearing the three bulls of Ameena Noani and the red cord of the Hasheers. Gaining access to the site requires getting past these guards. Asking for Abishai gets the Jackals nowhere, as neither the Hasheers nor the guards have seen Abishai for many weeks. Deception, Lore, Culture (Own or Other), or Influence checks – or a 50 ss bribe – can get the Jackals a short audience with Toara, a visiting Hasheer from the Scriptorium.

Toara is staying with Sari Namgidda benna Amar, as she is an important visitor to Rataro. Toara is a Hasheer inna Sarmom, chief among the learned of the Hasheers. The depth of her knowledge extends back millennia. She arrived in Rataro a week ago, after Abishai contacted her using a bonded scriptorium tablet Toara made for her. As Toara's client, Abishai routinely checks in with Toara, keeping Toara abreast of her research. The breakthrough in dealing with Mealil came recently, and when Abishai stopped answering Toara's messages, the Hasheer inna Sarmom came to Rataro to investigate for herself.

When the Jackals meet Toara, the older woman is breaking her fast with Namgidda. The two woman look to be related (cousins), both older with hair the colour of silver. Although Namgidda is the Sari of Rataro, it is clear she defers to Toara – to the point that when the Jackals explain they are looking for Abishai, Toara asks Namgidda to leave the room.

Toara, after questioning why the Jackals are there and how they know Abishai, can impart the following information:

- Most of the material in the introduction and above, save that concerning Mealil's whereabouts and activities.
- Toara is impressed if the Jackals tell her they were the ones who dealt with Atem's mine. 'Impressive, few this day could stand unaided against one of the Rathic.'
- She can reinforce the fact that Mealil is a Labasu – a Rathic of disease that typically resides in the Silent Lands yet is present here on the earth. She is unsure why or how that is possible, but believes it has to do with the medium of the corrupted oil.
- She has not seen Abishai for almost a year – not since her last visit to the Scriptorium. At that time, Abishai searched the archives for how to bind and exorcise a Rathic from the earth. She also researched the old lands of Sardon and Lukka, looking for a city by the name of Kibeth-Albin and a place known as Mirim Mahazra.
- How does Toara know what Abishai researched? She makes it her business to know.

- She does not think it is a coincidence Abishai is missing. They both knew this Mealil would move against Abishai at some point, and Toara kept insisting Abishai take the warning seriously. In one of her missives, Abishai let Toara know she prepared a refuge should the Rathic come looking for her.
- Toara can sense Abishai's tablet, the other half of her own, is still in the town, but cannot pin down where. However, this does mean Abishai is alive, as the tablet goes dead when its owner dies.
- Toara recommends they start at the dig site, and she can give them access to Abishai's research and her chambers on site. She gives the Jackals a token, a small lacquered wooden stick, which grants them access.
- Toara warns that the guards found two other Hasheers dead this week, under mysterious circumstances. This is the reason she sealed the site and posted some Kahri (a group of Hasheers who specialise in guarding the more scholarly of their order). It is unclear what caused the deaths – it could be Mealil, but it could also be something recently uncovered in the dig. She warns them to be careful.
- Toara needs to know what happened to Abishai and is willing to pay 350 ss if the Jackals can return her, alive. Should the Jackals find her too late to save her, Toara can give them 250 ss for their time.

When the Jackals are ready to start the search for Abishai, proceed to Act 2.

ACT 2: THE STREETS OF RATARO

Upon returning to the site with Toara's token, the Kahri give the Jackals access to the site. The demeanour of those Hasheers still working in the site is grave. The noise and the sounds the Jackals experienced during the **Mine of Atem** are muted. Instead, the Hasheers nervously grasp their staves at the sight of the Jackals. The Jackals are easily able to find Abishai's workshop, but can also choose to investigate the death sites, which the Kahri can show them.

1. Abishai's Workroom

The workroom looks much the same as the Jackals remember it (see page 20). There are several new features which are of interest:
- There are several tablet fragments, which seem to make up a map, spread out on a woven mat. Seven fragments are missing from the map. A Lore or Survival check identifies the map as the western slopes of the Vori Vana. There are strange markings along the sides – bulls, lightning bolts, and the weeping woman. A successful Culture (Luathi) check identifies these symbols as belonging to the Ishfalim, a group of tribes that the *Shalapher* states refused to join the Grand Kingdoms of old and accept the revelation of Alwain. These tribes continued to worship the gods of their ancestors, one of which was a bull-headed storm god. An Ancient Lore check enables a Jackal to recognise one of the symbols – a crescent moon over a mountain – as the symbol of an ancient chief of the Ishfal, Mahazra. He united several of the Ishfal tribes into a small kingdom in the north, and raided Sardon and Lukka. Upon his death, the confederation splintered apart, and the Ishfalim were driven north, beyond the Zaharets, by the Hulathi of the Grand Kingdoms and their Hannic allies.

- There is a new workbench shoved into a corner. An inlaid golden circle takes up much of its surface. Within the circle sit golden plates – offering plates – and small braziers. A successful Craft or Trade check reveals these objects are Gerwa in origin. A Hekas instinctively recognises them as imbued items, per the Imbue Lesser Elements rite. A Craft or Trade check also reveals they are worth at least a talent of silver! A Perception check reveals a slight, oily residue on one of the braziers, which looks like the same residue from the mines!
- A wooden box, with a fine lock of Gerwa manufacture. A Thievery check allows access to the box. A failure causes a small, poisoned pin to lodge itself in the would-be thief's hand [vector: blood; cycle: instant; intensity: 5; damage type: Mettle]. Jackals can break the wooden box using the rules found on page 69 of *Jackals*, but this breaks the materials inside (see below). Inside the box, the Jackals discover:
  › A tarnished silver bull figurine, worth 75 ss.
  › A small dagger, the bronze blade pitted and scarred. This was the dagger of the Hasheer who was slain in the Fragment Repository. It cut the fingers off Mealil's host.
  › A clay snake votive – this breaks into unrecognizable fragments should the Jackals break the box. It was part of an apotropaic rite Abishai placed on herself. Should the Jackals break the votive, Mealil is able to sense Abishai clearly, and might find her earlier (see below).
  › A clay tablet – this breaks if the Jackals break into the box. Reassembling it takes time (see below). The tablet is a note from Abishai. It details her fear that the Rathic is close to finding her. She cannot leave the town – she fears for her research – but relocated 'where earth and water meet, beneath Kauma's daughter, yet above Gai's sign'. This is a reference to the Red Maiden, a Melkoni redsmith, located at the river's edge. She has rented a room that overlooks a small garden.
- If the Jackals brought back any amphora fragments from Atem's mine, they are conspicuously missing.

2. Fragment Repository (Death Site 1)

This is the site of one of the murders – the one that happened six days ago. Mealil snuck into the dig site twice; each time, a Hasheer discovered it. In this room, where the Hasheers store uncatalogued fragments, it looked through the tablet fragments, attempting to discover the missing pieces of Abishai's map. There is a large, dark stain on the stones of this room's floor, but also on the walls and on some of the fragments. The acolytes moved the bloodstained fragments to the side and are attempting to recreate them. A Perception or Healing check reveals something ripped the body apart. A Deception check gives the Jackals the feeling something else was covered up here. A successful check following the Deception check reveals several fingers among the tablet fragments. Each is rotten, but not from decay. Sores and disease bloat the fingers, but they are still warm, and they twitch every so often. The Hasheer Mealil killed managed to sever the Rathic's fingers (or those of its host's body) before being slain. Abishai found the knife, but not the fingers, and took it to study it (see the box in Area 1).

3. Dig Site Gimel (Death Site 2)

This is the other murder site. Two Kahri stand as guards, as the murder occurred recently – just two nights ago. This site is a room that sunk under the weight of what was above, and the Hasheers excavated about half of it. The Jackals must enter the area through a small window. Inside, there are buckets and several small hand shovels. The Kahri can tell the Jackals an acolyte discovered Hasheer Namen here two nights ago with a broken neck. They had to partially dig him out from under the dirt that occupies the other half of the room; his arm was buried up to the shoulder. The Hasheers believe the mound shifted, and the falling debris killed Namen. Should a Jackal use a Perception check to investigate the area in which the Kahri say they discovered Namen's body, they find a tablet and a new bronze shod for a staff buried in the dirt. A Lore check reveals the tablet contains a ritual of exorcism, which can temporarily send a Rathic back to the Silent Lands. Namen was aiding Abishai in her research, and Mealil slew him for it. The shod has a small maker's mark along the inside, an X crowned with three stars. A Craft check lets a Jackal recognise the shod was cast recently, probably by a local redsmith.

Finding Abishai

By now, the Jackals have several clues as to where Abishai might be, but they must continue to search and ask around Rataro to find the Hasheer. Time is of the essence, as Mealil is also here hunting for Abishai. The Jackals need to accumulate **eight successes** (with critical successes counting as two successes) before they incur **four failures** to find Abishai before Mealil does. At the Loremaster's discretion, these checks might start to apply during the search of the site if the Jackals begin to try to work out where Abishai is at that point.

The Jackals receive one automatic failure for each of the following: spending time to rebuild the message tablet if they smash the chest in Abishai's work area; breaking the apotropaic votive when they smash the chest; and investigating both murder sites – if they investigate only one, they do not suffer a failure.

Jackals receive one automatic success for each of the following: possessing Abishai's message and discovering the staff shod with the maker's mark. Jackals can use Culture checks to discern where the redsmith foundries are in Rataro, Survival and Perception checks to try to hunt for signs of Abishai, Lore checks to unravel the message, and Influence or Deception checks to ask around about Abishai.

Should the Jackals accumulate eight successes before they gain four failures, they discover Abishai's hiding spot at the Red Maiden, ahead of Mealil. The Jackals have plenty of time to invoke the ritual before Mealil appears.

Should the Jackals accumulate four failures before they gain eight successes, but have at least five successes, they partially succeed. They arrive at the Red Maiden at the same time as Mealil, and a fight ensues. Otherwise, if the Jackals accumulate four failures before they gain eight successes; they arrive at the Red Maiden too late, and Mealil murders Abishai.

Once the Jackals discover the Red Maiden is Abishai's hiding place, proceed to Act 3.

ACT 3: EXORCISM OR ENDINGS

The Red Maiden is a bronze foundry owned by Glaucona, a recent arrival in Rataro. Her foundry is on the Asa Amwa, overlooking the bridge. Here, Abishai hides from Mealil. As stated above, when the Jackals get to the foundry what happens next depends on how quickly they discovered it.

If the Jackals succeed in Act 2: the foundry is active, and Glaucona and her three Luathi apprentices, Abner, Keilah, and Zella, are hard at work. Glaucona initially denies that Abishai is there. A difficult Influence check, or showing Glaucona the tablet, allows the Jackals to gain access to the upper room where Abishai hides. Abishai looks worse for the wear, even though she has only been hiding for a couple of days. Mealil sends horrific nightmares, which keep the Hasheer from sleeping. Abishai has only a few of her ritual components and maintains a failing ward. She is excited to see the Jackals, and can relate the following information:

- She discovered more about the Rathic, Mealil.
- She knows where the last amphora is buried; it was taken by a Luathi chieftain and sealed in his tomb.
- Although she does not yet know where the tomb is, she is working on it.
- The amphora is necessary to banish the creature to the Silent Lands.
- Mealil hunts her now, sending horrific yet tempting dreams.
- A companion Hasheer was researching rituals to temporarily deal with the Rathic.
- She has her notes on the final banishing rituals with her. They outline what is necessary.

If the Jackals recovered Namen's tablet from the site of his murder, Abishai can invoke the ritual for them. It is similar to the ritual she plans on using to permanently banish Mealil, but less potent. Any Hasheer, Priestess of the Eight, or Kahar can learn this rite. At this point, Abishai can accomplish the ritual in minutes, and the Jackals hear a nearby howl of anger which abruptly ends. Proceed to the *Aftermath* section below.

If the Jackals fail in Act 2 but acquire at least five successes: the Red Maiden is as above; however, Mealil attacks as the Jackals begin to talk to Glaucona. The attack involves Mealil, one Mouathenic, and three Wolves (plus one Wolf for every Jackal above five).

MEALIL

Type:	Rathic/The Dead	Location:	Rataro
		Wounds:	80
Defence:	75%	Protection:	4 (natural)
Combat:	100%	Move:	12
Knowledge:	95%	Initiative:	15
Urban:	60%	Clash Points:	5
Common:	60%	Treasure Score:	3
		Corruption:	20

Special Abilities

Inured to Darkness: Mealil suffers no penalties due to absence of light.

Chaotic Flesh: Mealil recovers 2d10 Wounds per round.

Chaotic Spirit: Mealil can take 1d6 damage to gain a Clash Point. Mealil automatically senses the Corruption in all creatures within 20 yards. This makes it impossible for a corrupt creature to sneak up on Mealil.

Heat of Fever: each round, opponents engaged with Mealil take 6 points of Valour damage.

Skill of the Rathic: the Loremaster can select a talent for Mealil before combat to represent how this creature fights uniquely.

Combat Range

1–15%	*Impart Disease:* Mealil inflicts the worst symptoms of its manifold diseases upon the area. All targets within 10 yards suffer 3d12 (20) damage.
16–30%	*Unnatural Strength (2 attacks):* Mealil's spiritual strength infuses the body it possesses. 5d8 (23) damage each.
31–55%	*Infectious Eruption:* buboes swell and burst over Mealil's body, showering the area with pus and infectious matter. 4d8 (18) damage. For each 8 rolled, the target suffers 1 Corruption and must make a save against exposure to The Touch of the Mines (see page 20). The Touch of the Mines' intensity begins at 2 and increases by 1 per 8 rolled for damage, in addition to the Corruption increases. A successful Endurance check against the attack roll reduces the Corruption taken by half, or to 0 for a critical success.
56–75%	*Speed of the Dead (4 Attacks):* unconcerned with the limits of the human form, Mealil assaults the Jackals with a flurry of blows. 4d8 (18) damage each.
76–90%	*Command the Corrupt:* like many Rathic, Mealil can claim dominion over all those with Chaos in their souls. It forces the target to make a hard Willpower check. If the Jackal fails, Mealil momentarily takes control of the corrupted creature for 1d4 rounds. Mealil can spend 3 Clash Points on the Jackal's turn to force them to take an action of its choice.

After slaying Mealil, any remaining enemies flee. Abishai comes down and speaks to the Jackals (see above), and performs the lesser exorcism rite to banish Mealil. Proceed to the *Aftermath* section below.

If the Jackals fail in Act 2: they arrive after Mealil and find the redsmith, her apprentices, and Abishai dead. The Rathic is gone, but it left its allies (see above) behind. Once the Jackals deal with the Mouathenic and the Wolves, they can search Abishai's body. The Hasheer is dead, torn apart by a rage-filled Mealil. The dying Abishai managed to write out a single message in her death throes: Mahazra. Proceed to the *Aftermath* section.

AFTERMATH

How this adventure ends depends on how the Jackals finish Act 3. Abishai, should she live, tells the Jackals what happened, filling in any of the details they wish to know. She is convinced that as tough as this creature is now, it would be far worse with the whole of its power. Toara can do the same, should Abishai fall. Either of the Hasheers can inform the Jackals Mealil is searching for the last of the amphorae. Based on Abishai's research, they believe Mahazra is the one who placed the sealing stone Atem discovered, and Mealil is searching for his tomb. Abishai's work on a Hulathi purification rite might render the oil which binds Mealil clean, allowing the Jackals a chance to stop Mealil from recovering its strength and spreading plague through the Zaharets. However, to do so, they must set out to Ameena Noani and find this burial site. See **Mirim Mahazra**.

Due to their efforts, Jackals can waive the normal seasonal action fee this month to gain Toara as a patron. They still must make an Influence check, on which they can spend shekels to gain bonuses to the roll, and have the required skill and Kleos to acquire Toara's patronage.

ADVANCEMENTS

- 1 for saving Abishai
- 1 for discovering what happened to Abishai, and what needs to be done
- 1 for discovering the exorcism rite

SOUTHERN TALE: ORSEM RECLAIMED

An adventure for Regarded Jackals, set during the month of Hamis, in the dry season.

OVERVIEW

Orsem Kitan lies on the eastern edge of Sentem's holds. Like its twin, Orsem Val, and other such orsems scattered along the War Road, it is an edifice of a previous age. Hulathi built the forts during the time of the Grand Kingdoms, and now other peoples claim them – save for Kitan. Lying beyond the reach of both Sentem and Densom, there was little reason to clear the orsem while the threat of Bartak Kentak existed. However, Sameel believes it is time to claim the fort and establish a strong eastern border, preventing Wolves and worse from using it as a home.

But worse has already come to Kitan. The rumours of the Dead wandering around it are true. Uoser, a Mouathenic in service of the Daughter Beneath the Earth, took possession of the orsem for his mistress. He worked to overcome some of the native protections the orsem's builders instilled in the stone, so he could help his mistress break free from the final bonds of her prison. In doing so, the Daughter taught him ancient rites for raising and binding the Dead. Their work complete, Uoser sent his final research to the Daughter, and now plans to launch an assault against Densom with the Dead he has raised from those who lie beneath the Aeco Plains.

Part of this adventure's background is fluid, depending on the Jackals' actions in previous adventures. It assumes the Jackals saved Sar Japeth with no complications. However, if the Jackals saved Sar Japeth with a cursed piece of hesoa, his deteriorating mental state starts to become evident. Colour the scenes below with comments about the Sar's intensity, and make it clear to the Jackals he wants these Dead put back to rest because the orsem is his family's birthright.

If Sar Japeth died in previous adventures, Sameel takes up the Sar title fully in Isten of this year. He is the leader of Sentem, and it is clear he takes the burden of leadership quite seriously. He raises Ba-en Nafar – or Naitgadda, if Ba-en Nafar is dead – to Nawsi.

ACT 1: SUMMONED BEFORE A SAR

The Sar of Sentem (see above) summons the Jackals to meet with him in Yesimal Keep. This message comes from one of The Thirty, who brings the Jackals to the same room in which they dined with Sameel in **The Moons' Road**. Sameel, Nabal, and Ba-en Nafar are there, as is Japeth, if he is still alive. The meal is much like the one before, with Japeth slowly questioning the Jackals about their involvement in Sentem's business over the past four years. Japeth is recovering, but still weak. His is thin and pale, and prone to lapses of silence as he ponders each thought carefully, but he manages to talk with the Jackals for the whole meal. As a man just reclaiming his wits and power, he is wary of any sarcasm or threats directed towards him. This is not a meal with a fellow traveller of the War Road, and the Jackals should not treat it as such.

Japeth can share the following information and ask the following questions over the course of the meal:

- He extends his thanks to the Jackals who helped him recover.
- He commissioned a special thank you – a series of bronze daggers (+10% to Melee Combat, +2 damage) – for each of the Jackals who walked the healing path for him.
- What do you know about the orsems?
- He can inform the Jackals concerning the nature and location of the orsems in the plains.
- For too long, Kitan has lain fallow, ignored by Sentem and Densom alike.
- He would like that to change – he wants the Jackals to claim the orsem in Sentem's (or his) name.
- He will pay the Jackals 450 ss to deal with the orsem and clear out the Dead, should they truly reside there.
- He also offers them a place in the orsem to call their own. A bed for as long as they want or need it.
- Although he believes the information on the Dead around Orsem Kitan to be accurate, he does think numbers are exaggerated. He still warns the Jackals to be careful. Recently, some of the shepherds say they have seen lights in the tower at night.

Should Japeth walk the tyrant's path, he mixes in the following questions over the course of the evening:

- Why are you here, in Sentem?
- Have you ever been to Ameena Noani?
- How has my son treated you? How has he treated the town?
- How did he speak of me while I was sick? Did he share the details?

Sameel is quiet, watching his father throughout the meal with compassion and pride (and a hint of concern should his father show strange signs of anger). He can share the following information:

- He hopes claiming the fort is the last piece to finally razing Bartak Kentak.
- The orsem secures Sentem's hold from the A'hule Asa to the sea.
- The rumours of the Dead have persisted for too long to be fanciful tales the shepherds and farmers share.
- Once the orsem is secure, Sameel wants to bring the Jackals into his plans for next year's raid on Bartak Kentak.

Once the scene draws to a close, Japeth excuses himself. The evening visibly wears on him, as he is not yet fully recovered. Sameel takes his father back to his room, and Ba-en Nafar and Nabal fall into conversation with each other. This is a perfect opportunity to introduce other hooks for any adventures a Loremaster plans to run this year.

Once the Jackals are ready to head to Orsem Kitan, proceed to Act 2.

ACT 2: ORSEM KITAN

Orsem Kitan lies four days east of Sentem, in the foothills of the A'hule Asa. If the Jackals experience any encounters, use the Dead of the Plains, Haunted Battlefield, or Horde of the Dead results from the Plains of Aeco Encounter Table in *Jackals* on page 163. As the Jackals approach, they see the shapes of great black birds taking flight and heading south towards the Aeco Wood.

Orsem Kitan, like its cousin Orsem Val and other such orsems along the southern War Road, is a remnant of the Hulathi kingdom of Lukka. Lukka built many towers along the southern edge of the War Road to watch the border with Ger, and to warn the north about invasions of Takan from the mountains and Jehumma's Gap. Kitan stands nearly 45 cubits tall, and like all traditional Hulathi buildings, it is made of hestul, which gives it a green glow at dawn and dusk. The Hulathi built Kitan with such craftsmanship that the seams between the stones are almost impossible to see, giving the tower the illusion of being carved from a single piece of hestul. They engraved the lower third of the tower with images of the sea – fish, waves, and ships – but these images are hidden by brambles. The middle third of the tower bears images of the mountains, while the top third is home to birds. At dawn and dusk, these engravings are highlighted and easy to see. Note the time of day the Jackals enter the orsem, as it affects the light situation on some levels.

Uoser can attack the Jackals at any point in the tower, joining in with other combatants and retreating further up into the tower. Feel free to add him into any fight and allow him to heal 4d8 Wounds between battles as he binds his wounds and calls upon his dark rites. The final confrontation with Uoser (see Act 3) takes place on the roof of the tower.

Areas of Orsem Kitan:

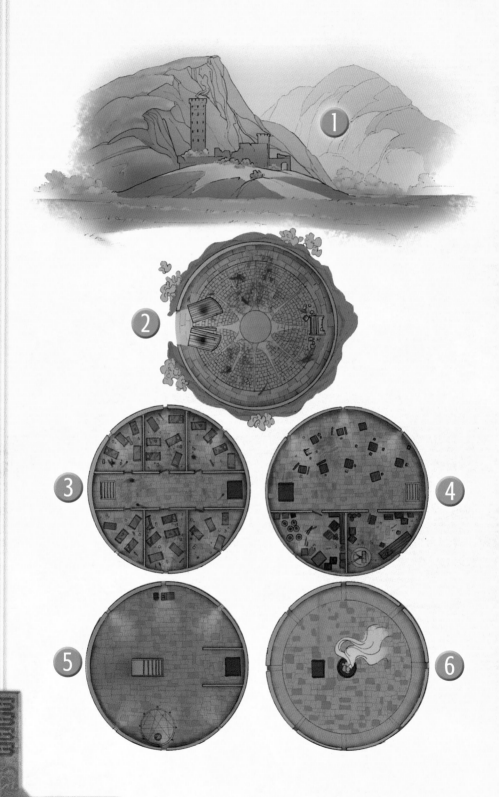

1. Outside the tower

The Aeco Plains break up into the foothills of the A'hule Asa just west of the orsem. Kitan sits on a small hill, adding another 100 cubits to the tower's height. The great doors of the orsem are missing from their hinges. Uoser, having sent his last missives to the Daughter, prepares to battle for his new home; the Mirror of Ashkagael (see below) warned him of the danger the Jackals present. Uoser summoned a horde of Rapiuma outside the tower through Mouathenic rites granted to him by the Daughter. Many of these Rapiuma stand much taller than the Jackals, as they are the remains of the Hulathi that fell defending this tower; others are Takan, or bear Gerwa or Mouadran treasures. Use the appropriate number of Rapiuma for the pack's Kleos level. Additionally, break the Rapiuma up into three groups, using the following group modifiers below:

- Hulathi: +2 Damage from tarnished silvered swords
- Takan: +4 Wounds
- Other: +1 Protection due to remnants of leather armour

These Rapiuma have standard treasure scores for their type and number. Additionally, Jackals can recover 1d6 blades from the Hulathi Dead. These swords inflict +2 damage due to their craftsmanship, but +4 damage to any creature with 15 or more Corruption. If a character with 15 or more Corruption attempts to use these swords, the blade burns them for 4 Wounds.

2. Level 1 – Great Hall

What a Jackal's senses reveal:

Sights – the wreckage of the doors, the remnants of the stairs, the portal leading up to the next floor, and the inlaid floor mosaic. Light from the doorway, but no windows.

Sounds – shuffling coming from above.

Smells – dry rot, an indistinct burning smell, and the faint smell of the sea

A large hall dominates the first level of Orsem Kitan. The wooden doors of the great fort lie on the floor, an oily black char mark in the centre of each. A mosaic of a shield with a golden sunburst dominates most of the floor on this level, although something defaced it with blood and excrement. With an Ancient Lore check, a Jackal can recognise it as the symbol of Lukka.

The stairs to the second floor no longer exist. The landing on the next level is just a dark portal in the ceiling. Getting through it requires climbing gear, an Athletics check, or some other clever plan. The blood and excrement on the mosaic covers a warding Uoser placed upon the seal during his attempts to overcome the orsem's natural protections. Any who cross the seal are overcome with a sense of dread and the fragility of mortal life. They must make a hard Willpower check. See the table below for the results of this check:

WARDING EFFECTS	
Check Result	**Outcome**
Critical success	Overcome the fear: no Mettle damage
Success	Shake off the fear: 2 Mettle damage
Failure	Afraid: 2d4 Mettle damage
Fumble	Terrified: 8 Mettle damage

A Lore or Craft check (by a Hasheer or Hekas) can identify the warding. A Craft or Thievery check can undermine the warding, as can a Touch of Law rite. A See the Unseen rite reveals the warding as a dark and terrible shape bound to the seal.

3. Level 2 – Barracks

What a Jackal's senses reveal:

Sights – total darkness in the halls, possibly some light from windows, the debris of a ruined guard's room, and strange symbols painted in blood on the walls.

Sounds – shuffling coming from above.

Smells – dry rot, and the faint smell of the sea.

The second level of Orsem Kitan held the sleeping quarters of the guards who manned the tower. Six rooms make up this level, each of which would have held four to six guards. Uoser gave these rooms a cursory search when he arrived, but he overlooked several things in his disinterest. The rooms still have a few treasures left:

- A pair of Hulathi spears. These one-handed spears add +5% to Melee and Ranged Combat, +1 damage, and +5% to Willpower checks.
- If the Jackals take 15 minutes to search the wreckage, they can find a silver necklace of a hawk (300 ss), as well as 60 Lukkan coins, each worth 15 ss.

Six Rapiuma and one Etemma guard this level for Uoser. The Rapiuma are armed with ritual implements – daggers, trowels, heavy bowls, and cups – instead of weapons. Uoser used them as assistants for his rites before sending them here to deal with the Jackals.

Uoser, in his attempt to corrupt the orsem, wrote his rites on the walls in his blood and that of his victims. An Ancient Lore check reveals the rites are in the language of Mouadah. Should any Jackal understand Mouadran, they can start to understand what the Uoser attempted to do. The rite calls upon something known as Imil-Ajas to free its daughter, bound beneath the earth. A Lore or Culture (Luathi) check reveals that binding beneath the earth is a punishment in the *Shalapher* for those who practise the Twisted Path: *And you shall separate those who practise the rites of the dark from the community to preserve the community. And they shall be bound beneath the earth, so that My light will never again shine upon their faces.*

The stairs of this level are intact.

4. Level 3 – Eating and Storage

What a Jackal's senses reveal:

Sights – total darkness in the halls, possibly light from windows, and the remains of rotted furniture.

Sounds – the breaking of clay fragments as the Jackals walk, and the scraping of bronze on stone from above.

Smells – dry rot, and the faint smell of the sea.

This floor is broken up into three great rooms. The first is a large room that once held the stores of food and supplies for the fort. Inside this room are six, wax-sealed amphorae containing an herb-infused honey. This honey, called *ahumarti* by the Hulathi, heals 1d8 Wounds when applied directly to the wounds. Eating a small handful of the honey grants an immediate Endurance check against disease and poisons and counts as a meal. Each amphora contains eight doses of the honey. The amphorae are bulky and heavy, each counting as 2 Encumbrance.

The second room is where the food was prepared. A large mill sits in one corner. Several bronze braziers and the remains of clay pots lay scattered in pieces across the floor.

The last room is a large hall where the guards took their meals. The passage of time has destroyed most of the furniture and trappings, but remnants of a few tables remain. The stairs leading up are intact, and a large pile of refuse is piled near the base of the stairs.

A group of Jackals and their hirelings came through here a year ago, intent on cleaning out the orsem. Uoser slew them and bound their spirits to this room. Use the appropriate number of Etemma for the pack's Kleos level. Foreshadow the treasure in the Nawsi's chambers by giving the Etemma similar weapons to those the Jackals bore in life.

5. Level 4 – Nawsi's Chambers

What a Jackal's senses reveal:

Sights – total darkness in the halls, possibly light from windows, chests, a bed mat, and ritual implements.

Sounds – the wind out of the mountains, and the faint sound of surf.

Smells – heady herbs, meat cooking, and the faint smell of the sea.

This was the room of the orsem's Nawsi, but Uoser has taken up residence here. His belongings are in a chest at the foot of his sleeping mat. A ritual area sits against a blank wall. The room looks lived-in, but tidy. A ladder in the centre of the room leads to the roof.

Examination of the chest reveals a fine Gerwa lock. A Thievery check allows access to the chest. Within the chest, the Jackals find:

- Uoser's personal gods: small votives of the Six and a strange Mouahalan throne, which those with the *Nightmares of the East* hook recognise!
- A candle of Anu. The light from this grey candle reveals the presence of corpses, spirits, and other beings and objects tied to the Silent Lands. It is half gone, meaning it has only 30 more minutes of use.
- The goods he took from the slain Jackals:
  - › One and a half talents of silver in bracelets, necklaces, rings, and hacksilver.
  - › Six items of Master quality (see page 164 of *Jackals*).
  - › A small token in the shape of a silver mask. The edges of the token are razor sharp. Shedding blood with this token for Mouathenic rites allows the ritualist to convert Wounds to Devotion Points on a 2 to 3 basis (see page 79 of *Jackals* for the rules about Blood Magic).

The ritual area contains a small bronze bowl – the Mirror of Ashkagael – identical to the one the Jackals found in in *The Lost Children* (see page 247 of *Jackals*). It is filled with foetid and cloudy water. Dropping some of one's own blood into the bowl activates it, and soon the water resolves into the image of a silver-masked figure. The mask is covered in hundreds of engraved teardrops that initially look like scales. The mask seems to smile and says: *"You are too late. My servant's task is already complete. I rise from the earth this night!"* The image then goes dead again.

The symbols of the Six are drawn in a circle around it, and the finger bones of humans and Takan lie scattered about, as if tossed against the wall. Should a Jackal take the bones, they can use them to ask a single yes or no question each season by spending 6 Devotion Points and gaining 2 Corruption. Finally, there is a small brazier, with the remains of a dove sizzling in the coals. The dove was ritually disembowelled. A Lore check reveals it is a simple divination ritual, used by most cultures (although forbidden to Luathi by the *Shalapher*), to provide an answer to a single yes or no question.

When the Jackals move to the roof, proceed to Act 3.

ACT 3: SERVANT OF A GREATER MASTER

6. Watchtower Roof

What a Jackal's senses reveal:

Sights – The towering shapes of the mountains and the green plains that stretch west to the sea.

Sounds – The mountain winds.

Smells – The faint smell of the sea, and herbs burning on a brazier.

Here Uoser waits, having just sent warning to his mistress. As the Jackals ascend the ladder, they see Uoser standing before a brazier – a brazier of sending (see page 170 of *Jackals*). He is whispering silently into a small cloud of smoke that is rising from it. The smoke does not dissipate, it remains over the brazier until it forms a small cloud. The cloud begins to drift south, against the wind, towards the Aeco Wood. Should the Jackals track it, they see it descend into the forest and disappear beneath the canopy.

Uoser is a solidly built Gerwa man, whose arms are a tapestry of scars. Beneath the scars, serpent tattoos writhe on his forearms. The Mouathenic is mad from years of practising the Twisted Path under the tutelage of the Daughter Beneath the Earth. His face twists into a manic yet silent laugh, and Uoser attacks the Jackals as soon as his rite is finished.

Uoser is a Mouathenic, with the following stats:

UOSER

Type:	Human	Location:	Orsem Kitan
		Wounds:	90
Defence:	65%	Protection:	5 (resilience of the grave)
Combat:	80%	Move:	13
Knowledge:	10%	Initiative:	18
Urban:	60%	Clash Points:	8
Common:	85%	Treasure Score:	4
		Corrupt:	13

Special Abilities

Inured to Darkness: Uoser suffers no penalties due to absence of light.

Dark Rites: Uoser has access to all the rites of the Mouathenics listed in this book. Whenever he can invoke a rite (see combat range), the Loremaster can choose to invoke a different rite from the one listed.

Chill of the North: Uoser's body is inhumanly cold. His touch causes 1d4 damage. Additionally, he is immune to cold damage. Fire damage bypasses his Protection.

Combat Range

1–10%	*Black Dagger (2 attacks):* Uoser lashes out with a corrupted dagger. 4d8 (18) damage each. Additionally, the poison on the dagger causes 2d6 (7) Wounds, which ignores Protection. The target can make an Endurance check to reduce the damage by half.
11–30%	*Invoke Darkness:* Uoser douses all the light in the area, plunging it into a supernatural darkness. Targets that are unable to see in the dark must spend 2 additional Clash Points for actions and reactions. The Mouathenic gains +20% to all Combat and Defensive targets that are unable to see and counts as having a positive trait for all attacks and defences.
31–45%	*Chaotic Lance:* with this rite, Uoser invokes dark energies against his foe. 3d8 (13) damage. For each 7 or 8 rolled, the target suffers 1 Corruption. A difficult Willpower check reduces the Corruption taken by half, or to 0 on a critical success. Double the Corruption on a fumble.
46–60%	*Draining Thrust:* through dark invocations, Uoser can steal the essence of those he wounds. 2d12 + 2d6 (20) damage. Additionally, the Mouathenic heals for half the damage he inflicted. If the Mouathenic absorbs damage which would take him above his maximum Valour, it stops at 60 Valour and he can immediately invoke any rite he knows for free.
61–80%	*Serpent's Bite (2 attacks):* the serpents on Uoser's arms leap out to attack those near him. 4d8 (18) damage each. For each 7 or 8 rolled, the target suffers 1 Corruption. A successful Willpower check against the Mouathenic's attack roll reduces the Corruption taken by half, or to 0 on a critical success. Double the Corruption on a fumble.

Uoser is silent, due to sacrificing his tongue to the Daughter Beneath the Earth in a ritual years ago. His black dagger is mouahalan. It inflicts +4 damage in the hands of Jackal, as well as the 2d6 poison damage. Possessing the blade inflicts 3 Corruption per season. After the Jackals slay Uoser and leave the orsem, proceed to the *Aftermath* section.

AFTERMATH

Japeth, Sameel, and Ba-en have questions for the Jackals when they return. Although they are thrilled that Orsem Kitan is now Sentem's, the ominous circumstances of the message, the rites, and the presence of an as-yet-unknown threat does not sit well with them. They set Arishat and Nabal to discovering what they can about this masked figure, while rewarding the Jackals. Sameel wishes for Sentem to know of the Jackals' great work; he sends runners through Sentem proclaiming their deeds and offers them a place among his guard for next year's raid (see **Raid of Raids** on page 135).

The Daughter Beneath the Earth is indeed free, and she will play a larger part in the in years to come. She begins by fleeing into the east for the moment and hiding among the Trauj. However, if it fits the tone of your campaign, harrowing nightmares, taunts, and messages are not inappropriate 'rewards' to bestow on the Jackals for their brief contact with the Daughter. Any Kleos dreams from this point on should centre around her emergence and plans.

ADVANCEMENTS

- 1 for slaying Uoser
- 2 for clearing the tower

HOOKS

From the Ashes: Toara summons the Jackals to the Scriptorium in Ameena Noani and draws them into her investigation of the murders and the fire.

What Lies Beneath: Clearing Kitan might not be as easy as dealing with Uoser. As the guards are clearing the first level, they discover a series of cellars where darkness dwells. Norakan warrens, Aburrisanu tunnels, or more Dead could threaten Sentem's hold on the orsem.

CHAPTER 6
YEAR OF
TESTED BONDS

I made the paths and straightened the land,
I made the wolf and the jackal flee before my people.
The cool of the shade, I moved, the beauty of the garden I established.
Those who rise from below and those who look down from above,
Those who travel the breadth of Lukka,
Do so in the palm of my hand, and they find rest.

~ Hymn of the Queen of the Zaharets ~

INTRODUCTION

The Year of Tested Bonds is Year 5 of *The Fall of the Children of Bronze* campaign, and the first of the 'dimming years' before war. This year sees the Jackals put down Mealil in the north, perhaps for good. In the south, Sameel asks the Jackals to join him on his annual raid of Bartak Kentak. Aiding the prince (or Sar, if Japeth is dead) is an honour, and this raid might prove to be different than previous raids, as forces that have lain dormant are struggling to awaken.

THEME

The theme of this year is loyalty. In the Zaharets, loyalty to clan, tribe, city, and pack form the bonds that connect the peoples of the area together. When those bonds are tested, they snap as often as they emerge stronger. In both adventures, the Jackals see their loyalty – or that of those around them – tested. Offers of power, coin, and security are powerful lures, and that is just when mortals tempt their fellows. When supernatural beings offer these things, the abundance and the fallout are staggering. Forces old and new are drawing lines in the sands of the Zaharets; this year tests the Jackals to see on which side they stand.

In the north, the theme plays out in two ways. First, in the tomb of Mirim Mahazra, the Jackals learn that the Luathi people split over the revelation of Alwain in the past. Belief severed loyalties, and war broke out. Second, the Jackals discover that Rakel of Orsem Honess is dealing with Glykera of Kroryla. What does such a move mean for the area? Will Honess turn away from Ameena Noani and towards Kroryla? What do the Jackals do with such knowledge? In the south, the Jackals go on a deadly raid into a Takan-controlled ruin. This is complicated by the raising of the Black Banner by forces loyal to the Daughter Beneath the Earth. However, the Daughter has need of Jackals, and offers them the kingdoms of this world for their help.

Additionally, if Japeth is walking the tyrants' path, he tries to have Sameel and his loyal pack killed in the raid, to end any attempt at usurpation. Do the Jackals side with the Sar they know or the Sar they saved?

IMPORTANT NPCS

Daughter Beneath the Earth, Hulathi Mouathenic: finally free from her prison beneath the Aeco Woods, the Daughter seeks to establish a kingdom for herself in the Zaharets once more. Although she is in convalescence in the A'hule Asa, she is in continual contact with the Black Tree tribe of Takan, and she prepares a surprise for Sentem during its annual raid on Bartak Kentak.

Glykera: see *Jackals* page 135. Glykera sees writing on the walls of her city. Within a decade, there will be more Melkoni in Kroryla, and they will need space. For this reason, coupled with the inevitable war between the Luathi cities to the east, Glykera seeks to create security and stability for her people. As such, she has begun wooing Orsem Honess and its Sar. This is fomenting discontent with Ameena Noani and creating more ties between Kroryla and Honess. The great western tower of Ameena Noani could become the great eastern tower of Melkon.

Rakel: see *Jackals* page 135. Nawsi Rakel of Orsem Honess is in an unenviable position. Her people are suffering, owing to Takan raids out of the Vori Vana, and much of Ameena Noani's support for the orsem has been diverted to Orsem Ven. Promises of renewed support have gone unrealised for five years. Rakel entered secret negotiations with Kroryla for said support, and Yahan's market is awaiting the arrival of the first shipment of goods.

Toara: see page 100. Toara understands the threat Mealil poses and aids the Jackals in their journey to Mirim Mahazra. She directs them north in the hope they might deal with Mealil, as well as uncover some of the plots she sees brewing there.

EVENTS IN THE NORTH

- Murders begin to take place in Kroryla. Ryla's followers are the targets, and nearly a dozen people are slain before the ritualistic nature of the killings is noticed.

EVENTS IN THE SOUTH

- Gerwa traders bring word that the fighting against the Ungathii is nearing its completion. The Kiani brought victory to Ger.
- If the Jackals renewed Barqan's fidelity to Sentem in **The Moons' Road**, they catch word that an Adept of Anu, one of the dread Gerwa cultists dedicated to death, is stalking Barqan.

RETIREMENT BENEFITS

If a player retires their Jackal in this year, their new Jackal gains +3 advancements due to the pack's renown attracting more skilled Jackals. They can also begin the game with any skill above 100%.

NORTHERN TALE: MIRIM MAHAZRA

An adventure for Regarded Jackals, set during the month of Isten, in the rainy season.

OVERVIEW

Toara summons the Jackals to the Scriptorium in Ameena Noani. Abishai, should she have survived the events of **Relapse**, is there as well. The Hasheers inform the Jackals that the time to strike at Mealil is now. After giving the Jackals the location of Mirim Mahazra and the ritual to cast the Rathic back into the Silent Lands, they send the pack north. However, Toara has a secondary goal in mind for the Jackals. Her agents in the Zaharets bring word to her of rebellion in Orsem Honess. She wants the Jackals to see what they can find along the way to shed light on these rumours. To that end, the route she advises them to take sends them close to the orsem and the caravans that run between it and Kroryla to the west.

ACT 1: THE SCRIPTORIUM'S SUMMONS

The Jackals either accompanied Toara to Ameena Noani in **Relapse** or receive a summons to meet her in the Scriptorium. (See *Jackals* page 123 for an overview of Ameena Noani and the Scriptorium.) Kahri move about the halls, keeping a watchful eye on all non-Hasheers after the riots of two years ago. The meeting takes place in the Vaults, a series of grand and warded chambers beneath the Scriptorium where the Hasheers protect the fruits of their labour. There, Toara meets with the Jackals amid thousands of clay tablets, bronze discs, and papyrus scrolls.

After thanking them once again for their aid in Rataro, especially if Abishai survived, Toara shares the following information:

- This is one of the most secure locations in the Zaharets, so they should be able to speak freely. They are not certain Mealil does not have corrupted agents in the Scriptorium.
- Why is it seeking the mirim (tomb/sacred hill in old Luathi)? Abishai believes the Ishfal chieftain who raided the Hulathi temple in the **Mine of Atem** took one of Mealil's amphora with him, and such a treasure would be buried with him. Mealil, during its attack on Abishai in Rataro, surely discovered its existence in her research.

- Should it recover the last of its power, Mealil will be free, and the rites of exorcism will not work on it.
- Abishai is terrified of that happening; from the accounts she read from Kibeth-Albin, Ameena Noani would fall in weeks should Mealil set its power against the city.
- The mirim is in the coastal mountains, west of Orsem Honess.
- They have a potent ritual of exorcism from Ger, which should work against a weakened Mealil. The ritual will banish Mealil from the earth for 14 generations. If or when it returns, Toara hopes the Scriptorium will have a better solution.
- It is a complicated ritual (see Act 3), one which requires a ritualist. Should the Jackals not have a ritualist in their pack, Toara provides the following:
- Training on the mundane aspects of the ritual, which enables any Jackal to set it up with a Lore check.
- A bronze rod with small buds protruding from one end. The rod is the Rod of Phineaon, a Kahar who served the Luathi after Shumma.
- Obviously, stopping a Rathic is the sort of thing a Hasheer hires a pack of Jackals to do. Toara promises the pack two talents of silver (total) for their aid. Additionally, the Scriptorium will buy any items or records the Jackals can recover from Mirim Mahazra.
- Additionally – and privately – if the Jackals agree to stop Mealil, Toara presents a second job. She knows Orsem Honess is struggling and that Kroryla is said to be coming to its aid. Unless she is the patron one of the Jackals, Toara does not reveal this directly, but instead asks the Jackals to bring back any unusual information on the situation in the northwest. For any such rumour gathering, Toara will pay the Jackals 250 ss each. If one of her clients is in the pack, she tells them of her concerns.

THE ROD OF PHINEAON

The Rod of Phineaon is a bronze rod with small buds protruding from one end – seemingly the buds of a Shalla Tree. Phineaon is a Kahar named in the *Shalapher* who served the Luathi after Shumma. Phineaon's stories revolve around his zeal for Alwain, often at the expense of his own safety. The rod possesses Phineaon's zeal, and it provides its wielder with the Devotion needed to invoke rites, allowing them to convert Mettle to Devotion on a 2 to 1 basis.

When the Jackals are ready to head out, proceed to Act 2.

ACT 2: CARAVAN IN THE WILDS

The journey from Ameena Noani to Kroryla takes 11 or more days, requiring five or more travel checks. Takan roam these lands, and are growing bolder, so encounters should include these beasts. As the Jackals near Orsem Honess, the sight of smoke on the horizon to the west draws their attention. Should they investigate, they come across a large Takan band attacking a large caravan. A dozen Warriors of Lykos are spread thin to protect the wagons, which contain many Melkoni families.

For a pack of four Jackals, use one Oritakan, four Mavakan, and one Atakan. Increase the number of Takan for higher Kleos levels or party numbers. Adding an additional Atakan or a pair of Tsutakan makes this fight tougher, but appropriate for the situation. This is the group the Jackals fight, while the Melkoni attempt to hold off another group of equal size. Each round, roll on the Caravan Battle table to see how well the fight goes for the Warriors of Lykos, adding +1 to the roll for each Takan the Jackals slay in this battle:

CARAVAN BATTLE TABLE	
d10	Result
1–3	Warrior Falls: the Takan rip one of the Melkoni to pieces. This result can happen three times before the Takan start taking prisoners. Each additional result gives the Takan 1d8 prisoners from the wagons. The Takan take these prisoners into the wilds immediately.
4–5	Hold your ground: the Melkoni fight the Takan to a standstill this round.
6–7	Steady!!: the Melkoni injure the smallest remaining Takan (Mavakan < Oritakan < Atakan). If they roll a second Steady result, they slay that Takan.
8+	Take it down: inspired by the Jackals, the Melkoni slay one of the Takan engaged with them. Should all the Takan by the wagons die, the Melkoni launch javelins into the Jackals' melee, inflicting 2d8 damage to 1d4 Takan.

After the battle, the oka (captain) of the warriors, a Melkoni by the name of Phaedo, approaches the Jackals to thank them for their aid. His people are wounded, and any offers of healing are greatly appreciated. The caravan consists of a dozen wagons, drawn by hand or mules, and nearly 40 Melkoni, about a third of which have suffered wounds from the attack. A Trade check reveals that personal possessions, not trade goods, fill some of the wagons. It seems some of these people are migrating to Orsem Honess.

Phaedo can relate the following information:

- He offers his gratitude for their intervention.
- They are a caravan out of Kroryla. They left there about a week ago (wagons do not make great time) and were heading towards Orsem Honess.
- They spotted the Takan two days ago. The caravan raced for Orsem Honess, but the Takan cut them off and forced them south. They made their stand here, but they would have perished if the Jackals had not arrived.
- They carry mostly trade goods from Kroryla – barley, olives, oil, other food stuffs, rope, and wine.
- With a hard Influence check, the Jackals can tell Phaedo is hiding something concerning what they are bringing to Orsem Honess. A second check – made with a trait if the Jackals provided healing to the caravan – causes Phaedo to add that he is transporting shields and armour for the fort, as well. As for why Kroryla would be trading such goods with a Luathi fort, he cannot say. Phaedo's

gratitude goes far, but he shuts down any more questions about this, saying he does not know more than that.

- He asks the Jackals to continue to journey to Orsem Honess with the caravan, as Takan roam the hills, and there is safety in numbers.
- If they ask him directly:
  › Yes, some of the people here are moving to Orsem Honess, the Sar (he says this as if the word is still new to him) offered space for them inside the walls.
  › Some are refugees from further west, from the wars. Others are those who seek life in a new place.
- Phaedo offers the Jackals 300 ss in trade goods (food, jewellery, and pottery) or a single well-crafted Melkoni Shield (+3 Protection (total), +10% to Influence). The shield's face depicts the world as the Melkoni envision it: divided into thirds – the top third dominated by a mountain, the middle third by vast plains and forests, and the lower third by waters and the underworld.

Should the Jackals stop in Orsem Honess, they immediately notice the Melkoni population, which makes up nearly a third of the city. Guards from the orsem ride out to meet Phaedo and the caravan while they are still some distance from the city. With them is Nawsi Rakel, who seems relieved at the sight of the caravan but anxious due to the presence of Jackals. The guards take the wagons, the people, and the warriors, and escort them quickly into the city. Rakel thanks the Jackals for their aid, then informs them she is now in control of the situation. If any Jackals comment on the Takan, and why they were so close to the Orsem, Rakel snaps back that the orsem's ability to keep its people safe is dependent on the quality of its support. Phaedo thanks the Jackals one last time, before disappearing into the fort. A Stealth, Influence, or Trade check reveals the caravan seems to have disappeared, most likely into the keep.

Orsem Honess is a good place for the Jackals to rest, recuperate, and resupply should they need to do so before heading out to search for Mirim Mahazra. Should the Jackals stay in the orsem, they can make one check (Loremasters should determine the difficulty of the check based on the skill chosen, but it should be at least difficult) each day to recon the fort for Toara. Possible information the Jackals might discover includes:

- The Melkoni are not visiting – they are building houses inside and outside the orsem.
- The Nawsi's guards have Melkoni among their number.
- A small shrine to Areton can be found in the market.
- Access to the Nawsi and the main fort is restricted by Warriors of Lykos.
- Hard checks reveal small supply depots of Melkoni weapons and armour.
- Foundations for new walls surrounding the new buildings are being laid.

The journey to the barrow takes another four days of travel, through the coastal mountains. Once there, it takes a week to find the hill of the king. Jackals can reduce this time with Ancient Lore, Lore, Perception, or Survival checks. Each Jackal can make one such check, reducing the search time by half a day on a success, or by a full day on a critical success. Once the Jackals find the mirim, proceed to Act 3.

ACT 3: MIRIM MAHAZRA

Mirim Mahazra, or the Grave of the Chieftain in the old tongue, is an ancient burial tomb of a Luathi chieftain from before the time of Barak Barad. Its history extends back to the founding of the Grand Kingdoms by the Children of Silver. When the Hulathi landed in the Zaharets, they converted many of the Luathi to the worship of Alwain, an act referred to as the Summons of Heaven. However, not all the tribes submitted to the Hulathi's rule or acknowledged Alwain's supremacy. The Ishfal tribe refused the Summons of Heaven, and the Hulathi pushed them to the outskirts of the Grand Kingdoms. Centuries later, Mahazra arose as a great king of the Ishfal. He gathered other tribes to him and began to raid the Grand Kingdoms, and he continued in the worship of his ancestors and the Balim of Keta. When he died, his followers buried him beneath the earth in the hill of his ancestors.

The mirim is a low hill in the coastal mountains, unlikely to stand out unless one was specifically looking for it with the aid of a Hasheer. The mirim looks like a hill, smaller than its neighbours and, after centuries, just as covered with trees and vegetation. One of the trees on the mound seems to be dying – its leaves are a sickly yellow colour. A strange rock protrusion, like an underbite of stone jutting up from the ground, is the only indication that there is something odd about the mound. When the Jackals get closer, they see this slab is nearly identical to the one they found in the mines (see page 28). Additionally, there is a bloated and rotting Melkoni corpse. A Healing check shows the signs of Mealil's Touch. If a Jackal turns it over, the corpse is revealed to have the black mark on its forehead. However, handling the corpse exposes the Jackal to Mealil's Touch of the Mines (see page 20).

The door seems to be in place, but there are signs of a recent disturbance around its edges. A Lore or Culture (Luathi) check reveals the door has a warding prayer around its edges to prevent graverobbers from disturbing the king's resting place. These wards kept Mealil from removing the slab, but the Rathic found a way around it by passing its spirit into the tree and entering through the roots. A hard Lore check removes the warding. If the Jackals do not remove the warding, they feel the curse settle upon them. In the short term, the Jackals suffer a 1d6 penalty to Mettle while in the mirim. The long-term effects of the curse are up to the Loremaster, or roll on the table below:

	LONG-TERM CURSE EFFECTS	
d10	Result	
1–2	*Corruption of Spirit:* increase all Corruption gains by 1 point	
3–4	*Baal Turns His Face from You:* wherever the Jackal goes, the rains cease to fall within 20 miles	
5–6	*Ill Fortune:* –1 Fate Point	
7–8	*Spirits of Reprisal:* any spirits in the area target this character first and most often	
9–10	Charge!: all bulls are enraged by the presence of the Jackal and go berserk, attempting to kill them	

The Jackal can remove the curse by taking a Remove Corruption seasonal action, which usually removes at least 2 points of Corruption. In this case, it does not remove any Corruption, it removes their curse instead.

A difficult Athletics check moves the slab enough to pull it free from the hill.

What a Jackal's senses reveal:

Sights – completely dark. The walls are made of fitted stones and are covered with paintings and carvings. The fine roots of trees and grass grow between the stones.

Smells – dank earth and stagnant water.

Sounds – the echoes of the Jackals' movements. Occasionally, a dull clatter.

1. Entrance Hall

The hall extends into the hill. The paintings on the wall tell the tale of the Balim creating the world by slaying a great multi-headed dragon, cutting it apart, and forming the world from its body. Studying the paintings for an hour grants the Jackal +5% to Ancient Lore, as they learn about the Balim of Keta and the cosmological origins according to the ancient Luathi. Halfway down the hall, a statue of a massive bronze bull stands in an alcove. The bull is a trap, cunningly stolen from the Hulathi of Sardon and repurposed to guard the kings of old. A Perception check reveals something strange about the bull. A second hard Perception check reveals the pressure plate in front of the bull. A Craft, Thievery, or Lore check can disarm the trap; however, doing so does not prevent its magics from activating later (see below).

- *Bull trap:* if the Jackals do not disarm the trap, when a person passes in front of it, the bull magically charges out of its alcove and crushes them against the wall, inflicting 2d20 damage. A hard Dodge check allows the Jackal to avoid the damage.
- *Bull statue:* should the Jackals find some way to remove the bull and get it back to civilisation, it is worth four talents of silver.

2. Main Room

Four broad stairs descend into this room, the walls of which are covered in paintings that tell the story of Mahazra, the last and greatest chieftain of the Ishfal tribe (see page 103). In the images, Mahazra has the head of a bull and the body of a powerfully built man. Studying these paintings for an hour gives a Jackal +3% to Ancient Lore. A small square altar stands in the centre of the room. Although it is similar in appearance to an Alwainic altar, the position of the horns is wrong, and the proportions are off. This is where the priests of the Luathi would offer sacrifices to the chiefs of old.

A great bundle of roots broke through the ceiling stones long ago, leaving small piles of stones and dirt throughout the room. One of the root groupings has swollen and burst, leaving an oily residue on the floor. Three archways lead out of this room. The portals to the left and right are level with this room, but the one opposite the entrance stands at the top of eight stairs, forcing any in the room to look up to where the chieftains lay.

3. Treasury Room

Through the left portal lie the burial goods of several of the Ishfal chiefs. These include piles of small silver coins, like those found in the mines, as well as weapons, armour, and jewellery. Disturbing the treasures summons the Dead from the Ossuary. All in all, the treasures of the mirim include:

- 3,000 shekels of silver in ancient silver coins.
- 12 ceremonial masks, 50 ss each.
- A silver war mask, 600 ss.
- Five necklaces worked with bull motifs, 50 ss each.
- Ten trinkets (rings, armlets, bangles, and signet seals), 55 ss each
- Two well-crafted leaf-bladed swords (both +2 damage and +5% to Melee Combat).
- Two sets of leather armour with bull motifs worked into the leather (3 Protection and +10% Endurance each).
- A golden shield rimmed with horn (2 Protection and +1 Clash Point).
- A strange sling made from Yammim hide (2d8 damage).
- A dozen small amphorae, each worth 50 ss.
  - › One of the dozen is Mealil's amphora – if a Jackal touches this amphora, Mealil possesses Mahazra (see below) and combat ensues.

4. The Ossuary

The bones of the chieftains and their servants were placed into this room by the reigning chieftain's priests. As the centuries passed, the Ossuary pit filled with bones, especially when the chieftains began to place the sacrificed bones of their conquered foes here as well. The curses of the mirim ensure any who violate the tomb summon these Dead from their graves to add the grave robber's bodies to the mass of bones. Until the Jackals loot the tomb, or until Mealil takes possession of Mahazra's body, the pile seems to be a dusty pit with bone fragments poking out of it. Once either of those two events occur, the Dead begin to reconstitute themselves. The Dead of the mirim fight with the following stats:

THE DEAD OF THE MIRIM			
Type:	Dead	Location:	Mirim Mahazra
		Wounds:	20
Defence:	35%	Protection:	2 (natural)
Combat:	85%	Move:	11
Knowledge:	10%	Initiative:	12
Urban:	10%	Clash Points:	1
Common:	15%	Treasure Score:	1
		Corruption:	11

Special Abilities

Inured to Darkness: the Dead of the Mirim suffer no penalties due to absence of light.

Chill of Death: at the start of each round, opponents engaged with the Dead of the Mirim suffer 5 Valour damage.

Combat Range

1–10%	*Bony Head-butt (2 attacks):* with jerky motions, the Dead slams its skull into its target, for 2d6 (7) damage each.
11–30%	*Savage Rend:* the claw-like fingers of the Dead easily rend the flesh of the living. 2d8+2d6 (16) damage.
31–55%	*Claws of the Dead (2 attacks):* even the Dead can be incited to a murderous rage. 2d8+2d6 (16) damage each.
56–85%	*Bone Snap:* the Dead seek to add bones to their own forms and to the Ossuary. They break the Jackal's bones for easy absorption. 2d12 + 2d8 damage (22). The target must make a hard Endurance check. If they fail, their bone breaks and they suffer –2 Clash Points for the rest of the fight.

The Ossuary summons two Rapiumas for each Jackal if they steal from the treasure room, or one each when they engage with Mealil. However, the Rapiuma only fight those who attack Mealil or those who have taken treasure (throwing the treasure down does not stop these attacks, only leaving the tomb for good).

5. Mahazra's Final Rest

Ascending the stairs, the Jackals can see this room is a broad oval, with a stone slab in the middle surrounded by votives, amulets, clay jars, and dried-out herb bundles. On the slab rests Mahazra. The dead chieftain was preserved in his bronze armour, and holds his two fabled maces: Ayamur and Yahrush. Time has withered the corpse, drying out its skin into a mottled grey colour. Upon entering the resting place, any Jackals with a Devotion score immediately feel the wrongness of the place. Rites, such as See the Unseen, reveal there are two spirits at war over the body. One can only be Mahazra – tall and vital, possessing a long beard plaited with rings. The other is Mealil, its form hazy with malice and oozing with infectious vitriol. Witnessing this scene in the Silent Lands requires a Jackal to make a difficult Willpower check or gain a point of Corruption. When the Jackals enter the room, Mealil possesses Mahazra with a burst of desire – the corpse's eyes fly open and radiate a sickly green light.

"Mortals. A thorn in my flesh. At least, the flesh I wear. I will have the last of my essence now, and then I shall grant you such terrible pleasures of the flesh that your bones burst and your bellies burn with my fire. You shall be the first of my feast." The body of the dead Luathi chieftain attacks almost immediately. If one of the Jackals is carrying the amphora, Mealil targets them until it scores a critical success (breaking the amphora) or slays them, in which case it breaks the amphora as its next action. If none of them have the amphora, it attempts to move past them to get to the room with the amphora. Do not forget the Dead from the Ossuary that awaken, as well!

MEALIL

Type:	Rathic/The Dead	Location:	Mirim Mahazra
		Wounds:	140
Defence:	75%	Protection:	8 (Mahazra's armour)
Combat:	140%	Move:	12
Knowledge:	95%	Initiative:	18
Urban:	60%	Clash Points:	8
Common:	60%	Treasure Score:	3
		Corruption:	20

Special Abilities

Inured to Darkness: Mealil suffers no penalties due to absence of light.

Chaotic Flesh: Mealil recovers 2d10 Wounds per round.

Chaotic Spirit: Mealil can take 1d6 damage to gain a Clash Point. Mealil automatically senses the Corruption in all creatures within 20 yards. This makes it impossible for a corrupt creature to sneak up on Mealil.

Heat of Fever: each round, opponents engaged with Mealil take 6 points of Valour damage.

Skill of the Rathic: a Loremaster can select two talents for the Rathic before combat to represent how this creature fights uniquely.

Combat Range

1–15%	*Impart Disease:* Mealil inflicts upon the area the worst symptoms of its manifold diseases. All targets within 10 yards suffer 4d12 (26) damage.
16–30%	*Unnatural Strength (2 attacks):* Mealil's spiritual strength infuses the body it possesses. 5d8 (23) damage.
31–55%	*Infectious Eruption:* buboes swell and burst over Mealil's body, showering the area with pus and infectious matter. 4d8 (18) damage. For each 7 or 8 rolled, the target suffers 1 Corruption and must make a save against exposure to The Touch of the Mines (see page 20). The Touch of the Mines' intensity begins at 2 and increases by 1 per 8 rolled for damage, in addition to the increases for Corruption. A successful Endurance check against the attack roll reduces the Corruption taken by half or to 0 on a critical success.
56–75%	*Speed of the Dead (4 Attacks):* unconcerned with the limits of the human form, Mealil assaults the Jackals with a flurry of blows. 5d8 (23) damage each.
76–90%	*Command the Corrupt:* like many Rathic, Mealil can claim dominion over all those with chaos in their souls. It forces the target to make a hard Willpower check. If they fail, Mealil momentarily takes control of the corrupted creature for 1d4 rounds. Mealil can spend 3 Clash Points on the creature's turn to force it to take an action of its choice.

The Chief of Old

Mahazra hates the Rathic of disease as much as the Jackals. He is fighting it in the spiritual realm as much as they are in the physical realm. Every time the Jackals score a critical success or Mealil fumbles, give them a clue to this fact. A deeper voice rings out of the corpse: *"Kill it, I will hold it here"* or *"This abomination must be ended"* or *"Do not let it reach [the treasury or the Jackal with the amphora]!"*

Lore checks reveal there is a spirit fighting Mealil from within. There might be a way to aid it. An Ancient Lore check suggests they can perhaps grant the spirit of the chief aid in the form of Devotion Points. Every 3 Devotion Points spent in this way reduce Mealil's Clash Points by 1 for one round. If the Jackals reduce its Clash Points to 0, they stun Mealil for the round, leaving it unable to take actions. Additionally, for the rest of the fight, the Jackals can spend 7 Devotion Points to allow Mahazra to command one of the Dead to attack Mealil.

If the Jackals defeat Mealil before it gets the amphora, the deeper voice returns. Mahazra whispers: *"I have it. I have it bound within me. We must not let this abomination free upon the world. What can we do?"* This is the time for the Jackals to enact the ritual Toara gave them (see below). If it is successful, the corpse disintegrates, its armour and weapons falling to the ground, and the Jackals banish Mealil from this world for 14 generations. If the ritual fails, the corpse cries out in a bellow of agony: *"It's not working!"* Grant the Jackals one more attempt; otherwise, Mealil flees the body of Mahazra into the Silent Lands. It is gone, for now, but returns to hound the Jackals later.

If the Jackals defeat Mealil after it breaks the amphora, Mahazra wrestles with himself as he struggles to contain the essence of Mealil. The Jackals get one chance to enact Toara's ritual before Mealil overcomes Mahazra and flees the mirim (see below). Even if the rite is successful, it does not work completely, instead banishing Mealil for a year and a day into the Silent Lands. There, the Labasu plans its revenge on the Jackals.

If the Jackals fail to defeat Mealil after it breaks the amphora, the Labasu touches each of the Jackals, giving them The Touch of the Mines. It then discorporates and heads out into the world to spread its corruption. Where it decides to target first – the Trauj enclaves, Ameena Noani, or Eastern Melkon – is anyone's guess.

The Ritual of Expelling

The ritual Toara gave the Jackals involves symbolically purifying the essence of the Labasu and sending it back into the Silent Lands. She gave the Jackals two figures – one of tamarisk and one of cedar – each of which stands in as a representation of Mealil. They must pour the amphora oil over the figurines, burn them, douse the ashes with water from the sea and the Asa Amwa, and finally bury the paste in the earth where the sun can shine upon it. If you want to add more to the ritual, the Jackals must also speak the following incantations at each step:

Pouring of Oil

Hear me, oh Labasu, oh Rathic
Whose touch inflicts sickness upon us.
I have seized your roaming eyes,
I have seized your sickening touch,
I have seized your wandering feet,
I have tied your arms.
May Alwain bring your body to an end –
He will cast you into fire, water, and earth.

Lighting of Fire

I am lighting the fire as the sun lights the darkness.
You, oh Labasu, oh Rathic
Melt, dissolve, render!
The smoke of your foulness shall rise to the heavens –
The sun will burn brighter than your embers.
Alwain will cut you off from the land of the living.

Dousing with Water

May the purity of the sea smash your essence
May the waters of the Amwa release your sickness
And may the land, like the river,
Become pure once again.

Burying in Earth

May the earth hold you,
May the earth calm you,
May the earth hide you,
May the earth hold you back,
May the earth cover you
And keep you from the light of Alwain.

Treasures of the King

Mahazra was a mighty chieftain of the Luathi, and his followers buried him amid his panoply of war. The finest priests and crafters of his age made his weapons and armour in the likeness of those carried and worn by their patron god.

- *Armour of the Bull:* 7 Protection, requires 21 Strength to wear. Once worn, the armour has an Encumbrance of 1.
- *Ayamur:* a one-handed mace that smells faintly of ozone. The bronze head of the mace has scenes of a bull-headed man ascending and descending a majestic mountain, as well as scenes of this same creature fighting and slaying a dragon from the sea.
    - › +5 Devotion Points to followers of the Balim.
    - › +1d10 damage to Yammim.
    - › Three times a day, the wielder can call upon the lord of storms to unleash a bolt of lightning up to 50 yards away for 4d12 damage. The target can spend 2 Clash Points to Dodge for half damage.
- *Yagrush:* a two-handed mace with a shorter handle (requires 18 Strength to wield, and a Jackal can wield it one-handed with 21 Strength). This mace's head depicts the Rider on the Clouds summoning or banishing the rains, depending on how the mace is rotated.
    - › +6 damage against Yammim and the Dead.
    - › Ride on the Clouds – move up to 30 yards on a gust of wind for 1 Clash Point, up to three times a day

- Those who wield both maces can intuit the Call Rider on the Clouds ritual by studying the mace heads for a day. This ritual costs 12 Devotion Points and summons a thunderstorm to the mace's location. The invoker must plant the mace upright in the ground during the ritual, which takes one hour. The invoker can add additional affects to the ritual by spending more Devotion Points.
  - *Fertile Rains (+5 Devotion Points):* the rains summoned are especially good for crops, doubling the yield for that season.
  - *Scouring Hail (+10 Devotion Points):* the summoned hail destroys all crops within a five-mile radius.
  - *Storm God's Fury (+15 Devotion Points):* the thunderstorm is especially terrible and is under the invoker's control. For the duration of the rite (one hour), the invoker can spend 5 Clash Points to strike a target with lightning for 4d12 damage. The target can spend 2 Clash Points to Dodge for half damage.

AFTERMATH

If the ritual is successful, even partially, it banishes the spirit of Mealil to the Silent Lands for a time. Toara is interested in how the ritual went and probes the Jackals to see how successful it was. Should she receive any inkling that the measure is temporary (due to the Jackals describing fumbles, missteps, or failures), she is disappointed, but begins preparing almost immediately for Mealil's inevitable return. Should the Jackals banish the Labasu for 14 generations, Toara is extremely amenable to having the Jackals as clients. The cost to initiate patronage with Toara is waived, and the cost to increase status with her is halved for the rest of the campaign. Toara warns the Jackals that more trouble is on the horizon; she has seen it in the Sky Road. War is coming to the Zaharets. Perhaps from the west, should the Jackals inform her about the state of the orsem. Perhaps from the south. She also mentions Sari Phamea needs Jackals, and that she would be glad to put them in touch with the ruler of Ameena Noani.

ADVANCEMENTS

- 1 for discovering evidence of something more than trade between Honess and Kroryla
- 1 for clearing Mirim Mahazra
- 1 for exorcising Mealil, which also increases each Jackal's Kleos by 1

SOUTHERN TALE: RAID OF RAIDS

An adventure for Regarded Jackals, set during the month of Isten, in the rainy season.

OVERVIEW

The annual raids on Bartak Kentak come to a violent conclusion in this adventure. Sameel, bolstered by recent events, decides to try to end the threat of the Takan lurking in the city once and for all. He hires a small group of Trauj and Gerwa mercenaries with the aid of Barqan, combining them with the men and women of Sentem and Densom, The Thirty, and the Jackals. This raid will not only scour the Takan for good, but provide the southern War Road with a new city – Eridu – named for Sameel's son.

The Daughter Beneath the Earth knows of the coming raid. She uses her rites to reach out to Ozamog, the Oritakan leader of the Black Tree tribe, and warn it about this raid of raids. Additionally, she sends two gifts to Ozamog. The first, the Heart of Belih, is an ancient and corrupted Hulathi artefact to aid in the destruction of the forces of Sentem. The second is a warrior by the name of Sanghulhaza. This warrior, devoted to the Daughter Beneath the Earth, seeks to slay those of the Yesim line. Adding to the chaos is the chance Japeth sees this as an opportunity to rid himself of the Jackals, and perhaps his heir (see above).

WHAT HAPPENED TO HIRROM

Japeth's eldest son, Hirrom, is presumed dead, but now serves the Daughter Beneath the Earth. She plans to have Hirrom – now called Sanghulhaza – slay his brother (and father, should Japeth not walk the tyrant's path) and claim Sentem in her name. She plans to have him reveal himself to the people of Sentem as a saviour after the raid. He supports Ozamog's plans, but serves the Daughter, not the Takan. Should a Loremaster want him to escape from this adventure, Hirrom is a sword pointed at the heart of the War Road, revealing the sort of long-term planning and cruelty of which the Daughter Beneath the Earth is capable.

ACT 1: THE OUTER WALLS

The adventure begins when Sameel summons the fighting forces of Sentem. The town swells with the influx of Jackals, mercenaries, and fighters from the surrounding areas. The Jackals, assigned to Sameel's own force, are invited to the planning sessions in the fortress. Sameel, Japeth and Ba-en Nafar (should they both be alive), Nabal, Sar Avi, and a large Trauj woman by the name of Sekata all are present for the meeting, where Sameel outlines his plan for this raid of raids.

Sameel shares the following information:

- The annual raids were effective at keeping the Takan contained, but that is not enough anymore.
- With the taking of the orsems last year, and with the trade flowing in from Mayrah Vedil and Ger, it is time to end this threat to the War Road once and for all.
- The plan is simple: scour the ruins of Bartak Kentak of all Takan and claim the city for the Luathi.
- The plan involves taking and holding the outer walls; then, over a series of days, raiding deeper and deeper into the ruined city, until all the Takan are wiped out.
- The Trauj will head to Densom to attack the city from the east, while The Thirty, the Gerwa, and the Jackals provide the main assault from the west.
- He asks the Jackals to lead the raids into the warren beneath the city, as they have experience in this area.
- Nabal's Kahar will aid in the cleansing of the city after taking it.
- Sameel is hopeful the city will be theirs within the season, and they can strike the name of Bartak Kentak from their memories. He plans to raise the Yesim banner over the newly claimed city of Eridu.

Other general items of note about the meeting:

- Sameel is exuberant – ready to claim the city for his people and end the threat of the Takan so close to Sentem.
- Ba-en Nafar is cautious, he knows the Takan are cunning foes. He remembers the events of **The Lost Children** and will be on the lookout for traps, ambushes, and misdirection.
- Sekata, the Trauj, is overjoyed her Alkitar will see battle against the Takan. She is hopeful this will be the battle that ensures her name will live on forever in the stories of her people.
- Nabal seems reserved but is filled with a zeal for the cleansing of the city. His Kahars outwardly show this, as well. If Japeth's curse has begun to affect him (see **The Moons' Road**), Nabal appears exhausted and is short with the Jackals. He speaks more about reclaiming what was lost than cleansing what may be gained.
- Japeth's attitude ranges from optimistic to sullen (if the curse of the Istanil holds sway upon him). Should the curse be in play, he might reach out to the Jackals to see whether they notice anything strange about Sameel. He hopes to plant doubts in their minds about the raid – doubts he might play upon later (see below).

Ba-en Nafar's scouts bring back the following information (labelled according to veracity):

- Although the city seems quiescent, the Takan are preparing for a battle (true).
- The western gate stands rebuilt! (False, although it is blocked with rubble and hastily erected fortifications.)
- The Takan were moving something large, carrying it by long poles threaded through the sides (true).
- A Nephilim is aiding the Takan (partially true – it is a corrupt Annubi).
- The Black Tree banner flies over the ruined ziggurat in the centre of the city (partially true, the tarnished mask emblem of the Daughter Beneath the Earth also flies).
- A strange human warrior is commanding the Takan (partially true, Sanghulhaza is under Ozamog's command, but has a contingent of Takan under his personal command).

When the Jackals are ready and have exhausted their questions, the raid begins. The journey from Sentem to Bartak Kentak takes three days, during which the Jackals can continue to question Sameel, Ba-en Nafar, Sekata, or Nabal. A camp is set up outside the city while Sameel waits for the Trauj to meet up with the forces of Densom. Five days after leaving Sentem, at dawn, the shofar trumpets sound, and the forces of humanity assail the ruined Takan city. (See *Jackals* page 132 for more information on Bartak Kentak.) The Jackals' first goal is to take the outer walls by making it to the western gate and unblocking it.

SIEGE WEAPONS

In the Bronze Age of the Zaharets, there are few aids to those who assault a fortified position. Siege towers, ladders, and battering rams are the main tools constructed to take a wall. Siege towers are slow-going (Move 8), and although they provide great protection to those within (Protection 8), they are susceptible to fire attacks, trapping those inside in a towering inferno. Siege ladders reduce the difficulty of Athletics checks to climb a wall by one degree, but they are cumbersome (Encumbrance 5). Battering rams aid in assaulting gates, but they are also quite heavy (Encumbrance 10). A four-person ram reduces the Athletics check difficulty for breaking a gate by one degree. A 12-person ram reduces the difficulty by two and inflicts one extra success on a success.

The Walls

The walls are short and squat, having fallen into disrepair due to the erosion of time and the constant raids by Sentem; yet, they still pose a threat. Ozamog reinforced the main gate of Bartak Kentak, and Mavakan guard the gate and the walls. Sameel leaves it up to the Jackals to decide how to take the western gate, and when and where to attack. There are two other groups on similar missions, with the goal of at least one causing enough damage to force the gate open.

When to Attack

Attacking at night does not necessarily help the Jackals, as the Takan are inured to darkness. With the dawn, Sentem's arrows and javelins rain down on the walls. This causes chaos upon the walls, which could create an opening for the Jackals. Sneaking up on the walls requires difficult Stealth check. If the assault happens at dawn, the shift in light and Sentem's assault change this to a regular Stealth check. Should the Takan spot the Jackals, they attack with their own counter-barrage of arrows. Sameel can concentrate fire on the area of the wall the Jackals plan to climb. His archers have a 45% chance each round after the Takan start attacking the Jackals to slay one defender on the wall. The Jackals, of course, can also attempt to drop the defenders.

Gaining the Walls

The walls of Bartak Kentak vary in height, but still pose an obstacle to most assaults. Ozamog stationed more Takan on the lowest parts of the wall. The Jackals must choose where to stage their assault. A Perception check shows the taller sections of the wall are not as well-guarded as the shorter sections. Climbing the walls of the city requires one Athletics check for the shorter sections, and two for the taller ones. Failing a check causes the Jackal to take damage as they fall. (See *Jackals* page 159 for rules on damage from falling.) Failing a check on (or falling from) the shorter sections is a normal intensity, while the taller sections are a difficult intensity. These checks are unopposed, unless the Takan spot the Jackals. In that case, the Jackals might have to ascend the wall under fire. Increase the Clash Points needed to Dodge attacks by 2 while on the wall. Additionally, a hit that causes Wounds provokes an Endurance check to see whether the Jackal remains on the wall. Once one Jackal makes it to the top, they can hold the section, drop a rope (one Jackal per round can ascend the wall using the rope without an Athletics check), or aid their fellows in any other manner they see fit.

Use the following encounter strengths:

- Tall sections – three Mavakan, one Oritakan, two Norakan (plus one Mavakan per Jackal over four).
- Shorter sections – four Mavakan, one Oritakan, one Retakan (plus one Mavakan per Jackal over four).

The Gate

Ozamog packed the western gate with rubble taken from the city, as well as remnants of items taken from caravan raids. A group of Takan holds the gate. If the Jackals remove them, they can clear the gate, allowing Sameel's forces to easily move inside.

- The Gate – three Mavakan, two Oritakan, one Gadakan (plus one Mavakan per Jackal over four).

Before combat, roll randomly to see how the other groups Sameel sent to take the gate fair:

OTHER GROUPS	
d10	Result
1–2	*Deadly Outcome:* the others perished in the assault; no help arrives.
3–4	*The Lone Survivor:* only one other person survived the assault to make it to the gate. On the second round of combat, this ally joins the fight. Use Guard stats.
5–8	*Harried but Still Here:* one of the groups survived, but Takan are attempting to chase them down. Roll a d4. At the end of that round of combat, the group appears on the far end of the gate map and makes five Ranged Combat attacks against the largest of the Takan. 85% skill, 3d8 damage. Roll the d4 again at the end of the round to see when they return.
9–10	*Not Down Yet:* a group of four guards shows up to aid the Jackals in claiming the gate. They act at the end of the initiative. Use Guard stats.

Once the Jackals secure the gate, proceed to Act 2.

ACT 2: WHAT LIES BENEATH

Sentem's forces rush through the gate and establish a major foothold in the city, and the green and gold banner of Yesim flies over the western gate. The skirmishes continue for five days, with the Jackals participating in raids, as well. (If you are so inclined, use these raids to play out mini-combats or assignments to attack supply caches in the city; assassinate Takan leaders, Annubi, and Shamans; or other adventure ideas you might have.) The fighting is fierce, but word quickly comes that the forces of Densom and the Trauj took the northern gate. After this, it becomes clear to Sameel that the tunnels beneath Bartak Kentak are a source of trouble. They allow the Takan to travel about the city almost unseen, and there are rumours of a power growing beneath the Sentem army's feet.

Over the next few days, tensions in the camp begin to grow. Starting on the third day, dark dreams trouble the sleep of Sameel's people, including the Jackals. Have each Jackal make a difficult Willpower check to see whether they sleep well enough to recover Wounds or Mettle. If they fail the check, they recover 1d4 less of each than they should. On a fumble, they recover nothing. On the fourth day of the raid, the Jackals witness an argument break out between some of The Thirty and the Gerwa mercenaries (use stats for two Guards and three Wolves, respectively, from *Jackals*). If the Jackals do not intervene, the two groups eventually drag others into the argument, which turns into a fight. On day five, the heavy mists of Bartak Kentak roll in, blanketing the city in an obscuring haze. Even the plains disappear, and everyone can hear the howls of Retakan stalking the streets.

Sameel tasks the Jackals with scouting the tunnels and discovering what lies beneath the streets of Bartak Kentak. Nabal confirms something is working on the hearts of those in the city – although to what end, he cannot tell. The Kahars are working on rites to shore up the army and their minds, but it will take some time.

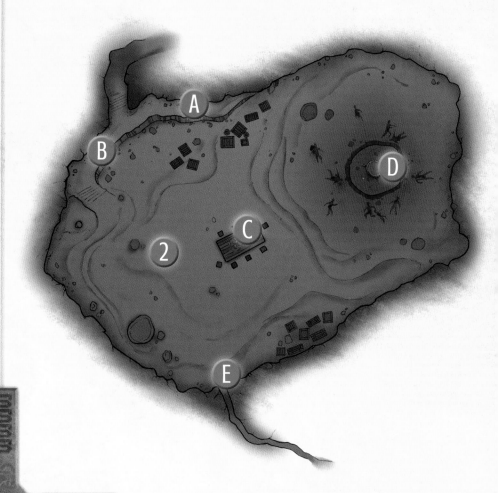

1. The Tunnels

What a Jackal's senses reveal:

Sights – completely dark. The tunnels quickly fill with smoke from torches. Decades of Takan tracks cover the dirt floors. Norakan claw marks show where they carved the tunnels from the dirt and stone of the plains.

Smells – the foul, trapped odour of the beastfolk.

Sounds – dripping water, shuffling in the dark, and the occasional scraping sound of the Takan tongue.

The easiest way to access the tunnels is through one of many house cellars. However, the tunnels are a labyrinth, carved out by the Takan over centuries. Finding anything in there is a daunting task. How the Jackals find the source of the Takan's aid is up to them. Have the Jackals describe what they find and how they are moving past the obstacles they encounter. For example, Survival and Perception checks can help interpret the tracks on the tunnel floors or spot dangerous traps. Lore checks can help interpret the signs and markings on the tunnels. Athletics, Craft, or Thievery checks can help clear cave-ins or aid the group past traps or blockades. Stealth checks can aid the group with scouting ahead, perhaps warning of ambushes. The difficulty for these checks should be difficult or hard, as the Loremaster sees fit.

The Jackals need to accumulate **ten successes** (with critical successes counting as two successes) before they incur **five failures** to navigate the tunnels.

Four checks account for a day's worth of exploring. Jackals can attempt to come back to the surface, requiring a Survival check that does not count towards navigating the tunnels, or stay in the tunnels for the night. A second Survival check is required to return to where they left off; a success does not count towards the navigating, but a failure does.

For every three checks (including any checks to retreat or find their way back), there is a 20% chance of an encounter in the tunnels. Roll on the table below to see what the Jackals discover:

TUNNEL ENCOUNTERS	
d6	Encounter
1	Ambush: four Retakan
2	Death for You, Jackal: three Atakan
3	Warband: five Mavakan and one Oritakan
4	Subcommand Group: two Oritakan and three Mavakan
5	Swarm: four Norakan per Jackal
6	Hunters in the Tunnels: four Tsutakan

Every two failures inflict 1d4 Mettle damage on the Jackals, due to the exhaustion of working their way through the tunnels. Whether the Jackals succeed or fail at the test, they move to The Cavern in the Deep.

2. The Cavern in the Deep

What a Jackal's senses reveal:

Sights – a faint, blood-red glow fills the cave, emanating from a broad, silver bowl that sits on a rock ledge. A dark liquid fills the bowl.

Smells – the foetid smell of unwashed Takan trapped in a small space, with a coppery stench underneath.

Sounds – chanting by the Mavakan priests.

A. Upper Ledge

This small ledge overlooks the rites the Takan are performing next to the Heart of Belih. Jackals can only access it by succeeding at their trek through the tunnels.

B. Broad Path

This is the primary access way for Takan to head into the tunnels from this cavern. There are hints of stairs here along the path, but the centuries of Takan using them have worn them down.

C. Council Chamber

This broad cavern is where Ozamog sheltered the bulk of his forces during Sameel's raids for the past decade. Now, it is the Oritakan's war council and site of the rituals with the Heart of Belih. Ozamog, his retinue of three Mavakan, and Sanghulhaza are currently here, gathered around table that holds a model of the ruins above. Ozamog and the human, who is garbed in a strange hauberk of black rings and a heavy boar tusk helm, speak in hushed tones as they plan their next attack on Sameel. This is also where the Takan commander keeps some of the spoils of his raids and war:

- 4,000 ss in various trade goods, jewellery, gems, and mouahalan coins
- *A Gerwa two-handed sceptre mace of exceptional quality:* +10% to Influence and Melee Combat, + 1 Clash Point.
- *The Horn of Yasafel:* this curled drinking horn is carved from the horn of a Yammim. The rim and plug are silver, and they call upon the light and the Law to re-establish those who drink from the horn within the arc of the world. This inscription is, strangely, written in Howls. The horn does a poor job of containing liquid, as the one holding it seems to always fumble with its weight and shape. To fill and drink from the horn, the person holding it must make a successful Athletics check. Those who drink from the horn recover 1d8 Wounds. However, the chaotic nature of the Yammim lingers, even after death. Anyone who drinks more than once a day has a cumulative 30% chance per additional drink of gaining Corruption equal to half the healing they receive.

D. Summit

Six Mavakan stand around this natural summit to the cavern. A stalagmite with its top sheared off serves as a pedestal, where rests a large silver bowl. Bodies of captured Luathi lie about the summit, their throats slashed. Six Mavakan chant over the silver bowl and occasionally bleed themselves into it, but the bowl never overflows.

E. Path to the Surface

The far side of the cavern leads up and back, beyond which is a tunnel to the surface, which emerges near the centre of the city.

If the Jackals successfully navigate the tunnels, they arrive in the cavern where the Heart of Belih lies without the Takan noticing. They emerge on the upper ledge (A) and can observe the cavern unseen.

If the Jackals fail to navigate the tunnels, they arrive in the cavern through the broad path (B), and the Takan spot them. Initiate the combat below immediately.

Fight in the Cavern

As soon as the fight begins, Ozamog's Mavakan (3) rush the Jackals and the human warrior (Sanghulhaza) turns and heads out of the northern tunnel. Howling in rage, Ozamog screams at the Mavakan priests (6) to aid him, before drawing his iron-studded whip, a gift from the Daughter Beneath the Earth, and trying to put an end to the troubling Jackals.

OZAMOG				
Type:	Takan		Location:	Bartak Kentak
			Wounds:	75
Defence:	70%		Protection:	5 (breastplate + shield)
Combat:	90%		Move:	14
Knowledge:	50%		Initiative:	15
Urban:	40%		Clash Points:	5
Common:	70%		Treasure Score:	3
			Corruption:	10

Special Abilities

Inured to Darkness: Ozamog suffers no penalties due to absence of light.

Commanding Presence: Ozamog's high-pitched howls and orders inspire the Takan. Each non-Oritakan Takan in the battle counts as having a trait that applies to their combat skills, as well as +5 Wounds.

Combat Range

1–15%	*Rallying Laughter:* Ozamog howls with laughter, exulting in the battle. Each Takan recovers 1d8 Wounds.
16–30%	*Flail of Ignorance (2 attacks):* up to two targets take 2d8 + 2d6 (16) damage each. Or Ozamog can inflict this damage on an ally to grant them a free attack at +15%.
31–55%	*Dance of Slaughter (multiple attacks):* Ozamog makes an attack on each adjacent enemy for 2d8+2d6 (16) damage each.
56–60%	*I Know Your Name:* Ozamog mimics the voice of a loved one or friend, sowing confusion. Each target must spend a Clash Point to make a difficult Willpower check. If they fail, the chaotic cry causes the target to spend an additional Clash Point to lash out at an ally.
61–90%	*Flay You Alive:* Ozamog lashes out with the whip, sticking the iron studs deep into the flesh of its target, before ripping it free. 4d8 (18) damage. The target must make a difficult Endurance check against Ozamog's initial attack or begin to bleed. At the start of each round, the target takes 2d6 (7) damage, which ignores Protection. If the bleeding inflicts more than 5 damage, the target is at –2 Clash Points for the round. Ozamog can spend 1 Clash Point to make this attack again against the same or a different target, up to three times per round.

MAVAKAN RETINUE

Type:	Takan	Location:	Bartak Kentak

Defence:	80%	Wounds:	45
Combat:	70%	Protection:	5 (breastplate + natural)
Knowledge:	40%	Move:	10
Urban:	40%	Initiative:	12
Common:	40%	Clash Points:	1.5
Intimidate:	75%	Treasure Score:	2
		Corruption:	10

Special Abilities

Inured to Darkness: the Mavakan suffers no penalties due to absence of light.

Howling Fury: the Mavakan possesses a barely contained fury, which it often releases in intimidating howls and other displays of aggression. This fury often causes lesser foes to flee. Once per battle, after inflicting damage, the Mavakan forces the target to make a difficult Willpower check. On a failure, the Mavakan inflicts 2d8 (9) Valour damage (normal combat rules for critical successes and fumbles apply). If this reduces the target to 0 Valour, the target must make a second Willpower roll or flee the combat for 2d4 rounds.

Combat Range

1–15%	*Glancing Blow:* the Mavakan strikes a glancing blow with its bronze weapon. 1d10 + 2d6 +4 (16) damage.
16–25%	Shield Bash: the Mavakan slams its shield powerfully into its target. 3d6 + 4 (14) damage. The target must make an Endurance check or lose 1d4 Clash Points. On a fumble, the target loses all Clash Points until their next turn.
26–55%	*Hammering Blows (2 attacks):* the Mavakan pummels its foes with brutal blows. 1d10 + 2d6 + 4 (16) damage each.
56–80%	*Ruining Strike:* the Mavakan's strength damages the armour of its targets. 2d10 + 2d6 + 4 (22) damage. Additionally, reduce the target's Protection by 2 points (4 on a critical success), as their shields and armour fail. Apply this damage to any shield the Jackal possesses first, then armour. A successful Craft roll after the battle allows a field repair and restores 2 points of lost Protection.

MAVAKAN PRIEST

Type:	Takan		Location:	Bartak Kentak
Defence:	80%		Wounds:	15
			Protection:	0
Combat:	70%		Move:	10
Knowledge:	40%		Initiative:	17
Urban:	40%		Clash Points:	1.5
Common:	40%		Treasure Score:	2
Intimidate:	75%		Corruption	10

Special Abilities

Inured to Darkness: the Mavakan suffers no penalties due to absence of light.

Howling Fury: the Mavakan possesses a barely contained fury, which it often releases in intimidating howls and other displays of aggression. This fury often causes lesser foes to flee. Once per battle, after inflicting damage, the Mavakan forces the target to make a difficult Willpower check. On a failure, the Mavakan inflicts 2d8 (9) Valour damage (normal combat rules for critical successes and fumbles apply). If this reduces the target to 0 Valour, the target must make a second Willpower roll or flee the combat for 2d4 rounds.

Ecstasy: the Mavakan is in an ecstatic rite, communing with the Heart of Belih, and will not defend itself.

Takan Rites: for every three Mavakan (or fewer) take one action below.

Takan Rites

Heal a Takan for 2d12 Wounds.

Grant 2d4 Clash Points to the Takan pool.

Provoke a hard Willpower check in a Jackal. If the Jackal succeeds, nothing happens. If they fail, increase the Clash Point cost any time the Jackal spends Clash Points by 1d4 until the end of the priests' next turn.

Force a Takan into a berserk rage. While it is in this state, reduce the Takan's Protection by 2 and its Combat skill by 25%, and increase its damage by +2d10 (11). At the end of the round, the Takan takes 1d8 damage. This effect lasts until the blood is spilled from the basin.

The Heart of Belih

The Heart of Belih is a large, shallow, silver basin, with the phases of the moons in intricate etchings along the edge. It is a Hulathi artefact, which the Daughter Beneath the Earth brought out of the west – during the fall of the blessed isle. Only the Daughter knows the basin's original uses – its current use is only one of three – but she taught Ozamog rites he finds advantageous. Ozamog used the heart to communicate with the Daughter Beneath the Earth (similarly to the bowls in **The Lost Children** and **Orsem Reclaimed**) and to spy on Sentem. This is how he knew about the coming raid.

The Heart has the following properties:

- When filled with water, the Heart reflects the Dream Road, and an invoker can use the Heart of Belih as a scrying bowl. For 5 Devotion Points, the invoker can view a location within 50 miles. They can see and hear the location as if they were standing there. Every additional 5 Devotion Points increases the range by 50 miles. For an additional 4 Devotion Points, the invoker can speak with someone they see in the bowl or speak broadly to anyone present.

- The Daughter also corrupted the Heart, turning its access of the Dream Road into a method of torment. When filled with blood, nightmares pour forth from the basin. These nightmares plague enemies of the invoker for a 10-mile radius. They suffer from lack of sleep, per the Nightmare Token rite (see *Jackals* page 87). Invokers can use this effect at the cost of 10 Devotion Points a day and by filling the basin with 15 Wounds' worth of blood a day. Invoking this ability inflicts 1d8 Corruption each day.

- Touching the bowl causes a brief connection between the Jackal and the Daughter. She can sense what is happening in the city and now knows who is behind it. The Daughter makes the Jackal an offer: make a covenant with her and receive power beyond their dreams – power to save their loved ones, and to forge a strong, bronze kingdom under a silver crown – or become marked for death. If the Jackal accepts, they are given a vision of the Daughter's fastness on the eastern slopes of the A'hule Asa and a command to bring her Sameel's head. Accepting this covenant immediately gives the Jackal 8 Corruption. If they refuse, they gain the Tsutakan's mark from a Marked for Death attack (see *Jackals* page 227).

Ozamog fights until it is clear the fight is turning against his Takan. Make morale checks as usual; when Ozamog fails his check, he attempts to flee into the deeper tunnels. If any of the priests are alive and see their commander fleeing, they incite him into a blood rage. This prevents Ozamog from fleeing unless someone disrupts the ritual by spilling the basin. If the Jackals slew the priests or disrupted the ritual, Ozamog flees, unless the Jackals choose to capture him.

When the Jackals leave the cave to go to the surface, proceed to Act 3.

ACT 3: THE FIGHT AT THE WELL

The tunnel out of the cavern leads the Jackals through many twists and turns, yet always with the hint of fresh air on the horizon. Soon, the muffled sounds of battle reach their ears. The tunnel ends in a solid brick wall, yet the Jackals can feel the movement of air. A hard Craft, Thievery, Lore, or Athletics check opens the secret passage, and deposits the Jackals in the cellar of a house much like the one through which they entered the tunnels days ago.

Upon exiting the house, the Jackals find they are near the centre of the ruins. The ziggurat in the centre of the city looms ahead. In the light of the setting sun, they can see the square before them – which holds one of the city's wells – is the site of a battle. Sameel, Ba-en Nafar (should he still live), and two of The Thirty battle for their lives against Sanghulhaza, a Gadakan, and a pair of Atakan.

Sameel and Sanghulhaza face off, while Ba-en Nafar and the two Luathi attempt to keep the Takan away from their master. The forces of Sentem have wounded the Takan (the Atakan start the fight at 41 and 37 Wounds, respectively, and the Gadakan at 50), but the fight will end soon unless the Jackals intervene. Use the round chart below to see how the NPCs act during the fight:

FIGHTING AT THE WELL	
Round	**NPC Actions**
1	Ba-en Nafar inflicts 10 Wounds (ignoring Protection) on one of the Atakan with his blades. The two Luathi drive their spears deep into the Gadakan for 15 Wounds total (ignoring Protection). The Gadakan, enraged, slays one of The Thirty with his own spear.
2	Ba-en Nafar inflicts 10 Wounds (ignoring Protection) on one of the Atakan with his blades. The Gadakan takes an additional 8 Wounds from the remaining Luathi before it slays them as well (should it be alive at this point).
3	Ba-en Nafar inflicts 10 Wounds (ignoring Protection) on one of the Atakan with his blades. However, one of Atakan (should either still stand) slays Ba-en Nafar.
4	Sameel knocks Sanghulhaza's boar tusk helm away, revealing his identity as Hirrom. Sameel is stunned by the revelation that his brother yet lives.
5	Sanghulhaza slays Sameel.
6	Sanghulhaza escapes.

SANGHULHAZA			
Type:	Humanoid	Location:	Bartak Kentak
Defence:	80%	Wounds:	100
Combat:	160%	Protection:	4 (hauberk)
Knowledge:	60%	Move:	15
Urban:	75%	Initiative:	18
Common:	70%	Clash Points:	6

Special Abilities

Fashioned Beyond the Shore: Sanghulhaza's arms and armour are a gift from the Daughter Beneath the Earth. The Smiths of Ouwathia Oulermo fashioned them at the height of their craft. His weapons may not be sundered, nor can his Protection be reduced in any fashion. However, if an attack ignores Protection, it still ignores his.

Rending Strike: Sanghulhaza can attempt to destroy an opponent's shield or armour. He must make an attack roll at half skill. If the Clash is successful, he reduces his opponent's shield or armour (in that order) by 2 Protection. If Rending Strike reduces armour to 0 Protection, it renders the item useless until a successful Craft roll is made during a seasonal action. Sanghulhaza inflicts half damage.

Skilful Strike: Sangulhaza can re-roll any damage dice with a result of '1'.

Combat Range

1–20%	*Flickering Blade:* Sanghulhaza flicks his blade out, drawing a thin line of blood the metal of his sword quickly absorbs. 2d12 (13) Valour damage (ignoring Protection) from a blow which does zero damage but instils fear in the target.
21–50%	*Flensing Strike (2 attacks):* Sanghulhaza cuts away a chuck of flesh from his target, delivering a deep and bleeding wound. 2d10 (11) damage each. The target must make a hard Endurance check or suffer 1d4 damage (which ignores Protection) at the start of their turn until they can bind their wounds. This bleeding effect stacks with other Flensing Strike attacks.
51–80%	*Sword Dance (3 attacks):* Sanghulhaza's sword is everywhere, dancing among the fighters, leaving death in its wake. 2d10 + 2d6 (18) damage each.
81–90%	*From Beyond Death:* the Daughter Beneath the Earth blessed Sanghulhaza's blade with rites unseen in this age of the world. 4d10 (22) damage and Sanghulhaza heals Wounds equal to the damage done.

Should Sanghulhaza drop below 15 Wounds, he cries out the name *"Wihatia!"* A bolt of lightning strikes from the clear night sky, slamming into Sanghulhaza and obliterating the well. The ground around the well collapses into itself, taking with it the body of Sameel's brother.

Once the fight at the well is concluded, proceed to the *Aftermath* section below.

If Japeth has fallen to tyranny, now is when he reveals his treachery. Warriors sent by Japeth enter the square, charging Sameel with the betrayal of Sentem and of Japeth. The leader gives the Jackals one chance to abandon Sameel before the warriors open fire with their bows. Depending on how the last two fights went for the Jackals, this could be a slaughter. Escape into the tunnels, or even abandoning Sameel, might be their only options.

AFTERMATH

There are several possible paths through this adventure.

Should the Jackals slay Ozamog, the forces of Sentem win the day. It takes another three weeks of fighting, and two seasons of ritual cleansing, but Bartak Kentak is rededicated as Eridu after the next Zadon's Week. Sameel (should he survive) plans to relocate the administrative power of Sentem to Eridu over the next few years. Japeth and Sameel offer the Gerwa and Trauj mercenaries, as well as the Jackals, places in Eridu. Halve the Establish Home seasonal action cost for these Jackals should they decide to build in Eridu. Sameel, should he survive, starts to rebuild The Thirty, offering places to his Jackal clients first.

If Ozamog survives, he flees to the Aeco Woods. Densom becomes plagued by Takan raids over the next three years, and Ozamog will burn Densom in five years if the Jackals do not stop him from raising the Black Tree banner again.

If the Jackals capture Ozamog, under torture over the next year, he reveals much about the existence of the Daughter Beneath the Earth – including the location of her resting place in the woods. It is a dark complex built by the Daughter's rites and servants from the Silent Lands. Who knows what the Jackals might find there?

If the Jackals fail to slay or capture Ozamog and Sameel dies, the Takan rally and push the forces of Sentem out of Bartak Kentak. The raid is a failure, and although there is plenty of blame to go around, the Jackals take a lion's share. No raids occur for the next decade, allowing the Takan the luxury of entrenching deeper into their old home. Within five years, Densom is a ghost town, as most of the townsfolk die from Takan raids or relocate to Sentem's walls. The southern end of the War Road becomes wilder and weaker for the coming war.

If Japeth slays Sameel, the official story is that Takan slew him in the final moments of taking the city, perhaps with his Jackal bodyguards. Japeth honours Sameel's wishes and renames the city after Sameel's son. Within the next season, however, the people of Sentem are introduced to a warrior Japeth promotes to Nawsi and proudly announces as his son, Hirrom. Both father and son are firmly under the Daughter's power, and Sentem grows darker and more brutal.

ADVANCEMENTS

- 1 for taking the gate, which also increases each Jackal's Kleos by 1
- 1 for slaying Ozamog
- 1 for saving Sameel

HOOKS

A Tower Under Siege: What is going on at Orsem Honess? The Jackals who investigate could become embroiled in Kroryla's attempts to annex the orsem. Or they could disappear without a trace for meddling.

The Scent of Prey: If the Jackals are cursed, they might find these curses draw spirits to them. What dark powers sense this and come to speak with the Jackals?

An Old Burial Site: The Daughter Beneath the Earth emerged from somewhere. Nabal would like to hire the Jackals to investigate rumours of the Daughter, while he searches for clues in the Hulathi tablets and scrolls at the Temple of the Morning Lord. There, he eventually discovers the Hulathi of Ouwa Ejo buried her alive in the Aeco Woods, at a place called 'Darkness Deserved'.

CHAPTER 7
YEAR OF GATHERED CLOUDS

My son, if you are owed a sum by a man of no means, split what is owed into three and forgive two of them. In doing so, you will be a good king.

My daughter, if a weak man holds something your kingdom requires, break him in the taking. In doing so, you will be a strong queen.

~ *The Instructions and Meditations of Fuenton IV, the Wise Tyrant*

INTRODUCTION

The Year of Gathered Clouds is Year 6 of *The Fall of the Children of Bronze* campaign and marks a difference in the format of the adventures going forward. There are no longer two adventures each year. As each growing power of the War Road turns to face each other, they focus on Tjaru, a fortress located near the centre of the coastal plains. Each moves to capture this fortress, sparking the events of the final five years. As such, each adventure is designed to be played by Jackals from either end of the War Road. There are notes and advice on how to tailor the adventures based on where the Jackals come from, but the adventures in and around Tjaru and the war are 'global' adventures, at least in relation to the War Road.

Additionally, the adventure frameworks below are a bit more fluid and flexible than the ones above. There are two reasons for this. First, Loremasters are at least six years into their game of *Jackals* at this point, which means their stories have developed differently from those outlined in the campaign, and their Jackals have made choices that echo in these stories. Second, although some choices are built into some of the preceding adventures, anticipating every outcome as the choices mount is nearly impossible. This campaign assumes the looming war is inevitable, and the looser story structure of the last five adventures gives Loremasters as much freedom as possible when approaching this arc of the campaign.

THEME

The theme of this year is the inevitable conflict between Ameena Noani and Sentem. Adventures, events, and hooks all point to Sari Phamea's need, in her mind, to claim the tin of Mayrah Vedil so her plan for a Luathi hegemony can continue safely. Sari Phamea fears what the lack of tin means for her city's future, and seeks to claim it out of self-interest, while Sentem, fearful of this move and acting out of pride and self-interest, moves to stop her. The key to both plans lies in taking the fortress of Tjaru, an old Gerwa fort which lies just south of the halfway point between Ameena Noani and Sentem.

The central conflicts for this year are the central conflicts in all wars – fear, resources, and pride. Both sides are fearful about what the other means to do with Mayrah Vedil's tin. Rather than come to some sort of agreement, they instead choose to see the coming war as inevitable and take steps that make it a self-fulfilling prophecy.

IMPORTANT NPCS

Sari Phamea: see *Jackals* page 186. The Sar of Ameena Noani has a vision: the Luathi people, free from the threat of the Takan and from reliance on foreign powers; all, of course, under the watchful guidance of Ameena Noani. To that end, she sets her eyes on Tjaru; and from there, the tin of Mayrah Vedil.

Sar Japeth: Japeth continues to worry about the threat from the north. Rumours surrounding Hirrom (and his death if the Jackals did not prevent it) concern him. Flush from a victory against the Takan at Eridu, Japeth seeks additional protection in the form of Tjaru. (This applies to Sameel if he is Sar of Sentem.)

Hen-he-net: the Gerwa trader is important to this story, as she often camps in the old Gerwa ruins of the War Road and knows quite a bit about them.

EVENTS IN THE NORTH

- Rumours of a Yammim trickle south out of the Vori Wastes. If a chaos serpent indeed moves, what does that bode for Ameena Noani? Additionally, if it could be slain, what riches could be gained?

EVENTS IN THE SOUTH

- A clan of the Nahunum of the mountains is spotted around Orsem Kitan. What are the giants doing near one of the old Hulathi forts?

RETIREMENT BENEFITS

If a player retires their Jackal in this year, their new Jackal gains +8 advancements due to the war on the horizon attracting mighty warriors from far and wide.

THE TAKING OF TJARU

An adventure for Welcomed Jackals, set during the month of Hamis, in the dry season.

OVERVIEW

The fortress of Tjaru is a Gerwa fortress, established in the same period as Mayrah Vedil. The fortress sits on a small tor and overlooks the coastal road. It was a city of the Takan during the days of Barak Barad, and fell during the Uprising, when the Takan put it to the torch rather than let it fall into Luathi hands. It remains uninhabited for three reasons. First, it sits far from the coast and the mountains. Although fortified, those fortifications need repair, and it is a hunting ground for Atakan and Retakan.

Second, there are few settlements in the area. Most of the Luathi villages and towns are closer to the mountains or further north and south, closer to other areas of civilisation.

Third, the site is haunted. In the closing days of the war, a long-forgotten Gerwa Kiani slew his Ketian prisoners as examples to prove Keta was broken. One of those prisoners was a Skesshic priest of Yasabah, and it let a powerful curse flow into its spilled blood to stain the stones of the fortress. The curse has several effects, the most recent being the luring of a Nyssalis to Tjaru. The beast roams the plains and is said to have claimed at least one of the Jackal packs a forgotten village hired to slay it. To claim the fortress, the Jackals must break this curse and deal with the Nyssalis.

ACT 1: THE NEEDS OF SARS

This adventure begins in the fortress of a Sar. Which fortress depends on the Jackals: it can be either Gilead or Yesim. The brokering of this meeting also depends on the Jackals. In the north, Toara introduces the Jackals to the austere court of Sari Phamea of Ameena Noani – perhaps for the first time. In the south, the Jackals are embedded in the lives of the Yesim family: Japeth, Sameel, or both are in attendance depending on the previous actions of the Jackals in this campaign. The scene in the north is described below, and the Yesim family continues to meet with the Jackals in the same hall as before (see page 85).

The court room of Ameena Noani lies in the Fortress of Gilead, in the heart of the city. At the far end of a colonnaded hall is the Bulls' Seat, a bronze throne topped with the three bulls of Ameena Noani. Arranged in a semi-circle from the throne are the chairs and stools of the Sar's council. However, this first meeting is small. Just Toara, Sari Phamea, and a few guards are in attendance, giving the hall an empty feeling. Toara makes her introductions, while Phamea listens intently, breaking the silence only to ask pointed questions about the Jackals' time on the War Road. Assume Sari Phamea knows all but the most intimate details of the Jackals' excursions. Her accuser (a combination advisor, spy, and prosecutor) is second to none when it comes to procuring information about the War Road, although few know the accuser's identity.

No matter which Sar meets with the Jackals, they relay the following information (themed for the appropriate end of the War Road):

- Each welcomes the Jackals and shares the tales of their exploits in the city.
- Each thanks the Jackals for all they have done for their end of the War Road.
- They explain that war looms on the horizon.
- Ameena Noani needs tin to survive.
    › The cost of lives and skill in claiming the dust of the Vori Wastes mounts each year.
    › The Takan raids grow worse, and bronze is needed to keep them out of the areas the Luathi claim.
    › The mines to the north, while rich, contain no tin.
    › The southern end of the War Road holds rich tin mines – Mayrah Vedil is the key example of this.
- Each Sar spins the events of two years ago differently.
- North: Ameena Noani wished to purchase tin from Mayrah Vedil, but Barqan of the city rebuffed its advances. Perhaps there is more tin in the area waiting to be claimed.
- South: Ameena Noani attempted to cut off Sentem's supply of tin and then attempted to kill Barqan for it when he refused.
- If Barqan is an Agent of Ameena Noani, Phamea uses that as the precedent for taking Tjaru, to protect Ameena Noani's interests.
- If Barqan is dead, the new Sar fills one of these roles, as the Loremaster sees fit.
- Something must be done to protect the city's interests. Each Sar sees the old fortress of Tjaru as the first step in this plan. Toara or Nabal fill the Jackals in on the pertinent information from the overview. The Sar would like the Jackals to investigate the possibility of taking the fortress in the name of their city, so they can establish a wilderness foothold to guard their interests. For this deed, the Sar is willing to pay each Jackal a talent of silver! They will be paid after they scout the fortress and investigate and deal with the rumours of the curse and the Nyssalis.
- Each Sar loans the Jackals a method of communicating with them. Toara loans the Jackals one of the tablets of the Scriptorium, whereas Japeth gives the Jackals the bronze brazier from Orsem Kitan, along with the rites Nabal established to use it.

If the Jackals agree to scout and take Tjaru, the Sar supplies them accordingly (with food, water, mules, and up to 500 ss of gear) and send them on their way. Toara asks them to keep an eye out for any active Gerwa rites or relics, whereas Nabal is interested in any Ketian artefacts the Jackals might sniff out for him.

The journey from Ameena Noani to Tjaru takes 10 days, whereas from Sentem it takes 5 days. The journey is along the coastal road and should be planned accordingly. When the Jackals reach Tjaru, proceed to Act 2.

ACT 2: TJARU ABOVE

The fortress of Tjaru sits atop the Aeco Plains. It is built deep into the stone of the hill, with walls extending high above it. Rubble and debris left behind when the Takan destroyed the city during the days of the Uprising choke the old ramp that once led up to the gates. Clearing or navigating a path is a challenge for the Jackals, as several treacherous surprises await them – both natural events and those of devious intent. The following obstacles lie in store for those who climb the path:

- Cyclopean stones block the path where the Takan pushed over the fortress wall onto the Luathi in the early days of the siege. Moving the stones out of the way, or scaling them, is the first obstacle. However, time has fractured the already damaged stones, and they are unstable. Each Jackal must make a difficult Athletics check to get over or past the rubble. Those who fail find the rock they are attempting to climb or move is weak, and breaks under the strain. The tumbling debris causes difficult damage (see *Jackals* page 159).
- Sinkholes abound on the trek – natural and parts of ancient traps left by the Gerwa and the Takan. These cause medium damage, directed against 1d4 random Jackals, and require a hard Dodge check to avoid.
- Annubi left active wards, known only to them, scattered throughout the gatehouse and the upper levels of Tjaru. They invoke them as part of their pilgrimage to Tjaru. When the Jackals enter a new area, there is a 35% chance it contains unseen wards. Spotting these wards requires hard Perception checks. A ritualist can attempt to deactivate a ward with a difficult Lore or Ancient Lore check. When a Jackal fumbles a skill check or fails to see a ward in an area, roll on the table below:

WARDS EFFECTS	
d6	Result
1–2	*Dead Ward:* the Jackal steps somewhere they should not, but the ward fails to ignite. Whether this is due to age, duplicity, or simple failure is unclear.
3	Bone-deep Fear: the ward grips the Jackal with a powerful fear of Tjaru. They suffer a loss of 4 Mettle for the remainder of their time in Tjaru, even if the ward is later deactivated.
4	*Anu's Touch:* nothing happens the moment the Jackal trips the ward; it appears to be dead. However, Anu caresses the Wounds of the Jackal when they suffer them, causing them to bleed for an additional 1d4 (3) damage, which ignores Protection. This bleed effect lasts only one round, but it occurs each time the Jackal suffers Wounds. This curse lasts until the Jackal takes an Atonement seasonal action – instead of removing Corruption, it removes the curse.
5	*Damage Burst:* with a hiss, the ward flares with light and damages the Jackal and those within a 10-cubit radius. The Jackal who triggered the ward takes 2d10 (11) damage, and those within the radius take 1d10 (6) damage as energies flare from the ward. A hard Dodge check allows the targets to take half damage (or zero damage on a critical success).
6	*Trapped!* The ward flares and the Jackal is gone! The Jackal is stuck between Kalypsis and the Silent Lands. A ritualist may attempt to bring them back with another Lore or Ancient Lore check. On a success, the Jackal returns unharmed. A failed skill check brings back the Jackal (albeit with 1d12 (7) Wounds), but also fails to close the door. That Jackal is cursed and plagued by spirits, the Dead, and Rathic for a year and a day, or until the ward is deactivated.

The Curse

The curse of Tjaru is a subtle one. Invoked by a sankunniyant (tender or priest) of Yasabah (one of the Skesshic deities), the curse settled in the ground of Tjaru. The wording of the curse is lost to the ages, but the effect is simple: nothing that walks upon two legs and reveres the sun can rest here. Their wounds do not heal, sleep eludes them, and their dead bodies rise again. None of these effects is immediately noticeable; however, for each month a person stays within the walls of Tjaru, they have a cumulative 10% chance of succumbing to the curse. In such cases, the following happens:

- Should the person die within the walls of Tjaru, their body and spirit return as one of the Dead.
- Sleep is less restful than it should be and provides none of its usual benefits.
- Healing is impossible in Tjaru. Wounds continue to bleed and fester, even with magical healing or acalana resin.

Breaking the curse is no simple action. Its power seeped into the stones of Tjaru and lingered there for centuries. No one alive knows what caused it or how to break it. There are three major links that bind the curse to Tjaru:

- First is the charnel pit on the north side of Tjaru's walls. This is where the sankunniyant brought down the initial curse. It is outside a sally-port on the north wall (see below). Below this space, at the base of the hill upon which Tjaru rests, is the charnel pit. There, the bones of the sankunniyant are mixed with the bones of Takan victims, slaves, and others. Putting the bones to actual rest requires two days of work and purification rites, which any invoker can enact with a Lore check and the spending of 10 Devotion Points for the whole pit.
- Second is the altar to Zadon. Here, the Takan built their unholy altar and stained it with the blood of Luathi. The pain, suffering, and death poured onto it served as a magnet for the initial curse. A Culture (Luathi) check reveals the typical way to destroy such altars: shatter it from its moorings, break it into a least 12 large pieces, and haul those pieces into the sun. The altar is basalt and, therefore, difficult to break (see *Jackals* page 69). Once the Jackals strike the first blow against the altar, it draws a pack of Retakan to itself for protection [one Retakan per Jackal – one of which wears a tarnished silver necklace worth 57 shekels]. After exposure to the sun from sunrise to sunset, the magics dissipate and the link is broken.
- The third and final link is the Nyssalis below the fortress. The curse lured this creature of chaos into the bowels of the fortress. A cleft in the cliffs allows it ingress, a piece of knowledge the Jackals would do well to discover before handing Tjaru over to their Sar. The Takan of the fortress bring offerings, and the Nyssalis often hunts wild ox or the occasional caravan out on the plains. Slaying a Nyssalis is no mean feat; doing so breaks the third link in the curse.

Should the Jackals break all three links, the curse slowly dissipates over the next year. By that time, the effects of the curse fade from all who dwell within Tjaru.

I. The Gatehouse

No enemy ever managed to breach the massive gates of Tjaru. It was the Takan who destroyed the great gates, choking the gatehouse with rubble from the inner fortress. It is unknown who or what pulled the massive blocks that once blocked access to Tjaru free, but their size is staggering. The gatehouse complex is typical Gerwa work, and an integral part of the defence of Tjaru. The gatehouse contains two chambers and likely held three gates during its heyday. Now, it is the resting place of a pack of Retakan that worship Tjaru as *omprak tegal* ('the sheltering darkness'). They notice any of the Jackals' failed attempts to scale the ramp and lie in ambush in the second chamber.

Use one Retakan per Jackal.

In the small guard station just off the second chamber, the Retakan have a nest. It contains the loot from their raids:

- 670 ss worth of worked goods:
  - › 100 ss in baskets and wooden products of Densom
  - › 500 ss in tin ore from Mayrah Vedil
  - › 70 ss in dry grain and wine from Sentem
- A set of leather vambraces, with a strange orange gem set in the leather over the wrist on the left one. A Luathi used Yammim scales to make the armour, and the gem is an eye he took from one of the Yammim's heads. The gem heats up in the presence of items and people with greater than 15 Corruption, warning the wearer of their presence. Additionally, they add 1d4 damage to Melee attacks per 5 Corruption points the target possesses.

2. The Walls

The walls of Tjaru stand 8 cubits thick and over twice that tall, with a 6-cubit ditch carved into the bedrock at their base. Time and weather have filled the ditch with debris, which the Jackals must clear for the defensive structure to become usable. Bastions stand out from the wall every 100 cubits. From their heights, the Jackals have a commanding view of the Aeco Plains. Far to the south, the Jackals can make out the settlement of Mayrah Vedil. Bones of Takan and humans litter the walls, bleached white and transitioning to dust from exposure to the Zaharets' sun. Although the walls are in good shape, there are parts which need to be shored up. Cracks in the façade indicate deeper issues, and some of the sections contain dangerous areas where small sections threaten to collapse (use the sinkholes above to approximate this danger.) Embrasures mark the wall along its course at regular intervals overlooking the ramp.

Additionally, the north wall holds the curse that festers in Tjaru. Here, the Jackals find the sally-port that leads to the sacrificial ledge, where the Kiani of Tjaru slew the Ketian prisoners. Finding and accessing the sally-port is difficult, as the heat of the fires the Takan set within the city sealed it. A difficult Craft, Lore, Culture (Gerwa), or Perception check enables the Jackals to work out where the Gerwa would slay their enemies and learn of the existence of such ports. An Athletics, Craft, or Thievery check is necessary to open the port. Beyond the port is a large, natural shelf, over 100 feet in the air. The wide rock ledge provided a perfect place from which to cast prisoners or kill them within view of besiegers. Below it, at the base of the cliff, is the charnel pit (see above). Invoking See the Unseen grants a vision of a snake-like creature falling from this ledge, hissing dark and potent words as it falls to its death.

3. The Well

Six wells dot the inner courtyard, where the remains of the Takan structures lay in ruin from age and flame. The wells provided water for the fortress and its soldiers; at this point, only two have collapsed. The remaining four still pull water, although rot claimed their ropes and buckets long ago. The presence of the Nyssalis fouled the two on the eastern site of the fort. Should a Jackal drink from either of those wells, they must make a hard Endurance check. On a failed check, they take 1d12 Wounds, twice that on a fumble, and half that on a success. Each of the wells is large enough for two people to climb down at the same time, providing access to Tjaru Below (see below).

4. The Town

The remnants of the Takan town lie outside the inner fortress. The fire they set consumed nearly all evidence of their presence in Tjaru, save for the foundations. The Sars will need this wreckage cleared before the fortress can truly be re-manned. Within the wreckage, Jackals can discover signs of Barak Barad: mouahalan coins (800), a pair of mouahalan heavy fighting blades stamped with the image of a black tree, and several votives altogether worth 200 ss to a non-Luathi merchant.

5. The Inner Fortress

The impressive inner keep has housed Gerwa Kiani, Oritakan warlords, and even stranger folk over the centuries. A companion fortification to the outer walls, the inner fort is broken up into eight sections that house the barracks, temples, and administrative facilities. The inner fortress possesses secret doorways that allowed the fortress commanders to access the cisterns of Tjaru Below (see below). A hard Perception check allows Jackals to notice one of these doorways (taking them to a random cistern below). Currently, it is home to a Gerwa Hekas and her bodyguards. Iset, the Hekas, travelled to Tjaru seeking information about Ger's past. She believes the Kiani who built and ruled from Tjaru became Mernptah the Eighth, the Great Unifier. She scours the inner fortress seeking some piece of knowledge that can provide the insight she needs to find Mernptah's tomb. Iset hopes that if she can find Mernptah's tomb, her patron, Neferu, can unify Ger under strong leadership and allow the nation to take its rightful place in the world once more.

She stays in the area assigned to the fort commander while her people explore Tjaru. She spends most of her time in the temple to the Eight, trying to decipher mosaics by torch light and glean the knowledge she desires. (Studying these cosmological images and the history of the Ketian wars for an hour grants the Jackals +5% to Ancient Lore.)

The information Iset seeks does not reside in Tjaru, as the unnamed Kiani of Tjaru is not Mernptah. However, should any of the Jackals look at Iset's notes, they might recognise their *Family Heirloom* or a feature from their *Treasure Map*. If these features have not yet come up in the campaign, they hold the key to finding the lost tomb of Mernptah in Jehumma's Gap to the south. Despite the strangeness of her party, Iset has no interest in starting a fight. She is warm to Gerwa Jackals and is comfortable and open with them. Should the Jackals be willing to talk, she can relate the following information:

- Her allies helped get her into Tjaru; the Takan do not bother the Annubi and those of Anu's path have secret ways into Tjaru.
- She wants to finish her research and return to the south, to civilisation.
- As a Hekas, Iset connects with the Jackals' outsider nature and discusses Tjaru.
- She is keenly interested in what the Jackals want with the old fortress.

- She is here in Tjaru seeking information from the past.
- She will tell a Gerwa Jackal that her mistress, the High Priestess Neferu, seeks the tomb of the Great Unifier for a plan to quell the independent Kianis.
- Her companions know of darkness below, and have kept her from disturbing it, physically or spiritually.
- She can relate the story of the sankunniyant's cursing of Tjaru and how it fell into disuse within several decades after the Kiani won the battle. She can also point the Jackals in the direction of the charnel pit.
- She informs them of the tunnels beneath Tjaru – where supplies, water, and other necessities were kept.
- She does not know how to access the tunnels beneath Tjaru. Anarak, her Annubi guard, told her his people closed the access points long ago. Nahi and Bet, the twin Adepts, believe that if they could access Tjaru Below, they could find a way to reopen the lower gates.

Should a fight break out, use Iset, two Adepts of Anu, and two Annubi.

ISET			
Type:	Human	Location:	Tjaru, Ger
Defence:		Wounds:	60
Combat:	45%	Protection:	2 (leather armour)
Knowl-edge:	60%	Move:	13
	90%	Initiative:	15
Urban:	60%	Clash Points:	4
Com-mon:	85%	Treasure Score:	4
		Corruption:	3

Special Abilities	
Hekas Rites: Iset has access to all the rites of the Hekas listed in Jackals (pages 84–87).	

Combat Range	
1–30%	*Dagger:* Iset lashes out with an imbued dagger. 4d4 + 4 (14) damage.
31–50%	*Dust of Geb (rite invocation):* Iset blows the Dust of Geb into the face of her target. The target takes 3d6 (11) damage, which ignores Protection. A successful Endurance check against Iset's attack roll reduces the damage taken by half, or to zero for a critical success.
51–60%	*Unguent of the Ukuku:* Iset brings forth a small jar and throws or smashes it on her target. The jar is filled with a thick unguent, which immediately begins to smear and sting. 2d12 + 2d6 (20) damage. The unguent burns the flesh and is highly flammable. As an action, Iset can set the target alight with a torch, causing the target to burn for 1d6 rounds, causing 4d12 (24) damage at the start of each of their turns.

Once the group decides to descend into Tjaru Below, continue to Act 3.

ACT 3: TJARU BELOW

There are three ways into Tjaru Below. The first is through the wells, the second is through the Nyssalis' exit in the cliff base, and the third is through the hidden cistern access (see above). The Jackals can attempt to discover the exit by spending time around the base of Tjaru; however, it is cunningly hidden. It was once one of the Deep Gates (see below) which the Nyssalis worked open. Spending an hour looking around the base of the cliff allows the Jackals to find the entrance with a successful hard Perception check. Should they discover it, they are able to enter Tjaru Below, near The Lair.

What a Jackal's senses reveal:

Sights – completely dark. With a light source, the Jackals can see the worked stone of non-human construction. The halls stand nearly 12 cubits tall and are broad. Rats scurry across the floor, spiderwebs cling to the walls, and the rotting remains of unidentifiable creatures adorn the larger chambers. Some seem to have been placed there, arranged in an offertory pattern. Others seem to have been haphazardly left behind.

Smells – cool, damp air with a foetid tang. Foulness.

Sounds – dripping water, shuffling in the dark, and the sound of something large moving from time to time.

1. The Cisterns

The wells descend into one of three large cisterns that collect the water Tjaru needs to survive a protracted siege. The last 15 feet of the descent is into open air, requiring the Jackals to descend by rope. Should any Jackal fall while descending the well, they take only 1d8 (5) damage from the bumps and bruises along the fall inside the well, as the water breaks their fall. However, should the Jackals fall into the eastern cistern, they discover the Nyssalis' venom has fouled the water. Jackals who fall into or drink from the water must make a hard Endurance check. On a failed check, the target suffers 3d12 (19) damage and loses 2d4 Clash Points for 1d4 rounds, due to the pain of the poison. On a success, the damage, Clash Point penalty, and duration are halved. Falling into this cistern alerts the Nyssalis to the Jackals' presence.

Each cistern has access to the fort via a set of stairs that spiral up the side of the walls. This was to ensure the commanders of the fort could accurately estimate their water reserves. The cisterns are all full, from centuries of collection. Each cistern holds approximately 130,000 gallons, enough for a thousand soldiers to hold Tjaru for a year.

2. The Halls

The passages and rooms beneath Tjaru are myriad. The Gerwa used them to store provisions and weapons, as additional barracks, and eventually as homes for soldiers and their families. Currently they are home to many creatures that love the cool and the dark. For each hour of exploration, there is a 25% chance the Jackals encounter something in the halls. Roll a d6 on the Tjaru Below Encounter Table to see what they stumble across. Roll for treasure normally for these encounters.

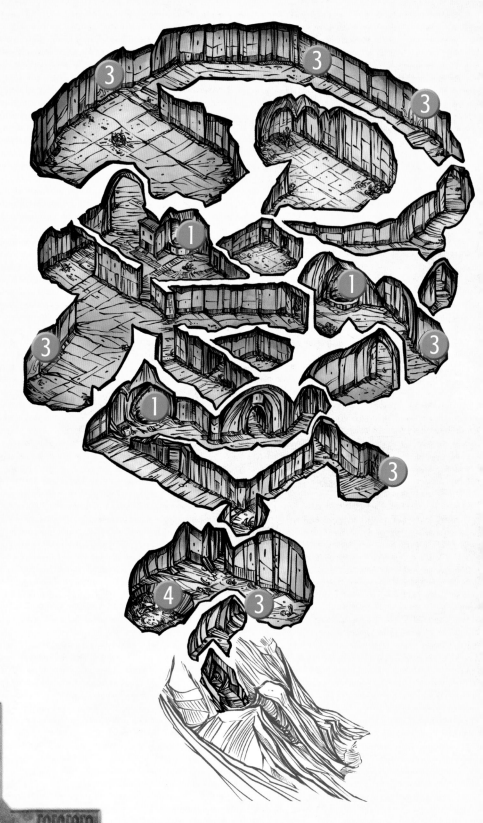

TJARU BELOW ENCOUNTER TABLE	
d6	Encounter
1–2	*Dangerous Webs:* two Ankabar per Jackal
3	*Poisonous Nest:* one Aburrisanu, plus one per Jackal
4	*Ambush!:* three Norakan per Jackal
5	*Blood in the Darkness:* one Retakan for every two Jackals
6	*Altar of Zadon:* see below

The Takan keep the Altar of Zadon in the Halls. Finding the altar requires a Survival or Perception check to determine its location, or a result of 6 on the Tjaru Below Encounter Table. Three Atakan crouch around the altar, casting out their worship into the night. The thing itself is a rough carving of a throne, about 4 cubits tall, topped with a bone crown and several Luathi necklaces (worth 200 ss), and stained with blood. See The Curse above for ways in which the Jackals can break the curse and deal with the altar.

3. The Deep Gates

The Gerwa did not build Tjaru Below, as evidenced by the cisterns and the halls. It is the work of Nahunum hands. Once, a great city stood here – home to many clans of Nahunum. They worked their gates into the stone of the hill, cunningly crafted and hidden, so that when they were closed, they were invisible and as inviolate as the rock of the hill. Seven of these gates exist; the Gerwa used them as sally-ports. The doors are evident from inside Tjaru. Each door is carved with the image of a great wave rising from the base of the door. On the western gates, ships carrying warriors can be seen in the carvings. The doors require little effort to open, once the Jackals remove the massive bars of iron that hold them. These bars sit 6 cubits up on the doors and weigh close to 400 lbs each. Removing them is a feat of strength, requiring a hard Athletics check. The south gate is unbarred and is the entrance the Nyssalis uses. Jackals find the remains of lions, humans, and other inhabitants of the plains near this gate.

4. The Lair

This is where the Nyssalis lives. It knocked down several walls, creating a large space for itself, and nested on the rubble. The beast is currently sleeping, unless the Jackals fell into the waters of the cistern or have made other noise, such as having a battle or encounter nearby. In such cases, make a Common Skill group check to determine whether the noise woke the Nyssalis. A Nyssalis is a dangerous foe – one the Jackals should take seriously, as it can kill even the most experienced travellers of the War Road.

Once the Jackals slay the Nyssalis, they can return to their Sar. Proceed to the *Aftermath* section.

AFTERMATH

Upon the Jackals' return, if they slayed the Nyssalis, the Sar is pleased. They shower the Jackals with feasts and rewards (something worth 1,000 ss and a well-crafted piece of Luathi equipment). The Sar immediately begins to send troops and craftspeople to Tjaru to renovate the fortress. Within the year, they man Tjaru, and the Zaharets moves one step closer to war.

As an additional reward for such a great service, Loremasters are free to wave the shekel cost of the Acquire Patron seasonal action this year with the appropriate Sar, and halve the cost of the Establish Home seasonal action if the Jackals establish in Tjaru.

However, if the Jackals did not break the curse, it takes hold of the new occupants soon after they occupy the fort.

ADVANCEMENTS

- 1 for taking Tjaru
- 1 for cleansing the curse
- 1 for slaying the Nyssalis, which also increases each Jackal's Kleos by 1

HOOKS

Messengers on the War Road: The Sars must gather aid from every corner of their Luathi holdings. In the north, Phamea sends Jackals to Mikro and Rataro, while in the south, Japeth does the same with Densom and other villages north of Sentem. Councils of war are held, and Jackals are needed as both messengers and protectors for leaders travelling the Takan-infested roads.

The Emissaries: The Sar needs mercenaries and allies to hold Tjaru. Sari Phamea sends emissaries to Kroryla, not knowing how Glykera will receive them. Jackals who have ties to the Melkoni are perfect for this. Sari Phamea might even be willing to let the troublesome Orsem Honess go in exchange for aid in holding Tjaru. Sar Japeth (or Sameel) turns south towards Ger and the southern tribes of the Trauj in a similar fashion.

Rivers to the People: The reclamation of Tjaru requires more than just warriors. The Sar needs to gather craftspeople, supplies, and other materials. They send Jackals out as envoys and guards for caravans and craftspeople and give them numerous other tasks to shore up and rebuild Tjaru. Perhaps they are sent to find Hen-he-net to entice the merchant to add Tjaru to her route.

Beyond the Walls: Clearing the area surrounding Tjaru is a task in and of itself. Annubi dwell not far from the fortress, seeing it as a holy site. Anu's Adepts often visit it for much the same reason.

A Forgotten Tomb: Iset wants to hire the Jackals to seek out Mernptah's Tomb.

CHAPTER 8
YEAR OF CORDED ARMS

Rejoice, ye of the Zaharets, for the blessed times have come.
The Sar ascends, on the car of glory, the son of Light –
Peace and order flow from his train and thunder and fire from his hands.
Rejoice, ye of the Zaharets, for the blessed times have come again;
Truth overcomes falsehood in the eyes of the king,
Darkness is cast away, and the flood waters retreat to their proper place,
For the Sar ascends, on the car of glory, the son of Light

~*Psalm of Victory*, **a maskil, a song of Kaom the Debarite**~

INTRODUCTION

Last year, the Jackals opened Tjaru for their Sar. In the intervening months, they helped establish the fort as a viable location for the Luathi. The population begins to swell as Tjaru prepares for war. In this adventure, the Jackals protect caravans coming to Tjaru, meet the new Nawsi of Tjaru, and have their first clash with the Luathi who oppose their Sar's designs.

THEME

The theme of the year of Corded Arms is us versus them. The Sars of the War Road are on a path of war, one that will lead to the unification of the Luathi in the Zaharets. The way through is paved in blood and bone. Both Sars are too independent to submit, and the move to claim Tjaru was the point of no return. Skirmishes break out, and it is only a matter of time before Luathi blood is spilt by Luathi blades.

Still, the Takan remain the true "them". These inhuman beasts are the physical manifestation of the chaos and darkness which threatens the Zaharets and all humanity. Next year, the Jackals once again turn towards their ancient foes and decide whether to stand against them or use them for their own gain.

IMPORTANT NPCS

Deborah of the Torch, Nawsi of Tjaru: A former Jackal, who is now a highly placed agent for the Sar's court, Deborah is known for being a canny warrior and gifted scholar. The songs attributed to her and about her exploits are numerous. She wears the scars of her story along her forearms and across her face. As Tjaru's Nawsi, she is loyal to the Sar, and will see Tjaru stand in the face of those who oppose it. She knows of the Jackals, and she will use them to these ends. [Note: Loremasters, this is a perfect position for a retired Jackal to step into, if appropriate.]

EVENTS IN THE NORTH

- Nawsi Namar retires after a Takan raid on Orsem Yahan. The Nawsi lost much of his leg defending the wall from the scaling Mavakan. It is unclear who Sari Phamea will send to replace him. Perhaps a retiring Jackal?
- Glykera breaks ground on a new village to the north of Kroryla. The unnamed town is on the western slopes of the Vori Vana.

EVENTS IN THE SOUTH

- The city of Eridu throws its gates open to all settlers. The Sar of Sentem welcomes all newcomers with the promise of aid and land for settling.

EVENTS ANYWHERE

- The year is unseasonably hot and dry. It does not affect crops this year, but the folk grumble at the possibility of another year like this.
- Caravans bring rumours of migrating Trauj.

RETIREMENT BENEFITS

If a player retires their Jackal in this year, their new Jackal gains +3 advancements due to the pack's renown attracting highly skilled Jackals. They start with a level 2 home in the city of their choice, representing the call to war spreading through the populace.

THE WAY THROUGH

An adventure for Favoured Jackals, set during the month of Ebre, in the dry season.

OVERVIEW

New challenges await those who dwell in Tjaru. The Sar of the city needs the Jackals to deal with everything from raids by the Moon Mask tribe of Takan to skirmishers in the plains. Additionally, the Sar has appointed a new Nawsi, Deborah of the Torch, who has more insight into the long-term goals of the fort. Knowing the other side of the War Road is putting agents into the field, Deborah sends the Jackals out into the plains to scout, which leads to the first true skirmish of what will eventually be called the War of Unification.

ACT 1: ALL ALONG THE WAR ROAD

For months, the Jackals have guarded the paths from their city to Tjaru against sorties from Takan skirmishers and those from the other end of the War Road. Tjaru receives word that Takan are harassing a caravan holding much-needed supplies, and the Jackals must head out to aid them. From the north, the wagon holds Hasheers and materials to strengthen the walls of Tjaru with wards; from the south, it holds a brazier of sending, a new redsmith, and bronze for the foundry established in Tjaru.

The Takan of the Moon Mask tribe target the caravans not for their goods, but for their seklah – their people.

Use one Oritakan, one Gadakan, two Atakan, four Mavakan, and six Norakan. Among those who fight are Deborah, the new Nawsi of Tjaru. She rallies the caravanners to circle the wagons, takes swings at Takan who get too close, and shouts orders to the Jackals. She can grant 1d4 Jackals one of the following bonuses each round:

DEBORAH'S BONUSES	
d6	Effect
1	Look Out: +2 Clash Points
2	Don't Just Stand There: restore 3d8 (13) Valour
3–4	Get Them: +4 damage for the round
5	Stand Your Ground: +1 Protection
6	I've Got This One: 4d8 damage to a random enemy as she spears it

The caravan contains a half-dozen wagons, including Hen-he-net's. When the Jackals have time to speak with the caravan, they learn the following information:

- The war effort continues to grow in both cities.
- Mercenaries, Jackals, and volunteers are responding to the call for war.
- Sentem opened Eridu's gates to settlers from Ger, Jackals, and the Trauj. They expect to enlist fresh soldiers from among the settlers.
- The Moon Mask tribe continues to cause trouble for the middle paths of the War Road. They are growing in number and answer to an Oritakan by the name of Shargot.
- Most of the merchants and craftspeople are heading to Tjaru because the Sar is paying good silver to get it up and running.
- From the north: the Hasheer, Abishai, leads the Scriptorium representatives, if she survived the events of Mealil's outbreak. She is quite excited to see the Jackals again and looks forward to working with them. The Hasheers refined some of their warding rites and seek to apply them to the walls of Tjaru to strengthen them. Also, if the Jackals failed to break the curse, Abishai and her Hasheers are there to attempt it. She leans on the Jackals for such matters, as she has in the past.
- From the south: the new redsmith is none other than Taom, son of Gan, the redsmith of Sentem (see **The Lost Children** in *Jackals*). He is excited to see the Jackals, and to start his new position in the fort. He mentions that he learned his craft not only from his father, but from Kahar Nabal, who taught him techniques discovered within the Temple of the Morning Lord. He is working on several pieces and would be glad to show them to the Jackals once he is settled in Tjaru.

When Deborah finishes ensuring the caravan is safe, she speaks with the Jackals:

- She greets each of them by name and reputation. She tells them how highly the Sar speaks of them.
- She is the new Nawsi of Tjaru, on her way there to take command. She hopes the Jackals continue to work with the fort and with her.
- The Sar's plan for the region require a lot of resolve, but loyalty will be rewarded.
- In fact, she will pay the Jackals 600 ss once they get to the fort, as a token of appreciation for the caravan duty.
- She plans to ride ahead and would appreciate the Jackals taking over the caravan escort for the last leg of the trip.
- She answers any questions they have to the best of her ability, save for any about the Sar's plans for Tjaru. *"Those questions are best answered within the walls of Tjaru."*

The caravan is still a day out from Tjaru. Should the Loremaster wish, they can add another encounter along the road – one with the Takan or the Dead of the Aeco Plains would not be out of place. When the Jackals get to Tjaru, proceed to Act 2.

ACT 2: WITHIN AND WITHOUT

Tjaru continues to grow. New homes and merchant stalls fill the courtyard, and the inner fortress' renovations are nearly complete. Guards move about the fort and along its walls, and redsmiths mount the last of the great hinges of Tjaru's new gates. There is now enough of an economy that Jackals can purchase any of the gear from *Jackals* here in the fort. Once the redsmith gets established, they may commission gear, as well.

Taom: specialises in spears, axes, and leather armour. He can add +2 damage, +5% Melee Combat, or +10% Influence to weapons, and +1 Protection or +5% Stealth to leather armour.

Gailious: a Melkoni redsmith from Ameena Noani, he specialises in spears, shields, and breastplates. His gear is heavy, with +1 Encumbrance, but is of fine quality. He can add +2 damage or +10% Melee Combat to spears, +2 Protection to shields, and +10% Athletics or +5% Dodge to breastplates.

When the Jackals arrive, Tjaru heralds them with cheers. New caravan arrivals mean more supplies and a better chance Tjaru continues to thrive. Word soon reaches the Jackals that Deborah wants to see them. She has set up her space inside the inner fortress. When the Jackals arrive, Deborah is unpacking her gear inside the fortress commander's barracks. She continues to do so as she speaks with the Jackals. She relates the following information:

- Deborah reiterates her thanks for the Jackals' aid. She suspects there will be more raids on the fort and its caravans over the coming seasons, and not just from Takan.
- She pays the Jackals the 600 ss she promised them.
- Rumour has it the other side of the War Road has organised sorties, as well.
- She suspects war will reach Tjaru within the year.
- In response to any questions about peace, she says, *"I think the time for that has passed. Soon, both will command armies. Our job here is twofold: ensure our side wins, and ensure it does so quickly. The longer the battle goes on, the weaker both sides will be afterwards. We must ensure our hold on the War Road remains intact."* Which is why the Jackals are here. She has plans and wants to include them.

- She needs eyes out in the plains to see what the other side is doing. Deborah is careful not to call other Luathi 'the enemy'.
  - › If the Jackals took the fort for Ameena Noani, she wants them to scout Mayrah Vedil, enter the town, and see what is happening. It is the closest city, and she wants to see what Japeth and Sameel are doing. Some reports say Barqan has a thousand warriors or more in the city.
  - › If the Jackals took the fort for Sentem, she wants them to head to Mayrah Vedil and search the area around it for northern scouts. She suspects Sari Phamea will put Jackals on the plains, as Mayrah Vedil is her goal.
- She promises to pay good silver for any information they recover, starting with another 500 ss just for going to Mayrah Vedil.

Mayrah Vedil

Mayrah Vedil lies three days away from Tjaru, requiring one travel check. Once the Jackals arrive at Mayrah Vedil, they might want to scout the surrounding area, investigate the town, or speak with the Sar. No matter which side of the War Road claims the Jackals' loyalty, there are those in Mayrah Vedil who oppose them.

North: the Razored Fangs are Japeth's trusted pack. They are keeping a wary eye on all new and known packs who arrive in Mayrah Vedil, as they know that Sari Phamea might slip them into the city to spy for her.

South: scouts from the north are surveying the city and have been doing so for a month. They have yet to find the exit points along the wall, but they know something strange is going on in the mines. Additionally, one merchant is in Sari Phamea's employ, a Luathi named Hephzi-Bah. She is a retired charioteer from Ameena Noani, and Phamea set her up as a trader along the War Road as a reward for her career. She is fiercely loyal to Phamea, and she sends messages north on small clay tablets hidden within her wagons. Hephzi-Bah is currently hiding two spies in her house, who await the night of the third Fireday of this month, when the darkness will allow them to sneak into the mines.

Beyond the Wall

The plains around the walls of Mayrah Vedil are strangely bare. Perception or Survival checks reveal freshly cut grasses, cropped short to the point of burning under the seasonal sun. Also, what few trees grew here were chopped down, and the flocks that once grazed are nowhere to be seen. It is as if the city contracted and pulled within its walls. The view from the walls is unobstructed for miles.

- Survival checks reveal the presence of many tracks, both human and animal. Many of them head into the city from the south, and only a few head back south. Those that do are wagon tracks. However, there are strange things afoot in the area.
  - › There are many muddied tracks, ones which cannot be read easily (see below).
  - › There are a few tracks that seem to be close to the walls and head around the city. The Jackals can discover the remains of small campsites – with no fires – concealed about a mile out from the city.
- Perception checks reveal at least a dozen guards atop Mayrah Vedil's walls, along with barrels at regular intervals.

- Lore checks reveal there is something wrong with the tracks, it is almost as if the party was attempting to hide its numbers. With a critical success, the Jackal determines Takan are moving about the plains, disguising their passage on the well-travelled roads.
  › Survival checks then enable the Jackals to track the Takan back to several tunnel entrances and mountain paths. They are all marked with the Moon Mask.

Within Mayrah Vedil

Mayrah Vedil has grown since its description in in Chapter 4. Sentem reinforced it with a group of Trauj mercenaries of the Ashan Haluzanrab, who work for bronze that is shipped back to the Luasa for their tribe. Barqan (if he is still Sar) reinforced the city, for example by fortifying the gates with bronze earlier this season. Barqan is canny and knows a war is coming. Much like Tjaru, Mayrah Vedil bustles with activity. The redsmiths smelt bronze and Jackal packs walk the streets, some as guards, others as shoppers.

- Perception checks reveal merchants flush with wares, as if they brought enough for a much larger city. Many of those who roam the streets are not looking at the goods but at the people. They act more like caravan guards than city-goers. Additionally, the Jackals notice certain parts of the city now have reinforced gates, as well. The buildings that house the foundries and the mines are no longer accessible and remain under guard.
- Influence checks get merchants talking. They can share the following information:
  › The Sars of Sentem and Mayrah Vedil put out the call for merchants last year.
  › They know Tjaru did the same.
  › The Sars are grilling those who come through this way from the north. They want information about Tjaru, Ameena Noani, and any troops coming down from the north.
  › No matter the time of day, there is always about the same number of people in the streets. They pack the city. I have no clue where everyone stays.
  › Barqan is a canny Sar. He is paying the merchants tin to be here. Just for coming here with goods, merchants receive several shekels of gems. Barqan also purchases information with tin, as well as weapons, armour, and foodstuffs.
- Trade checks reveal the markets are flush with weapons, armour, and food, but no jewellery, pottery, or any other trade goods. It is a war camp.
- Culture checks reveal most of the goods here are Gerwa or Trauj. Luathi trade goods are strangely absent.
- Deception or hard Thievery checks can help acquire goods at a reduced price (up to 40% discount) or free (with Thievery).

Meeting Barqan

The Jackals blend in when they arrive in Mayrah Vedil, but each day there is a chance someone recognises them based off their Kleos (see *Jackals* page 176).

When this happens, a guard brings the Jackals to Barqan's attention, who immediately sends for them. When the Jackals arrive, if they dealt with Barqan previously (or if they saved his life) and present themselves, he greets them warmly and puts them up in his own home.

WHO IS SAR OF MAYRAH VEDIL?

It might be that Barqan is not Sar of Mayrah Vedil anymore, or that he is not loyal to Sentem. In that case, what is a Loremaster to do? Do not panic. This far into any campaign, your story will drift from the suggested plotline. Here are some helpful tips to navigate this chapter with a disloyal or dead Barqan.

If Barqan is dead, who is the new Sar? If they are loyal to Sentem, you can use most of this chapter with a simple name change. If they are loyal to Ameena Noani, use the information below, again with a name change.

If Barqan is loyal to Ameena Noani, he is working for Sari Phamea. He is one of Phamea's spies and has secretly sent shipments of tin north for the past several years. Ameena Noani is better equipped, and Barqan extends the same welcome to Phamea's agents that he would extend to those who saved his life. Additionally, he will provide Ameena Noani with intelligence next year prior to the war. At this point, Barqan has made peace with his situation and just wants to get himself and his people safely through the next couple of years.

Barqan is forthcoming to those Jackals who serve the same Sar he does. If he is meeting Jackals he does not know, he is accompanied by a group of Jackals known as the Razored Fangs (five Jackals of Gerwa and Luathi heritage, see below), who act as his guards. He can relate the following information:

- He offers to hire the Jackals, assuming he does not know they are associated with the opposing city (make a Recognition check).
- He asks what they are doing here in the city.
- He becomes suspicious of them and, depending on their attitude, asks them to leave the city.
- Barqan immediately sends a message to Sentem about the Jackals; the messenger leaves before dawn the next day.

When meeting Jackals he does know, he will meet in private and relay the following information:

- Mayrah Vedil is preparing for war.
- Sentem sends troops here as Japeth acquires them. Barqan houses them throughout the city, and many stay in the mines to prevent spies from seeing them.
- Barqan has expanded the mines over the past couple of years, and not along the veins of metal. His tunnels now thread the A'hule Asa, and some exit into the plains, miles from Mayrah Vedil. They provide ingress and egress into the plains, and they will hopefully aid the city if it comes to a siege. He gives this information to the Jackals, so long as he trusts they work for the same Sar as he does.

- Barqan offers what aid he can, up to 1,000 ss in bronze goods. He is concerned about his city and his people, and latches onto the Jackals as people who can do something about his fears.
- Rumours have reached his ears about spies within the city. His people are on it, but he could use aid. He suspects one of the Jackal packs (north) or one of the merchants is selling information to the other side (see Gathering Information below).

In the Mines

Japeth saw the writing on the wall and began marshalling troops in Mayrah Vedil several seasons ago. It quickly became more difficult to hide the additional people. He and Barqan began to move people into the mines, working to clear and expand the old Hannic tunnels as barracks. Currently, Barqan has approximately 600 men and women in the city who are there to fight for Sentem, and at least that many inside the caves. Getting into the caves should quickly become the number-one priority of Jackals spying for Ameena Noani (see Gathering Information below).

The guards outside the mines have strict orders to stop anyone who does not bear one of Barqan's tokens. Jackals from the south or those working with a defecting Barqan gain access to these tokens.

Gathering Information

Once the Jackals are aware of the nature of the information they need, they might want to start tracking it down for the powers that be. The Jackals need to accumulate **eight successes** (with critical successes counting as two successes) before they incur **four failures** to discover the spies or gain access to the mines. Below are some ideas for which skills might be useful. Each skill check is a day's worth of legwork.

Finding the spies:
- Influence and Perception checks (one per day) to determine who is here for more than work and trade.
- Influence checks to investigate rumours, and to see who is buying and selling information.
- Culture checks to see whether someone stands out from the crowd.
- Deception checks for bribes or to spread rumours.
- Thievery checks to search the merchant's wares, stalls, and carts for evidence.
- Craft checks to determine whether someone is lying about where their goods are from.

Infiltrating the mines:
- Perception checks to notice guard rotations and food deliveries.
- Perception or Craft checks to notice the rocks being brought out, and to intuit that a lot of mining is going on inside.
- Deception or Influence checks to bribe a guard or convince them the Jackals belong inside the mines.
- Perception checks to notice the token; Thievery checks to steal it.
- Perform checks to distract the guards.
- Stealth checks to sneak in; Athletics checks to force a way in.

For every two failures, there is a chance Hephzi-Bah or Barqan notice the Jackals' activities. See below for the effects of the failures.

If the Jackals succeed in finding the spies:

- *With one or fewer failures* – the Jackals learn of the spies and Hephzi-Bah. If they consult Barqan, he suggests they leave Hephzi-Bah alone, but take the spies when they leave the city, as it is unclear what they know.
- *With two or three failures* – the Jackals learn of Hephzi-Bah, but she knows they know. The spies leave immediately, requiring the Jackals to chase them down (see below). Hephzi-Bah attempts to leave discretely.

If they succeed in infiltrating the mines:

- *With one or fewer failures* – the Jackals get into the mines without standing out. They sneak or bribe their way past the guards and can count the warriors in the mines, who number another 800, bringing the total fighting force of Mayrah Vedil to approximately 1,500. They also hear mention of the tunnels out into the plains. If they wish to investigate those, there is a second challenge to do so, as they are heavily guarded.
- *With two or three failures:* they get into the mines but do not get an accurate count before the guards notice them. Their cover is not blown, but they should get the feeling they need to leave, or it will be. If a fight breaks out in the mines, it is difficult for the Jackals to escape due to the presence of nearly 1,000 warriors. Their best estimate places 400 warriors in the mines, and they hear nothing of the tunnels.

If the Jackals fail:

- *At finding the spies* – the spies and Hephzi-Bah escape and the Jackals find out too late. Although they can still track down the spies (see Act 3) Hephzi-Bah escapes with full knowledge of the warriors in Mayrah Vedil and the tunnels of Barqan. Sari Phamea will use this knowledge in later years when she besieges Mayrah Vedil.
- *At infiltrating the mines* – the Jackals are unable to determine how many warriors are in the mines, save for 'many'. It becomes clear the guards and the Razored Fangs are aware of them, and the chase is on.
- The Jackals might have an additional opportunity to discover more information if they take a captive, but the Fangs and the spies are unwilling to be captured alive.

Once the Jackals have their information, the location of the spies or the number of warriors in the cave, proceed to Act 3.

ACT 3: FIRST STRIKES

In the final act, the Jackals must either race to capture the spies who fled Mayrah Vedil or must fight their way free from the Razored Fangs, a pack of Jackals loyal to Sentem. The chase involves a series of three checks. Each check provides advantages or disadvantages for the Jackals when the chase is over. Any critical successes allow a Jackal to mitigate a loss from one ally. Any fumbles cause a Jackal to increase the effects of a failure to the maximum die roll.

1. *Pursuit:* each Jackal must make a Survival check as they travel into the Aeco Plains. The plains are fraught with dangers, which are important to note even when one is involved in a chase. Should a Jackal fail this roll, they take 1d4 Mettle damage from a bad fall, sprained ankle, etc. Additionally, Loremasters should check to see whether they encounter something on the plains.

2. *Unrelenting:* the Jackals must make an Endurance check as the chase extends. Muscles burn, but the chase is unrelenting. Should a Jackal fail this roll, they take 1d3 Mettle damage.

3. *Ambush:* the end is in sight. Each Jackal must make a Perception check to detect an ambush or find a good spot for the fight. Use the rules for ambushes (*Jackals* page 62).

Once the Jackals catch up to the spies or find a good spot for an ambush, the fight begins. After the initial ambush round, the leader of the opposing side gives the Jackals an opportunity to surrender or switch sides. They talk about how the other Sar treats their people, how they reward those loyal to them, and how inevitable the war's end is. During this time, the spies try to slip one of their number away. This requires a hard Perception check to notice. A critical success allows the Jackals to notice the freshly turned dirt where the spies buried a hastily written report.

Each group consists of five Jackals loyal to their city. Three are Luathi (spies or Razored Fangs) and two are either Melkoni (spies) or Gerwa (Razored Fangs).

The Spies: Nahash, Qeshet, Sara'el (Luathi); Cleon and Elpis (Melkoni).

The Razored Fangs: Nahash, Qeshet, Sara'el (Luathi); Menes and Hatshepsut (Gerwa).

Once the Jackals kill or capture the spies/Razored Fangs, the adventure comes to an end. The Jackals return to Tjaru with information and possibly captives. Proceed to the *Aftermath* section.

NAHASH (LUATHI SPY OR RAZORED FANG)

Type:	Human	Location:	Aeco Plains
		Wounds:	36
Defence:	75%	Protection:	4 (leather + shield)
Combat:	90%	Move:	12
Knowledge:	65%	Initiative:	18
Urban:	75%	Clash Points:	3
Common:	70%	Treasure Score:	3
		Corruption:	4

Special Abilities

Dirty Tricks: when Nahash targets someone an ally also targets, he can spend a Clash Point to ignore 2 Protection after rolling an attack.

Disarming Strike: Nahash can make an attack roll at half skill in Melee Combat. If successful, he tosses the opponent's weapon 1d10 yards away. 2d10/2 (6) damage.

Combat Range

1–10%	*Retreat:* Nahash breaks from combat and retreats a full move, while firing his bow at his target. 2d10 (11) damage. If he rolls two consecutive Retreats, he flees from the fight.
11–25%	*Savage Blow:* Nahash attacks the nearest target with either his sword or his bow. 2d10 + 2d4 (16) damage in melee, 2d10 (11) damage at ranged.
26–50%	*Bolstering Strikes (2 attacks):* Nahash attacks the nearest target twice with either his sword or his bow. 2d10 + 2d4 (16) damage each in melee, 2d10 (11) damage at ranged. Should Nahash inflict 5 or more points of damage (after Protection), he heals 5 Wounds.
51–65%	*Bring Them Down (2 attacks):* Nahash attacks the nearest target twice with either his sword or his bow. 2d10 + 2d4 (16) damage each in melee, 2d10 (11) damage at ranged. Additionally, after Nahash successfully makes this attack, each of his allies engaged with the target can spend 1 Clash point to make an immediate attack.
66–90%	*Might Thews:* Nahash attacks his opponent with savage abandon. 2d10 + 2d4 +3d6 (27) damage. If the attack causes Wounds, they bleed for 2d4 (5) damage a round until a successful Healing check is made to staunch the wound.

QESHET (LUATHI SPY OR RAZORED FANG)

Type:	Human	Location:	Aeco Plains
		Wounds:	36
Defence:	75%	Protection:	4 (leather + shield)
Combat:	90%	Move:	12
Knowledge:	65%	Initiative:	18
Urban:	75%	Clash Points:	3
Common:	70%	Treasure Score:	3
		Corruption:	4

Special Abilities

Dirty Tricks: when Qeshet targets someone an ally also targets, she can spend a Clash Point to ignore 2 Protection after rolling an attack.

Piercing Thrust: Qeshet ignores 2 points of Protection with her melee attacks.

Combat Range

1–10%	*Retreat:* Qeshet breaks from combat and retreats a full move, while firing her bow at her target. 2d10 (11) damage. If she rolls two consecutive Retreats, she flees from the fight.
11–25%	*Savage Blow:* Qeshet attacks the nearest target with either her sword or her bow. 2d10 + 2d4 (16) damage in melee, 2d10 (11) damage at ranged.
26–50%	*Bolstering Strikes (2 attacks):* Qeshet attacks the nearest target twice with either her sword or her bow. 2d10 + 2d4 (16) damage each in melee, 2d10 (11) damage at ranged. Should Qeshet inflict 5 or more points of damage (after Protection), she heals 5 Wounds.
51–65%	*Bring Them Down (2 attacks):* Qeshet attacks the nearest target twice with either her sword or her bow. 2d10 + 2d4 (16) damage each in melee, 2d10 (11) damage at ranged. Additionally, after Qeshet successfully makes this attack, each of her allies engaged with the target can spend 1 Clash point to make an immediate attack.
66–90%	*Might Thews:* Qeshet attacks her opponent with savage abandon. 2d10 + 2d4 +3d6 (27) damage. If the attack causes Wounds, they bleed for 2d4 (5) damage a round until a successful Healing check is made to staunch the wound.

SARA'EL (LUATHI SPY OR RAZORED FANG)

Type:	Human	Location:	Aeco Plains
		Wounds:	36
		Protection:	3 (leather + shield)
Defence:	75%	Move:	12
Combat:	90%	Initiative:	21
Knowledge:	100%	Clash Points:	3
Urban:	75%	Treasure Score:	3
Common:	70%	Corruption:	4
		Devotion Points:	25

Special Abilities

Dirty Tricks: when Sara'el targets someone an ally also targets, she can spend a Clash Point to ignore 2 Protection after rolling an attack.

The Heat of the Flame: when Sara'el uses the Crack of Flame rite, all targets also take 1d8 damage, which ignores Protection.

Combat Range

1–10%	*Retreat:* Sara'el breaks from combat and retreats a full move, while firing her bow at her target. 2d10 (11) damage. If she rolls two consecutive Retreats, she flees from the fight.
11–25%	*Savage Blow:* Sara'el attacks the nearest target with either her sword or her bow. 2d10 + 2d4 (16) damage in melee, 2d10 (11) damage at ranged.
26–50%	*Bolstering Strikes (2 attacks):* Sara'el attacks the nearest target twice with either her sword or her bow. 2d10 + 2d4 (16) damage each in melee, 2d10 (11) damage at ranged. Should Sara'el inflict 5 or more points of damage (after Protection), she heals 5 Wounds.
51–90%	*Rite:* Sara'el uses a Hasheer rite.

CLEON (MELKONI SPY)

Type:	Human	Location:	Aeco Plains
		Wounds:	36
Defence:	75%	Protection:	6 (breastplate + shield)
Combat:	90%	Move:	12
Knowledge:	65%	Initiative:	18
Urban:	75%	Clash Points:	3
Common:	70%	Treasure Score:	3
		Corruption:	4

Special Abilities

Dirty Tricks: when Cleon targets someone an ally also targets, he can spend a Clash Point to ignore 2 Protection after rolling an attack.

Interpose: Cleon can spend Clash Points to react and attempt to take a blow for another character within 3 yards. This costs 2 Clash Points. Cleon is treated as the target of the original attack. Cleon can then spend additional Clash Points to react as usual to that attack.

Combat Range

1–10%	*Retreat:* Cleon breaks from combat and retreats a full move, while firing his bow at his target. 2d10 (11) damage. If he rolls two consecutive Retreats, he flees from the fight.
11–25%	*Savage Blow:* Cleon attacks the nearest target with either his sword or his bow. 2d10 + 2d4 (16) damage in melee, 2d10 (11) damage at ranged.
26–50%	*Bolstering Strikes (2 attacks):* Cleon attacks the nearest target twice with either his sword or his bow. 2d10 + 2d4 (16) damage each in melee, 2d10 (11) damage at ranged. Should Cleon inflict 5 or more points of damage (after Protection), he heals 5 Wounds.
51–65%	*Bring Them Down (2 attacks):* Cleon attacks the nearest target twice with either his sword or his bow. 2d10 + 2d4 (16) damage each in melee, 2d10 (11) damage at ranged. Additionally, after Cleon successfully makes this attack, each of his allies engaged with the target can spend 1 Clash point to make an immediate attack.
66–90%	*Shield Bash:* Cleon slams his shield into his opponent, damaging and potentially stunning them. 4d8 (18) damage and the target must make a hard Endurance check or lose 1d6 Clash Points each round for two rounds. A successful check reduces the loss to one round, a critical success to no Clash Point loss, and a fumble doubles the duration of the stunning.

ELPIS (MELKONI SPY)

Type:	Human	Location:	Aeco Plains

		Wounds:	36
		Protection:	3 (leather + shield)
Defence:	75%	Move:	12
Combat:	90%	Initiative:	21
Knowledge:	100%	Clash Points:	3
Urban:	75%	Treasure Score:	3
Common:	70%	Corruption:	4
		Devotion Points:	25

Special Abilities

Dirty Tricks: when Elpis targets someone an ally also targets, she can spend a Clash Point to ignore 2 Protection after rolling an attack.

Orichalcum Blade: when Elpis is under the effects of Ryla's Blessing, she ignores 4 points of Protection.

Combat Range

1–10%	*Retreat:* Elpis breaks from combat and retreats a full move, while firing her bow at her target. 2d10 (11) damage. If she rolls two consecutive Retreats, she flees from the fight.
11–25%	*Savage Blow:* Elpis attacks the nearest target with either her sword or her bow. 2d10 + 2d4 (16) damage in melee, 2d10 (11) damage at ranged.
26–50%	*Bolstering Strikes (2 attacks):* Elpis attacks the nearest target twice with either her sword or her bow. 2d10 + 2d4 (16) damage each in melee, 2d10 (11) damage at ranged. Should Elpis inflict 5 or more points of damage (after Protection), she heals 5 Wounds.
51–90%	*Rite:* Elpis uses a Rylareia rite.

HATSHEPSUT (GERWA RAZORED FANG)

Type:	Human	Location:	Aeco Plains

		Wounds:	36
Defence:	75%	Protection:	3 (leather + shield)
Combat:	90%	Move:	12
Knowledge:	65%	Initiative:	18
Urban:	75%	Clash Points:	3
Common:	70%	Treasure Score:	3
		Corruption:	4

Special Abilities

Dirty Tricks: when Hatshepsut targets someone an ally also targets, she can spend a Clash Point to ignore 2 Protection after rolling an attack.

Disarming Shot: Hatshepsut can make an attack roll at half skill at range. If successful, she knocks her opponent's weapon 1d10 yards away. 3d8/2 (7) damage.

Combat Range

1–10%	*Retreat:* Hatshepsut breaks from combat and retreats a full move, while firing her bow at her target. 3d8 (13) damage. If she rolls two consecutive Retreats, she flees from the fight.
11–25%	*Savage Blow:* Hatshepsut attacks the nearest target with either her sword or her bow. 2d10 + 2d4 (16) damage in melee, 3d8 (13) damage at ranged.
26–50%	*Bolstering Strikes (2 attacks):* Hatshepsut attacks the nearest target twice with either her sword or her bow. 2d10 + 2d4 (16) damage each in melee, 3d8 (13) damage at ranged. Should Hatshepsut inflict 5 or more points of damage (after Protection), she heals 5 Wounds.
51–65%	*Bring Them Down (2 attacks):* Hatshepsut attacks the nearest target twice with either her sword or her bow. 2d10 + 2d4 (16) damage each in melee, 3d8 (13) damage at ranged. Additionally, after Hatshepsut successfully makes this attack, each of her allies engaged with the target can spend 1 Clash point to make an immediate attack.
66–90%	*Arrow Storm (X attacks):* Hatshepsut launches a volley of arrows into her opponents for 3d8 (13) damage each. She can spend a Clash Point after an attack to make an additional attack with her bow, for up to three attacks.

MENES (GERWA RAZORED FANG)

Type:	Human	Location:	Aeco Plains
		Wounds:	36
		Protection:	3 (leather + shield)
Defence:	75%	**Move:**	12
Combat:	90%	**Initiative:**	21
Knowledge:	100%	**Clash Points:**	3
Urban:	75%	**Treasure Score:**	3
Common:	70%	**Corruption:**	4
		Devotion Points:	25

Special Abilities

Dirty Tricks: when Menes targets someone an ally also targets, he can spend a Clash Point to ignore 2 Protection after rolling an attack.

My Will Made Solid: when Menes uses Summon Lesser Ba, the Ba gains 2 Protection and +5 Wounds.

Combat Range

1–10%	*Retreat:* Menes breaks from combat and retreats a full move, while firing his bow at his target. 2d10 (11) damage. If he rolls two consecutive Retreats, he flees from the fight.
11–25%	*Savage Blow:* Menes attacks the nearest target with either his sword or his bow. 2d10 + 2d4 (16) damage in melee, 2d10 (11) damage at ranged.
26–50%	*Bolstering Strikes (2 attacks):* Menes attacks the nearest target twice with either his sword or his bow. 2d10 + 2d4 (16) damage each in melee, 2d10 (11) damage at ranged. Should Menes inflict 5 or more points of damage (after Protection), he heals 5 Wounds.
51–90%	*Rite:* Menes uses a Servant of the Eight rite.

AFTERMATH

Upon returning to Tjaru, the Jackals meet with Deborah. She wants a full debrief. If the Jackals have captives, Deborah questions them to discover what they know.

North: the revelation of the tunnels and the presence of troops in the mines is a shock to Deborah. That is a large enough group to swing the tide of a battle.

South: if spies infiltrated Mayrah Vedil, they most likely have done the same in Tjaru and Sentem.

Deborah rewards the Jackals and thanks them for their assistance. Dealing with information and counterintelligence is sure to aid Tjaru and Deborah in the upcoming years. She mentions that when the Hasheers arrive, she will enlist the Jackals to aid in some divinations concerning the war.

ADVANCEMENTS

- 1 for saving the caravan
- 1 for succeeding at discovering the spies/information in the mines, and 1 additional advancement if this was done with one or no failures
- 1 for killing or capturing the spies/Razored Fangs

HOOKS

To Darken the Moon: The Moon Mask tribe needs to be investigated. The Takan tribe is growing bolder in its assaults on caravans, Tjaru, and Mayrah Vedil.

Spy versus Spy: The Sars need Jackals to root out and take care of spies in Tjaru, Sentem, and the plains.

CHAPTER 9
YEAR OF
DISCARDED VEILS

Just as there is a cycle to the seasons,
So is there a rhythm to the lives of all.
Crops arise and crops are reaped,
Sars seek peace, Sars go to war.
Time flows on, the mountain rises tall,
Old men fall, and children arise.
Just as there is a rhythm to the lives of all,
So is there a cycle to the seasons.

~ **The Wisdom of Beniel** ~

INTRODUCTION

This year's adventure sees the Jackals aid a divining ritual to seek wisdom from beyond the mortal world, followed by the fallout of that rite. The Sar of their city, through the Hasheers and Deborah, places a terrible burden on the backs of the Jackals. Do they use the information gained to cripple their 'foes' by using the Takan tribe against them? Or do they stand against a dark deed that could stain their efforts and their souls?

THEME

The theme of the Year of Discarded Veils is the ends sometimes justify the means. Using Takan against Luathi is a horrible act to even contemplate, let alone put into action. However, the temptation is great. Let the beastfolk soften up the enemy prior to the battle, and there will be less loss of life for those loyal to the Jackals' Sar. How do the Jackals wrestle with the morality of this act? Do they? Can they go along with it, or do they defect? This could be a moment when the Jackals, faced with what their side is willing to do, switch sides in the war.

IMPORTANT NPCS

Beket, Gerwa Hemet-Netjer: Ba-en Nafar sent for Beket, a relative of his from Ger. She is a powerful Hemet-Netjer of Djhutemos, the Gerwa god of knowledge. He hopes she can divine something to aid Sentem. He did not inform Sameel, knowing Sameel's devotion to Alwain would prevent him from using a diviner, as the *Shalapher* prohibits such acts.

Hasheer Zamira: Zamira is the ambitious Hasheer of the Scriptorium in Ameena Noani, who is willing to explore fringe rites to ingratiate herself among the Court of the Bulls. She discovered ancient Ketian rites of darhrin (divination through sacrifice or reading of entrails) and is willing to use them, despite what the *Shalapher* says.

EVENTS IN TJARU

- More caravans arrive, including new materials for the altar of Alwain. Kahars set up a worship area in the courtyard of the fortress.
- The Moon Mask tribe has claimed three more caravans over the past year, leaving the fortress short of the estimated number of warriors, stores, and resources.

EVENTS IN THE NORTH

- There are rumours of a black-haired warrior defending a band of Melkoni refugees from a Takan attack. The rumours say this warrior slew 100 Takan by herself.

EVENTS IN THE SOUTH

- Nabal finishes the restoration of the Temple of the Morning Lord.

EVENTS ANYWHERE

- Two eclipses of Gai signal the intense heat will result in a sparse crop this season.
- Hatsaa means even more this year, in the hope the rainy season crop will be more bountiful than that of the dry season.
- Heavy rains fall in Tise and Eser.

RETIREMENT BENEFITS

If a player retires their Jackal in this year, their new Jackal gains +12 advancements if they make a Gerwa, Melkoni, or Trauj Jackal, representing mercenaries flooding the War Road.

THE PRICE OF VICTORY

An adventure for 'Defenders of Jackals, set during the month of Samane, in the dry season.

OVERVIEW

The Year of Discarded Veils punishes those living in the Zaharets with relentless heat (increase all Mettle loss by 1 for adventures this year). Unseasonably hot weather beats down, and tempers rise. Perhaps that is why, when given a dire warning through divination, Deborah's thoughts turn bloody. She wants the Jackals to track the Moon Mask tribe back to its home and lure the Takan tribe against a massing of troops from the other side. The resulting raid would cripple many enemy troops and rid the plains of the largest Takan tribe which threatens it. Are the Jackals willing to do whatever it takes to ensure their side is victorious in the upcoming battles, or are there some lines they are unwilling to cross?

ACT 1: THE DANCE OF THE HEAVENS

The adventure begins on the Second Gai Day, at the end of an exceptionally hot dry season. Deborah summons the Jackals to her chambers, where the Hasheer or Hemet-Netjer wait. The room is slightly cooler, due to its size, but is still uncomfortably hot. After introducing them, Deborah explains her plans. The Hasheer or Hemet-Netjer is going to attempt a rite of darhrin – divination through the reading of a sacrifice. Any Luathi can make a Culture (Own) check; a success means they know the *Shalapher* forbids this act. Deborah knows this, too, but does not care. If – and it is a big if in her mind – it works, the potential reward outstrips the potential curse. Between the loss of troops to the Takan, and the reports of the scouts, Tjaru's hold on the plains seems tenuous. Without intervention, it seems as though the other side might take it within the year.

Both Zamira and Beket are willing to explain the simple rite to Jackals who wish to understand what they plan to do. After ritually purifying themselves through washing, eating, and anointing, they will prepare the doves for sacrifice. With each sacrifice, they will ask a single yes-or-no question. Then, through the examination of the doves' livers, Alwain (Zamira) or the Eight (Beket) will answer the questions. Zamira assures the Jackals the Children of Silver performed this rite long ago (false, it is a Ketian ritual). Even if this was true, Luathi now know it is forbidden to them. Zamira argues the merits with any who question her, while Beket simply states their proscriptions have no hold on her.

Eventually, Deborah brings the meeting to an end, stating she has already given the order and the ritual will take place tonight. She does not want the Jackals to participate in the ritual (although they are welcome to watch). What she wants is help in crafting the questions. According to Zamira or Beket, the darhrin can only divine yes-or-no questions. Deborah's current questions are:

- Will battle begin this year?
- Will it occur at Tjaru?
- Will Ameena Noani/Sentem be victorious?

She is open to the Jackals' input on the first two questions, but is adamant about the third. Slight variations are acceptable to her, but the question's essence must remain. The ritual will take place this night, as the eclipse of Gai adds weight to the divination. Whether the Jackals decide to witness the divination or not does not affect the ceremony. Deborah places guards on the rooftop to ensure these rites happen. If the Jackals try to stop it, Deborah takes measures to restrain them. In this case, the Act 2 mission takes on a tone of penance or a chance to get rid of troublemakers by placing them where the fighting is thickest.

The Ceremony

If the Jackals participate in or witness the ceremony, it takes place on the roof of the inner fortress when the eclipse of Gai begins, and it lasts until the eclipse ends – approximately two hours. The officiant climbs the stairs to the roof, carrying six doves in a bronze cage. Earlier in the day, she prepared a small altar, brazier, and worktable with a bronze basin, an ewer, small leather pouches, bronze blades, and pincers.

The rite begins with a prayer:

- *Beket:* She asks that the Six keep their eyes away from this place, while invoking Djhutemos to attend, grace this place with his wisdom, and place his answers within the doves.
- *Zamira:* She invokes the Lord of Time's presence here, to shed light into the darkness, and illuminate his people. While all the trappings of Alwainism are here, a Culture (Luathi) roll reveals it is all a bit off. Nowhere in the *Shalapher* is Alwain referred to as the Lord of Time. Luathi who make this roll feel uncomfortable with the rites, and if the Jackal asks, the Loremaster should tell them something is very wrong here. They feel as if they should leave or interrupt the ritual. This might bring them into conflict with the guards Deborah placed here. [Use Guard stats – One per Luathi Jackal.]

After the invocation, the officiant washes her face and hands in the basin with water from the ewer. Then she rinses her mouth with water from the ewer, takes pinches of herbs, spices, and ash from the pouches, and anoints her tongue with them. More prayers asking for the guidance of the gods/god continue while this happens. Once Gai is fully eclipsed, the officiant sacrifices the first of the doves. It is a simple ritual. The officiant deftly lets the blood fall on the altar, removes the liver, and places the remains on the brazier to roast. With each dove, the officiant invokes Djhutemos or the Lord of Time again, calls out their question, and begs them to inscribe the answer within the dove. The officiant asks each question twice, in slightly different ways, to ensure accuracy of the answer.

The answers to the questions are as follows:

- *Will battle begin this year?* No. The reading is clear, enemies will clash but war will not begin this year.
- *Will it occur at Tjaru?* Unclear. Some of the signs point to yes, but they also point to something greater which will not occur here. The officiant believes this means a battle will occur here, but it will not be the deciding factor.
- *Will Ameena Noani/Sentem be victorious?* Unclear. The signs point to overwhelming force brought to bear against Tjaru. But certain markings on the liver point to victory through a crooked path.

The rite is over when the eclipse of Gai ends. Deborah is not thrilled with the rite's outcomes, although it seems to bring an end to some inner debate. If the Jackals are present, she asks to see them in the morning. If they are not, she summons them in the morning and gives them the high-level view of what happened during the ritual. Luathi who witness Zamira performing the rite gain 1d4 Corruption, as they knew it was wrong and did nothing to stop it.

The Summons

The next morning, Deborah summons the Jackals to walk Tjaru's walls with her. Her guards stay back and keep all from approaching within earshot of the Nawsi and the Jackals. Here, she outlines her plan.

- The situation is more desperate than the Jackals may know.
  › Either Ameena Noani possesses more power due to their alliance with Kroryla...
  › Or Sentem called in many favours with Ger and their allies among the southern Trauj tribes in Jehumma's Gap.
- The Takan attacks continue to increase as the Moon Masks grow bolder with each season. She fears a horde is coming, with the Moon Masks in the middle of it.
- The divinations from the previous night seem to confirm her worst suspicions. Tjaru will lose the war for their Sar.
- Deborah has a plan involving the 'crooked path' from the oracles.
- The first step is to deal with the Moon Masks. So far, Tjaru has only reacted to their attacks. She wants the Jackals to go out into the plains to locate the Takan and find out how many there are. This is a scouting mission, not one to wipe out the Takan. She fears there are too many for the Jackals to handle, anyway.
- She had the quartermasters prepare food for the Jackals for the rest of the month, as well as 18 acalana resins from the supply.
- She trusts the Jackals know she will reward them handsomely for this. Should her plan work, a talent of silver is just the beginning of the rewards the Sar will gift them.
- As for the second part of the plan, she must first speak with the Sar and her advisors. She will have news for them when they return.

When the Jackals head out to track down the Moon Masks, proceed to Act 2.

ACT 2: THE THRILL OF THE HUNT

The problem with the Moon Masks is they seem to appear out of nowhere and then disappear back into the plains. Thus, tracking down the Takan is the Jackals' first task. They know of several attack sites within several days to the east of Tjaru. These sites are the places to start.

Tracking the Takan

The Jackals need to accumulate **ten successes** (with critical successes counting as two successes) before they incur **five failures** to discover the trail of the Takan. Each skill check is a day's worth of legwork. No more than four attempts can be made at any one site, requiring the Jackals to travel 1d4 days between the sites of the attacks. Below are some ideas for what skills might be useful.

- Ancient Lore: there are several ruins scattered among this region of the plains. Some are from the Children of Silver, whereas others are from Barak Barad. It seems unlikely the Takan would have the gall or ability to squat within a Hulathi ruin.
- Drive: some of the wheel tracks here are not from the wagons, but from chariots.
- Lore: Takan this organised are following either an Oritakan or a Mouathenic. Eventually, that leader draws enough attention for the Takan band to become a horde, drawing other, smaller bands into a massive army.
- Perception: it would seem from the wreckage that the attacks happened swiftly, without the defenders having much chance to react.
- Ride: the Takan, or at least some of them, were riding horses. This is a nearly unheard-of occurrence, but it might explain why the raids happened so quickly. These are large horses, like those of the Trauj.
- Stealth or Thievery: insight into the raid makes it clear to the Jackal the Takan were after lives and goods. This was a raid, not a bloodletting. In most of the raids, the Takan slaughtered the caravanners completely. But they may have captured some and led them away.
- Survival: gaining the lay of the land shows – although the coastal plain is flat – there are ravines and hills that could hide forces. Especially in the foothills.

If the Jackals succeed:

- Several facts become clear when the Jackals look at the sites together: the Takan are taking prisoners, they are mounted, and there is not much space in the area to hide a large force, save for in the ravines. Following the trail, the Jackals find their way to the old Takan fastness of Kek-bel-kala.

If the Jackals fail:

- The Jackals begin to piece information together, but not before the Takan ambush them! Use two Oritakan and two Mavakan per Jackal, as well as 2d6 Norakan. These Takan are marked with Moon Masks and automatically flee at 50% casualties (not counting the Norakan). This enables the Jackals to follow their trail back to Kek-bel-kala.

Kek-bel-kala

Kek-bel-kala is a redoubt from the early days of Barak Barad. As the Grand Kingdoms fell, Lukka held on the longest in the face of the great Takan hordes. During that time, the Takan carved out this fortress in the walls of the plain's ravines to provide a refuge and a redoubt in the face of the failing armies of Lukka. During the Takan's centuries of dominance, Kek-bel-kala became a retreat for Oritakan and those among the Takan who walked the Twisted Path. Its location became a secret, another shadow of fear on the minds of the Luathi. The sun never shone again on those the Takan took to Kek-bel-kala. A grain of this terror is captured in the Book of Freedoms in the *Shalapher*:

> And the lament of the Luathi ascended from the land, the earth itself joining with their cry.
> For the weight of their slavery pressed down upon both and the terror of the altar in Kek's
> house gripped them.

During the Uprising, the Luathi searched for Kek-bel-kala, but whether due to its hidden nature or some dark grace, the Nehanu's armies never discovered it. The Takan retreated from the Aeco Plains to less dangerous ground, and Kek-bel-kala lay hidden for 150 years. It was when Tjaru once again sprang into the minds of the Luathi that the Takan turned theirs to Kek-bel-kala. Urged on by the Daughter Beneath the Earth, the Moon Mask tribe returned to the redoubt and quickly saw the benefits of the place. The Daughter sends each new tribe or tattered remnant of Takan that comes under the influence of the Moon Masks here. Inside, the Takan discovered many ancient altars, armouries, and darker powers that enhance their strength. The call goes out through whatever ill-understood path of the Dream Road the Takan travel, a horde instinct grows in the minds of the beasts, and more will soon arrive.

A horde champion has yet to emerge at Kek-bel-kala, but it is only a matter of time. Until it does, the Takan do not operate as one entity, but as several camps within the cliffs. This plays to the Jackals' advantage, as the various camps see each other as rivals, and tensions run high. The primary factions are listed below.

The Black Nails: lead by Oritakan triplets, this band is the largest. They also arrived the most recently and inhabit the outer areas of Kek-bel-kala (the plains and area 2). Mixed in among them is a score of humans, corrupted and joined with the Takan to serve the Daughter Beneath the Earth. Members of the Qayim and Tamu's group are among them. In total, there are 150 humans and 350 Takan of various breeds.

Sessu Umari: Led by a human Mouathenic called Umari (Exalted) in the Takan tongue, these Takan scar their faces with long vertical lines. Umari claimed the temple complex (area 10) when she arrived. Shargot has not slain her yet, primarily due to her power, which only waxes as she communes with the Rathic in the temple. While rare, it is not unheard of for a human to be a horde champion. Indeed, this is how the Priest-Kings of Mouadah used them in the deep reaches of the past. Sessu Umari contains all types of Takan, and Umari's will keeps them cohesive and focused. In total, there are a dozen Mouathenics, and 100 Takan of various breeds.

Moon Masks: led by Shargot (an Oritakan), this was the first group to retake Kek-bel-kala 30 years ago. They preyed on War Road caravans in secret for most of that time, slowly building their numbers, before bowing their heads to the Daughter Beneath the Earth. They hold the deep areas within the complex (areas 7–9). The Moon Masks primarily contain Mavakan, Tsutakan, and Oritakan, and are highly organised. In total, there are 600 Takan, including 400 Mavakan, 40 Tsutakan, 10 Oritakan, and 150 Otsakan (half-breeds).

Sunqu Ilutu: led by the Grey Taker – a massive Atakan – this band is the smallest, but the most vicious. They claimed a spot in Kek-bel-kala by killing and eating another band three seasons ago. They hold the middle area of Kek-bel-kala (areas 3–6), although not well. They have some Norakan among their numbers and are using them to reopen one of the side tunnels on the western side of the complex. Sunqu Ilutu primarily contains Retakan, Atakan, and Norakan. This area is a chaotic mess, where the strong prey on the weak. In total, there are 80 Takan, including 15 Atakan, 40 Norakan, and 25 Retakan.

Once the Jackals find Kek-bel-kala, what happens next is up to them. Takan and humans occupy the ravine, going through the daily routines of an armed camp. From the outside, the Jackals can see nearly 100 Takan and about half that many humans. Who knows how many more wait inside?

Additionally, the Jackals see:

- All the humans working the in ravine bear the mark of the Black Nail. Aside from that and some obvious signs of Corruption, they look like a gathering of Jackals.
- Thirteen humans are hanging from the upper galleries. A Perception check reveals they are still alive! They hang from a Gordian Noose, a complicated knot of rope which constricts the body with its own weight, forcing the victim to agonisingly contort themselves to breathe fully. Although not deadly, the pain is excruciating, and most victims slowly start to choke. A critical success reveals the bottoms of the victims' feet are cut. The blood stains the walls of Kek-bel-kala.
- A chariot stands on the outskirts of the camp, unharnessed but also untouched. The chariot possesses a high bronze rim and thick, menacing wheel blades. Its harness looks to be made for something massive. (A Gadakan would pull this.) Should the Jackals inspect the chariot, they can see it is a piece of Ketian work. The bronze plating is worked with massive snakes, whose jaws face forwards, as if to consume those the chariot charges. It is large enough to carry three people into battle, or five if comfort and fighting are not a concern. This heavy chariot is Dunan Imtu – it grants all within it an additional +1 Protection. It possesses a speed of 24, if pulled by two Trauj horses or a Gadakan, as they are lent speed by the magic of the chariot. It also lends weight to their charge, granting them 2d12 damage on a trample. The chariot can travel in the Silent Lands if the driver spends 10 Devotion Points. The journey takes one hour per day of travel. A Lore check is required in place of the Survival check for travel. A failure results in the driver taking 1d6 Corruption and any riders gaining 1 Corruption. Additionally, there is a one-in-ten chance of encountering a Ba, Lesser Rathic, or Rapiuma during the journey. This climbs to a two-in-ten chance if the driver fails their Lore check. Finally, the blades of the chariot are imbued with an extreme poison [vector: blood; cycle: instant; intensity: 10; damage type: physical].

Infiltrating Kek-bel-kala

Getting into Kek-bel-kala is doable, if dangerous. If they mark themselves with a black nail, the Jackals should find entering the outer areas simple enough. Most of the Takan of the Black Nails ignore them, although the humans might find some interest in their passing and attempt to strike up a conversation. Should the Jackals try to find out more about Kek-bel-kala from them using Influence or Deception checks, they might hear the following:

- I joined up for the same reason you did. The voices called me here.
- No champion has emerged yet, but my shekels are on Umari.
- Umari is the Daughter Beneath the Earth (false).
- The horde will choose its champion soon; then, we march.
- The fortress holds many secrets.
- The prisoners bleed to consecrate the fortress. Better them than us!
- Shargot's pack holds the rest of the caravanners deep in Kek-bel-kala.

As the Jackals head deeper into the site, it becomes more difficult to remain anonymous. After all, those in the Zaharets know of the Jackals' deeds – friend and foe alike. With a successful Deception check, the Jackals can steal gear marked with the Black Nail, which provides +25% to all Deception and Stealth checks in Kek-bel-kala and –25% to all Reputation checks. Each time the Jackals move between areas inside Kek-bel-kala, the Loremaster rolls against the highest Recognition in the group (see *Jackals* page 176). For each level of Recognition, a Takan has a 25% chance of noticing the Jackals, modified by whether the Jackals are in disguise (–10% to the check) or are wearing Black Nails gear (–25%), as well as by the area's attention modifier (the Takan have a more difficult time recognising anything in the more chaotic areas of Kek-bel-kala):

- *Moon Masks:* Normal (+0%)
- *Sessu Umari:* Difficult (–25%)
- *Sunqu Ilutu:* Hard (–50%)

Should the Recognition check fail, no Takan will recognise the Jackals in this area for the next hour. Should the Recognition check succeed, the next time any Takan sees them, they recognise the Jackals for who they are. If this ends in combat, each subsequent Recognition check over the next two days moves up a category, as the fortress is on higher alert.

Combat in Kek-bel-kala

The fortress is large, so if the Jackals are swift and silent, they might get away with one or two fights before they must flee the fortress. Use the following examples for battles in the ruins, or use a specific room description from below:

- *Moon Masks:* one Oritakan and one Tsutakan, plus two Mavakan per Jackal.
- *Sessu Umari:* one Mouathenic and one Wolf (bandit), plus one Norakan per Jackal.
- *Sunqu Ilutu:* one Atakan, plus one Retakan per Jackal.

Black Nail Territory

What a Jackal's senses reveal:

Sights – an intricate carved façade gives the ravine wall the look of a mighty fortress. Small gatherings of humans and Takan.

Smells – unwashed bodies. Campfires.

Sounds – chaotic noises of an armed camp, the sounds of a fight or murder happening just out of sight, and whoops and yells of excitement or outrage.

1. Gatehouse

At nearly 40 cubits tall, the gates of Kek-bel-kala are half the height of the ravine walls. The gatehouse façade extends to the full height of the walls. The Black Nails hold the gate, but there are signs of multiple skirmishes between them and Sunqu Ilutu. The Black Nails hang grisly trophies (heads, hands, etc.) from the gatehouse to warn the Sunqu Ilutu against crossing the threshold, save in dire need. Two Atakan crouch in the darkness on the inside of Kek-bel-kala, while the Black Nails sit on barrels near the exit to the ravine. Today seems to be a day of truce. Perhaps.

2. Main Gallery

This massive hall is an armed camp. The Black Nail command, consisting of the Oritakan triplets – Bakenet, Tenekab, and Nekabet – as well as their concubines, human officers, and two Gadakan chariot pullers reside here. Several large bronze braziers made from Melkoni shields provide light, as does the sun streaming in through the façade's windows.

Sunqu Ilutu Territory

What a Jackal's senses reveal:

Sights – this area possesses no light sources, as all the Takan are inured to darkness. With a light source, friezes depicting the Takan at the height of Barak Barad are revealed. The walls bear glorified images of humans being enslaved, killed, and worse.

Smells – blood, rotting meat, and the stink of sweat.

Sounds – rumbles in the dark, challenges being called out, and claws scraping against stone.

3. The Nest

This room was once the waiting area. Those called before the throne or who sought to visit the temple waited here before continuing. Now, it is the den of those who follow the Grey Taker. The statues that once lined the walls now lie broken and scattered. The plunder the Sunqu Ilutu gathered from raiding caravans and others in the temple lies scattered throughout. An extreme Perception roll reveals 50 minas' worth of silk that is still usable, a fine silver sword etched with horses (useless in a fight, but a fine gift for a Trauj) worth 1,000 ss, and a fine bronze spearhead (+2 damage, +15% to Melee Combat).

4. Throne Room

This area holds the great throne of Kek-bel-kala. The Takan of old carved the massive black throne in imitation of the onyx throne of Mouadah. Currently, the Grey Taker holds the throne room as its personal den. The skins of humans it has killed drape the arms and back of the throne. The wall carvings behind the throne depict a great mountain range, and an inhuman fortress that rises over the throne. The eastern wall, opposite the throne, shows a scene of fertile plains and a great, gated city.

Ancient Lore checks suggest the northern wall is Enekgotaru, a fortress of legend from the *Sagas*, an ancient epic from the time of the Grand Kingdoms. Enekgotaru is said to be the home of Imil-Ajas, the great enemy. The western wall depicts the plains of Shimar, home to Mouadah.

A half-dozen humans are chained to the floor of the throne room, their chains bound to great iron rings set into the flagstones. Many of the doors from this room lead to what were storage rooms and treasury chambers, but the Takan plundered them long ago.

The throne grants anyone with a Corruption score of 10+ the ability to cast their sight beyond the walls of the throne room and view the whole of the War Road. They have a Wisdom × 3 chance of finding an image they want to see. A fumble shows them something horrific or terrible, inflicting 2d4 Corruption.

The Grey Taker stacked his plunder along the south wall. Intermixed with bleached skulls and rotting limbs is a portion of Tjaru's wealth stolen by this beast. Approximately three talents' worth of silver jewellery, diadems, helms, and trade goods line the wall. Additionally, a fine Melkoni shield (+3 Protection and +10% to Influence), a Gerwa bow (+2 damage), and a pair of Trauj scimitars (+2 damage, +1 Clash Point) sit among the piles.

At any given time, the Grey Taker, 1d6 – 1 Atakan, and 2d6 Retakan are in the throne room, eating, sporting, or tormenting the human prisoners. Should a fight break out, the Grey Taker is an Atakan with the following stats:

THE GREY TAKER			
Type:	Takan	Location:	Kek-bel-kala
		Wounds:	100
Defence:	75%	Protection:	5 (natural)
Combat:	125%	Move:	20
Knowledge:	60%	Initiative:	18
Urban:	60%	Clash Points:	5
Common:	40%	Treasure Score:	1
		Corruption	10

Special Abilities

Inured to Darkness: the Grey Taker suffers no penalties due to absence of light.

Crimson Maw: the Grey Taker is always taking bites and snaps at those around it. This rending is accounted for in the extra d8 on all attacks below. The taste of blood riles them into a frenzy. The Loremaster should take the result of the d8 roll and add it to the Grey Taker's Wounds (in addition to the damage it causes). This can take the Grey Taker above its maximum Wounds.

Piercing Thrust: the Grey Taker's attacks ignore 2 points of Protection.

Skilful Strike: the Grey Taker can re-roll any damage dice results of '1'.

Combat Range

1–15%	*Dismissive Backhand:* the Grey Taker delivers a stunning backhand to its target. 3d8 (14) damage and the target loses 2 Clash Points immediately.
16–35%	*Just a Taste:* the Grey Taker unhinges its jaw and takes a chunk out of its target. 1d10 + 2d8 (14) Wounds.
36–55%	*Rip You Apart! (2 attacks):* the Grey Taker attempts to rend its target in two with massive blows. 2d10 + 2d8 (20) damage each.
56–80%	*Dislocating Grab:* the Grey Taker grabs its target, pulling limbs from sockets while it holds them. 5d8 (23) damage. The Grey Taker grabs the target. (–6 Clash Points and unable to take actions, save for Unarmed Combat or Athletics checks.) The target must spend an action to make an Unarmed Combat or Athletics Clash against the Atakan's Combat to break free. While grabbing a target, the Grey Taker can make attacks against the target without them being able to react, and enjoys +15% to Combat rolls.
81–90%	*Seklah!:* the Grey Taker attempts to consume its target in a ravenous expression of hunger and violence. 3d12 + 2d8 (28) damage.

5 & 6. The Pen

These two main halls, and the rooms attached to them, are where the Grey Taker keeps its prisoners, nearly all of which are Trauj. They can roam the rooms and set up what defences they can. Indeed, the Grey Taker often gives them weapons. They crouch in the darkness, waiting for the Atakan to hunt them. Currently, there are nine prisoners in this area, all emaciated and nearly mad from the terror.

Shargot Territory

What a Jackal's senses reveal:

Sights – darkness, Mavakan sparring in the hall, and humans in chains doing menial work or fighting unarmed against smaller Takan.

Smells – spices, unwashed flesh, and the stink of penned-up beasts.

Sounds – sounds of sparring, discussions in Howls about the best way to take Tjaru, and the cries of agonised prisoners.

7. The Deep Halls

The deep halls were once the palatial portion of Kek-bel-kala. The sculptures and friezes still stand here, showing mighty Oritakan girded for war, humanity enslaved, and scenes of battle in which the Takan tower over the forces of the Luathi. It is now split between the quarters for Shargot's followers, t heir brood, and the bulk of the human prisoners from the caravans. Nearly 100 people are chained along the halls, between doorways, or shackled to the floor – much like those in the Grey Taker's throne room. The room at the far end of the halls is the vault, where Shargot keeps his band's weapons, armour, and treasure. None of the weapons or armour are exceptional; Takan who have such gear keep it with them, but there is enough here to arm a force twice the size of that in Kek-bel-kala. The vault also holds two talents' worth of trade goods, spices, and jewellery taken from caravans all over the War Road.

8. The Proving Ground

This is where Shargot holds court, as well as where his band trains. Shargot is an Oritakan, cast in the mould of the leaders of Barak Barad, with a keen mind and strong will. He is moulding his band into an army. At any given time, 2d12 Mavakan run drills. There is a 55% chance Shargot is here, overseeing the training. Most disturbing is the presence of Otsakan – half-breed abominations. They stand as tall as Trauj, while possessing the bestial physiques of their Takan parentage. Shargot revived the ancient practices of Barak Barad to breed the Otsakan as shock troops. Some force within Kek-bel-kala is amicable to the practice and blesses the Otsakan to be fruitful and multiply. There are 1d4 × 10 Otsakan here at any time. Shargot has begun to work with Umari, and Jackals can find Otsakan in her areas, as well.

Should a fight break out here, Shargot is an Oritakan with the following stats:

SHARGOT			
Type:	Takan	Location:	Kek-bel-kala
		Wounds:	70
Defence:	100%	Protection:	4 (breastplate)
Combat:	105%	Move:	14
Knowledge:	50%	Initiative:	15
Urban:	40%	Clash Points:	6
Common:	100%	Treasure Score:	3
		Corruption:	10

Special Abilities

Inured to Darkness: Shargot suffers no penalties due to absence of light.

Commanding Presence: the high-pitched howls and orders of Shargot inspire the Takan around it. Each non-Oritakan Takan in the battle counts as having a trait that applies to their combat skills, as well as +10 Wounds.

Skilful Strike: Shargot can re-roll any damage dice results of '1'.

Rattling Will: when Shargot makes a successful Willpower check, the originator of the effect takes a –20% penalty to any subsequent skill check that affects Willpower against Shargot for the rest of the adventure. On a critical success, Shargot deals 2d6 Wounds (ignoring Protection) to the originator.

Skilful Challenge: when Shargot successfully challenges an opponent, the Clash Point cost to react to anyone but Shargot increases by an additional 1.

Combat Range

1–15%	*Rallying Laughter:* the Oritakan howls with laughter, exalting in the battle. Each Takan recovers 1d8 Wounds.
16–30%	*Flail of Ignorance (2 attacks):* up to two targets take 2d8 + 3d6 (19) damage; or, the Oritakan can inflict this damage upon an ally to grant them a free attack at +15%.
31–55%	*Dance of Slaughter (multiple attacks):* Shargot makes an attack on each adjacent enemy for 2d8+3d6 (19) damage each.
56–60%	*I Know Your Name:* Shargot mimics the voice of a loved one or friend, sowing confusion. Each target must spend a Clash Point to make a difficult Willpower check. If they fail, the chaotic cry causes the target to spend an additional Clash Point to lash out at an ally.
61–90%	*Darkness Will Come Again:* Shargot sends a vicious blow across the brow of his target. 2d8 + 3d6 (19) damage, and the target must make an extreme Endurance check or become blind for 2d4 rounds.

OTSAKAN				
Type:	Humanoid/Takan		**Location:**	Kek-bel-kala
			Wounds:	45
Defence:	75%		**Protection:**	3 (leather + shield)
Combat:	90%		**Move:**	15
Knowledge:	50%		**Initiative:**	15
Urban:	60%		**Clash Points:**	2
Common:	50%		**Treasure Score:**	2
			Corruption:	3

Special Abilities

Inured to Darkness: the Otsakan suffers no penalties due to absence of light.

Inbred Hatred: the Otsakan hates humanity in a way that outshines even the Takan. When fighting against humans, the Otsakan has a trait for all combat rolls.

Combat Range

1–20%	*Glancing Blow:* the Otsakan strikes a glancing blow with its bronze weapon. 1d10 + 2d6 (12) damage.
21–45%	*Shield Bash:* the Otsakan slams its shield powerfully into its target. 3d6 (10) damage. The target must make a hard Endurance check or lose 1d4 Clash Points. On a fumble, the target loses all Clash Points until their next turn.
46–65%	*Shield Trap:* the Otsakan brings its khopesh across those engaged with it in a slashing strike, attempting to catch shields. 1d10 + 2d6 (12) damage. If the target is using a shield, they must roll a difficult Athletics check or see the straps snapped by the Otsakan. The shield is useless until repaired with a successful Craft check and 30 shekels' worth of components.
66–75%	*Savage Blows (2 attacks):* the Otsakan savagely hacks at its target, attempting to drive them to their knees. 2d10 + 2d6 (18) damage each. If both attacks hit, the target is knocked prone.
76–90%	*Hateful Ending:* the Otsakan seeks to take the head of a prone enemy. 4d10 + 2d6 (29) damage. Hateful Ending can only target prone creatures.

9. The Passages

The passages lead to the upper balconies and galleries of Kek-bel-kala, many of which have collapsed over the centuries. This is the route to get to the prisoners the Jackals spotted hanging outside. The tunnels also lead to the deeper parts of the fortress, which Shargot's forces have yet to explore. Some say there are ways out of the fortress into the mountains, while others report receiving dreams from something beneath the ground – something calling to them.

Sessu Umari Territory

What a Jackal's senses reveal:

Sights – Small, lit braziers which cast light and have small smouldering packets on them.

Smells – Spikenard (an essential oil) from the braziers, which nearly masks the stench of death and decay.

Sounds – Soft chants and prayers, the rushing of wind, and incoherent whispers just at the edge of perception.

The temple complex lies deep within the fortress. There are no prisoners here. Instead it is a camp of Takan, spread throughout the temple, occupying the former adherents' cells. Umari took the chambers of the high priest, and recently used prisoners from the Grey Taker to consecrate the statues here. She spends much of her time communing with the Rathic of Kek-bel-kala, the Daughter Beneath the Earth, and a terrible presence to the east. This presence slowly reveals to her how she can aid it in raising the Iron Gates of the East once more. Due to the profane nature of the temple, the three-dozen slain captives have risen as Etemma. Umari will not engage in a fight with the Jackals in the temple. She commands her Takan and Etemma to slay the intruders, while she retreats to the high priestess' chambers. Should the fight go poorly for her forces, she escapes into the mountains, to join with the Daughter Beneath the Earth.

An Ancient Lore check reveals the Takan built this temple to the worship the three prime Rathic of Bartak Kentak: Nabim-Sin, Orakenu, and Moktal. A Jackal who spends an hour in the temple with a light source increases their Ancient Lore skill by 5%. At any given time, there are 30 Etemma, 4d6 Norakan, and 2d6 Mavakan in the main temple area.

Kek-bel-kala is a death trap, should the Jackals go in swinging. There are nearly 1,000 Takan, Dead, and humans in this old temple. The size of the nascent horde should be worrisome to the Jackals. Some might attempt to rescue the prisoners, but even that could be a fool's errand. How such an attempt plays out is up to you, but it should be deadly and dangerous.

When the Jackals return to Tjaru to report their findings, proceed to Act 3.

ACT 3: BLOODY SUNRISE

Upon returning to Tjaru, Deborah wants a debrief about what they discovered. She grows worried and strangely excited at the news of a Takan horde that large so close to the fortress. She interrupts the Jackals' tale, asking for clarifications on numbers, types, dispositions, etc. Once the Jackals complete their report, Deborah begins to share the second part of her plan:

- Scouts report a large army of Luathi moving towards Tjaru.
- It seems the time for the first battle of this war has come.
- Tjaru is not yet ready, they need at least one more season get everything in place.
- Deborah needs the Jackals to buy the fort time to finish getting prepared. She wants them to lure the Takan horde into the other army. She knows where they should be. It should be easy enough to kick their nest and go running towards the other army.
- She knows it is a shocking plan, but without it, her people are going to die. There is no time to get a message to the Sars – the other army will arrive at Tjaru within the week.

This is a strange moment for all the Jackals. They have spent the last nine years working with one of the city-states, defending their people, slaying Takan to keep them safe, and strengthening the rule of Law. However, this is a different sort of decision – this is the wilful use of chaotic beings to slay Lawful ones. What do the Jackals do? What are the consequences of their actions? The remainder of this chapter looks at three possible outcomes to Deborah's request: follow her orders, warn the Luathi, or defect.

Like Wolves to the Slaughter

Following Deborah's order is the practical choice. The Takan are a threat to Tjaru, as are the Luathi. The two threats cancel each other out, and the forces of Tjaru can then march in to clean up the stragglers. Everything works out... Right? But there are two problems with this plan.

The first is that it undermines the rule of Law in the area. Using Takan as a weapon against other humans is a despicable act, causing 6 Corruption per participating Jackal. Should it come out that the Jackals took part in this action, their names live in infamy for the rest of their days, and possibly for centuries to come.

Second, it destabilises the region. Should the Takan win, they will coalesce into a true horde, bound to a singular will. This is a danger the Zaharets has not seen for centuries. They will turn their eyes to Tjaru next, and the siege next season will be orders of magnitude worse. Even if the opposing Luathi win, their side of the War Road will be devastated by the loss of so many soldiers. True, it leaves them ripe for more invasions by Tjaru, but it also means they are defenceless against the things that wait in the darkness. Takan, Melkoni, or Gerwa all stand to claim a piece of the War Road if this happens. Instead of uniting the two city-states into one kingdom, Deborah's plan could fracture the War Road even more.

If the Jackals take this course, Deborah provides them with solid intelligence on where the enemy camp lies. Then, it is a matter of luring the whole of the Takan camp out into the field. There are many ways to do this, but here are two possibilities.

Deception

The Jackals, posing as Black Nails, can inform Kek-bel-kala of the approaching army. This spurs the leaders of the factions into action, forcing a champion to emerge. Currently, the strongest contenders are Shargot and Umari. There is a 40% chance that Umari becomes the champion, a 30% chance Shargot does, and a 30% chance they ally, slay the Grey Taker, and lead together. Once informed, the horde forms within two days, and they set out to meet the army. This force marches at 1,100 strength.

Assassination

It might be enough, from what the Jackals saw, for them to slay the leader(s) of one of the bands and escape, leaving a trail for the horde to chase (this means the triplets, in the case of the Black Nails). This involves a fight somewhere in Kek-bel-kala. The issue with this plan is that the deeper the Jackals go inside to assassinate a leader, the better chance they have of riling the horde, and the quicker it coalesces.

- Killing the triplets has a 40% chance of triggering the horde immediately. If it does, there is a 60% chance the Grey Taker emerges as the champion, absorbing the Black Nails and using its newfound strength to slay Shargot and force Umari to yield. This horde is ready to fight within 1d4 + 4 hours and marches at a strength of about 850. If the Grey Taker does not emerge as the champion, the Shargot/Umari alliance does – after slaying the Grey Taker. This force marches at 900 strength.
- Killing the Grey Taker is perhaps the best solution. The throne room is isolated, so slaying the Grey Taker without too much intervention is possible. The void left between the Black Nails and Shargot is quickly discovered and filled, triggering the horde immediately. There is an 80% chance of a Shargot/Umari alliance forming, with a 10% chance either will emerge as the individual champion. The horde coalesces in 1d3 + 2 hours. This force marches at nearly 1,000 strong.

- Killing Shargot or Umari is the most difficult path for the Jackals. They are deepest in the fortress, so fighting without detection and escaping without notice is practically impossible. However, should either die, the horde coalesces immediately, and the remaining leader slays the Grey Taker and two of the three triplets. The horde emerges over 1d6 + 4 hours but takes great casualties. They march at 800 strong.

The Horde

A horde is not just a group of Takan larger than most bands. When a group that large comes together, a champion eventually emerges – one with a supernatural link to those under it. No one living knows whether this is a part of the Takan nature or something Keta bred into them. It means the horde operates as one organism, with the champion as its head. As stated above, the horde accepts and somehow instinctually prefers a Mouathenic as champion.

Once the horde coalesces, it is up to the Jackals to lure it to the approaching army. This involves a series of hard Survival rolls, as the Jackals must stay close enough to provide the lure but far enough ahead of the Tsutakan packs that attempt to run them down. Each Jackal must pass three such checks, with failures costing them 2 Mettle (fumbles count as losing 4 Mettle). Every three failures result in a Tsutakan pack attacking (use one Tsutakan per Jackal). This might mean the Jackals must fight multiple times before they arrive at the enemy army.

The Luathi army is easy to locate, as it contains over 2,000 warriors (over twice as many as Tjaru possesses), plus its baggage train. If the army marches south from Ameena Noani, it consists of 65% Luathi warriors, 25% Melkoni heavy infantry, and 10% Trauj riders, all marching beneath the banner of the Three Bulls. If the army marches north from Sentem, it consists of 55% Luathi warriors, 30% Trauj riders, and 15% Gerwa mercenaries, beneath the banners of Hawk (Sentem) and Hart (Densom). Chariots rumble across the plains, with Trauj riders acting as scouts. If the Jackals arrive during the day, the army is on the march and ready for a fight. If the Jackals arrive during the night, the army is encamped and not prepared for an ambush.

In this scenario, it is unnecessary for the Jackals to even get involved. Once the horde sees the Luathi army, it naturally attacks. The Jackals can watch from a safe distance, removed from the slaughter.

Read or paraphrase the following:

From where you watch, the thunderous clash of bodies and the screams of the dying fall muted on your ears. This vantage point abstracts the chaotic melee of war. To your eyes, it plays out in a scrambling, ant-like parody of the carnage you know churns below. The day wears on, but you know the outcome. Death.

The rapine nature of the Takan means the Luathi can expect to suffer 30% casualty rates. Compare this to the average casualty rate of approximately 5% for ancient battles. Six hundred warriors lie dead in the Plains of Aeco, with twice that many wounded. Once again, the War Road claims its toll, paid in bones and blood. The Luathi army curls in on itself, and begins to retreat, taking what wounded it can with it.

However, the army breaks the horde, which scatters; 70% of the survivors return to Kek-bel-kala. How many Takan the army slays depends on the champion:

- **The Triplets:** these three Oritakan are tacticians and blunt the worst of the losses. The Takan suffer 25% losses.

- **The Grey Taker:** the Atakan whips the horde into a frenzy, costing them more lives. The Takan suffer 40% losses.
- **Shargot:** Shargot is no fool, but neither is he a tactician. The Takan suffer 30% losses.
- **Umari:** Umari supplements the Takan's force with dark and terrible rites. The Takan suffer 20% losses.
- **Shargot/Umari Alliance:** the two working in tandem is terrifying. The Takan suffer only 15% losses.

Proceed to the *Aftermath* section below.

A Voice in the Wilderness

This scenario starts much like the previous one. The Jackals must still kick the horde's nest and lead it to the Luathi army. However, in this scenario, they choose to warn the opposing army. When the army comes into view, after the Survival checks, the Jackals must rush to warn the Luathi. A final hard Endurance check is necessary to cross the remaining distance in time. Failure here inflicts 2 points of Mettle loss (4 on a fumble).

The army's scouts, probably Trauj, are the first to meet the Jackals. Honesty gets the Jackals captured or slain, but it is a simple Deception check to inform the scouts about the horde, without any mention as to how they know about the horde. The scouts split – some ride ahead to see the horde, while some return to the army with the Jackals. The commander, Abner, listens to the reports of the Jackals and the scouts. Abner is a canny commander, so any Deception checks with him are difficult. Should the Jackals come under suspicion, Abner places them under arrest, requiring them to escape in the chaos of battle. Use the Guard stats from *Jackals*.

Otherwise, Abner gives them his thanks, the thanks of the Sar of the city, and the promise that their names will be known. He also tells them that should they survive this day, he will find some way to repay them, then asks if they will join his bodyguard to fight in the battle. Should the Jackals refuse, Abner is disappointed but accepts this, as the Jackals did race to warn them. Should they agree, see the battles in *To Turn Traitor*, below.

The Jackals' warning has a substantial effect on the battle. It reduces the casualties among the army to 15%, while the Takan suffer an additional 15% in losses. From wherever the Jackals watch the battle, it is closer and more visceral. Read or paraphrase the following:

It is the sound that hits you first. The roar of the Takan, the sounds of spears on shields, the thunder of the charging chariots. The forces of the army blunt your view of the battle. But you know they battle the true enemy out there in the plains.

If the Jackals stay for the battle, Abner finds them afterwards. A Takan claw has wounded the commander, whose arm streams blood. A Hasheer works on the wound while the commander talks with the Jackals. He tells them of the bloody fight, and that they routed the enemy with an acceptable loss of life. He could not have done it without the Jackals, and he worries aloud about how bad it could have been. Abner rewards the Jackals with two fine robes each (+10% to Influence), a talent of silver, and a fine Trauj horse. He also offers the Jackals a place in the army, where they would draw a captain's share of the plunder. They plan to attack Tjaru, although they must regroup and rest first. If the Jackals refuse, he grudgingly accepts their decision and allows them to leave with accolades of the army. If they accept, see *To Turn Traitor*.

Once the Jackals escape, leave, or flee from the Luathi army, proceed to the *Aftermath* section below.

To Turn Traitor

This scenario assumes the Jackals cannot or will not enact Deborah's plan. If they defy her to her face, Deborah throws the Jackals into a cell, from which they must escape or fight their way out. Use the Guard stats from *Jackals*. If they do not, Deborah assumes the Jackals mean to carry out her plan.

Finding the army is not a difficult task, and the Jackals encounter the scouts of the army as above. Soon, the Jackals find themselves before Abner. The commander listens to the Jackals, and everyone present is horrified by Deborah's plan. For a Luathi to use Takan in such a fashion against fellow Luathi is beyond the pale. Convincing Abner of Deborah's plan and the Jackals' defection requires the Jackals to gain **four successes** before they incur **two failures**.

Abner wants the Jackals to scout Kek-bel-kala, not to use the beasts in his upcoming assault, but to see how large the threat is. When the Jackals return, Abner makes the decision to attack Kek-bel-kala before moving on to Tjaru. He cannot abide a Takan army at his flank or rear. Abner enlists the Jackals to help scout the fortress and aid in the assault, using Kek-bel-kala as a crucible for the Jackals. If they prove themselves in the battle (for example, bringing back the heads of the Takan leaders), he sees them not only as defectors, but as Jackals willing to do the right thing for the right reasons. After the battle with the Takan, proceed to the *Aftermath* section below.

Battles in Jackals

Although future supplements may focus on rules for mass combat, this adventure focuses on the actions of the Jackals, not those of leaders. For some of the possible scenarios in this and the next adventure, the Jackals could find themselves in pitched battles. *Jackals* handles this by focusing on the Jackals while the rest of the combat happens off-screen. The Loremaster should keep the action focused front and centre on the Jackals. In Kek-bel-kala, this means they battle with the leaders of each section. Use the Jackals as the gauge to see how the rest of the combat is fairing for their side. Each round, describe what they see off in the distance: a flash of combat tumbling through the halls, a group of soldiers taking down an Atakan, etc. If you prefer a bit of randomness in your fights, roll on the following chart every other round of combat, starting on round two:

VAGARIES OF WAR	
d10	Effect
1	*A Turn for the Worse:* a horn sounds, and reinforcements arrive. Add 1d4 of the weakest creature or one of the strongest to the battle.
2–3	*An Arrow in the Back:* a random Jackal suffers an arrow strike from a passing Takan. Ranged Combat 85%; 1d8 + 1d6 (8) damage. Jackals can spend Clash Points to Dodge, as usual.
4–5	*Scrum:* a Luathi soldier knocks a Mavakan into a random Jackal. Add one Mavakan (with 20 Wounds) into the battle. The Jackal in question must spend a Clash Point and succeed on a hard Athletics check or be knocked prone.
6–7	*A Thousand Arrows:* 2d8 random Takan lose a Clash Point and take 2d8 damage (ignoring Protection) from Luathi arrows.
8–9	*The Dread of Combat:* the Takan must make a morale check as if they suffered 75% casualties. If they are above 50% in numbers, the check is a simple one.
10	*A Turn for the Better:* two Luathi running past stop to aid the Jackals in their fight. They each provide one Jackal with +2 Clash Points and +1d10 damage, as they help distract and slay the creature. They move on after the next die roll.

In this case, after combat, you determine how well the Jackals' side did with a d100 roll, modified by the items below. As per the scarring rules, each modifier is cumulative. The Loremaster should make one check at the end of combat.

- Each Jackal who ends the battle in Kek-bel-kala with no Wounds in the second row: –10%
- Each Jackal who dies: +10%
- Each leader the Jackals slay
  › Triplets: –5% each
  › Grey Taker: –20%
  › Shargot: –10%
  › Umari: –15%
- Each leader who escapes
  › Triplets: +5% each
  › Grey Taker: +5%
  › Shargot: +15%
  › Umari: +20%

	MASS COMBAT RESULTS		
dIOO	Result	Jackals' Side Casualties	Enemy Casualties
Less than 50%	Fate Be Praised: the Jackals' forces suffer only minor casualties and wounds	2%	45%
51–75%	An Easy Victory: the Jackals' forces easily triumph over their foes	4%	30%
76–100%	The Cost of War: the Jackals' forces suffer what was expected by the scribes for this battle	8%	20%
101–125%	The Toll of the War Road: the Jackals' forces struggle to eke out a victory	12%	12%
126–150%	Pyrrhic Victory: the Jackals win, but at great cost	20%	8%
151–175%	Loss: the Jackals' forces lose the fight	30%	4%
176%+	Rout: the Jackals' forces are brutally slaughtered as they run	45%	2%

AFTERMATH

Like Wolves to the Slaughter

Depending on the outcome of this option, the Takan massacre the opposing army, forcing Abner to retreat. Twice the number of casualties listed scatter into the plains, with only about half that number eventually regrouping with Abner. There is still the matter of the Takan horde. Deborah wants to slaughter them before the next dry season, to ensure they are removed from the planning. Tjaru is safe, for now, and the Jackals dealt a severe blow to the enemies of their Sar, but at what price? The final adventure is easier for Tjaru, as the enemy forces are unable to regroup. But the Jackals are left with the memory of their choice and the Corruption it caused. There is always the chance others hear about what the Jackals did and come looking for revenge.

A Voice in the Wilderness

This middle-of-the-road solution allows some to see the Jackals as heroes. Abner's army survives, and if the Jackals help, the army heralds them as heroes. The Takan still inflict their damage, and Tjaru still has the upper hand in the battles to come, but to a lesser extent. Additionally, Deborah is furious. While she understands the moral difficulties of the situation, she no longer trusts the Jackals as she once did. She has them followed and places them in the hottest parts of next year's battles, attempting to remove them as liabilities. The Jackals can take the time to appeal to a higher authority to mitigate this by speaking with their Sar. The news horrifies Phamea and Sameel, but Japeth (especially if corrupted) sides with Deborah. A corrupted Japeth might order the Jackals to be imprisoned, or worse, condemn them as traitors.

To Turn Traitor

In this scenario, the battle next year goes against Tjaru. Abner possesses both his army and the Jackals. He thanks them and rewards them for their aid. Abner also questions the Jackals about Tjaru, its weaknesses, entrances, Deborah, and her plans. If the Jackals proved themselves in the Battle of Kek-bel-kala, Abner gives them positions similar to those they held with Deborah – advisors to the captain of the host. A feast is held in their honour during the next seasonal action, and they benefit from 50% off new Acquire Patron actions. However, they also lose any Homes or Patron levels with the other side, at least until the end of the next adventure (see the *Aftermath* section below).

In any case, the war for the Zaharets and the emerging kingdom of Luathi reaches its crescendo in the next adventure. The heavy rains of the season, especially after the heatwaves, turn the War Road to mud – forcing both sides to stand down until Salas next year.

ADVANCEMENTS

- 1 for finding Kek-bel-kala
- 1 for freeing the captives
- 1 for leading the Takan to slaughter Tjaru's enemies
- 1 for warning Abner's forces, which also increases each Jackal's Kleos by 3
- 1 for defecting, which also increases each Jackal's Kleos by 5

HOOKS

To Raze a Fortress: Kek-bel-kala cannot stand. While the horde may have been averted, there is still a festering pit in the plains! Delving the depths of Kek-bel-kala requires resources and will, something the Jackals might find in short supply.

Seeking Deeper Mysteries: What is the Moon Mask, and how is it behind the Takan of Kek-bel-kala?

The Dweller Beneath: Something lies beneath Kek-bel-kala, something that has not been seen in this world for an age. What is it? A long-forgotten Rathic? A servant or messenger from the Frost-rimed throne? Whatever it is, Deborah seeks to put an end to it.

The Remnant: Deborah needs the Jackals to hunt down the remnants of the army scattered by the horde. They are to capture and turn any they can, or imprison or slay any they cannot.

CHAPTER 10
YEAR OF GOLDEN GRAIN

The Sar of the Morning will come
Let the Luathi make a joyful noise.
Light will be the boss of their shield
Wrath the edge of their blade.
The land will stand with them,
Against the chaotic seas.
Hail will fall like siege stones
And the sea will assail their foes.
The sun's spears will blaze in the sky,
And lightning shall fall like arrows.
Let the Luathi rejoice, salvation is at hand,
for the Sar of the Zaharets will arise.

~ Kaharic Psalm of Coronation ~

INTRODUCTION

This is the final adventure in *The Fall of the Children of Bronze*. Here, the war for the Zaharets comes to its completion with one side falling under the sway of the other. Although the Jackals play a major part, theirs is not the only part, and Fate decides what becomes of the Luathi of the War Road. Can the Jackals lead their side to supremacy, or will they fall beneath the bronze of their sisters and brothers? What is the shape of the Zaharets at the end of this year? That is in the hands of the Loremaster and the Jackals.

Why *Fall*? Here, at the end of the campaign, it might seem strange to title the book *The Fall of the Children of Bronze* when a new Luathi kingdom is about to be born. However, the reality of the situation is the status quo of the Zaharets has radically changed, and one of the city-states will fall and many Luathi lives will be lost in the raising of a new kingdom. Finally, it remains to be seen whether this new kingdom can hold together. Are the Luathi stronger for this conflict, or is the new kingdom a shell that collapses under the pressures of Kalypsis? These are questions outside the scope of this campaign, but ones that may be covered in future supplements or played out at your tables.

THEME

The theme of this year is unity through conflict. The conflict between the two sides, the plans of the Sars, and the machinations of those in power all come to a head this year. The Jackals find themselves, once again, at the fulcrum of these events and must navigate them as best they can. Although war is inevitable, there is the chance for something greater to come from it than simple material gains. There is a chance for unity, and the birth of the first Luathi kingdom in the Zaharets for centuries.

IMPORTANT NPCS

Abner, Nawsi of the Army: Abner is the Nawsi of the Sar's army (see above). He is wise enough to see the potential in a unified War Road and seeks to work towards that end. This includes granting mercy to those he captures, or surrendering in the face of overwhelming odds, so Luathi survive.

Deborah, Nawsi of Tjaru: Deborah is in a flexible position, based on the Jackal's decisions in the previous adventure. The more powerful she is, the fairer she is willing to play. The worse her position, the more desperate she becomes. Her loyalty to her Sar is nearly an obsession, and this leads her to put her people's lives and interests above those of any other Luathi.

EVENTS

- Heavy rains initially look to wash out crops, but the harvest is good. It does not replenish the lost crops of previous years, but it provides a solid basis for recovery.
- Abner begins to raid the areas around Tjaru, taking pastures, flocks, and small towns like Jabalem.
- Other battles spring up along the War Road. Settlements begin to take sides, old grievances flare up, and feuds reignite under the pretence of war.
- As the year rolls on, the heat returns, and the famine begins to settle in. Avsalim, using dark rituals far to the north of ruined Keta, is behind the strange weather.

RETIREMENT BENEFITS

There are no retirement benefits for this year. Fate has delivered the Zaharets to war, and each person must stand on their own.

THE FALL OF THE CHILDREN OF BRONZE

An adventure for 'Defenders of' or Champion Jackals, set during the month of Hamis, in the dry season.

OVERVIEW

The Sars go to war at the start of the dry season in the Year of Golden Grain, as it is unclear whether the brutal weather of the last two years will continue. In this adventure, the final battle of what will come to be known as the Wars of Unification comes to an end, with one Sar becoming the Malekh or Malekeh (king or queen) of the new Luathi kingdom on the War Road. However, that victory lies on the other side of two bloody battles – from Tjaru to Mayrah Vedil – in which the Jackals find themselves fighting against their sisters and brothers. In the end, the War Road stands unified and (hopefully) strong against that which would threaten it.

This adventure is the most fluid of all adventures in this campaign; it requires additional information and preparation by the Loremaster due to the campaign nature. There is framework for the final adventures here, which requires Loremasters to hang their own campaign consequences on it to bring *The Fall of the Children of Bronze* to a satisfying conclusion. The base assumption of this adventure is the Jackals stood with Deborah's plan and used the Takan to assault Abner's army. The changes noted below show how the outcome of the other adventure affects this one. If the Jackals defected, Loremasters must adapt the adventure to reflect the flipside of the battle. Notes to aid Loremasters are provided below.

> **Jackals in the South:** Battle of Mayrah Vedil → Battle of Tjaru
> **Jackals in the North:** Battle of Tjaru → Battle of Mayrah Vedil

The order in which the first two acts of this year play out is flexible. If Abner represents the armies of Ameena Noani, the first battle takes place at Tjaru, with Deborah falling back to Mayrah Vedil. If he represents the armies of Sentem, the first battle is at Mayrah Vedil, with the forces of Ameena Noani retreating to Tjaru. Both adventures start the same way. Deborah summons the Jackals to her chambers in the pre-dawn hours. The Nawsi holds a small scrap of parchment. Word came this morning (by way of a Tablet of the Scriptorium or the Brazier of Sending) that Abner's forces are on the move. They move ever closer, like vultures circling their prey. Deborah plans to march out against them, bringing with her the armies of Tjaru. She wants the Jackals to leave with her immediately.

Abner's forces, although decimated by the Takan attack, have recovered somewhat in the previous seasons. They are 20% stronger than they were at the end of the battle with the Takan (somewhere between 900 and 1,900 warriors). Meanwhile, Deborah's forces stand at just over 1,400 warriors. This does not include the warriors Barqan secured within the mines, which – depending on the arc of your campaign – might belong to Abner or Deborah, determined by the side of the War Road to which Barqan's forces are loyal.

Ameena Noani's Forces

Phamea's preparation and foresight paid off. She managed to assemble a large force consisting of Melkoni and Luathi. Luathi make up a larger portion of this army than they do Sentem's army, because the north has more towns from which to draw. Melkoni phalanxes anchor the right flank of her army. The bulk of her forces are the Luathi – primarily slingers and spear wielders – with Jackals filling out the remainder of her forces. The presence of Kahars and Hasheers also bolsters Ameena Noani's forces. Additionally, the army fields heavy chariots.

- 800 Luathi slingers and spear wielders
- 350 Melkoni phalanxes
- 150 Jackals
- 60 Kahars and Hasheers
- 40 heavy Luathi chariots

Sentem's Forces

Japeth and Sameel recruited more mercenaries than Ameena Noani, due to their smaller population. Luathi shields and Gerwa soldiers protect slingers and Gerwa archers, while the Trauj harass the enemy's flanks. Jackals make up about a quarter of their forces. Additionally, the army fields light chariots.

- 400 Luathi shields
- 150 Gerwa soldiers
- 150 Luathi archers
- 100 Gerwa slingers
- 220 Trauj cavalry
- 350 Jackals
- 24 light Gerwa chariots

ACT 1: BATTLE OF MAYRAH VEDIL

The battle for Mayrah Vedil is a battle in the plains.

It is a three-day journey between Tjaru and Mayrah Vedil. Five days after the initial news, the armies of Ameena Noani and Sentem meet. However, Mayrah Vedil is too valuable to both sides to risk destroying it during a siege. Neither side is willing to put its foundries, mines, and skilled labourers at risk. The battle takes place on the plain of Negeddo, just west of the city, allowing the sides to flee into Mayrah Vedil or back to Tjaru, as needed.

When the Jackals arrive, forces move into position.

If Mayrah Vedil's battle happens first:

- *Ameena Noani's Forces:* Deborah attempts to take the city by first crushing the army outside it. Recognising the folly of a rush up the ridge, Deborah attempts to swing wide with her forces and threaten the gate, forcing Abner to meet them on the plains or against the wall. If Deborah knows of the hidden passages, she sends the Jackals into the mountain with a small force to prevent the soldiers hiding there from engaging.
- *Sentem's Forces:* Abner and the armies of Sentem are at their full strength described above, complemented by Barqan's warriors. Abner arrays them along the ridgeline just outside Mayrah Vedil, so his warriors have the advantage of height and momentum while charging downhill. If Barqan's warriors have yet to be discovered, they emerge from the mountains near noon, an hour after the battle begins, to attack the northern front.

If Tjaru's battle happens first:

- *Ameena Noani's Forces:* Abner presses his advantage, aiming to take the city as quickly as possible. He leaves a token force in Tjaru (10% of his army) and establishes it as a hold, giving Deborah time to fall back to Mayrah Vedil.
- *Sentem's Forces:* Deborah, harried by Abner, makes for Mayrah Vedil. She does not possess enough time to enter the city, so she arrays her forces on the ridgeline.

Timeline of the Battle of Mayrah Vedil

Below is the timeline of the battle of Mayrah Vedil. Think of this as a possible order of events for the battle, which allows Loremasters to showcase certain events in the background or use them as set pieces for the fights.

TIMELINE OF THE BATTLE OF MAYRAH VEDIL		
Hour	Deborah (Ameena Noani)	Deborah (Sentem)
1	Abner breaks camp and arrays his forces	Armies arrive at Mayrah Vedil. Deborah's army regroups, bolstered by Barqan's forces. Assemble on the ridgeline, as Abner's army arrives.
2	Deborah's army arrives. Not waiting for any communication, Deborah's army attacks. Battle begins. Trauj horsemen harry the archers, while Deborah attacks the path leading to the gate.	Abner sends messages to Deborah and Barqan demanding their surrender. They reject his offer, although Barqan keeps it in his heart.
3	Chariots engage on the plains while the fighting grows fierce.	Battle begins. Barqan initiates the attack. The bulk of his forces assault the ridge, while the Melkoni swing around to try to take the road and the gate leading into the city.
4	Deborah sends the Jackals into the mountains if she knows of the tunnels.	Chariots engage on the plains while the fighting grows fierce.
5	Shadow of Doubt upon a Soul invoked (see below).	Shadow of Doubt upon a Soul invoked (see below).
6	Barqan's forces join the fray, attacking Deborah from the north.	Barqan's forces join the fray, attacking Abner from behind.
8	Battle ends	Battle ends

Trickery and Tactics

1. Hidden Tunnels

Barqan has control of the tunnels within the mountain. If no one else knows about them, Barqan plans to send his 1,000 warriors out through them to flank the enemy. Thus, one hour into the battle, these reinforcements arrive. If the Jackals (or Abner, due to his spies from **The Way Through**) know of the tunnels, they use them to circumvent the defences of the city, allowing a pincer manoeuvre from behind the enemy's forces. In such a case, the Jackals might be sent to fight in the tunnels, either to defend or to take them.

2. Shadow of Doubt upon a Soul

The Hasheers of Ameena Noani discovered a rite in Rataro which they attempt here. Shadow of Doubt upon a Soul is an old Lukkan rite, but treads into the shadowy paths of magic. This rite requires four hours and two-dozen Hasheers to enact. The Jackals can clearly see the tent where the Hasheers perform this rite (see below). The nuances of the rite are unknown, but Go-el, the ranking Hasheer, worked out enough of it to attempt an invocation. The rite invokes the Silent Lands into this world, causing what is normally deep below to rise to the surface. The rite requires either a large number of sacrifices or a site of great death. Go-el believes the battle will suffice. The Hasheer is correct; however, the knowledge he possesses on this rite is lacking. It does summon the Silent Lands here, but it releases torments and nightmares on the souls and minds of all who battle beyond the tent. The resulting chaos ravages both sides, unchecked, and causes terror to rule the field. When the rite is invoked (see below), all Jackals must make a hard Willpower check to keep fighting and not flee in terror. Those on both sides who can see the tent when the rite is invoked must make a morale check. Assume both sides possess a Defence Skill group of 60%, modified by how the Jackals have handled the battle. Every two Jackal successes decrease the difficulty of their side's check, while increasing the opposition's difficulty by the same amount. If a side fails, they break and attempt to flee the combat. If both sides fail, proceed to *Ending the Battle*. If only one side fails, increase their casualty percentage by 10%. The rite consumes the Hasheers and their tent, leaving a dead patch of earth which never heals.

3. Chariot Battles

It would not be a battle of the War Road without chariots. As stated above, there are 64 chariots rumbling around the battlefield, the sounds of their wheels and collisions rumbling over the thickest din of combat. If the Jackals do not get involved in the chariot combat, the chariots act as colour, adding sight and sound to the battle raging around them. If the Jackals do get involved, chariot combat is fast, furious, and dangerous for all involved (see below).

Battle Scenes

The focus of this battle is not on the thousands of nameless NPCs that rage across the plains, but the efforts and events of the Jackals. Much like the previous adventure, the Jackals' tale follows several smaller scenes which act as a guide for how the rest of the battle is going. Below are four scenes in which the Jackals can become embroiled. As Loremaster, it is up to you to pick and choose which to use, or to add your own into the chaos of the battle. You know your group and how much combat and variety they enjoy better than we do.

Each scene takes between one and two hours of time. Between each scene, the Jackals must make an Endurance check to see how they fare after hours of combat. The first check is easy, the second normal, the third difficult, and the fourth hard. For each failure, the Jackal suffers 1d6 Mettle damage, due to the stress and exhaustion of battle.

1. The Hasheers' Tent

The crimson tent of the Hasheers sits on a small rise to the west of the battlefield. The Hasheers set up braziers in the tent, causing its interior to become sweltering and unbearable. Still, they press on. The Jackals either defend the tent from a sortie or attack the tent to interrupt the rite. Depending on the situation, Kahri guard the tent or Gerwa soldiers attack the tent – use the following stats for either:

WARRIORS				
Type:	Human		Location:	Mayrah Vedil
Defence:	65%		Wounds:	45
Combat:	85%		Protection:	3 (leather + shield)
Knowledge:	40%		Move:	14
Urban:	50%		Initiative:	18
Common:	50%		Clash Points:	2
			Treasure Score:	2

Special Abilities

For the King and the Gods: when a warrior is reduced to 25 Wounds or less, they receive +3 damage until they flee.

Combat Range

1–10%	*Form Up:* the warrior moves in closer with another of their squad, shoring up the line. They can use a ranged attack while doing so. 2d10 + 2 (13) damage.
11–25%	*Savage Blow:* the warrior attacks the nearest target with either of its weapons. 2d10 + 1d6 (15) damage in melee, 2d10 + 2 (13) damage at range.
26–50%	*Hold the Line (2 attacks):* the warrior attacks the nearest target twice with each of its weapons. 2d10 + 1d6 (15) damage each in melee, 2d10 + 2 (13) damage each at range. Should the warrior inflict 10 or more points of damage between both attacks (after Protection), they cause each ally within 5 yards to heal for 8 Wounds.
51–65%	*Count on Your Companions (2 attacks):* the warrior attacks the nearest target twice with either of its weapons. 2d10 + 1d6 (15) damage each in melee, 2d10 + 2 (13) damage each at range. Additionally, the Loremaster can spend 1 Clash Point to increase the warrior's Protection by 1 for each other warrior within 2 yards, as they shield each other.
66–85%	*The War Road Tithe:* the warrior strikes a savage blow to end the fight. The warrior attacks the nearest target twice with either of its weapons. 2d10 + 1d6 (15) damage each in melee, 2d10 + 2 (13) damage each at range. Additionally, the target must make a hard Endurance check, or suffer 2d6 bleed damage for a number of rounds equal to the initial bleed damage roll. Half damage and duration on a success; no damage on a critical success.

The Jackals have four rounds to triumph in this scene. If the Jackals have not defeated the warriors by then, reinforcements arrive to aid those who oppose the Jackals. Either more warriors ignite the tent while the Jackals are distracted, or more come to aid their fellows against them. This might provoke the Willpower check above if the ritual goes off.

2. Chariot Battle

Should the Jackals wish to join, the chances for a chariot battle are many. Chariots in Kalypsis serve one of three roles: transportation, mobile artillery platforms, or weapons of chaos and shock. This scene has three parts: acquiring a chariot, accomplishing its role, and dismounting. Acquiring a chariot could be as simple as stepping onto one of the chariots the Jackals' side possesses, or it could mean taking an occupied one from an enemy combatant. Taking a chariot requires dealing with the driver (through archery or by charging dangerously close to the vehicle) and removing them without getting run over by the chariot or scythed by its blades. Light chariots can hold two Jackals (a driver and a passenger), whereas heavy chariots can hold a driver and three passengers. Use the warrior stats above for any enemies, and the following rules for chariots:

CHARIOTS			
Chariot	Move	Trample Damage	Protection
Light chariot	18	1d10	1
Heavy chariot	13	1d12	3

Once the chariot is under the Jackals' control, they must determine their goal. Do they want to get to another battle scene, harass the enemy's flank with arrows and spears, or drive deep into an enemy force to break it up?

- *Transportation:* the chariot driver can quickly get the Jackals where they want to go. A Drive check allows the Jackals a bonus for the next scene appropriate to arriving early. Perhaps it allows them to lay an ambush, or they gain a temporary Valour bonus of 2d8 as they are rested and ready to fight. However, there is always the chance Trauj cavalry or opposing chariots see the Jackals and decide to attack them!
- *Harassment:* the Jackals can choose to harass their enemies' flanks. In this case, a difficult Drive check by the driver allows the passengers to make Ranged Attacks at the enemy. If the Jackals deal 30 or more damage in a single pass, they provoke a morale check in that unit (use the warrior's Defence of 65%). Every 10 points of damage above 30 increases the Defence check by one step (from normal to difficult, from difficult to hard). Should they fail the morale check, the Jackals rout their enemy!
- *Impact!* The Jackals can choose to drive their chariots through the enemy lines. This is a hard Drive check. On a success, the passengers can make a single Melee Combat check against the warriors, adding the chariot's trample damage die to their own. If the Drive check is a critical success, the warriors cannot make a Clash check; otherwise, the opposing warriors can defend. If the enemy suffers 30 or more damage in a single round of combat, it provokes a morale check as above. Should the check fail, the Jackals rout their enemy!

3. The Tunnels

No matter which side the Jackals end up fighting for, the mines of Mayrah Vedil are likely to become a battlefield. If the Jackals defend the city, they may stand with the hidden troops or move to counter an assault to take the tunnels. If they attack the city, they may lead sorties to take the tunnels, the mines, or the city. If the tunnels are undiscovered, the Nawsi might call upon the Jackals to counter the sudden appearance of new forces.

Fighting in the tunnels is difficult, as Barqan only widened them enough for lightly armoured warriors to fit through. Use of any two-handed weapon, one-handed heavy weapon, or shield imposes a +2 Clash Point cost for all actions and reactions because of the limited space. Barqan is hiding over a thousand warriors in the tunnels. What forces the Jackals to meet the troops in the tunnels depends on when their Nawsi commands them to act.

- *Claiming/Defending the Tunnels:* the Jackals and a group of warriors enter the tunnels to prevent Barqan's warriors from joining the fight. The Jackals face two warriors per Jackal, with the rest of their warriors engaged around them. Use the Vagaries of War table (page 207) to add to the battle. If the Jackals defeat the warriors, this affects the battle (see below).

- *Claiming the Mines/City:* if the fight goes well for the Jackals, they can press their advantage into the city. Barqan and the Nawsi defending the city left a token force inside to guard the retreat. If the Jackals can take the city, they might be able to close the gate and trap the forces of the enemy outside Mayrah Vedil's walls. This entails taking out the warriors of the city, closing the city gates, and holding them while the rest of their forces crush the enemy against the walls. The fight inside the city should be difficult (two to two-and-a-half times the normal difficulty), as the defenders are focused and willing to fight to the last person. Refer to the section on Mayrah Vedil (page 87) to see the layout of the city.
- *Counterattack:* if Barqan's forces are not dealt with, they exit the tunnels and attempt to flank the attacking forces (see Timeline of the Battle of Mayrah Vedil, above). The Jackals are either part of these attack forces or stand to intercept the attack. Barqan has 1,000 warriors, so the Jackals are outnumbered. With 300 warriors behind them, the Jackals are told to hold the line long enough for the Nawsi to redeploy some troops to engage with the enemy. Use the Vagaries of War table from the previous scene (page 207) to add to the battle.

Use one-and-a-half warriors (round down) per Jackal, plus two Hasheers and either a Melkoni or Gerwa Invoker (depending on the side). Use the stats for Sara'el, Elpis, or Menes on pages 179–183.

If the Jackals win their fight or last for at least four rounds against the enemy, they buy their army enough time, despite the losses.

4. Claim the Standard

Sars and Nawsis use standards to organise and signal forces on the battlefield. Claiming one creates chaos in the opposing army. The Jackals, tasked with claiming a standard from a unit of archers that is devastating their army, must sneak through the chaos to cut down the bearer. The Jackals need to accumulate **eight successes** (with critical successes counting as two successes) before they incur **four failures** to claim the vital standard.

Jackals can use any skill the Loremaster accepts, but they should describe how the check aids them in moving towards the standard. Most skill checks should be at least difficult, representing the scale of the conflict. Some examples are:
- Deception checks to disguise their movements.
- Stealth checks to sneak through the battle.
- Perception checks to track where the standard and enemies are.
- Martial skill checks to represent the fights which happen along the way.
- Endurance checks to struggle through the slog of the battle.
- Culture checks to give orders to units on the battlefield, whether they are yours or not.

For every failure, the Jackals take 2d12 (13) damage, representing the incremental Wounds suffered by wading through a battlefield.

If the Jackals succeed, they steal the standard. If they fail, they get to the standard but must fight the standard bearer and retinue. Use a number of warriors (see above) appropriate to the Jackals' Kleos level.

Capturing a standard removes that unit from battle, effectively making it safer for the Jackals' own troops.

End of Battle

After four scenes, the battle ends. As before, the Loremaster makes a d100 battle outcome check using the modifiers below:

- Each Jackal who ends the battle with no Wounds in the second row: –10%
- Each Jackal who dies: +20%
- Shadow of Doubt ritual results
  - › Defended/burned the Hasheer tent: –20%
  - › If both sides fail the Willpower check against the Shadow of Doubt ritual: +25%
  - › If only the enemies fail the check against the ritual: –10%
  - › If only the Jackals fail the check against the ritual: +10%
- Captured a standard: –15%
- Routed a unit due to chariot use: –15%
- Won the battle in the tunnels/mines/city/counterattack: –10% each
- Lost the battle in the tunnels/mines/city/counterattack: +15% each

d100	Result	Jackals' Side Casualties	Enemy Casualties
Less than 50%	*Fate Be Praised:* the Jackals' forces suffer only minor casualties and wounds	2%	45%
51–75%	*An Easy Victory:* the Jackals' forces easily triumph over their foes	4%	30%
76–100%	*The Cost of War:* the Jackals' forces suffer what was expected by the scribes for this battle	8%	20%
101–125%	*The Toll of the War Road:* the Jackals' forces struggle to eke out a victory	12%	12%
126–150%	*Pyrrhic Victory:* the Jackals win, but at great cost	20%	8%
151–175%	*Loss:* the Jackals' forces lose the fight	30%	4%
176%+	*Rout:* the Jackals' forces are brutally slaughtered as they run	45%	2%

MASS COMBAT RESULTS

If this is the second battle, proceed to Act 3. If this is the first, then Abner's forces return to Tjaru. This is either because Abner retreats as a result of heavy losses or because the defenders of Mayrah Vedil hole up inside the city, while the carnage attracts a large group of Takan (perhaps the horde or its remnants from the previous year). Proceed to Act 2.

ACT 2: BATTLE OF TJARU

The Battle of Tjaru is a siege. The forces of Ameena Noani surround the ancient Gerwa fortress, attempting to take it as quickly as possible. However, sieges in the Ancient Near East were not quick battles, so this battle takes place over the course of several weeks (possibly months). Loremasters need to calculate the numbers of the armies based on previous casualties.

When the Jackals arrive, the forces move into position:

If Tjaru's battle happens first:

- *Ameena Noani's Forces:* Abner settles in around the fortress to set up the siege. He begins with sorties to probe the strength of the gates and defenders, and searches for an alternate way into the city.
- *Sentem's Forces:* Deborah and the armies of Sentem are at full strength (see above). They man the walls and the gates, while raiding out through the posterns (side or back entrances) and Deep Gates (see pages 157–163 for a description of Tjaru).

If Mayrah Vedil's battle happens first:

- *Ameena Noani's Forces:* Deborah presses her advantage, and rushes to take the fortress as quickly as possible. She left a token force in Mayrah Vedil (10% of her army) and established it as a hold, giving Abner time to fall back to Tjaru.
- *Sentem's Forces:* Abner returns to Tjaru, either in retreat or to regroup. Abner sets the defenders as best as he can (if his army was forced to retreat, he fears his warriors are ill-prepared for a protracted siege).

Timeline of the Battle of Tjaru

Below is the timeline of the Battle of Tjaru. Think of this as a possible order of events for the battle, which allows Loremasters to showcase certain events in the background or to use them as set pieces for the fights.

TIMELINE OF THE BATTLE OF TJARU		
Week	Deborah (Ameena Noani)	Deborah (Sentem)
1	Encampment around Tjaru	Abner arrives
2	Creation of siege works	First sortie against Tjaru's gate
3	First sortie against Tjaru's gate	Sortie beyond the walls
4	Murder in the camp	Second sortie against Tjaru's gate
5	Second sortie against Tjaru's gate	Murder in the camp
6	Sortie beyond the walls	Third sortie against Tjaru's gate
7	Battle ends	Battle ends

Trickery and Tactics

1. Sneaking in or out of Tjaru

As mentioned, Tjaru's builders hid many posterns and sally-gates in the rock of the walls and the tor. The defenders can move beyond the walls to strike at siege works or enemy forces, or even to launch counterraids. Soon, the attacking forces begin to watch and search for these gates. The Nawsis rely on the Jackals for either defending the gates or searching them out.

2. Murder in the Camp

The Nawsis strategically placed men and women in the enemy camps in and around Tjaru. During the fourth week, these infiltrators begin to sabotage foodstuffs and slay key personnel. The Jackals must discover the traitors and deal with them before they force the siege to an end.

Battle Scenes

Much like the previous scene, the Jackals' tale follows several smaller scenes that act as a guide for how the rest of the battle is going. Below are four scenes in which the Jackals can become embroiled. As Loremaster, it is up to you to pick and choose which ones to use, or whether to add your own into the chaos of the battle. You know your group and how much combat and variety they enjoy better than we do.

Each scene takes between one and two hours, and plays out over the course of a week. You can bookend each scene with preparation and fallout, as the Jackals' tasks affect and shift the tide of the siege.

1. Assassinate a Nawsi!

The Nawsi of their camp sends the Jackals out to infiltrate the enemy lines and slay one of the rival Nawsis. This is not an attempt at throwing away the lives of the Jackals; therefore, their commander does not send them after the rival army's commander. However, the following targets are deemed acceptable:

- Nawsi of chariots (besieging army only)
- Nawsi of archers
- Nawsi of scouts

In any of these cases, the Jackals must enter the camp (or Tjaru), find their target, slay them, and escape unseen. The Jackals need to accumulate **six successes** (with critical successes counting as two successes) before they incur **three failures** to find the Nawsi.

Jackals can use any skills the Loremaster accepts, but they should describe how their check aids them in moving towards the enemy Nawsi. Most skill checks should be at least difficult. Some examples are:

- Deception checks to disguise their movements.
- Stealth checks to sneak through the camps.
- Perception checks to track where the Nawsi and enemies are.
- Athletics checks to scale walls.
- Martial skill checks to represent the fights that happen along the way.
- Endurance checks to struggle through the slog of the battle.
- Culture checks to find their way through the camps.

For every failure, the Jackals take 1d6 (4) Mettle damage, representing the cumulative stress and exhaustion suffered during the hunt.

If the Jackals succeed, the Nawsi has only two warriors as guards when found. If they fail, the Nawsi has a retinue of six warriors when found.

Use the following stats for the Nawsi:

NAWSI			
Type:	Human	**Location:**	Tjaru
Defence:	75%	**Wounds:**	60
Combat:	95%	**Protection:**	5 (leather + shield)
Knowledge:	50%	**Move:**	14
Urban:	60%	**Initiative:**	18
Common:	60%	**Clash Points:**	4
		Treasure Score:	2

Special Abilities

For the King and the Gods: when the Nawsi is reduced to 25 Wounds or less, they receive +3 damage until they flee.

Leader of Warriors: the Nawsi grants all allied warriors a trait on attack checks.

Combat Range

1–10%	*Form Up:* the Nawsi moves in closer with another of their squad, shoring up the line. They can use a ranged attack while doing so. 2d10 + d6 + 2 (17) damage.
11–25%	*Savage Blow:* the Nawsi attacks the nearest target with either of their weapons. 2d10 + 2d6 (18) damage in melee, 2d10 + d6 + 2 (17) damage at range.
26–50%	*Hold the Line (2 attacks):* the Nawsi attacks the nearest target twice with each of their weapons. 2d10 + 2d6 (18) damage each in melee, 2d10 + d6 + 2 (17) damage each at range. Should the Nawsi inflict 10 or more points of damage between both attacks (after Protection), they cause each ally within 5 yards to heal for 8 Wounds.
51–65%	*Count on Your Companions (2 attacks):* the Nawsi attacks the nearest target twice with either of their weapons. 2d10 + 2d6 (18) damage each in melee, 2d10 + d6 + 2 (17) damage each at range. Additionally, the Loremaster can spend 1 Clash Point to increase the Nawsi's Protection by 1 per ally within 2 yards of them, as they shield each other.
66–85%	*The War Road Tithe:* the Nawsi strikes a savage blow to end the fight. The Nawsi attacks the nearest target twice with either of their weapons. 2d10 + 2d6 (18) damage each in melee, 2d10 + d6 + 2 (17) damage each at range. Additionally, the target must make a hard Endurance check, or suffer 2d6 bleed damage for a number of rounds equal to the initial bleed damage roll. Half damage and duration on a success; no damage on a critical success.
86–90%	*Sound the Trumpets!* The Nawsi gives a rallying cry or blows on their trumpet, granting courage to their companions. All the Nawsi's allies heal 2d8 (9) Wounds There is a 40% chance of summoning 1d3 more warriors to fight on the Nawsi's side.

2. Scale the Walls

The besiegers must get a foothold in Tjaru. They attempt to do so in two ways: assaulting the gatehouse (see below) and scaling the walls. The Jackals must either defend the walls or scale them! Scaling the walls is a hard Athletics check. A success means a Jackal scales the walls of Tjaru before the defenders can spot them. A failure means they scale the walls, but the defenders spot them. A fumble means the defenders get a free attack before the Jackal can crest the wall. If the Jackals win this fight, they can move to open the main gates (see *The Gatehouse* below).

If the Jackals are defending the walls, detecting the scaling warriors requires an extreme Perception check, as the attackers are scaling the walls in secret and at night. A success means the Jackals spot the warriors as they crest the wall. A critical success allows for one roll per the ambush rules (*Jackals* page 62). A failure means the Jackals are ambushed!

Use one-and-a-half warriors (round down) per Jackal, plus two Hasheers and either a Melkoni or Gerwa Invoker (depending on the side). Use the stats for Sara'el, Elpis, or Menes on pages 179–183.

If the Jackals fail to stop the attack, or retreat, the warriors move to open the gates (see below).

3. The Deep Gates

Scouts and raids slip in and out of the Deep Gates beneath Tjaru. Jackals either participate in these raids or hunt for ways into the fortress. As hunters, their Nawsi tasks the Jackals with working out where the raids are coming from. The Jackals need to accumulate **four successes** (with critical successes counting as two successes) before they incur **two failures** to find the Deep Gates.

Jackals can use any skills the Loremaster accepts, but they should describe how this check aids them in finding the gates. Most skill checks should be at least difficult (other difficulties are noted below). Some examples are:

- Stealth checks to lie in wait.
- Perception checks to track where raids emerge or to locate the door (hard difficulty).
- Survival check to track footprints back to near where the doors are.
- Lore check to identify the doors (extreme difficulty).

If the Jackals succeed, they discover a set of doors. They can attempt to force the doors open (extreme difficulty) or lie in wait for the next raid and attempt to slip into the fortress.

If the Jackals fail, they discover the doors right as 15 warriors led by a Hasheer or a Hekas emerge. The defenders fight for three rounds, then attempt to retreat into the tor. If they do so, they seal the gate and do not use it again during this siege.

If the Jackals are participating in raids, they must ensure this gate remains a secret. After a raid heads out, it is the Jackals' duty to watch the gate and slay any enemies who discover it. This is a hard Perception check. On a success, the Jackals notice a group of six Trauj warriors riding close to the gate entrance. Use the following stats:

TRAUJ WARRIORS

Type:	Human	Location:	Tjaru

Defence:	75%	Wounds:	45
Combat:	85%	Protection:	4 (leather + shield
Knowledge:	40%	Move:	14
Urban:	50%	Initiative:	18
Common:	95%	Clash Points:	2
		Treasure Score:	2

Special Abilities

For the King and the Gods: when a Trauj warrior is reduced to 25 Wounds or less, they receive +3 damage until they flee.

Trample: a Trauj warrior gains the ability to trample their foes. Any time they move over an enemy, they inflict 2d12 (13) damage. An enemy can spend a Clash Point to Dodge or to make a Clash attack. If they make the attack, they still take the damage.

Born to the Saddle: a Trauj warrior has a trait for all attacks made from horseback.

Combat Range

1–10%	*Form Up:* the Trauj warrior moves in closer with another of their squad, shoring up the line. They can use a ranged attack while doing so. 2d10 + 2 (13) damage.
11–25%	*Savage Blow:* the Trauj warrior attacks the nearest target with either of their weapons. 2d10 + 1d6 (15) damage in melee, 2d10 + 2 (13) damage at range.
26–50%	*Hold the Line (2 attacks):* the Trauj warrior attacks the nearest target twice with each of its weapons. 2d10 + 1d6 (15) damage each in melee, 2d10 + 2 (13) damage each at range. Should the warrior inflict 10 or more points of damage between both attacks (after Protection), they cause each ally within 5 yards to heal for 8 Wounds.
51–65%	*Count on Your Companions (2 attacks):* the Trauj warrior attacks the nearest target twice with either of their weapons. 2d10 + 1d6 (15) damage each in melee, 2d10 + 2 (13) damage each at range. Additionally, the Loremaster can spend 1 Clash Point to increase the warrior's Protection by 1 per warrior within 2 yards, as they shield each other.
66–85%	*The War Road Tithe (2 attacks):* the Trauj warrior strikes a savage blow to end the fight. The warrior attacks the nearest target twice with either of their weapons. 2d10 + 1d6 (15) damage in melee, 2d10 + 2 (13) damage at range. Additionally, the target must make a hard Endurance check, or suffer 2d6 bleed damage for a number of rounds equal to the initial bleed damage roll. Half damage and duration on a success; no damage on a critical success.

If the Jackals fail, they do not notice the riders, and the besieging forces (15 warriors, led by a Hasheer or a Hekas) spot them and attack. If the Jackals fail to hold the door, the attackers invade the fortress from below. Loremasters can adapt the gatehouse scene to take place in Tjaru Below, instead.

4. *The Gatehouse*

The gatehouse of a fortress is dichotomy written in stone. It is a necessary hole in the wall, which makes it the weakest and most vulnerable point. Therefore, it needs to paradoxically be the strongest point. Tjaru's repaired gatehouse stands as the choke point for both the attackers and defenders. As described above, the approach to Tjaru's gate is a broad path that exposes the attackers' right side to the defenders' javelins, slings, and arrows. Beyond that, Tjaru's gatehouse possesses three great gates, with two chambers between them, which leaves the attackers vulnerable to assault from all sides. However, both sides know that taking the gates is the best chance the attackers have (assuming the Deep Gates go unnoticed).

The easiest way to take the gates is to coordinate scaling the walls with a gate attack (or an assault from below – see above). Opening even one or two of the gates and dealing with the gatehouse guards can save dozens of lives. This act assumes the battle eventually comes to the gatehouse, with the Jackals either defending it or attacking it.

The attack comes in three phases. The first two are attempts to draw defenders off the gates, and – if successful – lead an attack on the gate itself. These attempts occur at multiple points at the same time, as 40 to 50 attackers assault the walls. The main group consists of 200 warriors attacking the gate. Collectively, this band has 400 Wounds. At 200 Wounds, the band must make a morale check to see whether it flees. Jackals can attempt to make hard Perform, Lore, or Culture checks – which represent speeches, songs, or inspiring stories – to have the warriors hold their ground. At 100 Wounds, the group breaks and flees.

The attackers come up the ramp, attempting to defend themselves with large wicker shields as they prepare to ram the door. The bearers soaked these shields to prevent them from igniting, and they are large enough to provide overlapped protection to the attackers. The rams are heavy logs sheathed with bronze heads in the shape the Yammim, the Nyssalis, and the lion. The attackers make their way up the ramp as quickly as they can to shelter in the shadow of the gate as they attack it. The truth of the matter is the gates will fall. It is not a matter of if, but when. When attackers assault the gates, if the Jackals are not part of a sortie attempting to open them, they can serve one of three roles in the attack:

Shields: Jackals can hold the shields up for their allies. Each minute of the fight requires a hard Endurance check to ensure the shield is in place. For each failure, the Jackal suffers 1d4 Mettle damage, and the ram crew takes 1d12 damage (maximised on a fumble).

Bows/Javelins: gaps in the shields give arrows and javelins a chance to slip in, but their bearers can also coordinate openings to allow the ram crew to counterassault the walls. Once per minute, these Jackals can make a difficult Ranged Combat check to attempt to lead some of the warriors under their command to take out the defenders on the wall. A success inflicts damage on the defenders' Wounds equal to the Jackal's ranged weapon damage ×5. For each failure, the Jackal suffers 1d4 Mettle damage, and the ram crew takes 1d12 damage (maximised on a fumble).

Rams: teams of 20 wield the heavy rams against the gate. Each minute, the rams inflict 6d12 (39) damage upon the gates. The outer and middle gate are each made of wood, reinforced with bronze, and possess 250 Wounds. The inner gate is only wood and possesses 150 Wounds. Each Jackal manning the ram can make an Athletics check each minute to aid in the attack. On a success, the Jackals add their Strength score to the damage. On a critical success, they add double their Strength score. On a failure, they add nothing to the attack round, but suffer 1d4 Mettle damage (maximised on a fumble).

Gatehouse: each time a gate breaks, the attackers start the siege process over again with the next gate. First, they must secure the new gate chamber, clearing out the defenders who man both it and the murder holes above. If the defenders force the attackers to retreat after they break through a gate, the defenders choke the ruined gate with rubble; four Athletics or Endurance checks are required to clear the rubble. Fifty warriors (with 100 Wounds total) guard each gatehouse. Rather than fight the warriors individually (although if that is your group's style, feel free to do so), assume the fight lasts for 30 minutes as the Jackals and their warriors fight off the enemy warriors. Have each Jackal describe how they are participating in the battle and make an appropriate hard skill check. On a success, the defenders suffer damage equal to the damage of the Jackal's attack ×5 (representing multiple attacks by multiple warriors over the course of the battle). The Jackal must then make a hard Endurance check. On a failure, they suffer 1d4 Mettle damage (maximised on a fumble). Their own side then suffers 5d10 (27) damage, although Jackals who spend their action describing how they defend the warriors can reduce this damage by 1d12 (doubled on a critical success). The damage done to each side might provoke a morale check (see *Jackals* page 63).

Once the Jackals' warriors breach the third gate, the battle for Tjaru is over.

The defence phases correspond to the attack phases. Jackals can participate in defending the outer walls or the gatehouse. If they attend to the walls, use a similar scene to the scaling the walls scene above. Each phase takes an hour, and for every phase the Jackals spend defending the walls, roll a d100:

- 1–25% – attackers breach two gates.
- 26–75% – attackers breach one gate.
- 76–100% – attackers do not breach any gates.

If they defend the gatehouse, the main defensive group consists of 300 warriors. Collectively, this band has 600 Wounds. At 300 Wounds, the band must make a morale check to see whether it flees. Jackals can attempt to make hard Perform, Lore, or Culture check – which represent speeches, songs, or inspiring stories – to have the warriors hold their ground. At 150 Wounds, the group breaks and flees into the city, looking for ways to escape.

While defending the gates, Jackals can take any of the following three actions:

Death from Above: the Jackals take part in the defenders' attempts to bring down the attackers' battering ram. Gaps in the shields give the Jackals a chance to slay attackers with arrows and javelins. Once per minute, these Jackals can make a hard, Ranged Combat check to attempt to take out the attackers at the gate. A success inflicts damage on the attackers equal to the Jackal's ranged weapon damage. For each failure, the Jackal suffers 1d4 Mettle damage, and the defenders take 1d12 damage (maximised on a fumble) from an ill-timed attack.

Defend the Gate: the Jackals can choose to fight where the action is thickest, in the gatehouse. Loremasters can use this scene each time a gate breaks. The defenders rush to attack from hidden sally-ports and murder holes, while the attackers attempt to start the siege process over again with the next gate. These sorties into the gatehouse have the element of surprise, but they can quickly turn into disaster. Jackals must remain aware of the danger. The Jackals and 50 warriors guard each gatehouse. Each sortie lasts approximately 30 minutes, as the Jackals and their warriors fight off the enemy warriors. Have each Jackal describe how they are participating in the battle and make an appropriate hard skill check. On a success, the attackers suffer damage equal to the damage of the Jackal's attack × 5 (representing multiple attacks by multiple warriors over the course of the battle). The Jackal must then make a hard Endurance check. On a failure, they suffer 1d4 Mettle damage (maximised on a fumble). Their own side then suffers 5d10 (27) damage, although Jackals who spend their action describing how they defend the warriors can reduce this damage by 1d12 (double on a critical success). The damage done to each side might provoke a morale check.

Attack the Ram: the Jackals might become desperate enough to launch an attack directly against the ram. This is dangerous for two reasons. The first is that the Jackals must leave the protection of Tjaru to get to the ram. This involves using sally-ports, climbing down into an attacking force, or ambushing the attackers. Additionally, the ram is amid the attacking forces, requiring the Jackals to fight through the horde to get to the ram. If things fall apart, the Jackals risk losing their lives. Second, the ram is harder to break than a body. To successfully assault the ram, the Jackals need to accumulate **six successes** (with critical successes counting as two successes) before they incur **three failures.** Jackals can use any skills the Loremaster accepts, but they should describe how this check aids them in moving towards the ram. Most skill checks should be at least difficult (others are noted below). Each failure costs the Jackal a point of Mettle damage. Some examples are:

- Stealth checks to lie in wait.
- Athletics checks to scale down the walls.
- Deception checks to blend in with the attackers.

If the Jackals succeed, they are in position to reach the ram. They can attempt to slay the ram wielders or lie in wait for them to arrive (depending on their goal and plan).

If the Jackals fail, they start further away from the ram than they hoped. Perhaps the attackers see them, or the press of attackers forced them back. They each suffer 2d12 damage upon entering the fight below (ignoring Protection) to represent the toll this failure inflicted on them.

The Jackals must now fight to claim the ram. Use one-and-a-half warriors (round down) per Jackal. Additionally, Loremasters could add in some of the named Invokers from above, or any humanoids (Anu's Adepts, Wolves, Guards, etc.) from *Jackals* to mix up the fight. This fight lasts five rounds. If the Jackals slay their foes before the end of round five, they have time remaining to damage the ram. The ram has 100 Wounds, a Protection of 4, and is immune to ranged weapons. If the ram is reduced to below 50 Wounds, it cannot be used until it is repaired, which costs the attackers one week to replace the wood of the ram. If it is reduced to 0 Wounds, the ram is useless and the Jackals can recover the ram's head, worth 1,000 ss. In this scenario, it takes the attackers two weeks to build a new ram.

If the Jackals do not slay their foes within five rounds, the attackers force them to retreat. During this retreat, if they still have a functioning ram, the attackers have time to breach a single gate.

End of the Siege

If the defenders force the attackers to flee three times before they can breach the gates, it means the defenders managed to defend Tjaru long enough for reinforcements to arrive and break the siege. If this was the first battle, Deborah chases Abner as he retreats to Mayrah Vedil. If this was the second battle, proceed to Act 3.

If the attackers break through the main gate or the Deep Gates, the battle for Tjaru is nearly over. If this was the second battle, proceed to Act 3. If this was the first, Deborah's forces retreat to Mayrah Vedil – as a result of a breach or the siege breaking – and Abner takes his warriors south to the easier target of Mayrah Vedil. Proceed to Act 1.

ACT 3: UNIFICATION

What happens after the battles? The first step is to determine the results of the War of the Plains. This campaign assumes the Jackals turn the tide in favour of their side of the War Road. But fate is not always so kind, and the vagaries of war might work against them.

There are two factors to consider when determining which side wins what the Luathi will call the Wars of Unification: casualties and Tjaru. The Loremaster may decide to let each Jackal tell of their legendary deeds during the battle. Once all have done so, the Jackals can nominate one player to make the roll for their side to determine the outcome of the war. It is a d100 roll modified by the following factors:

- Percentage of casualties on the Jackals' side (see Mass Combat Results table above) during the battle for Mayrah Vedil: +(X)%
- Each Jackal's tale: –5%
- Each Jackal's death: +20%
- If the Jackals fought alongside Abner
  - › If they took Tjaru: –30%
  - › If they failed to take Tjaru: +30%
- If the Jackals fought alongside Deborah
  - › If they defended Tjaru: –30%
  - › If Tjaru fell: +30%

If the final modified total is 50% or less, the Jackals' side wins the war. If it is greater than 51%, the opposing Nawsi led their army to victory.

If the Jackals wish to spend Fate Points on this roll, a reroll requires 1 Fate Point from each Jackal.

Even after the outcome is determined, the fight for the War Road continues for some time. The battles rage for the next month, as the winning side moves through the Zaharets putting the land in order. Deborah (or Abner) does not give up easily, fighting a retreating battle along the War Road; but the writing is on the wall, and the Luathi are now one people.

In Tise, the victorious armies finally arrive to surround the opposing stronghold (Ameena Noani or Sentem). The Nawsi of the armies sends the Jackals as envoys to speak with the Sar of the city and deliver the message of surrender and unification. The victorious Sar has no desire to burn a Luathi city to the ground, and so sends the Jackals with a message of peace.

Read or paraphrase the following:

My dear sister (or brother), may Alwain's light fall on you like the rains we so desperately need. The years have not been kind to us – famine and war take a toll on the children of Shumma. Already, I hear the sounds of Takan as they wait in the hills. We must bring this conflict between us to an end. For too long have the ends of the War Road stood opposed to each other, and for too long have Luathi fought Luathi. To this end, I claim the Zaharets for our people, in the name of Alwain. We shall be one people, in one kingdom, with one Malekeh (or Malekh). Alwain has raised me up for such a time as this; going forward, I will rule our people.

But my sister (or brother), we are brother and sister – I will not forget you. If you would but bow before me, I will give back to you the seat of your family. It will be to you and your descendants a garden to tend and rest in, so long as you serve the kingdom. If you do not bow, I will pull you up, root and leaf, and cast you into the Luasa, where the heat will wither you.

These here serve as my ears, my eyes, and my strong right hands. Speak to them as you would to me. I give you until the 3rd Udsar of Tise to decide.

The Loremaster should take note that the Jackals could stand before a ruler they betrayed here. If this is the case, getting them to accept the Sar's offer might involve an extreme Influence check. If the ruler does not accept the offer, the Jackals or the army forcibly take them into custody and send them into the Luasa desert, never to be heard from again in the lives of the Jackals.

If the Jackals were on the side of defeat, they stand with their Sar while other Jackals deliver the above message. They might influence their Sar one way or another, but the outcome is certain: opposing the rise of the king or queen is futile. Should their Sar acquiesce, the Jackals might remain as their advisors, aids, or Jackals. Should they convince their Sar to resist, they follow their Sar into exile.

Once the message is delivered and the Sar chooses to either bow to the victor or enter exile, the Jackals' active part in this story is over. The army continues its takeover of the city. The new Sar is crowned Malekh or Malekeh on the 3rd Udsar of Tise, which becomes a new holy day for the Luathi people. The new kingdom of Adaanshummar is, for now, a kingdom in name only; the long process of extending the rule of Alwain over the whole of the Zaharets has just begun. Although many of the Children of Bronze fell in the war, the Kingdom of Adaanshummar begins the process of rising once again.

AFTERMATH

This concludes *The Fall of the Children of Bronze* campaign. The Jackals fought a war and were pivotal in the birth of a nation of their people. For the first time since the Grand Kingdoms, a kingdom of light encompasses the whole of the War Road. What does this mean for the Zaharets, the Luathi, and the Jackals?

Zaharets: the Kingdom of Adaanshummar does not coalesce in a single night, or even a single year. It takes years to become established. At the start, the northern end's wealth is slow to trickle south, but it soon stabilises. Tjaru and Eridu become more important as cities in the centre of the new kingdom, and soon join Ameena Noani and Sentem as some of the great Luathi cities. In several generations, Tjaru might even become the capital of Adaanshummar. The rest of the Zaharets cannot ignore Adaanshummar. Glykera initially accelerates her plans for Orsem Honess, but if they do not come together quickly, she might seek an alliance with the new Malekh or Malekeh. Ger, on the other hand, will not stand for a unified kingdom on its border and begins to prepare for war. Furthermore, the threat of the Iron Bound Tree still looms, and a unified Luathi kingdom is not in its plans. Internal rebellions and external threats will anneal the new kingdom or break it.

Luathi: for the next decade, the tribes of the Luathi move from sharing a cultural identity to sharing a national one. The two sides of the War Road learn to work together, sharing in Alwainic rites, taxes, and levies of the Malekh. The above-mentioned rebellions and external threats draw the Luathi closer, as they fight for a national identity in a world where they have not ever possessed one.

Jackals: depending on the Jackals' relationship with the new Malekh/Malekeh, they might seek new positions in the kingdom, continue their roles as Jackals to ensure the land inside the new borders is safe, or retire. In any event, the need for Jackals does not disappear, and the new kingdom requires their skills, talents, and natures to keep the War Road safe for decades to come.

ADVANCEMENTS

- 4 for surviving the war
- 1 for taking/defending Tjaru
- 1 for following their Sar into exile
- 1 for convincing a Sar they betrayed to bow
- 1 for deeds of valour, bravery, or legend during the war

HOOKS

Back to Work: The Zaharets is still filled with ruins, Takan, Mouathenics, and fouler things. Get back out on the War Road, Jackal!

In Service of the Throne: If the Jackals are tied to the new Malekh or Malekeh, they might find themselves in roles as ambassadors, guards, or kingdom-level troubleshooters.

War: What of the brewing conflict with Kroryla?

The City of Dust: Where is Kibeth-Albin, the city of dust, and what secrets might it hold?

Protect the Throne: Those who follow the Iron Bound Tree (Takan and others) do not want to see the Luathi unified. Plans to assassinate the Malekh or Malekeh are already being laid.

Rumours of War: Rumours of another Takan horde in the far north, across the Vori Wastes, reach the new Malekh or Malekeh's ears. Jackals are needed to investigate these rumours.

APPENDIX I
NEW PATRONS

The Fall of the Children of Bronze includes new patrons the Jackals might encounter and acquire over the course of the campaign. See page 181 of *Jackals* for rules on acquiring patrons.

GLYKERA		
Skill Requirement	Region	Sphere of Influence
Trade	Kroryla	Political

Glykera is the Anaxa (Lady) of Kroryla. Glykera left the eastern Melkoni cities with her family as a child and settled in Kroryla. The city is the only home she remembers, and as she grew, she rose quickly in status in the town. As a Warrior of Lykos, Glykera became part of the fabric of Kroryla, and now – as Anaxa – she plans to see it grow even more. She wants to start a new town to the north, as well as annexing Orsem Honess. Glykera worries about the new influx of refugees from the west, and fears what the end of the twenty-year war might bring for Kroryla and the Zaharets. She plans to ensure Kroryla endures, no matter the cost.

Known Benefit: Glykera is concerned with the growing numbers of refugees who fill Kroryla's streets. She looks to her Jackals to gather information about what is happening to the west (is the war over? What is Melkon's plan for the eastern colonies?), as well as determining what can be done to bind the new refugees to Kroryla more tightly. Additionally, she sends them north to scout possible locations for new settlements. To aid them in these tasks, she gives them Melkoni shields, engraved with one of the trials of Lykos. These shields are well-crafted, weigh 1 less Encumbrance than usual, and provide the bearers with +10% to Influence and Culture (Melkoni) checks.

Exalted Benefit: Glykera entrusts her Jackals with her most vital task, swaying Orsem Honess and Nawsi Rakel towards growing the kingdom. The nature of this mission changes, depending on where in the timeline of *The Fall of the Children of Bronze* it takes place. If Adaanshummar exists, Glykera risks war with the new Luathi kingdom. However, their triumph spurs her to create something similar. Glykera commissions new weapons for her Jackals, cast from orichalcum – the mystical metal of the west. Such weapons are heavier than usual (+1 Encumbrance), but they provide the wielders with +1d6 damage and ignore 2 Protection for creatures of darkness (the Dead and Rathic). Additionally, Glykera provides 1,500 ss towards a home within Kroryla for each Jackal.

SAR BARQAN		
Skill Requirement	Region	Sphere of Influence
Craft	Mayrah Vedil	Mercantile

Sar Barqan of Mayrah Vedil is a merchant through and through. His town of Mayrah Vedil is growing, thanks to its tin-filled mines. Barqan, loyal to Sentem, seeks to expand upon the mines' capabilities by employing Jackals to clear the Takan from the hills and the mines (the Norakan are a constant problem). Additionally, he is always looking for new redsmiths and techniques to ensure Mayrah Vedil's goods are the best on the War Road.

Known Benefit: Barqan sends his Jackals into the A'hule Asa to discover whether the old Luathi tales of the Nahunum enclave in the mountains is true. The Nahunum of old were renowned crafters in stone (see Tjaru), and Barqan greatly desires their knowledge. In return, Barqan commissions each of his Jackals a piece of Luathi-crafted gear with two traits of the Jackal's choice. Additionally, Barqan provides 1,500 ss towards a house for each Jackal, or 2,000 if the Jackal plans to build a foundry.

Exalted Benefit: Barqan wants to extend his redsmithing capabilities. To this end, he entrusts his Jackals to go to Ger and recruit one of their Hekas (or convince a renowned Hekas in the group or along the War Road to retire in Mayrah Vedil). His desire is to get the Hekas to open not only a foundry, but also a school to teach the ways of imbuing to Luathi students. He is not sure whether it is possible, or how the Kahars will feel about it, so he wants his Jackals to keep a low profile. Barqan gives Exalted Jackals one of a series of Hannic relics which his workers found in the tunnels. These relics appear as small silver basins, engraved with images of star patterns unfamiliar to the Luathi. When a Jackal fills the basin with water, its magical properties activate. The stars glow under the water, providing the Jackal with the following benefits:

- +20% to Ancient Lore, Lore, or Survival checks when knowledge of the stars would aid.
- Once per season, the Jackal can use the basin to divine a single answer to a yes-or-no question. The strict response to this is yes or no.
- A successful Ancient Lore roll reveals possible locations of additional paths of the Hannic moon roads, some of which might still be active, or point to old Hannic redoubts.

APPENDIX 2
GLOSSARY OF NPCS

Abishai (f). Luathi Hasheer of Rataro. Young Hasheer who becomes involved in Mealil's return.

Abner (m). Luathi leader of the opposing army of Luathi in the final years of the campaign.

Aldimir (m). Melkoni Mouathenic who violates the sanctity of Umbalna's forest, kicking off the events in **Forgotten Covenant**.

Arishat (f). Luathi Hasheer of Sentem. Aged advisor to the Yesim line of Sentem, key figure in the southern adventures for the first three years of the campaign.

Avi (f). Luathi Sari of Densom. Leader of Densom and loyal to the Yesim line. Possesses secret knowledge of the ayal in **The Sacred Hart**.

Ba-en Nafar (m). Gerwa advisor to Sameel of Sentem. Ally to the Jackals in the southern adventures for the first three years of the campaign, **Orsem Reclaimed**, and **Raid of Raids**.

Barqan, Sar (m). Luathi Sar of Mayrah Vedil. Opened the tin mines of Mayrah Vedil for Sentem, now rules in their stead. Although, his loyalties might be wavering.

Barqan (m). Luathi Kahar of Orsem Yahan. Tends the House of Healing in the fort.

Beket (f). Gerwa Hemet-Netjer in Tjaru. A priestess of the Six and the Eight who is installed in Tjaru.

Daughter Beneath the Earth (f). Hulathi Mouathenic. This mysterious figure is behind many of the troubles plaguing the southern end of the War Road.

Deborah of the Torch (f). Luathi Jackal turned Nawsi of Tjaru. Deborah is installed as the Nawsi of Tjaru and is desperate to defend her side of the War Road.

Diokles (m). Melkoni woodcutter in Orsem Yahan. This woodcutter's mind is trapped by the Hazukamna in **Forgotten Covenant**.

Eilene (f). Melkoni brickmaker in Mikro. Daughter of Philon, Eilene escapes Mikro to warn the Jackals in **Shadow Over Mikro**.

Gan (m). Luathi trader in Densom. Gan opens his home to Jackals, but he is spying for the Daughter Beneath the Earth.

Ganak of the Amar (m). Luathi Hasheer possessed by Mealil in **Relapse**.

Glykera (f). Melkoni leader of Kroryla. Glykera watches the War Road with interest and seeks to build a stronger colony around Kroryla. She has opened negotiations with Rakel of Orsem Honess.

Grey Taker (f). Atakan. Brutal warrior who leads one of the Takan tribes in Kek-bel-kala in **The Price of Victory**.

Hanni of the Geshrun (m). Luathi Wolf. Hanni leads a bandit group called the Qayim in the plains around Sentem.

Hanno (m). Luathi herbalist. Husband of Avi, Hanno is the herbalist of Densom.

Hen-he-net (f). Gerwa trader along the War Road. Hen-he-net is everywhere, selling her wares. She also passes on information and spies for Ger and others.

Hirrom (m). Luathi son of Japeth. Hirrom disappeared several years ago, leaving Sameel to step into his place as heir of Sentem. He was captured by the Daughter Beneath the Earth and transformed into the warrior Sanghulhaza.

Huldel (f). Luathi Hasheer of Orsem Yahan. Tends the House of Healing in the fort.

Japeth (m). Luathi Sar of Sentem. A strange malady afflicts the Sar of Sentem. Healing this man is the focus of the southern adventures for the first three years of the campaign.

Kinesh (m). Luathi Kahar in Mikro. A man broken by the power of Naahpasswee, Kinesh is now a vessel for a myriad of possessing spirits.

Leodias (m). Luathi shepherd and priest of Naahpasswee in Mikro. Leodias discovered the buried Skessh and began the events in **Shadow Over Mikro**.

Mahazra (m). Ancient Luathi king who led those who rejected the Hulathi and Alwain. Buried in Mirim Mahazra.

Mealil. Labasu-Rathic. Spirit of disease freed in **Mine of Atem**, hunts Abishai in **Relapse**, and is confronted by the Jackals in **Mirim Mahazra**.

Mellou (f). Trauj Mouathenic who violates the sanctity of Umbalna's forest, kicking off the events of **Forgotten Covenant**.

Nabal (m). Luathi Kahar of Sentem. Nabal is rebuilding and renovating an old Hulathi temple to Alwain near Sentem. It was there he discovered the ritual used to try to heal Japeth.

Namar (m). Luathi Nawsi of Orsem Yahan. Namar is the young captain of the eastern fort. Loyal to his people and to Ameena Noani, he sends for the Jackals in **Forgotten Covenant**.

Namgidda benna Amar (f). Luathi Sari of Rataro. Namgidda oversees the Hasheers' work in Rataro.

Naahpasswee (f). Skessh. Bound within her kella by the Hulathi of old, Naahpasswee's thoughts broke free, and she is the source of trouble in **Shadow Over Mikro**.

Ozamog (m). Oritakan leader of Bartak Kentak. Ozamog is the loyal servant of the Daughter Beneath the Earth and war chief of the Takan forces in **Raid of Raids**.

Philon (m). Melkoni brickmaker in Mikro. Philon falls under Naahpasswee's influence and begins to renovate the kella in **Shadow Over Mikro**.

Rakel (f). Luathi Nawsi of Orsem Honess. A Nawsi who is looking to Kroryla for support.

Sameel (m). Luathi Nawsi of Sentem. Son of Japeth and brother to Hirrom, Sameel works to save his father in the southern adventures for the first three years of the campaign and destroy Bartak Kentak once and for all in **Raid of Raids**.

Sanghulhaza (m). See Hirrom.

Sekata (f). Trauj Alkitar. Sekata leads the Trauj forces in **Raid of Raids**.

Shapan (m). Luathi/Melkoni woodcutter. The son of Diokles, Shapan helps the Jackals save his father from the Rathic in **Forgotten Covenant**.

Shargot (m). Oritakan. Leader of the Moon Mask tribe and possible ruler of Kek-bel-kala in **The Price of Victory**.

Toara (f). Luathi Hasheer inna Sarmom in the area around Ameena Noani. One of the Hasheer chiefs, Toara investigates Mealil in **Mirim Mahazra** and generally works to secure the lands of the Luathi from the forces of chaos.

Umbalna. Spirit of Ligna Hualla. A great spirit and ruler of the forests. In **Forgotten Covenant**, Umbalna holds the people of Orsem Yahan in violation of the covenant due to the malfeasance of Aldimir and Mellou.

Umari (f). Mouathenic in Kek-bel-kala. Umari heads one of the tribes in Kek-bel-kala and leads them in dark rites to ancient beings in **The Price of Victory**.

each element of that Product Identity. You agree not to indicate compatibility or co-adaptability with any Trademark or Registered Trademark in conjunction with a work containing Open Game Content except as expressly licensed in another, independent Agreement with the owner of such Trademark or Registered Trademark. The use of any Product Identity in Open Game Content does not constitute a challenge to the ownership of that Product Identity. The owner of any Product Identity used in Open Game Content shall retain all rights, title and interest in and to that Product Identity.

8. Identification: If you distribute Open Game Content You must clearly indicate which portions of the work that you are distributing are Open Game Content.

9. Updating the License: Wizards or its designated Agents may publish updated versions of this License. You may use any authorised version of this License to copy, modify and distribute any Open Game Content originally distributed under any version of this License.

10. Copy of this License: You MUST include a copy of this License with every copy of the Open Game Content You Distribute.

11. Use of Contributor Credits: You may not market or advertise the Open Game Content using the name of any Contributor unless You have written permission from the Contributor to do so.

12. Inability to Comply: If it is impossible for You to comply with any of the terms of this License with respect to some or all of the Open Game Content due to statute, judicial order, or governmental regulation then You may not Use any Open Game Material so affected.

13. Termination: This License will terminate automatically if You fail to comply with all terms herein and fail to cure such breach within 30 days of becoming aware of the breach. All sublicenses shall survive the termination of this License.

14. Reformation: If any provision of this License is held to be unenforceable, such provision shall be reformed only to the extent necessary to make it enforceable.

15. COPYRIGHT NOTICE

Open Game License v 1.0a Copyright 2000, Wizards of the Coast, Inc.

Modern System Reference Document, Copyright 2002, Wizards of the Coast, Inc.; Authors Bill Slavicsek, Jeff Grubb, Rich Redman, Charles Ryan, based on material by Jonathan Tweet, Monte Cook, Skip Williams, Richard Baker, Peter Adkison, Bruce R. Cordell, John Tynes, Andy Collins and JD Wiker.

System Reference Document, Copyright 2000–2003, Wizards of the Coast, Inc.; Authors Jonathan Tweet, Monte Cook, Skip Williams, Rich baker, Andy Collins, David Noonan, Rich Redman, Bruce R. Cordell, based on original material by E. Gary Gygax and Dave Arneson.

RuneQuest System Reference Document, Copyright 2006, Mongoose Publishing; Author Matthew Sprange, based on original material by Greg Stafford.

RuneQuest Companion System Reference Document, Copyright 2006, Mongoose Publishing; Author Greg Lynch et al., based on original material by Greg Stafford.

RuneQuest Monster System Reference Document, Copyright 2006, Mongoose Publishing; Author Greg Lynch et al., based on original material by Greg Stafford.

OpenQuest, Copyright 2009–2013, D101 Games; Author Newt Newport, Simon Bray, Paul Mitchner, Tom Zunder

Legend Copyright 2011, Mongoose Publishing; Author Lawrence Whitaker Pete Nash et al., based on original material by Greg Stafford.